Jury of Six

MATT BRAUN

St. Martin's Paperbacks

This is a work of fiction. All of the characters, organizations and events portrayed in this novel are either products of the author's imagination or are used fictiously.

HANGMAN'S CREEK / JURY OF SIX

Jury of Six copyright © 1980 by Matthew Braun.
Hangman's Creek copyright © 1979 by Matthew Braun.

Cover photo © Steve Terrill/Corbis.

ISBN: 0-312-94780-1
EAN: 9780312-94780-4

Printed in the United States of America

Hangman's Creek Pinnacle Books edition / March 1985
Jury of Six Pocket Books edition / May 1980
St. Martin's Paperbacks edition / July 2002

St. Martin's Paperbacks are published by St. Martin's Press, 175 Fifth Avenue, New York, NY 10010.

10 9 8 7 6 5 4 3 2 1

To Bill
Uncle, friend and Texan

CHAPTER 1

Ben Langham reined to a halt on the north bank of the Canadian. He looped the reins around the saddlehorn and fished a tobacco pouch from inside his greatcoat. His horse lowered its muzzle to the water while he stuffed and lit his pipe.

On the sundown side of sixty, Langham was nonetheless a man of imposing stature. Age had thickened his waistline, but he sat tall in the saddle, head erect and shoulders squared. With a mane of white hair, and wind-seamed features, he looked very much like a grizzled centaur. The pipe jutting from his mouth, he puffed cottony wads of smoke and slowly regarded the sky.

There was a bite in the air, unusually sharp for early December. A heavy overcast screened the afternoon sun, and beyond the river umber plains stretched onward like a burnt-out sea. Shifting in the saddle, Langham tested the wind, searching for the scent of snow. A slight northerly breeze was crisp and dry, but he'd weathered too many storms in the Panhandle not to recognize the signs of oncoming winter. Soon, he told himself, the blizzards

1

would howl down off the high plains and blanket the land with snow. Which meant today might very well be his last chance to inspect the line camps until spring melt-off.

To Langham, the line camps were a hedge that often spelled the difference between disaster and a profitable year. As the largest rancher in the Texas Panhandle, his LX spread was much too big to be manned from the home compound. Like a small nation, it needed outposts during the long plains winter. Spotted every six miles around the fifty-mile perimeter, these outposts formed a fence of sorts on the open range. Cattle had a tendency to drift with a storm, or to mindlessly gather in bunches, shivering and hungry, and starve to death rather than seek out graze. The line riders patrolled between their stations, holding the cows on LX land and driving them to hillsides where wind had blown snow off the grass. A grueling task, it was a job assigned to the most trustworthy men on Langham's crew. Without them, the winter-kill alone would have soon bankrupted the LX.

Yet, while Langham himself had handpicked the line riders, he understood that even the best of men occasionally needed prodding. Life in a line camp, which consisted of a one-room cabin and a log corral, was a solitary existence. With the onset of winter, a line rider often went for weeks at a time without seeing another human. The loneliness and the drudgery of herding stubborn cattle through snowdrifts could sour a man, slowly work on his spirit and turn him lax. A surprise visit and a word of encouragement would do much to bolster that spirit. And the uncertainty, never knowing when to expect another visit, gave the men something to ponder on cold winter nights.

Langham knocked the dottle from his pipe, thoughtful a moment. He was privately amused that the men considered him the original sonofabitch, far more demanding than Jack Noonan, the ranch foreman. At his age it was no small compliment, one he meant to preserve. He nurtured it at every opportunity.

Stuffing the pipe in his pocket, Langham gathered the reins and kneed his horse into the water. Once across the river, he turned west and rode along the shelterbelt of trees bordering the shore. His thoughts now centered on Shorty Phillips, who was stationed at a line camp several miles upstream. He debated staying for supper, then quickly decided against it. No slouch as a cowhand, Phillips's cooking could gag a dog off a gut wagon.

Some while later, Langham crested a wooded knoll and hauled back sharply on the reins. Below, where the treeline thinned out, several riders were hazing a bunch of cows away from the river. At first glance, he thought some of the crew were moving cattle to another section of range. Then he looked closer, and realized none of the men rode for LX. The bastards were cow thieves.

And they were rustling his stock!

Langham reacted instinctively, his hand moving

to the carbine in his saddle scabbard. But blind anger quickly gave way to cool judgment. He counted seven men, and forced himself to admit the odds were too great. He needed help, even if it meant allowing the rustlers to escape for the moment. His mind turned to Shorty Phillips, estimating time and distance. Within the hour he could have Phillips riding for the home compound; another three hours, four at the outside, and Phillips could return with most of the LX crew. By nightfall they would be on the rustlers' trail, and easily overtake them at first light. The conclusion, though delayed, would be no less satisfying. A stiff rope and a short drop always settled a rustler's hash.

The plan formulated, Langham shoved the carbine back in the scabbard and gathered his reins. So intent had he been on the rustlers that the whirr of a gun hammer caught him completely unawares. He turned, scanning the trees to his rear, and found himself staring into the muzzle of a cocked pistol. Not ten yards away a young boy, mounted on a bloodbay gelding, sat watching him over the gunsights. There was a haunting familiarity about the youngster's features, and for an instant the two men stared at each other. Then the boy wagged his head.

"Old man, you're too nosy for your own good."

"You're makin' a mistake," Langham warned him. "No way on God's earth you'll get away with it."

The boy's mouth twisted in a bucktoothed grin. "Wanna bet?"

"Well, I'll be damned." Langham blinked, suddenly recognized the misshapen face he'd seen on reward dodgers. "I know you!"

"Now you done spoiled it for sure."

The boy fired twice, one report blending with the other. Langham swayed, jolted by the impact of the slugs, then slowly toppled out of the saddle. He hit the ground on his side and rolled over, bright dots of blood staining his coat. He groaned, struggling to rise, and somehow levered himself to his hands and knees. His mouth ajar, head hung between his arms, he stared sightlessly at the hard-packed earth. He tried to speak, but produced only a distorted whisper.

The youngster watched his struggles with an expression of detached curiosity. Then he sighted carefully and shot Langham in the head. The rancher's skull exploded in a mist of gore and bone matter, and he collapsed. His leg twitched, and his foot drummed the dirt in a spasm of afterdeath. A moment passed, then he lay still.

At the last shot, his horse spooked, rearing away. The boy aimed, triggering two quick shots, and the horse went down in a tangle of hooves and saddle leather. Without haste, the youngster calmly reloaded and holstered his pistol. Then he reined the bay around and rode down the knoll.

Shorty Phillips discovered the body early next morning. A couple of hours later, still rattled by what he'd seen, he rode into the home compound. There, once Jack Noonan had him calmed down, he spilled out the story. While riding his regular patrol, he had spotted buzzards circling the knoll, and upon investigating, he'd found Langham's body. Other than covering the remains with his mackinaw, he hadn't waited around. He hit the saddle and rode.

The foreman immediately summoned Luke Starbuck. Headquartered at the LX, Starbuck was chief range detective for the Panhandle Cattlemen's Association. The news of Langham's death struck him hard, for he'd been a lifelong friend, and at one time foreman of the LX. But he listened impassively, revealing nothing of what he felt, and questioned Phillips in a cold, measured voice. Then he ordered horses saddled, and sent someone to fetch his assistant, John Poe. Within minutes, Starbuck and Poe, trailed by Noonan and Shorty Phillips, rode out of the compound.

Shortly before noon, the men reined to a halt atop the knoll. Buzzards had already begun working on the dead horse, but took wing as the riders approached. Starbuck sent John Poe to scout the outlying area, and told the other two men to remain with the horses. Then he walked forward and knelt beside Langham's body. When he lifted the mackinaw, his face turned ashen and for a moment it seemed his iron composure would crack. Yet he somehow collected himself and, after inspecting the grisly remains, climbed to his feet. Without a word, he began a careful examination of the knoll.

Noonan and Phillips watched in silence. Neither of them offered to help, for they saw that a quietness had settled over Starbuck. A manhunter for the past four years, tracking down rustlers and horse thieves, he had acquired a reputation for steel nerves and suddenness with a gun. Outlaws seldom surrendered when cornered, and in the time he'd served as a range detective, he was known to have killed eleven men. The number he had hung was a matter of speculation. The nearest peace officer was four days' ride to the south, and summary justice was widely practiced on the plains. Starbuck, according to rumor, had decorated a dozen or more trees throughout the Panhandle. But he was a private man, with no tolerance for questions, and the exact count was unknown. Those who had worked with him, however, told of an eerie quietness he displayed when pushed beyond certain limits. Some men called it a *killing quietness*, and the record seemed to bear them out. Today, watching him, Noonan and Phillips were aware he hadn't spoken since looking underneath the mackinaw.

Starbuck completed his examination as Poe topped the knoll and rode toward them. He waited, his mouth set in a grim line, with Noonan and Phillips standing beside him. When Poe dismounted, he wasted no time on preliminaries.

"How many?"

"I make it seven or eight," Poe informed him. "Found signs where they were drivin' a bunch of

7

cows, then all of a sudden they just stopped and hightailed it out of here."

"Figures," Starbuck observed. "One of them was posted up here as a lookout. The way I read it, Ben rode in from the north, and when he saw what was happening, the lookout killed him."

"So they ditched the cows to make better time. Whoever's leadin' them evidently wanted to be long gone by the time Ben was found."

"That's how it adds up."

"Ben have any chance at all?"

"None," Starbuck said tonelessly. "Bastard drilled him twice, then finished him off with one in the head. No way of telling, but I'd say he shot the horse so it wouldn't show up with an empty saddle and raise an alarm. Probably figured that'd buy them a little more time."

"That, or he's plain kill crazy."

"Crazy like a fox." Starbuck extended his hand, five spent cartridges cupped in his palm. "Found these over in the trees. He sat there and reloaded before he rode off. That tell you anything?"

"Offhand, I'd say he's not the type that spooks easy."

"Yeah, that's for sure." Starbuck paused, considering. "How about tracks?"

"I followed them maybe half a mile, no trouble."

"Which direction?"

"Southwest," Poe noted. "Straight as a string."

Starbuck nodded. "New Mexico."

"You thinkin' what I'm thinkin'?"

"Maybe, maybe not; but I know a place we can find out."

Late that night, Starbuck and Poe rode into Tascosa. An isolated trading post, the town was situated on the Canadian River, roughly halfway between LX lands and the eastern border of New Mexico. Apart from a few adobes, there was one saloon and a general store. Tascosa had no streets, only a handful of permanent residents, and no law. It was the perfect haven for outlaws, on the edge of nowhere.

When Starbuck pushed through the batwing doors, a measurable hush fell over the saloon. There were perhaps a dozen men standing at the bar and seated around crude tables. Some of them knew him on sight, and the others would have instantly recognized his name. Yet, even to those who had never seen him, his presence was a matter to be weighed with care. In Tascosa, where every man looked to his own safety, caution was the basic tenet of survival.

With Poe at his side, Starbuck walked directly to the bar. Outside, he had checked the horses tied at the hitch rack, and none of them had been ridden hard. A swift glance around the saloon further strengthened his hunch: the men he sought were by now across the border into New Mexico. He rapped on the counter, and the bartender hurried forward.

"Evenin', Mr. Starbuck."

"Ernie." Starbuck nodded amiably. "How's tricks?"

"Oh, you know, dollar here, dollar there. What can I get you gents?"

"A little information."

The barkeep gave him a guarded look. "I try to tend to my own knittin', Mr. Starbuck. Feller stays healthier that way."

"Ernie, you've got a choice." Starbuck paused, motioning around the room. "You can worry about these boys later, or you can worry about me now. Which way you want it?"

"Jesus." The barkeep licked his lips, shot a nervous glance over his shoulder. "That ain't no choice at all."

"Wasn't meant to be." Starbuck fixed him with a level gaze. "Last night, maybe the night before, eight men wandered in here for a drink. Tell me about them."

"How'd you hear about that bunch?"

"Let's stick to me asking the questions."

"Well, there's not nothin' special to tell, except maybe . . ."

"Yeah," Starbuck prompted him, "except maybe what?"

"The youngest one," the barkeep replied thoughtfully. "No more'n a kid, but the others treated him like he was meaner than tiger spit. Sorta strange."

"Describe him," Starbuck persisted. "Anything you remember."

"Oh, he was an ugly little scutter. Wouldn't stand

no taller'n your shoulder. And his face was all lop-sided. Looked like a jackrabbit when he grinned."

"You mean he was bucktoothed?"

"Near about as bad as I ever seen."

Starbuck turned to Poe. "What do you say, John? Think he fits the ticket?"

"In spades!" Poe agreed. "Couldn't be no one else."

"And I'll bet they called him Billy." Starbuck pinned the barkeep with a look. "Didn't they, Ernie?"

"How the hell'd you know that?"

"Took a wild guess." Starbuck stepped away from the bar. His eyes traveled around the room, moving from face to face. "This here's private business, just between me and Ernie. Anybody sees it different, now's the time to speak his piece."

A leaden stillness filled the saloon. None of the men spoke, and no one met Starbuck's gaze. After a brief while he dug a double eagle from his pocket and tossed it on the counter.

"A drink for my friends, Ernie."

Starbuck walked to the door. He waited there, watching the room, until John Poe was outside. Then he stepped into the night. A moment later the sound of hoofbeats slowly faded from Tascosa.

CHAPTER 2

Ben Langham was buried the next afternoon. His casket was borne to the graveyard by six cowhands. A few steps behind the pallbearers, Starbuck followed with Jack Noonan and John Poe. Several cattlemen, whose ranches bordered the LX, brought up the rear.

The procession entered the small cemetery north of the compound and halted. The casket was lowered onto planks laid across the grave, then the pallbearers stepped back and the men removed their hats. Vernon Pryor, one of the ranchers, walked to the head of the grave. Except for itinerant preachers, religion was a sometimes thing in the Panhandle; funeral services were always kept simple, the last words spoken by a close friend. Pryor opened a dog-eared Bible and began reading the Twenty-third Psalm.

Starbuck scarcely heard the words. The service was properly somber, and some ninety cowhands, almost all the LX crew, were gathered around the cemetery. But for him there was a sense of the unreal about the burial. He stared at a coffin which represented nothing, merely a rough-hewn wooden box. His mind was suspended in a void of bygone years, and he saw revealed there an image of all that had once been and would never be again. His grief, even now tightly suppressed, had not yet come to grips with an essential truth. Ben Langham was dead.

To him, there had always been a godlike quality about Langham. Olympian in manner, a white-haired monolith, the rancher had seemed indestructible. Other men lived and died, but Ben Langham went on forever, ageless and somehow immutable. Starbuck saw him that way still.

Some ten years past, Starbuck had hired on as a trailhand with the LX. A drifter, wandering the aimless life of a saddle tramp, he was a nomad without family or roots. But Langham, who was a keen judge of character, quickly brought a halt to his wanderlust. Assuming ever greater responsibility, Starbuck was promoted to head wrangler, and then jumped to trail boss a year later. Within three seasons, he went from fiddle-footed cowhand to segundo of the LX.

At the time, Langham's spread was located in the Rio Grande Valley, near the Mexican border. During the summer of 1874, however, tragedy struck the ranch. An outbreak of cholera claimed the lives of Langham's wife and three children, along with a score of cowhands. Devastated by the loss, and determined to outdistance memories of the past, Langham turned his gaze north, to the Texas Panhandle.

There, on the banks of the Canadian River, he established a new ranch. But he brought with him the LX brand and Luke Starbuck, who assumed the post of foreman.

Thereafter, a sense of closeness and kinship steadily developed between Langham and Starbuck. The old man looked on his young foreman with affection and pride, much as a father would treat a son. Working together, they created a prosperous ranch out of a raw wilderness. By the spring of 1876, the LX was running fifty thousand head of cattle and the crew numbered nearly a hundred men. That summer ten herds went up the trail to railhead, and the proceeds to the ranch totaled in excess of a half million dollars. Ben Langham, within the space of two years, had become the most influential stockgrower in the Panhandle. And he was quick to credit his foreman with having converted an ocean of grass into a top-notch cattle outfit.

Yet the summer of '76 had proved a crossroads in Luke Starbuck's life. Besieged by rustlers and horse thieves, the Panhandle Cattlemen's Association had been forced to take action. At Langham's urging, Starbuck had been appointed the Association's first range detective. His orders were to run the outlaws to earth, wherever the trail might lead, and see justice done. Since vast distances and poor communications stymied elected peace officers, his mandate from the Association gave him the power of judge, jury, and executioner. He was hindered neither by state boundaries nor the law itself, for the renegade bands respected no code except that imposed at the end of a gun. His credentials as a detective were quickly established, and with each outlaw hung or killed, his reputation took on added luster. Still, no sooner was one gang routed than another appeared to take its place, and what began as a temporary assignment evolved into a deadly vocation. He became a professional manhunter.

Over the past four years, Starbuck had grown cold and hard, brutalized by the sight of death. Today, staring at Ben Langham's coffin, he mourned the passing of a man who had befriended him and taught him the meaning of family. But his grief was inward, a white-hot coal that burned to the very core of his vitals. Outwardly he was stoic, somehow dispassionate, and curiously uninvolved in the ancient rites of burial. His thoughts were not of remorse, but of revenge.

Vernon Pryor finished reading and closed his Bible. Starbuck caught only the last few words, then the sound of ropes sawing on wood jarred him back to the present. He blinked and saw the pallbearers lowering the coffin into the ground. He forced himself to watch, but his mind was focused on the task ahead. As the top of the coffin disappeared, there was a moment of strained silence. Then, jamming his hat on his head, he turned away from the grave.

The four ranchers, all older men, immediately stepped forward to shake his hand. Each in turn offered condolences and expressed his sorrow, for it was widely known that Ben Langham had considered Starbuck the same as family. Their remarks were accepted without comment, and then, his voice deliberate, Starbuck addressed them as a group.

"We've got some things that need talking out. As long as you're here, I'd like to call a special meeting of the Association."

A statement rather than a request, his tone left the ranchers momentarily flustered. Before anyone could reply, he stepped past them and moved away. Outside the cemetery plot, the LX hands kept their heads bowed, their eyes averted. His expression was stony, and he looked straight ahead as they opened a path before him. A solitary figure, withdrawn into himself, he walked toward the main house.

Starbuck was waiting when they filed into the office. The ranchers were uncomfortably aware that he stood behind Ben Langham's desk. For several years, seated at that desk, the LX owner had ruled the Panhandle Cattlemen's Association. An aura of power still lingered in the room, and the men exchanged uneasy glances as they moved forward. Starbuck motioned them to chairs.

"Suppose we get to it," he said brusquely. "I'm short on time, but I thought it only fair that I advise you of a couple of things. One's got to do with the LX, and the other involves the Association."

Vernon Pryor and Will Rutledge were seated directly across from him. Oscar Gilchrist and Earl Musgrave had taken chairs at either end of the desk.

Early settlers in the Panhandle, they had established their own ranches shortly after Ben Langham staked out the LX. Yet, while they admired Langham, their feelings were mixed about Starbuck. In the beginning, he had earned their respect as ramrod of the LX; though not yet thirty, his knowledge of cows, and general ranch operations, surpassed that of men twice his age. Later, as a range detective, his methods had often disturbed them. He obtained results, but the ranchers were of the opinion that he overstepped himself, frequently exceeding his authority. Only Langham had been able to hold him in check, and now that steadying influence was gone. The prospect unnerved them more than they cared to admit.

Vernon Pryor cleared his throat. A man of glacial calm, he was tall and distinguished, and the other men attached a certain importance to his views. Over the years, whenever they were at odds with Langham, he had acted as their spokesman. Now, his fingers steepled, he peered across the desk at Starbuck.

"Luke, you seem to have us at a disadvantage."

"How so?"

"Well, for one thing," Pryor replied, "we'd like to know your position here today. Are you talking for the LX, or have you asked us here in your official capacity with the Association?"

"Both." Starbuck took a one-page document from the desk drawer and laid it before them. "For openers, there's Ben's last will and testament. It's right

to the point, so you might as well read it for your-
selves."

While the ranchers huddled around the will, Starbuck pulled out the makings and began rolling himself a smoke. The document, like the man who had
written it, was blunt and without equivocation. The
ranchers evidenced no great surprise as they read,
and it required less than a minute for them to scan
the contents. Starbuck struck a match and lit his
cigarette, waiting until they looked up.

"Ben wasn't much with words," he said quietly,
"but I reckon he spelled it out pretty clear."

"Very clear," Pryor remarked. "According to this,
you inherit everything he owned. No exceptions and
no conditions. You're to be congratulated, Luke."

"Damned right!" Earl Musgrave added. "Ben always said you was like blood kin, and by Christ, he
wasn't kiddin'."

The other men quickly endorsed the sentiment.
By conservative estimate, Starbuck was now a man
of enviable wealth. Then too, ownership of the LX
conferred on him a mantle of power, for it was the
largest, and easily the most prosperous, cattle operation in the Panhandle. That fact wasn't lost on
the ranchers, and it did nothing to quell their apprehension.

Starbuck sensed their concern. "You needn't
worry about me trying to fill Ben's boots. I only
showed you the will so we'd have all our cards on
the table. That and nothing else."

"Pardon me," Pryor said, tapping the will. "I notice this is dated May 1, 1876. If I'm not mistaken, that's about the time you accepted your first assignment as a range detective."

"To peg it exact, it was one day after I accepted."

"In other words," Pryor commented, "he told you about the will the day he wrote it."

Starbuck took a long drag on his cigarette. He exhaled, watching the rancher, and slowly nodded. "Ben always liked to sandbag the odds. He decided the Association needed me more than the ranch, but he wanted to make sure I'd stick around—and take over—after he was gone." He paused, inspecting his cigarette, then shrugged. "I guess he figured only a damn fool would walk away from a deal like that."

"Was he right?"

"Why do you ask?"

"Oh, nothing." Pryor gave him a crafty smile. "It's just that I get the feeling you're not all that concerned with the LX."

"Maybe later," Starbuck told him, "but not now. Tomorrow I'm headed for New Mexico."

"New Mexico!" Gilchrist blurted. "What the hell's in New Mexico?"

"The fellow that killed Ben."

A pall fell over the ranchers. Starbuck walked to the window and stood staring out at the compound. Briefly, he related the details of his search at the knoll, and then went on to describe what he'd uncovered in Tascosa. When he turned away from the window, his eyes were dulled and a small knot pulsed at his temple.

"Put it all together, and it spells the same name every time. Billy the Kid."

"Billy the Kid!"

Will Rutledge trumpeted the name, but the other ranchers were no less astounded. All four men shifted in their chairs, gaping at Starbuck, and for an instant they appeared struck dumb. Then Oscar Gilchrist found his voice.

"You can't do it, Luke. Gawddamnit, we won't let you do it! You're head of the LX now, and we need you here."

"Oscar's right," Musgrave chimed in. "It's too risky. Hell's fire, they're still fightin' the Lincoln County War! You get yourself mixed up in that and you're liable to wind up in New Mexico permanent."

"Save your breath," Starbuck said flatly. "I should have gone after the Kid a long time ago. If I had, Ben would be alive today."

"Judas Priest!" Musgrave protested. "It was Ben that always stopped you! I heard him myself, sittin' right there behind that desk. He told you to stay the hell out of New Mexico till they quit squabblin' amongst themselves. Ain't that so?"

"Hold on, Earl," Pryor temporized. "Maybe Luke has a point. For all practical purposes, the Lincoln County War is over and done with. I even hear they've got themselves a new sheriff. So maybe now's the time to rid ourselves of the Kid once and for all."

"One thing's for sure," Rutledge interjected.

"The little bastard knows Luke's got orders not to cross the state line. Hell, he has to know! That's why him and his gang keep hittin' our herds so regular."

Starbuck's mouth hardened. "Those orders died with Ben. Tomorrow, I'm heading out with John Poe and three or four good men. We'll stay till we get the job done."

"I still don't like it," Gilchrist said dourly. "New Mexico ain't like other places, Luke. Them people has turned killin' one another into a sport, and an outsider wouldn't have no more chance than spit on a hot stove."

"Oscar, you could talk yourself blue in the face, but it won't change a thing. I'm going, and the argument stops there."

"What about the LX?" Pryor ventured. "I know you feel bound to go after Ben's killer, but there's always the chance you won't come back. Have you thought about that?"

Starbuck's laugh was scratchy, abrasive. "Tell you what, Vern. If somebody punches my ticket, I won't have much use for the LX. You boys can divvy it up any way you please."

"Would you put that in writing?"

"Gawddamn, Vern!" Gilchrist admonished him. "You sound like you already got Luke measured for a pine box."

"No, he's right," Starbuck admitted. "Anything happens to me, it wouldn't be legal unless it was in writing." He hesitated, eyes squinted in a sardonic look. "Course, there's something I'd want in exchange."

"Oh?" Pryor said slowly. "What's that?"

"A letter of authorization from the Association."

"Dead or alive?" Pryor asked. "For Billy the Kid?"

"Why not?" Starbuck smiled. "Word it right, and it might just keep the law off my neck."

The ranchers glanced quickly at each other. It seemed a reasonable request, and while they wished Starbuck no harm, all of them were acutely aware that a new element had been introduced into the discussion. His death would profit them handsomely, and every man was obliged to look to his own interests. At length, Pryor nodded, once more the spokesman.

"Agreed," he said evenly. "But if I was you, I'd pay a call on John Chisum. He's president of the New Mexico Stockgrowers' Association, and it wouldn't hurt to have his support. If you like, I'll even write him a personal note."

"Which side of the fence is he on?"

"The winning side! Matter of fact, I hear tell he handpicked their new sheriff. Fellow by the name of Pat Garrett."

"Never heard of him." Starbuck stubbed out his cigarette in an ashtray, thoughtful a moment. "All right, I'll see what Chisum has to say for himself. But whichever way it goes, I still aim to get the Kid."

"Don't go off half-cocked," Pryor advised. "John

Chisum makes a lot better friend than he does an enemy."

"Well, Vern, I reckon that'll be up to him."

"Meaning you intend to play it your own way, regardless?"

Starbuck smiled. "What the hell, why spoil a perfect record?"

CHAPTER 3

On December 8, Starbuck forded the Pecos River. He was accompanied by John Poe and four LX cowhands. The men were a rough lot, all of them veterans of previous manhunts and intensely loyal to Starbuck. Once across the river, they turned south and rode toward the Jinglebob Ranch.

Starbuck now regretted his promise to call on John Chisum. Three days in the saddle had afforded time to think it through, and he questioned that anything worthwhile would come of the meeting. He'd dealt with cattle barons before, and Chisum, who was known as the King of the Pecos, would very likely try to exert some form of control over his actions. But he was determined to operate on his own, without constraint and answerable to no one. His purpose was to exact simple vengeance—an eye for an eye—uncomplicated by courts or legal technicalities. He foresaw problems ahead.

Late that afternoon, Starbuck and his men sighted the Jinglebob headquarters. Located in the southeastern quadrant of New Mexico Territory, the ranch was a day's ride from the town of Lincoln.

Everything about the Jinglebob was mammoth in scope. Natural landmarks, such as rivers and mountains, were used to measure its boundary lines. Over 100,000 cows grazed its range, and a crew of one hundred fifty cowhands was kept on the payroll year round. Thirty years before, John Chisum had laid claim to a sprawling empire, defending it against outlaws and marauding Indians, and successive waves of westward-bound settlers. A man who recognized no authority but his own, he ruled the Pecos like a feudal lord.

The *casa grande* was of a style befitting the man and his ranch. It was one story, constructed of native adobe, with broad wings extending off the central living quarters. Beneath a tile roof, hewn beams protruded from walls four feet thick. The window casements gleamed of tallowed oak, and the double doors were wider than a man's outspanned arms. The house, which overlooked the river to the west, dominated the ranch compound. Covering several acres, the buildings were grouped with a symmetry that was at once methodical and pleasing to the eye. Four bunkhouses formed a quadrangle, with a dining hall the size of an army barracks in the center. Corrals and stables, flanked by a line of storage buildings, angled south along a bend in the river. A commissary and an open-sided blacksmith shed were situated on a plot of open ground central to the entire compound. The effect was that of a small but prosperous village, bustling with activity.

All afternoon, since crossing the Jinglebob

boundary, Starbuck had expected to be challenged. A group of six strangers, appearing unannounced on open rangeland, was a matter to warrant questions. But no one had approached them, and now, as they rode across the compound, their presence attracted little more than passing interest. At the hitchrack, Starbuck and his men dismounted. He left Poe in charge, ordering them to stay with the horses until he returned. Then he walked toward the main house.

Before he could knock, the doors swung open. A girl, dressed rather formally in a lavender taffeta gown, stood just inside the entranceway. Her smile was tentative, and she fixed him with a steady, inquiring gaze.

"Good afternoon."

"Ma'am." Starbuck doffed his hat. "I wonder if I might have a word with Mr. Chisum?"

"Of course." She stepped aside, motioning him into the vestibule. "My father has been expecting you for some time."

Starbuck moved past her, struck by both her words and her unusual beauty. She had dark eyes and high cheekbones and raven hair wound in coils atop her head. Her skin was soft and creamy, untouched by wind or sun, and her mouth was a lovely oval. She was small and compact, with a stemlike waist and breasts that formed perfect mounds. She seemed to him something out of a storybook, ethereal and strangely out of place. As she closed the doors, he collected himself, turned to face her.

"Excuse my manners," he said, smiling. "I

should've introduced myself right off. I'm Luke Starbuck."

"Mr. Starbuck." She nodded pleasantly. "My name is Sallie Chisum."

Starbuck scarcely heard the words. Her voice was intimate, with the timbre of an old violin. Yet it was a trained voice, very proper and very correct. His head buzzed with questions, but he restrained himself.

"Pleasure, Miss Chisum. If you'll pardon my saying so, you sort of took me by surprise. We don't often see ladies like you over my way."

"Oh?" Sallie Chisum said, watching him. "And where is that, Mr. Starbuck?"

"The Panhandle," he replied. "North of Palo Duro Canyon."

"You've ridden a long way."

"Yes, ma'am, that's a fact."

"May I ask why you wish to see my father?"

"A business matter," Starbuck noted vaguely. "I represent the Cattlemen's Association."

"I see."

She paused, waiting for him to elaborate, but instead Starbuck's eyebrows lifted in question. "You say your father was expecting me?"

"Yes, indeed," she explained, suddenly amused. "You and your men have been under observation from the moment you rode onto Jinglebob. Father is about to perish of curiosity."

"Sounds like your hands keep their eyes open."

She merely smiled, indicating a hallway. "Shall

we? I suspect father's patience has about reached its limit."

"Oh, sure thing." Starbuck took a step back. "After you."

Sallie Chisum led him down the corridor. She walked quickly, with a sort of bustling vitality, and the rustle of silk seemed pitted in counterpoint to the clink of his spurs on the tiled floor. He was abruptly aware of the bearded stubble on his jaws, and the layer of trail dust covering his clothes. The delicate scent of her perfume made him wonder if he smelled as rank as he looked. He felt very much like a moth swooping along behind a butterfly.

At the end of the hall, she went through an open door and stopped. Starbuck entered, and found himself in a combination office-den. There was an odor of tobacco and saddle leather, and flames crackled in the fireplace. A massive desk occupied one side of the room, with a stuffed eagle mounted on a pedestal and gun racks lining the walls. Opposite the desk, directly before the fireplace, an old man sat slumped in a wing chair.

"Father," Sallie Chisum said graciously, "we have a guest. Mr. Starbuck, of the Panhandle Cattlemen's Association."

"Mr. Chisum." Starbuck crossed the room, his hand extended. "I'm Luke Starbuck."

"Welcome to Jinglebob." Chisum shook hands without rising, then motioned him to a companion wing chair. "Take a load off your feet."

While Starbuck removed his mackinaw, the girl

turned and walked to the door. She smiled, nodding to him, and looked at her father.

"If you need anything, I'll be in the parlor."

The door closed, and Chisum waited until he had seated himself. After a moment, the rancher waved a square, stubby-fingered hand toward a wall cabinet.

"Care for a whiskey?"

"No, thanks."

"Coffee?"

"Much obliged, but I'll pass."

"Luke Starbuck." Chisum's cordial manner became a swift look of appraisal. "I don't know you, but I know your name."

Starbuck shrugged. "I reckon bad news travels fastest."

"Well, I sort of like what I've heard so far. But, then, I get the feelin' I ain't heard it all. What's your business with Jinglebob?"

"Here." Starbuck dug out a soiled envelope and passed it to him. "That's from Vernon Pryor. He told me to tell you it'd pretty much explain things."

Chisum pulled metal-framed spectacles from his shirt pocket, tore open the envelope, and began reading. Starbuck studied him, betraying nothing, but frankly astounded by the rancher's appearance. A withered giant, his features were those of a fleshed skeleton bound with gray, chalky skin. He was completely bald, with bone china teeth, and he spoke with the slurred inflections of a man wasted by illness. Only his eyes were alive, and by exercise of sheer will, his mind remained attentive. Starbuck thought to himself that time was the cruelest of vandals. Other contests might end in a draw, but John Chisum had already lost his struggle with the years.

When he finished the letter, Chisum folded his spectacles and returned them to his pocket. He cleared his throat, slowly shook his head.

"Sorry about Langham. Our trails never crossed, but I always heard good things about him. Damn shame he had to get it that way."

Starbuck nodded. "He deserved better."

Chisum fell silent. He saw in Starbuck's cold, slate-colored eyes the look of a man who stayed alive by making quick estimates. He himself was no mean judge of character, and he sensed that accounts of Starbuck's work as a manhunter were in no way exaggerated. He speculated on the possibilities, weighing his next words carefully. At length, he tapped the letter with his finger.

"According to Pryor, you aim to run the Kid down and kill him."

"Yeah, I guess that's about the size of it."

"What about his gang?" Chisum asked. "Aren't you interested in getting them?"

"All things evened out, I'd be satisfied with the Kid."

"Well, Mr. Starbuck, the plain fact of the matter is—I wouldn't!"

Starbuck met his gaze. "I get the feeling you're trying to tell me something."

"Would it surprise you," Chisum said bitterly, "to

learn that the Kid and his gang only spend half their time in the Panhandle? The rest of the time they're figurin' out ways to rustle Jinglebob cows."

"If that's the case, why haven't you put a stop to it? You've got enough men on your payroll."

"Humph!" Chisum grunted. "Lemme ask you something, Starbuck. How much do you know about the Lincoln County War?"

"Not a whole lot."

"Then it's time somebody gave you an earful. Otherwise you won't get no closer to the Kid than we have."

Chisum quickly sketched events of the past three years. Essentially a political struggle, the Lincoln County War involved two factions. On one side were Chisum and another rancher, John Tunstall, and a local storekeeper, Alexander McSween. Challenging them were L. G. Murphy and his partner, Jack Dobson, whose interests included a ranch as well as the town's leading business establishments. More than twenty men had met their deaths during the fighting, including Tunstall, McSween, and L. G. Murphy. Several of them had been murdered in cold blood by Billy the Kid, who worked for Tunstall and McSween even though he detested Chisum. After the fighting had subsided, Chisum made his peace with Jack Dobson. Their compromise was a simple division of the spoils: Dobson controlled the town government and Chisum assumed command of county politics. Ironically, the truce transformed Billy the Kid from a hired gun into an outlaw leader. He vilified Chisum for having compromised, and quickly formed a gang of murderous renegades. For the last year, the Kid and his men had raided Jinglebob herds on an average of once a month.

"Small ranchers," Chisum concluded, "and especially the Mexicans, think the Kid's some sort of Robin Hood. Course, him robbing the rich to help the poor ain't nothin' but a load of horseshit! But they believe it—and they protect him—and catchin' the little bastard's like trying to grab a puff of smoke."

Starbuck considered a moment. "I was told you got your own man elected sheriff. What's he done about the Kid?"

"Not a goddamn thing!" Chisum said sternly. "Now, don't misunderstand me. Pat Garrett's a regular bulldog, and he's honest as they come. But so far he ain't cut the mustard as a lawman."

"Then why'd you put him in office?"

"Cause I could trust him," Chisum countered. "On top of which, he used to be pals with the Kid. Nothin' illegal, but they was real thick, and there ain't nobody knows the Kid better'n Pat Garrett. So he seemed like a natural."

Starbuck looked skeptical. "What's your point? You wouldn't be telling me all this unless you had a reason. Why not just get to it?"

"Awright," Chisum said gravely. "I've got a bum ticker. Already had two strokes and the Doc says I could go at any time."

"Sorry to hear it," Starbuck said with genuine concern. "But I still don't see your point."

"There's two things I want done before I cash in. I want my daughter married off to a decent man, and I want this rustlin' stopped cold. That's all it'd take for me to go out with the biggest goddamn grin anybody ever seen."

"Well, I'm sure no prospect as a son-in-law, so we must be talking about rustlers."

"What we're talkin' about," Chisum said firmly, "is exterminating the Kid *and* his gang. But I want it done before I die! Otherwise I wouldn't rest easy for fear Sallie might lose everything I've worked a lifetime to build."

Starbuck thought it sounded a bit flimsy. Some inner voice warned him that Chisum wasn't telling the whole story. Then, wondering if perhaps it wasn't his cynical streak at work, he decided to reserve judgment. He rocked his hand back and forth, fingers splayed.

"I see your drift, but you'll have to spell it out a little plainer."

"Nothin' real complicated," Chisum said with an affable gesture. "You're an experienced manhunter and Pat Garrett ain't. If you was to team up with him, I got an idea we'd get this thing settled muy damn pronto."

"I work alone," Starbuck remarked. "Not that I don't need help now and then, but I prefer to use my own men."

"Here in New Mexico, things would go a lot

smoother if you went about it legal. That's no threat; I'm just sayin' folks are still jumpy about strangers, what with all the trouble we've had the last few years. You let Garrett pin a deputy's badge on you, and you'll save yourself a world of grief."

Starbuck laughed. "You'll have to give me a better reason than that. I never needed a tin star before, and I don't see the need now."

A wintry smile lighted the old man's eyes. "Suppose Ben Langham was sittin' here today. Now, like I said, we never met, but unless I miss my guess, he'd tell you to take all the odds you can get. Course, maybe I'm all wet, but I figure that's just the way he would've put it to you."

Starbuck was silent for a long while. At last, still uneasy about Chisum's motives, he inclined his head in a faint nod. "I'll agree on two conditions. First, Garrett has to give me a free hand. So far as anyone else will know, he's still top dog. But either I do it my own way, or I don't do it at all. Second, he has to deputize my men. I trust them, and when the time comes, I want to make damn sure they're backing my play."

"Deal!" Chisum agreed without hesitation. "I'll write him a note and send it into town first thing tomorrow. More'n likely he'll bow his neck, but there won't be no problem. He'll go along."

"Fine." Starbuck uncoiled from his chair and stood. "I'll take it slow on the way into Lincoln. By the time me and the boys get there, maybe Garrett will have simmered down."

"Any idea where you'll start?"

Starbuck gave him a cryptic smile. "Downwind. Anybody that stinks as bad as the Kid, the smell's got to be plumb ripe."

CHAPTER 4

A brilliant sunset edged toward the mountains west of Lincoln. Entering town from the opposite direction, Starbuck was struck by the picturesque setting. To a stranger, unfamiliar with its history of bloodshed and violence, it would have appeared a peaceful community, thriving with commerce.

With John Poe at his side and the men strung out behind, Starbuck inspected the town's main thoroughfare. They rode past an adobe church, with a high bell tower, then the courthouse and several small establishments. A large general store, apparently the only one in Lincoln, dominated the business district. Nearby was a bank and a hotel; farther down the street were shops and saloons and a couple of cafes. Across from one saloon was a burnt-out ruin, obviously a structure of some substance before being reduced to charred rubble. Many of the buildings, notably the hotel and the general store, were pocked with bullet holes.

Starbuck reined to a halt before the hotel. He left Poe with instructions to get the men quartered and the horses stabled. Then he crossed the street and walked back along the boardwalk to the courthouse.

Only last night John Chisum had given him a brief rundown on Lincoln County's new sheriff. After a pleasant supper, seated once again in the den, Starbuck had sipped whiskey and listened while the rancher talked. Pat Garrett had drifted into New Mexico Territory not quite three years past. A former buffalo hunter and cowhand, he quickly evidenced the determination to settle down and make something of himself. With money he'd saved, he opened a saloon at Fort Sumner, and shortly afterwards, he married a local girl. Billy the Kid often frequented his saloon, and in time a friendship developed. The natives jokingly called them "Big Casino" and "Little Casino," for at six-four, Garrett was nearly a foot taller than the Kid. But Garrett had aspirations to bigger things; early in 1880 he moved his family to Roswell, and opened a general store. There he courted the respectable element, businessmen and politicians, and the most influential rancher in the territory, John Chisum. Backed by the Jinglebob owner for sheriff, he had won a landslide victory in the November elections. His one campaign promise was to rid New Mexico of its boy outlaw.

Yet, according to Chisum, the new sheriff had made little headway in the month since the election. There was talk he never would, due to his past friendship with the Kid. Chisum discounted such gossip, however, for he had satisfied himself that Pat Garrett was an ambitious man. One perfectly willing to use the Kid as a steppingstone into the larger arena of territorial politics.

A good listener, Starbuck had nodded and sipped his whiskey and offered no comment. He'd learned long ago that secondhand information was unreliable at best, and all too often misleading. Chisum's assessment of Garrett might very well prove correct. On the other hand, it was entirely possible the town gossips had stumbled upon the truth. So far as Starbuck was concerned, it was a toss of the dice, and a poor bet either way. But now, as he entered the courthouse and moved toward the sheriff's office, he had no qualms. Within a few minutes, he would determine the only truth that mattered. His truth.

Pat Garrett greeted him affably. Expecting resentment, Starbuck was immediately put on guard. But the sheriff pumped his hand, offering him a chair, to all appearances genuinely cordial. Once they were seated, Garrett took a sheet of paper from his desk drawer. He grinned, casually tossing it across the desk.

"I don't know whether you read it or not, but Chisum's letter sure don't mince words. He must've thought the idea would put my nose out of joint."

Starbuck merely glanced at the letter. "You're not sore?"

"Hell, no!" Garrett said earnestly. "I got more troubles than I can say grace over. Besides which, nobody ever accused me of being a dimdot."

"I don't follow you."

"Well, it's no secret that politics put me in office.

Politics and John Chisum. So there's no way I'm gonna start riding a high horse where he's concerned."

"That's it?" Starbuck prompted him. "One hand washes the other, and no questions asked?"

"Not altogether," Garrett replied. "See, I've got a long ways to go as a lawman. I figure you can help me get there, and I'd be a damn fool not to grab the chance. Boiled down, you've got the savvy and I need it. It's just that simple."

Starbuck wondered at the man's candor. Somehow his openness and mild tone didn't square with his rawboned looks. Aside from his towering height, he was broad-shouldered and full through the chest. His features were angular, with wide-set eyes and a straight mouth partially covered by a brushy mustache. All in all, he appeared tough as rawhide, hardly the amiable, easygoing giant. Starbuck thought he would bear watching.

"You're agreeable, then," Starbuck asked at length, "to me calling the shots? No bones now, no bones later?"

"Not a one," Garrett affirmed. "We both want the Kid hung, and for my money, that's all that counts. You've got your reasons and I've got mine—fair enough?"

"Fair enough." Starbuck took out the makings and began rolling a smoke. "Suppose you tell me about the Kid."

"There's not a helluva lot to tell."

"Start with his habits. Other than rustling cows

and killing people, what's he do in his spare time?"

"Oh, he's got the usual vices. Next to liquor and gamblin', he's always had an eye for women."

"Has he got a favorite hangout?"

"A couple," Garrett acknowledged. "Mesilla and Fort Sumner. But he's tricky, always on the move. No way to predict where he'll turn up next."

"Mesilla?" Starbuck struck a match, lit his cigarette. "I seem to recollect that's down near the border."

"Half a day's ride, maybe less."

"Any chance he holes up in Old Mexico after a job?"

"Hell, what's the need? Except for lawmen, he's got no worries north of the border."

"Most folks just naturally take his side, that it?"

"Some do, and them that don't are too scared to let on otherwise. Live and let live, that's their motto."

"Have you ever come close to nailing him?"

"No," Garrett admitted. "He's had me runnin' around like a fart in a bottle, and that's a plain fact. Course, maybe Chisum told you, I've only been in office a little more than a month."

"You mean to say nobody's spotted him? No reports at all?"

"Well—" Garret paused, obviously troubled. "Couple of weeks ago, him and his gang had a brush with the law over around White Oaks. But it was one in a million, strictly an accident. He got away without a scratch."

"Where's White Oaks?"

"Other side of the mountains; northwest of here."

"Northwest." Starbuck pondered a moment. "Suppose the Kid wanted to avoid Lincoln and the Jinglebob. Could he circle around the mountains and cut across to Fort Sumner?"

"Yeah, that'd be one way to do it."

"And from there, he'd have a straight run into the Panhandle, wouldn't he?"

"What're you gettin' at?"

"Nothing," Starbuck said quietly. "Just working my way backwards."

"Backwards to what?"

"Good question." Starbuck made an empty gesture with his hands. "Any idea where the Kid unloads all that rustled stock?"

"God A'mighty!" Garrett snorted. "If I knew that, we wouldn't have no problem, would we?"

"But it has to be someplace close around. Otherwise it doesn't make sense."

"Why do you say that?"

"Because he switches back and forth raiding Chisum and the Panhandle outfits."

"I don't see the connection."

"You would if you had to drive Jinglebob cows over any distance. He has to get rid of them in a hurry, and that means whoever he deals with probably buys everything he rustles."

"Panhandle stock included?"

"Sounds reasonable to me."

"So where does that lead us?"

Starbuck almost told him. Then, on sudden impulse, he changed his mind. "Maybe nowhere. I'll have to think on it awhile."

Garrett heaved himself to his feet. "If there's any heavy thinkin' to be done, I always say a man does it better with a drink in his hand. Care to join me?"

"Thanks, Sheriff." Starbuck rose. "Don't mind if I do."

"Call me Pat." Circling the desk, Garrett grinned broadly. "Hell, since I started politickin', I don't hardly answer to nothing else."

"Sure thing," Starbuck said without irony. "My friends call me Luke."

"Well, Luke, let's go get ourselves a dose of pop-skull."

Outside, the men turned west, angling across the street. As they walked, Garrett pointed out the charred ruin, explaining that it had once been the McSween Mercantile. With some relish, he went on to recount the end of the Lincoln County War.

Later dubbed the Three Day Battle, it began when the Kid led a band of hired guns into Lincoln. A direct challenge to the Murphy forces, it was designed to force a showdown. The Kid and his men took cover in the McSween Mercantile and the home that adjoined the store. The opposition, led by Sheriff George Peppin, occupied a store and hotel owned by Murphy and his partner, Jack Dobson. The battle raged for three days and two nights, with gunfire sweeping the street and the town's residents locked in their homes. On the third night the Murphy forces set fire to McSween's house, which quickly spread to the store. Silhouetted against the flames, the besieged men were forced to make a run for their lives. The Kid escaped, but Alexander McSween went down in a hailstorm of bullets. Altogether, the Three Day Battle resulted in ten killed and nearly twice that number wounded.

Ironically, only days before the showdown, L. G. Murphy had died a natural death in Santa Fe. With their leaders dead, the opposing factions gradually disbanded following the battle. Old animosities still existed, fanned anew when the Kid and his gang turned to rustling as a livelihood. Yet, in the ashes of the McSween store, an official end had been written to the Lincoln County War.

"Life's funny," Garrett concluded. "Nobody hardly remembers McSween and Murphy. But the Kid's still front-page news, and everybody from the governor on down wants to see him hung. Damn queer, the way things turn out."

Inside the saloon, Garrett led the way toward the bar. Then, suddenly reversing himself, he walked to a table where two men were seated. With a wide smile, he beckoned Starbuck over to the table.

"Luke, I'd like you to meet Jack Dobson and Judge Hough. Gents, this here's my new deputy, Luke Starbuck."

Starbuck sensed an instant of hesitation. Jack Dobson, like Chisum, was a survivor of the Lincoln County War. Yet he was politically opposed to the cattleman, and therefore no friend of Pat Garrett's.

After a round of handshakes, Starbuck moved to one side, watchful.

Garrett was in a bragging mood. He informed the men that Starbuck was only one of six new deputies. He went on to state that, with his expanded force, he would soon have the Kid under lock and key. Dobson, a paunchy, whey-faced man, waited until the sheriff paused for breath. Then he smiled, flashing a mouth full of gold-capped teeth, and shook his head.

"What if the Kid don't cooperate, Pat? Six men or sixty, you've still got to catch him."

"Hell's fire!" Garrett beamed. "I got myself some experienced manhunters! Luke and these other boys eat hardcases like the Kid for breakfast. You mark my word, we'll have him in the bag before Christmas!"

"Maybe you will," Dobson chuckled, "maybe you won't. Guess we'll just have to wait and see."

"Whatever the outcome," Judge Hough added quickly, "we wish you luck, Sheriff." He paused, glancing at Starbuck. "And, of course, you too, Deputy."

Starbuck merely nodded. A bloodless man in his late forties, the judge had bleached blue eyes and skin the lifeless texture of parchment. He was tall and rangy, with sallow features and an enigmatic gaze, as though the head of an eagle had been grafted onto the body of a whooping crane.

No one spoke for a moment. Dobson fell silent, while Starbuck and the judge inspected each other.

Then, with heavy good humor, Garrett addressed Judge Hough.

"We'll take all the luck we can get, and I appreciate the sentiment, Judge. Even if you don't mean it, you're a gentleman and a scholar."

With a bluff smile, Garrett turned and walked to the bar. Starbuck joined him, and the barkeep hustled forward with a bottle and glasses. The lawman poured, chuckling softly to himself.

"Bastards!" he grunted. "Sure did my heart good to rub their noses in it."

"I take it Dobson's pulling for the Kid."

"Oh hell, yes!" Garrett hooted. "He'd take sides with the devil himself if he thought it would fix my wagon."

"Seems sort of strange," Starbuck mused aloud. "When you consider the Kid was gunning for him not too long ago."

"Well, like I said, it's a queer world. The Kid used to side with Chisum, and now he rustles Jinglebob cows." He downed his drink, poured another. "Course, where Dobson's concerned, it's a matter of politics. If I don't catch the Kid, then him and his crowd won't have no trouble electin' themselves a sheriff next time around."

"What about the judge?" Starbuck asked. "Where's he fit into it?"

"One of Dobson's cronies," Garrett said without much interest. "His name's Owen Hough. Had himself a pretty fair law practice in Santa Fe at one time. Then Murphy hired him to look after their legal interests, and when the fightin' was over, Dobson got him elected to city judge."

"Seems a little bit like a comedown, doesn't it?"

"Damned if it don't! For my money, he would've been smarter to stick to Santa Fe. Christ, anything beats lickin' Jack Dobson's boots!"

Starbuck had a visceral instinct about such things. He sensed that Judge Owen Hough was no bootlicker. Moreover, he'd noted that Dobson quickly backed off once the judge entered the conversation. It occurred to him that there was more to the alliance of businessman and lawyer than appeared on the surface. But it was a passing thought, and he had no time to explore it further. Garrett's voice intruded with amiable mockery.

"You look like you done started that heavy thinkin' we was talking about."

"Yeah, some," Starbuck allowed. "Only trouble is, we keep adding pieces to the puzzle."

"Maybe so," Garrett commented. "But I get the feelin' you've already fit the first piece into place."

Starbuck nodded. "Suppose you tell me about Fort Sumner."

CHAPTER 5

A hunter's moon slipped out from behind the clouds. The landscape around Fort Sumner, blanketed by a light snowfall, was momentarily limned in an ice-blue brilliance. Then the moon faded, and a dull overcast once more bathed the settlement in darkness.

Starbuck and John Poe stood outside an adobe at the edge of the settlement. The building, like many of those at Fort Sumner, was deserted. But it commanded a view of the road leading west, toward the Jicarilla Mountains. For the past two nights, the adobe had served as a hideout for the lawmen and their horses. With no fires allowed, the thick walls also provided shelter from the bitter cold. Bedded down inside were Pat Garrett and his regular deputies, Jim Bell and Bob Ollinger. The four new deputies, Starbuck's men, completed the posse.

Starbuck was playing a hunch. From past experience, he'd learned there was a pattern to any manhunt. Outlaws who had evaded capture for any length of time often grew bold, and careless. The leader of a gang, after several successful jobs, inevitably developed an inflated opinion of himself. A by-product of that vanity was an ever-increasing contempt for lawmen. With time, simple audacity gave way to recklessness, and caution ceased to be a factor. Almost without exception, the leader of an outlaw band assumed a mantle of invincibility, and godlike arrogance.

All he'd learned to date convinced Starbuck that Billy the Kid had fallen into a similar pattern. Little known by his real name, William Bonney, the Kid had thumbed his nose at the law since age fifteen. Barely twenty-one now, he had killed eight men in the last six years, and never once come close to facing the hangman's rope. His exploits had brought him the adulation of the common people and the respect of a gang of ruffians feared throughout the territory. It was heady stuff, quite enough to turn any man cocksure and overly bold.

The information Starbuck had gleaned from Pat Garrett merely confirmed his hunch. The Kid alternated raids on Chisum's Jinglebob with forays into the Panhandle. While there was no set timetable to the raids, there was nonetheless a definite pattern. The Kid always struck each location once a month, and he *never* struck the same spot twice in a row. Which led to a very tempting conclusion.

The gang's aborted raid on the LX had occurred precisely two weeks past. Only three nights ago the Jinglebob had lost more than a hundred head to rustlers. Logic dictated that it was the Kid's handiwork, and it might be deduced that the gang would again skirt the Jicarilla Mountains on a gradual eastward swing to the Panhandle. Starbuck was convinced the eastward swing regularly included a layover at Fort Sumner.

An abandoned army post, Fort Sumner was remote and starkly uninviting. Pete Maxwell, one of the few ranchers in the area, had taken over several of the buildings as headquarters for his cattle operation. A small settlement had evolved, with a general store and the saloon previously owned by Pat Garrett. Most of the residents were Mexican vaqueros and their families, and the local economy revolved around Maxwell's ranch. The nearest law was in Lincoln, ninety miles southwest, and native-born Mexicans had small regard for gringo peace officers. As a result, the Kid was free to come and go as he pleased. He was widely admired—polite to the women and generous to the men who drank with him—and always welcome at Fort Sumner. No one there, Pete Maxwell included, would think of betraying him.

For two days and a night the lawmen had remained hidden in the adobe. The road was a narrow track, seldom used, and no one from the settlement had as yet discovered them. But now, early on the second night, Starbuck's concern was deepening. With no fire, and the men limited to cold rations, the chance of a storm posed serious problems. Even though the snowfall was still light, he questioned the wisdom of staying too much longer. At last, after searching the overcast sky, he turned to Poe.

"I'm thinking we'll have to call it quits."

"That wouldn't bother Garrett's boys none."

"Yeah, they're not much, are they?"

"Couple of peckerheads, if you ask me."

John Poe was a methodical man, stingy with words, but a dead shot and absolutely fearless in a fight. Somewhere in his late thirties, he was powerfully built, with ruddy features and an inscrutable manner. Aside from Ben Langham, he was the only man Starbuck had ever fully trusted.

"Suppose we stick it out till midnight." Starbuck paused, studying the clouds a moment. "If it hasn't cleared by then, we'll let the boys build a fire and cook some hot grub."

"Whatever you say."

"You got a better idea?"

Poe rolled his quid to the other jaw and spat a stream of tobacco juice. "Not unless you've got a bearskin coat handy."

"No such luck—"

Starbuck suddenly stopped. He peered through the swirling snow, listening. Then he heard it again, the faint jingle of saddle gear somewhere in the distance. He whirled to Poe.

"Quick, inside! Get the boys ready!"

While Poe awakened the men, Starbuck stationed himself at the window nearest the road. Within the space of a minute, Garrett was crouched beside the doorway, and the deputies were positioned by the windows fronting the adobe. No one spoke, listening intently as the sound of hoofbeats drew closer.

Then, one at a time, five riders materialized out of the snow. They were strung out in single file, their horses held to a walk. Hunched deep within their coats, the men were dim shapes, their features indistinguishable.

The riders were within yards of the adobe when Pat Garrett abruptly stepped through the doorway. He raised his hand, rapped out an order. *"Halt!"*

The lead rider jerked erect, clawing his coat aside. There was a gleam of metal as his gun cleared leather, then Starbuck shot him. He screamed, pitching sideways out of the saddle, and tumbled to the ground. Before Starbuck could lever another round into his carbine, the other riders reined sharply around and gigged their horses into a gallop. The remaining lawmen at last opened fire, but it was too late. The drifting snow closed in behind the riders, and an instant later the thud of hoofbeats faded away to silence.

Starbuck moved to the door, brushing past Garrett, and walked to the fallen rider. Garrett hesitated a moment, then the deputies crowded through the doorway, and they trooped along in a bunch behind Starbuck. As they crowded around, he struck a match, cupping it with his hands over the dead man's face.

"Anybody know him?"

"Tom O'Folliard," Garrett mumbled. "He's one of the Kid's men."

"So we had him," Starbuck rose, his voice edged, "and let him get away."

"Sorry." Garrett ducked his head. "I thought maybe they'd come along without a fight."

"Well, Sheriff, you damn near got your ass shot off! Of all the fool stunts—"

Starbuck turned away, furious. He stalked toward the adobe, staring straight ahead. At the doorway, he suddenly spun around, motioning to the deputies.

"Get saddled!" he ordered. "Poe, take a couple of men and go round up some lanterns."

"That's crazy!" Garrett protested. "We'll lose their tracks in the snow."

"We ride in ten minutes."

Starbuck turned and entered the adobe.

The trail twisted and dodged for a week. The Kid crossed mountain ranges and mesas, doubled back and circled, attempting every trick known to lose his pursuers. But the foul weather held and the skies remained overcast; for all his cunning, there was no way to erase horse tracks in fresh snow. The posse was never more than a few hours behind.

Starbuck drove the men with dogged relentlessness. The bitter cold sapped their spirits, and the chase, punishing to man and animal alike, slowly drained their vitality. By the sixth day, they were haggard and bleary-eyed with fatigue. Their grumbling had turned to surly ill-temper, and the slightest offense provoked an argument. Yet the men, despite their rebellious mood, were the least of Starbuck's worries. Their horses were spent, slogging heavy-footed through the snow, and their rations were running low. Without fresh mounts and adequate provisions, they were finished. Unless the Kid was caught quickly, he would not be caught at all.

Camp was pitched that evening on the windswept banks of a small creek. Supper consisted of boiled jerky and hardtack, washed down with coffee. Sitting off to one side, Starbuck pondered their situation, and found the prospects bleak. His one consolation was that the Kid faced an equally miserable predicament. Pressed hard, never allowed to pause or replenish their supplies, the gang would also be on short rations tonight. He took bitter comfort from the thought.

Starbuck drained the last of his coffee, and rose. He walked to the fire, where Garrett squatted with his hands held to the flames. Tossing his cup on the ground, Starbuck caught the lawman's eyes and nodded. Turning, he moved a short distance downstream, and Garrett joined him a moment later.

"I hate to admit it," Starbuck commenced in a sandy voice, "but we've about run out our string."

"No argument there," Garrett said bluntly. "Even good men can only be pushed so far."

"The hell of it is," Starbuck frowned, "I figure the Kid's only a couple of hours ahead of us. Galls me to quit when we're that close."

"We've got no choice," Garrett reminded him. "It'd take us another day to close the gap, and by then we'd be afoot. Horses got their limits, too."

Garrett's tone was waspish, disgruntled. Though he was nominally in command, even his own deputies understood that it was Starbuck who gave the orders. The arrangement grated on him, and day by day his mood had sharpened. Yet he needed Starbuck, and for all his simmering resentment, he continued to swallow his pride. The Kid was his ticket to bigger things.

Starbuck gave him a speculative look. "What's up ahead, the direction the Kid took?"

"Lots of open space."

"No towns, no ranches? Nothing?"

"Oh, there's an old shepherd's hut at Stinking Springs, but nothin' else within a day's ride. It's pretty sparse over this way, mostly sheep country."

"A shepherd's hut," Starbuck said slowly. "How far off?"

"Maybe—" Garrett stopped, eyes suddenly alert. "A couple of hours, three at the outside."

"You think the Kid—"

"Damn right he would!" Garrett interrupted. "He knows this country like he knows the back of his hand."

"That being the case, it makes sense he'd camp there to get out of the weather."

"Course it does! With dark comin' on, it'd be the most natural thing on earth."

"Suppose we let the horses rest till midnight. You reckon we could take it easy and still make it there by sunup?"

"Why, hell, yes! Even if we had to walk 'em

partway, we'd get there with time to spare."

Starbuck let the idea percolate a few moments. "It's a gamble, but we might just catch the Kid with his drawers down. You game?"

"I'm game." Garrett glanced toward the fire. "I don't know about the men."

"Well, Pat, if they're not, then we'll just handle it ourselves. How's that sound?"

"By God, you got yourself a deal."

The men heard them out. The idea of a night march brought some low grumbling, but no one seriously objected. Instead, like a lodestone freshly glimpsed, their thoughts turned to Stinking Springs, and the Kid.

By dawn, crouched low in an arroyo, the men were in position. The stone hut, located on a desolate stretch of prairie, had no windows and only one door. The gang's horses were picketed in front of the hut, and shortly before sunup, a tendril of smoke drifted from the stovepipe chimney.

A few minutes later, one of the outlaws stepped outside and began unbuttoning his fly. Without warning, Garrett fired, followed instantly by shots from three of the deputies. The outlaw reeled backwards, clutching his chest, and staggered through the doorway. From inside the hut there was a loud commotion, men shouting and cursing. Then a shrill voice, rising to a maddened pitch, drowned out the others.

"They've murdered you, Charlie! Kill some of the sonsabitches before you die!"

"That's the Kid," Garrett said quickly. "Watch 'em now!"

The wounded outlaw lurched through the door. The lawmen watched in disbelief as he hobbled toward them. His shirtfront was drenched with blood and he held a cocked pistol in his hand. Yet no one spoke, and without command, they held their fire. Some twenty yards away, the outlaw stumbled to a halt and his mouth opened. The words were lost in a gush of blood and his eyes rolled back in his head. He fell face down in the snow.

Starbuck raised his carbine, sighting carefully. He shot the horse nearest the door, and grunted with satisfaction as the animal went down, blocking the entrance. He worked the lever and placed three rapid shots at the base of the stovepipe. A fourth shot sent it flying off the roof, and within moments smoke began seeping through cracks in the door. He smiled, lowering the carbine, and turned to Garrett.

"Talk to the Kid. Tell him the show's over."

Garrett nodded, cupped his hands to his mouth. "Hey, Kid! It's me, Pat Garrett! Can you hear me?"

"I hear you, Pat. What's on your mind?"

"Gettin' a little smoky in there, is it?"

"Not bad. Whyn't you come on down and get a snootful?"

"You're boxed in, Kid! Nowhere to go! Call it quits!"

"Like hell! We'll just sit tight and let you freeze your balls off out there."

Starbuck whispered something to Garrett, and the lawman bobbed his head. "Won't work, Kid!" Garrett shouted. "You try waitin' till dark and we'll just kill your horses. Even if you bust out of that hut, you'd never make it on foot. Wise up and toss in your hand!"

Silence descended on the hut. Smoke continued to filter through the door, and gradually the sound of men coughing became louder. After several minutes the Kid's voice suddenly broke the stillness.

"You win, Pat! We've had enough!"

"No funny business!" Garrett yelled. "Shuck your gunbelts! Come out with your hands in the air!"

A few moments passed, then the door creaked open. One by one, dimly obscured by the smoke, the outlaws walked from the hut. At Starbuck's suggestion, Garrett ordered them to move forward, away from the picketed horses. The men complied, halting on his command, their arms raised.

With the deputies covering them, Garrett and Starbuck scrambled from the arroyo. Their carbines held at hip level, they separated and moved to within a few yards of the outlaws. Starbuck had no trouble identifying the Kid. He was runt-sized, with a lantern jaw and the look of a bantam gamecock. His eyes were the color of carpenter's chalk, and cold. He waited until they halted, then gave Garrett a lopsided grin.

"Don't shoot, Pat. We'll come peaceable."

"Cut the wisecracks," Garrett growled. "There's nothin' funny about where you're headed."

"Yeah, well, it ain't all that serious either. I've slipped away from some real lawmen, Pat. I don't guess you'll gimme too much trouble."

"Don't get me riled, Billy! I mean it now!"

"Wouldn't think of it, Pat." The Kid laughed, and his gaze shifted to Starbuck. "You the jasper that did the fancy shootin'?"

Starbuck regarded him without expression. "What makes you ask?"

"Just curious."

"You try to make a break," Garrett cut in, "and he'll sure enough show you some fancy shootin'."

"He'd have to do it," the Kid grinned. "You couldn't've hit that stovepipe if it was jammed straight up your butthole."

"By God, that's it!"

Garrett ordered one of his deputies to fetch the manacles from his saddlebags. Ten minutes later they had the outlaws mounted and were ready to move out. With Garrett in the lead, and Starbuck riding shotgun, they turned their horses toward Santa Fe.

CHAPTER 6

Three days before New Year's, Starbuck crossed the plaza and walked toward the territorial jail. Until a trial date could be set, the Kid and his gang were being held there for safekeeping. Only then, according to Garrett, would they be transported back to Lincoln.

Starbuck now had reason to believe otherwise.

The plaza swarmed with activity. A town built on commerce and politics, the territorial capital was once the terminus for the Santa Fe Trail. Winter was the slow season, but as a major trade center, Santa Fe was never really idle. Exchange between Mexico and the United States was its principal business, and tons of trade goods, arriving now by train rather than wagon caravan, were stored there year round. Shops around the square were crowded, and open-air markets on the plaza itself were thronged with people. The holidays had done nothing to slow the brisk pace of trade.

To Starbuck, all the clamor and hubbub was a vast annoyance. He felt nothing of the festive spirit, and the season of brotherly love seemed to him an ironic joke. His thoughts were on deception and double-dealing. And as he moved through the crowds, he was plagued by a sense of betrayal.

Arriving in Santa Fe the day after Christmas, he had been filled with quiet elation. Ben Langham's killer had been caught, and he'd completed the job in slightly less than three weeks. The fact that Garrett got credit for capturing the Kid—and evidenced no intention of sharing the limelight—bothered him not at all. The Kid had been charged with an old murder, the assassination of a Lincoln County sheriff some two years past. It was a strong case, with several eyewitnesses, and there was no question the Kid would be tried and hung. Though impatient to see the Kid mount the scaffold, Starbuck was satisfied with the arrangement. An eye for an eye would shortly be exacted.

Then, unwittingly, one of Garrett's deputies had talked out of turn. Night before last, with several drinks under his belt, Bob Ollinger let slip that the Kid had been offered a deal. Questioned by Starbuck, the deputy refused to elaborate. But he drunkenly implied the Kid could escape hanging by turning state's evidence against those behind the rustling. His last statement, though somewhat cryptic, was the most telling.

"The Kid spilled his guts before and he'll do it again."

Starbuck braced Garrett later that night and demanded an explanation. The lawman professed ignorance, claiming Ollinger was a blowhard and given to an overactive imagination when drunk. Pressed for details, he did admit that Chisum believed there was a mastermind behind the rustling. He declined to speculate, however, on whether Chisum would go so far as to offer the Kid a deal. Nor would he discuss the motives, personal or otherwise, that might prompt the cattleman to do so.

Unconvinced, Starbuck began an investigation of his own early next morning. Having failed with Garrett, he resolved to trick the Kid into an admission. But that would require a bold hand, and sufficient facts to give his bluff the ring of truth. He needed information about the last time the Kid had "spilled his guts," and his search began in the territorial records of the Lincoln County War. By late afternoon, the trail led to the former Attorney General of New Mexico. There, employing a discreet form of interrogation, he uncovered the full story.

Following the Three Day Battle in Lincoln, Governor Lew Wallace issued a general amnesty for all offenses committed during the "war." Some months later, a lawyer who had supported Alexander McSween was callously murdered by two former members of the Murphy—Dobson faction. Upon learning the Kid had witnessed the shooting, Governor Wallace promised immunity, and a full pardon, if he would testify. The Kid agreed, submitting to arrest, and gave testimony before a grand jury. Then, for no apparent reason, he escaped from jail and promptly returned to cattle rustling. The governor publicly denounced him and withdrew all forms of immunity. Since that time, flaunting the law, the Kid had grown even more vicious. He was known to have murdered three men in cold blood, including an unarmed Indian Agent on the Mescalero reservation. Why he'd broken his agreement with the governor, however, remained a mystery. One of the many surrounding Billy the Kid.

Late last night, reflecting on what he'd learned, Starbuck had found sleep impossible. He tossed and turned, trying to formulate a plan, and hadn't closed his eyes until shortly before dawn. But now, crossing the plaza, his confidence was restored. The answer had come to him at breakfast this morning, and it had come with startling clarity.

The Kid, like all outlaws, viewed any peace officer with suspicion and distrust. The trick was simply to make him believe he was being tricked.

Starbuck had no compunction about using subterfuge and guile. Experience had taught him that a certain breed of outlaw had no concept of morality. For reasons he failed to understand, the public made folk heroes of such men as Jesse James and Sam Bass. And Billy the Kid. Cast in the role of the underdog, these men were thought to have compassion for the downtrodden and an inborn hatred of injustice. But such attributes were the invention of dime novels, and the public's bizarre need to create legends larger than life. Four years as a range detective had convinced Starbuck that these mankillers lacked even the most fundamental code of decency. Only a fool dealt with them on the basis of fair play, and only by being utterly pragmatic had he survived their treachery and malice.

Contrary to popular belief, he knew the Kid was nothing more than a common murderer. Far from a gunfighter, the young outlaw had given none of his victims an even break. Of the eight men he'd killed, at least seven had been gunned down with no chance to defend themselves. Folklore and truth, where the Kid was concerned, had absolutely nothing in common.

To Starbuck, there was more than passing similarity to a rabid animal. If a mad dog was terrorizing the countryside, no one would hesitate to shoot it down on sight. The Kid was no different. And Starbuck now regretted that the Kid had allowed himself to be taken prisoner. Justice would have been more swiftly served if the young outlaw had chosen to make a fight of it. Starbuck would have then killed him quickly and efficiently, thereby ridding the world of one more mad dog. Yet the Kid still lived, and, given the chance he might elude the hangman's rope, Starbuck saw no alternative. He somehow had to trick the Kid into rendering his own death warrant.

Starbuck was admitted to the territorial jail without question. As one of Garrett's deputies, it was only natural that he would drop around to check on the star prisoner. The cell block was large, with a wide corridor, and he was relieved to see that the Kid had been segregated from the rest of the gang.

What he had in mind would work better without an audience.

Locked in adjoining cells, Dave Rudabaugh, Tom Pickett, and Bill Wilson watched passively as the guard led Starbuck down the corridor. Toward the rear, all the cells were empty; there were no prisoners on either side of the Kid or across the corridor. He lay sprawled on a rickety bunk, staring at the ceiling.

The guard halted before the door. "Look alive, Kid. You got yourself a visitor." Turning, he nodded to Starbuck. "Give a yell if you need anything."

"Much obliged."

Starbuck waited until he was out of earshot, then moved closer to the cell door. "Mornin', Billy. Thought I'd come by and see how they're treating you."

"No complaint."

"How's the food?"

"Tolerable."

"Glad to hear it." Starbuck pulled out the makings and began rolling a cigarette. "Care for a smoke?"

"Don't mind if I do."

The Kid rose from his bunk in one motion and stepped to the door. Starbuck passed the makings through the bars, and smiled. "Keep it, if you want. I can always get more."

"Thanks."

After the Kid had built himself a cigarette, Starbuck struck a match. They both lit up and stood smoking a moment in silence. Then the Kid regarded him with a crooked grin.

"You through dancin' around the Maypole?"

"Come again?"

"Whatever it is, whyn't you just get to it? You ain't here to shoot the breeze and we both know it."

Starbuck had seen his share of hardcases. In Texas, and elsewhere he'd ridden, there was no scarcity of the breed. The young outlaw was cast from a similar mold, and yet, there was something different about him. The pale blue eyes were steady and confident, and behind the gaze was a cocksure certainty more menacing than a bald-faced threat. The Kid was one of those oddities of God's handiwork, a man purged of conscience. He could kill with the icy detachment of an executioner, and never suffer a moment's remorse. If Starbuck had needed any justification, he found it staring at him through the bars. He decided it was time to trim the Kid's wick.

"I've got a message from a mutual friend."

"Yeah, who's that?"

"No names." Starbuck glanced over his shoulder. "Some of these places, the walls have got ears."

"So what's the message?"

"He says time's running out. If you figure to make a deal, you better do it pretty quick."

"Christ, the old bastard only contacted me day before yesterday. What's the rush?"

Starbuck had one of the answers needed, and it enabled him to proceed with greater assurance. He shrugged. "You might recall, he gives orders, not explanations. Hell, I don't even know who it was that contacted you! But the old man evidently thought the message wasn't strong enough. He sent word for me to have a talk with you."

"Tell him to get the ants out of his pants. I still got time to think it over."

"Not if they set an early trial date, you don't."

"Come off it," the Kid scoffed. "What's that got to do with anything?"

"Plenty," Starbuck said earnestly. "Once you're remanded to the Lincoln court, there'll be lots more pressure for the governor to keep hands off."

The Kid gave him a swift, sidelong look. "Who you tryin' to shit, Starbuck?"

"I don't follow you."

"In a pig's ass! You think I don't know who you are?"

Starbuck almost smiled. He cautioned himself to go slow, allow the Kid to swallow the hook on his own. "Suppose you tell me who I am."

"You're a goddamn range detective! You draw your pay from the Panhandle Cattlemen's Association!"

"That's not exactly a secret."

"Aww for Chrissake!" The Kid laughed suddenly, a harsh sound in the cramped cell. "Are you gonna stand there and tell me you're not tryin' to run a sandy?"

"Whoa, now!" Starbuck looked genuinely puzzled. "You just lost me going around the turn."

"Horseshit! You come to the territory to see me planted, and there ain't no two ways about it. You must think I'm some kind of fool to believe you'd take a hand in anything that would stop me from gettin' hung."

"You're talking about Langham—the fellow that was killed over in the Panhandle—aren't you?"

"Don't try puttin' words in my mouth. I'm saying you want me dead, and the reason don't matter."

"You're wrong," Starbuck insisted. "The Association wants the rustling stopped, and that's their only interest. The way they figure it, Langham's dead and gone, and there's not a helluva lot of profit in vengeance."

"Profit?" the Kid said scornfully. "What the devil's profit got to do with it?"

"Everything," Starbuck nodded gravely. "You know it yourself: the only thing that matters to the big boys is how much dinero they put in the bank. They're willing to trade you in order to get a shot at the head dog behind all this rustling."

"You're lying! I can smell it like you'd been dunked in sheep dip."

"Why would I lie? I've got no reason."

"I don't know," the Kid said doubtfully. "But I still say it stinks."

"Then you'd better take off the blinders and start thinking straight. Unless the Panhandle crowd was in agreement with—the old man—how would I even know you'd been offered a deal? I'm strictly a messenger boy, just following orders. That's all there is to it, plain and simple."

The Kid turned away. He was obviously confused and suspicious, not at all convinced he'd heard the truth. He took a long pull on his cigarette, staring at a spot of sunlight on the floor. Finally, with a look of sudden resolve, he glanced around at Starbuck.

"No soap," he said shortly. "Tell the old man I pass."

"Hold off—"

"Like hell! I got sold down the river once before, and I ain't gonna fall for it again."

"You mean a couple of years ago, when the governor got you to testify before the grand jury?"

"Damn right!" The Kid spoke in an aggrieved tone. "The sonovabitch spoon-fed me a bunch of promises, and after I delivered, he went ahead and pressed charges against me anyway."

"You're plumb certain about that, are you?"

"If I wasn't, why the hell would I've broke jail?"

"Well—" Starbuck hesitated, seemingly at a loss. "I suppose you've got a point, but of course that time around you were playing a lone hand. This time, there are some important people who'll bring pressure to bear on the governor. Believe me—with what's at stake—they won't sell you out."

"I don't trust none of 'em," the Kid said stubbornly. "Once I testified, they'd welch on the deal faster'n scat! So you just tell 'em I said to jam it up their butt."

Starbuck felt a surge of triumph. He set his features in a downcast expression, but inside he knew he had soured the Kid on any sort of deal. The trial would go forward, and all in due time, Ben Langham's killer would be hung. He was on the verge of letting it rest there, but on impulse, he suddenly changed his mind. Perhaps it was possible to dust two birds with a single stone. One last trick.

"You know," he suggested casually, "it wouldn't hurt your chances none to hedge your bet. Even if you mean to hold out, you could still play both ends against the middle."

"I don't savvy," the Kid said woodenly. "Hedge my bet how?"

"Give the old man a nibble, show your good faith. Name a few names."

"You're nuttier'n a fruitcake!"

"Wait a minute," Starbuck stilled his outburst with upraised palms. "I didn't say anything about testifying. You wouldn't even have to give a deposition. But if you named some names—and it turned out to be the straight goods—then it would sure leave the door open."

"Yeah, but I wouldn't have nothin' left to sell either."

"No, you're wrong," Starbuck told him. "Without your testimony, it's all hearsay, isn't it? So any way you cut it, you'll still improve your hand."

The Kid paused, as though weighing his words. After a marked silence, he dropped his cigarette on the floor, ground it out underfoot. Then he looked up.

"Joe Coghlin. Coghlin's Slaughterhouse in Lincoln."

"Are you saying he's the top dog?"

"No," the Kid stalled. "But he's the one that buys the rustled stock."

"Who calls the shots?" Starbuck pressed. "It's no good unless I've got the whole story."

"Well, let's just say Coghlin don't hardly take a leak till he checks with Jack Dobson."

"That's all?"

"All you're gonna get."

It was enough. Starbuck left the jail whistling to himself. Once outside, his thoughts turned to the Jinglebob and John Chisum. And he began planning the next step.

CHAPTER 7

The morning stage pulled into Santa Fe an hour late. The driver brought his team to a halt before the express office and set the brake lever with a hard kick. As the agent hurried outside, a band of street urchins gathered around. He waded through them, cursing their ancestry in broken Spanish, and hustled forward to open the coach door.

Judge Owen Hough was the first passenger to alight from the coach. Dusting himself off, he moved into the shade of the office portico. There he waited impatiently while the luggage was unloaded from the rear boot. After claiming his bag, he gave one of the Mexican *golfillos* a dollar to run it over to the hotel. Brushing the other children aside, he turned and walked quickly toward the east side of the plaza.

At the corner, Judge Hough slowed his pace. He took a cigar from inside his coat, snipping the end with one clean bite, and pretended to search his pockets for a match. While he lit the cigar, his eyes roamed the plaza, scanning the crowds for a familiar face. Satisfied he hadn't been seen, he snuffed the match and rounded the corner onto a side street. Ahead were several stores and warehouses, framed against a backdrop of the Sangre de Cristo Mountains. He strode to an alleyway separating a feed store and a livery stable, and carefully inspected the street in both directions. Then he turned into the alley.

Walking to the rear of the feed store, he mounted a short flight of stairs. He paused before a back door, rapping lightly with his knuckles, and entered. The room was windowless and sparsely furnished, empty except for two chairs and a wooden table. On the table was a kerosene lamp, the wick turned low. A large man, his features shadowed by the dim light, rose from one of the chairs. He seemed strangely out of place in the drab surroundings. His gray mustache was neatly trimmed and waxed, and he wore a frock coat and a stiff winged collar covered by a black cravat. His pearl stickpin gleamed in the umber lampglow.

He smiled and extended his hand. "Good to see you, Owen. I was beginning to think you wouldn't make it."

"The stage was late." Hough shook hands, tossing his hat on the table. "A rockslide outside Blue Springs held us up almost an hour."

"I assume you took the usual precautions?"

"Of course."

Once every month Owen Hough traveled to Santa Fe. On the pretext of personal business affairs, his trips seemed perfectly routine and aroused little interest in Lincoln. Only Jack Dobson knew the true nature of his business, and no one knew that his monthly reports were delivered in the dingy back room of a feed store. As a further precaution, the meetings were always held on random dates, selected a month in advance by the man who received his report. There was no correspondence between them, and no record existed of the meetings ever having taken place. Upon arriving in Santa Fe, it was Hough's responsibility to enter the back-alley storeroom without being observed. The penalty for failure, though never articulated by either man, was mutually understood.

"Well, let's get to it, shall we?"

Hough nodded, taking a chair across from the other man. He puffed on his cigar, waiting, aware that a certain protocol dictated how the meeting was to proceed. A moment passed, then the large man thoughtfully twisted one end of his mustache.

"Our meeting was well timed this month. The capture of Mr. Bonney and his cutthroats presents us with a delicate situation. One, I hasten to add, that has intriguing possibilities."

"Oh?" Hough said cautiously. "Such as?"

"We'll come to that later. For the moment, suppose you brief me on the state of things in Lincoln."

"There's been no great change. Chisum's health continues to deteriorate, but not alarmingly. He's just dying slowly, by degrees."

"Has his doctor visited the ranch?"

"Not to my knowledge."

"Are you saying you're not certain?"

"I'll rephrase it—no—the doctor has not visited him."

"Then we must surmise his condition remains unchanged."

"As a matter of fact," Hough replied, "our latest information has it that his spirits have improved somewhat. Apparently the Kid's capture gave him a boost, mentally if not physically."

"I see that as no consequence. In the long term, a momentary lift in spirits alters nothing."

"Perhaps not, at least where Chisum is concerned. But it's had a marked effect on our own situation."

"Would you care to be more specific?"

"Our associates have come down with a case of nerves."

"Dobson?"

"And Coghlin," Hough added. "They're frightened out of their wits the Kid will start talking."

"About the rustling operation?"

"Yes, primarily that. You see, Coghlin has dealt directly with the Kid on several occasions. And through him, that establishes an indirect link to Dobson. They don't trust the Kid and they don't trust each other—and despite all my assurances, it's evolved into a matter of fear feeding on fear."

"But that's ridiculous! The Kid has been charged with murder, not rustling."

"True enough. Of course, as Coghlin put it, the

Kid would weasel on his own mother to save himself."

"In other words, he might implicate them in exchange for a lesser charge. Or at the very worst, a commutation in the event he's sentenced to hang. Is that it?"

"Exactly."

"And you personally, Owen? Are you worried as well?"

"No, of course not," Hough said without conviction. "My hands are clean. So far as anyone knows, I'm just another political hack, a nobody."

"On the contrary. I detect a note in your voice, some slight apprehension. Are you perhaps concerned that the link tying Coghlin to Dobson extends equally to you?"

"You're mistaken, Warren. I have no reservations whatever. Absolutely none."

"Let us hope so. Conspiracy is a nasty charge, and as we both know, you are the only link connecting our associates here in Santa Fe to the affairs in Lincoln. They might well become nervous themselves if it was felt you were no longer reliable."

"I understand. And I assure you, Warren, there's no need for concern."

"But if there were"—a querulous squint—"let me be blunt. You were sent to Lincoln to do a job. Dobson and Coghlin are your responsibility, Owen. We depend on you to hold them in line, and see to it that they perform as directed. Any display of weakness on their part reflects adversely on your leadership. So, as the saying goes, a word to the wise. When you return to Lincoln, correct the situation immediately. Agreed?"

"Agreed," Hough repeated in a low voice. "Of course, it would help if I could return with something a bit more substantial regarding the Kid."

"Then you may inform our friends that Mr. Bonney will not talk."

"He won't?"

"You have my word on it."

"How can you be sure?"

"In exchange for his silence, Mr. Bonney will be offered a change of venue. Naturally, it won't make the slightest bit of difference in the verdict. But he'll be led to believe, through his defense attorney, that a change of venue represents his one hope. Like the proverbial drowning man, he will grasp at the idea of a trial anywhere other than Lincoln. The arrangements were concluded only this morning with the district judge, and Mr. Bonney will be so informed this afternoon. Do you approve?"

"It's—Warren, it's damn near Machiavellian!"

"Why, thank you, Owen. I consider that a rare compliment."

Owen Hough, by virtue of arrangements with unscrupulous men, had prospered greatly. Once a man of principle, his convictions had long ago been eroded by the practice of compromise. Slowly, trading his beliefs for position and material gain, he had become enmeshed in a web of obligations so unconscionable that he lost sight of conventional morality. Today, no less corrupt than the man across from him, he thought it a masterful stroke that the Kid would be duped into silence.

"One thing, though," he said at length. "A moment ago, you said the change of venue won't affect the verdict. I take it you mean the Kid will hang, regardless?"

"Yes, that's correct. Not only has he become a liability, but his execution will serve to distract Chisum. As we've discussed before, Chisum very likely suspects there is more to it than the rustling. With Bonney dead, however, those suspicions will be dampened considerably."

"On the other hand," Hough said hesitantly, "Chisum might look upon this as an opportunity. With the Stockgrowers' Association behind him, he could bring pressure to bear on the governor. Then, once the Kid's been sentenced to death, he could offer commutation in return for information. At that point, the Kid wouldn't hesitate to talk."

"There will be no commutation, Owen. I guarantee it! You just leave the governor to us, and go on about business as normal."

"You're saying, even if Chisum makes the offer there's no way he can deliver. So as a result, the Kid won't talk."

"Precisely."

Hough took a deep breath, blew it out heavily. "What about this fellow Starbuck? He has a reputation as a real bulldog. If Chisum hires him to dig deeper, he might just uncover something we've overlooked."

"Your Mr. Starbuck represents one of the intriguing possibilities I mentioned earlier."

"In what way?"

"As you say, he's an experienced detective. Because of that, Chisum will respect his opinion. We have only to convince Starbuck it's a simple case of rustling—nothing to do with politics—and he in turn will convince Chisum."

"How do we accomplish that?"

"Quite simple. We allow the rustling operation to die with William Bonney. In any event, it has already served its purpose: namely, to speed Chisum to his grave. So we let the rustling stop here, and everyone walks away believing it was the work of one man. Or in this case . . . a kid . . . Billy the Kid."

"I don't know." Hough sounded uncertain. "Maybe it's too simple. From what I've heard about Starbuck, he's not the type to be taken in easily."

"You correct me if I'm wrong, Owen. We've established that Bonney will not talk, regardless of the circumstances."

"Yes."

"The rustling operation has ended, and with Bonney's silence, there's no way to trace it to either Dobson or Coghlin."

"That's right."

"And aside from some unfounded suspicions,

Chisum has no way of connecting any of this to the political situation."

"Yes, that's correct, also."

"So there you have it. We've anticipated every contingency."

Hough made a small nod of acknowledgment. "Yes, it appears you have."

"Then I suggest you return to Lincoln and put our affairs in order. I needn't remind you that the Pecos Valley is all that lies between us and absolute control of the territory. We depend on you to have all the machinery in place the day John Chisum dies."

"I won't let you down, Warren."

"We never thought otherwise, Owen. Now, if, there's nothing else, suppose we depart in the usual manner. I'll see you here the twelfth of next month."

Owen Hough unfolded from the chair, tugged his coat smooth. He shook hands, not at all warmed by the other man's smile. Then he moved to the door and stepped outside. The winter air chilled the sheen of perspiration on his forehead.

Starbuck spotted him leaving the alley. On his way back to the hotel, he had paused to admire a center-fire rig in the window of a saddlemaker. As he turned to cross the plaza, he saw Hough emerge onto the side street. He quickly ducked inside the saddle shop.

Watching through the flyblown window, he sensed his instincts hadn't played him false. Not ten minutes ago the Kid had mentioned two names, Joe Coghlin and Jack Dobson. Now, by some quirk that beggared coincidence, the political crony of one of those men appeared in Santa Fe. There were, he told himself, perhaps a dozen explanations for the judge's presence in Santa Fe. Yet in the same instant he knew there was no reasonable explanation for what he'd just seen. Owen Hough was not the type to be skulking around in the alleyway of a feed store.

The judge turned the corner and walked west along the plaza. Starbuck waited until he had mingled with the crowd, then moved through the door of the saddle shop. He was torn between trailing Hough and investigating the feed store. But the debate lasted only a moment. He decided the feed store could await another time.

As he started across the plaza, he caught movement out of the corner of his eye. Something made him look around, his gaze directed to the side street, and he froze. A man emerged from the same alleyway, acting altogether too casual. From his dress, frock coat and striped trousers, he had no more business in a feed store than the judge. He walked briskly to the corner, looking straight ahead, and crossed to the south side of the plaza.

Starbuck followed him. The decision to do so was visceral, too compelling to ignore. Some gut instinct told him the man with the waxed mustache had, only moments before, parted company with Owen Hough. Their meeting, quite obviously, had been held in secret. And it was clear that they had left the feed store separately to avoid being seen together. All of which indicated they had something to hide. Something that might—or might not—have bearing on the rustling operation in Lincoln. But very definitely something that had to be explored further.

Hanging back in the crowd, Starbuck trailed the man to the Mercantile National Bank. There, turning into a stairwell, the man ascended to the second floor. Cautious now, Starbuck climbed the stairs without haste, listening as footsteps faded along a central corridor. He timed it perfectly, topping the upper landing in time to see the frock coat disappear through a door at the end of the hall. He walked down the passageway only far enough to inspect the door. The top half was frosted glass, and the word PRIVATE had been inscribed in gilt letters. His gaze swung to the adjoining door, which appeared to be the entrance to a suite of offices. He studied the legend painted there.

THE SANTA FE LAND & DEVELOPMENT CO.
WARREN F. MITCHELL
PRESIDENT

Starbuck turned and retraced his steps along the corridor. Outside the bank, he paused and rolled a smoke, pondering the strange turn of events. There were no answers, only hard questions, but one thing was clear.

His next stop was the Jinglebob, and a talk with John Chisum.

CHAPTER 8

Starbuck rode into the Jinglebob on New Year's Day. At the door, he was again met by Sallie Chisum. Her greeting was pleasant and seemingly guileless; but he wondered how much she knew of her father's affairs. By now, he had learned that her mother was dead, and despite her youth, she had assumed the duties of mistress of the house. He thought it likely that she knew a good deal more than she pretended.

John Chisum was seated before the fireplace. When Starbuck entered the den, it was as though the old man hadn't moved since his last visit. Even the cheery glow of the fire did nothing to improve the rancher's jaundiced color. He still looked wasted and frail, a husk of his former self. Yet there was a noticeable change in his manner. He was smiling, and there was a peculiar glint in his eyes.

"By golly!" Chisum boomed, pumping his arm with vigor. "Good to see you, Luke! We were mighty impressed with the way you jumped right in there and helped nail the Kid. Ain't that right, Sallie?"

"Yes, Father." Sallie paused beside his chair, smiling. "And very grateful, too."

Her hair was parted in the middle, pulled back in a tight bun. The effect was severe, but somehow accented her fine features when she smiled. She gently touched her father, placing a hand on his shoulder as if he were a fragile artifact beyond value. The gesture was natural yet revealing. Watching her, Starbuck had the impression she would never marry while her father lived. After he'd taken a seat, she excused herself and left the room. The instant the door closed, Chisum hunched forward, chortling softly.

"Tell me all about it! Skinned the little bastard good and proper, did you?"

Starbuck gave him a clenched smile. "The Kid sent you a message."

"Oh?" Chisum inquired. "What's that?"

"He said to take your deal and stuff it. He doesn't believe you'd keep your word, and he trusts the governor only about as far as he could throw him."

Chisum eyed him with a mixture of dismay and surprise. "How'd you find out?"

"Secrets of the trade." Starbuck lolled back, hooked one leg over the chair arm. "I suppose you had your reasons, but I didn't come all this way to see the Kid get a life sentence. I want him hung, and one way or another, I aim to get the job done. So I'll trade you some information in return for your promise not to interfere any further."

"What sort of information?"

"Dobson and a fellow named Joe Coghlin are behind the rustling. They use Coghlin's slaughterhouse to get rid of the rustled stock."

"The Kid told you that?"

Starbuck related the gist of his conversation with the Kid. Chisum merely listened, coldly silent. His frown deepened when he heard the Kid had refused to give evidence against Dobson and Coghlin. But he agreed, after some argument, to leave the young outlaw to the courts. He frankly admitted he'd never had much influence with the governor anyway. Then, almost as an afterthought, Starbuck casually changed the subject.

"You know anything about the Santa Fe Land and Development Company?"

"What makes you ask?"

"Curiosity." Starbuck watched for a reaction. "Got an idea there's a connection between Judge Hough and the president of that outfit, Warren Mitchell."

Chisum's face was arrested in shock. "Hough? Owen Hough? Are you sure?"

Starbuck briefly described the incident in Santa Fe. He told of spotting Hough, and then the man with the waxed mustache, slipping out of the feed store. He went on to relate how he'd followed the man to the offices over the bank. The facts, he concluded, spoke for themselves. Judge Hough and Warren Mitchell—whatever their reasons—were meeting in secret.

Chisum's features were now drawn and solemn.

"Have you ever heard of the Santa Fe Ring?"

"No." Starbuck shook his head. "Not that I recollect."

"They're a group of businessmen and bankers. A small group, but the real power behind the scenes. Their purpose is to gain political and economic control of the territory. All of it—including the Pecos Valley!"

"And I take it you've stopped them?"

"So far." Chisum was visibly shaken. "I always thought they were behind the Lincoln County War. But I couldn't prove it, and then the truce come along and I hoped we'd seen the last of it. Looks like I was wrong."

"You're saying Hough and the rustling are all tied in some way to this Santa Fe Ring?"

Chisum nodded. "Never occurred to me that Hough was their man, but it makes sense. Don't you see, they're afraid to kill me outright. Too much blood's been spilled around here already. So they'll wait for me to die, and Hough will have it all set up to take over control of the valley. Goddamn vultures!"

"Pretty cagey," Starbuck remarked. "Once you're gone, they'll own New Mexico kit and caboodle."

"Appears that way." The cattleman paused, looking Starbuck over like a prize bull he was considering buying. "Course, if you were willin' to lend a hand . . ."

"Not my fight," Starbuck said evenly. "I got the Kid, and that finishes it so far as I'm concerned."

"Does it?" Chisum studied his nails, thoughtful a moment. "You know, the Kid only pulled the trigger. The others—Dobson and Coghlin—their hands are just as dirty. If they hadn't made rustlin' worthwhile, then Ben Langham and the Kid probably wouldn't've never crossed trails."

"That's dirty pool."

"Maybe." Chisum's tone was severe. "But it's the God's truth, and you know it just as sure as you're sittin' there."

Starbuck stared at him, considering. "What was it you had in mind?"

"Look into things, investigate it. Maybe you'd figure some way to put the screws to Dobson and Coghlin. If they ever broke, we'd be plumb certain to send the others runnin'."

"Well—" Starbuck shrugged, one eyebrow raised. "I guess it would take up the slack time while I'm waiting on the Kid to hang."

"That's the ticket!" Chisum grinned. "You open up that can of worms and there's no tellin' where it'll lead!"

"Hold off!" Starbuck corrected him. "I'll look into the rustling operation, but it stops there. Your political squabbles—the Santa Fe Ring and all that business—that's none of my affair. Let's make damn sure we understand one another on that score."

Chisum readily agreed. He smiled, bobbing his head, not in the least concerned. Age had taught him that certain men never did anything by halfway measures. Luke Starbuck would go all the way, and stick to the very last.

Early next morning Starbuck and Garrett dismounted outside the slaughterhouse. Starbuck's insistence on a search had put the lawman in a crabby mood. According to him, Coghlin slaughtered no more than fifty head a month, supplying the butcher-shop trade in Lincoln and nearby towns. That accounted for less than half the cows rustled from the Jinglebob, not to mention an equal number stolen each month in the Panhandle. He thought the search was a waste of time, and altogether the wrong way to start an investigation. Starbuck, listening with only one ear, had remained adamant.

Entering the office, they found Coghlin poring over an accounting ledger. A squat, fat man with sagging jowls, he had deep-set eyes and a down-turned mouth. He looked up, stubbing out a cigarette with nicotine-stained fingers, and rose from the desk. His expression was neutral.

After a round of handshakes, Coghlin congratulated them on their capture of the Kid. He evidenced no surprise when introduced to Starbuck, commenting blandly that everyone in Lincoln had heard of the new deputy. On edge, Garrett cut short the small talk with a curt gesture.

"Mind if we have a look around, Joe?"

"Look around?" Coghlin suddenly frowned. "What for?"

"I'll tell you if we find it."

"C'mon now, Sheriff! That's a little high-handed, don't you think?"

"Not unless you got something to hide."

"No, I don't," Coghlin blustered. "On the other hand, you've got no right busting in here without some kind of authorization."

"Well, it's like this, Joe." Garrett paused, fixed him with a scowl. "You force me to get a search warrant and I'm gonna be awful put out. Why not cooperate and save yourself some grief?"

Coghlin stared at them for several seconds. Then he shrugged, still frowning. "All right," he said crossly. "Where would you like to start?"

"Your hide pile," Starbuck broke in, silencing Garrett with a look. "We'll skip the rest."

Coghlin mumbled an inaudible reply. He led them outside, and walked toward the rear of the building. Behind the slaughterhouse, stacks of dried cowhides awaited shipment to the tannery. In all, flattened stiff and boardlike, there were perhaps a hundred hides. Halting, Coghlin motioned with a disdainful wave.

"Help yourself."

Starbuck moved forward, and began a systematic inspection of the hides. One at a time, removing them from the stacks, he checked each hide front and back. His expression became increasingly somber as he worked his way from stack to stack. Then, near the bottom of the last stack, he grunted softly.

Holding a cowhide in front of him, he walked to where Garrett and Coghlin waited.

"There's your proof."

Tapping the hide, he directed Garrett's attention to the brand. On the hair side the marking was a distinct □X. He flipped the hide over, revealing a clearly legible LX on the underside. He dropped the hide on the ground.

"The brand's been altered," he said. "Somebody used a running iron to change the L into a box. Only one trouble, though. The original brand burns all the way through, and there's no way to change it on the back side." He kicked the hide with the toe of his boot. "That cow came off of Langham's spread, over in the Panhandle."

"Spot anything off the Jinglebob?"

"No," Starbuck admitted. "Only the one had been altered."

"One hide," Garrett said thoughtfully. "That ain't much in the way of evidence, Luke."

"Maybe." Starbuck turned his gaze on Coghlin. "I understand you've got a ranch a few miles outside town."

"So?"

"You have any objection to our taking a look-see?"

"A look-see?" Coghlin repeated, stealing a glance at Garrett. "What's all this about, Sheriff?"

"Seems pretty clear," Garrett observed. "Somebody's been rustlin' stock."

"You're accusing me of rustling?"

"Nope, never said that."

"Well, it's a damn good thing! I'm in the business of buying cows, but I'm no expert on altered brands. Outside of stock detectives and cow thieves, not many people are."

"Which clears you on both counts, don't it?"

"You bet your life it does!"

"Then you won't have no objection to my deputy ridin' out there, will you, Joe?"

"I guess not," Coghlin said grudgingly. "When did you have in mind?"

"Today," Starbuck told him. "Sooner the better, and it'd probably be a good idea if you tagged along."

Coghlin averted his eyes. "Sorry, but I have business here in town. I'll give you a note to my foreman, Earl Gantry. He runs the spread for me anyway."

"Whatever seems fair."

Starbuck gave the cowhide another kick, then walked off. He knew, almost instinctively, that Coghlin's foreman would receive two notes. One he carried, and one sent ahead in warning. He planned to ride within the hour.

By late afternoon Starbuck's case looked stronger. With John Poe and their four men, he had spent several hours combing the rangeland on Coghlin's spread. The tally was encouraging, if not altogether conclusive. From scattered bunches of cows, they had cut out eight head with altered brands. Three were originally Jinglebob stock, and five had once worn the brands of various ranches in the Panhandle.

Earl Gantry, Coghlin's ramrod, had dogged their tracks throughout the afternoon. As Starbuck suspected, he had been warned in advance, and he went out of his way to make their job more difficult. Any question was met with an evasive reply, and he flatly refused to discuss all matters pertaining to operation of the ranch. Like a shadow, he simply stuck with them, watching their every move.

Shortly before sundown, Starbuck halted the search and rode back to the ranch compound. He realized now that it would take time to comb Coghlin's entire spread. There was the further problem of holding the rustled stock until identification could be made and officially registered with the Stockgrowers' Association. Yet all that was secondary to the larger problem. The case against Coghlin was strong, but wholly circumstantial.

Several factors worked to Coghlin's advantage. The cowhide at the slaughterhouse was, in itself, not particularly damning. The rustled stock at the ranch proved possession but not intent. Coghlin would doubtless contend he had bought the cows in good faith, unaware of the altered brands. And to cap it, Starbuck himself had soured the Kid on turning state's evidence. There was no corroboration, and therefore nothing substantial to establish Joe Coghlin's guilt.

And there the link to Jack Dobson ended. Judge Owen Hough, whatever his complicity, seemed almost untouchable.

At the compound, Starbuck noticed an older woman and a buxom young girl standing outside the house. But his attention was quickly diverted. As he stepped down out of the saddle, Gantry kneed his horse closer.

"You got more business here, Deputy?"

"Lots more," Starbuck said quietly. "I aim to spend the night, and I'd appreciate some grub for my men."

"The hell you say!"

Gantry had cold gunmetal eyes, sleek muddy hair and weatherbeaten features. He was muscular, somewhat taller than Starbuck, and had the lean hips of a horseman. The challenge in his voice was unmistakable.

"Mr. Gantry," Starbuck said, eyes boring into him, "I'd advise you not to mess with the law. I intend to comb your herds and collect any cows with altered brands. That's called evidence, and you'll put yourself in the position of obstructing justice if you try to stop me."

"Well—" Gantry blinked, suddenly uncertain of his ground. "Have you cleared that with Mr. Coghlin?"

"I don't need to clear it with him. The cows are stolen and I'm within my rights as an officer of the law."

"By God, we'll just see about that!"

Gantry reined his horse sharply around. He spurred hard and rode off at a gallop toward town. Watching him disappear down the road, Starbuck was tempted to lag back and follow him into Lincoln. A war council would almost certainly be called tonight, and a roster of those who attended might prove useful at some later date. Aside from Judge Hough, Starbuck was curious if there were other townspeople who still supported the Dobson faction. Then, out of the corner of his eye, he saw a man approach the house. The woman and the girl greeted him, and together they trooped inside. Any thought of trailing Gantry suddenly vanished. Instead, his thoughts turned to the older couple and the girl, obviously a family.

He wondered if they'd ever met Billy the Kid.

CHAPTER 9

Ellen Nesbeth was twenty years old. A girl in the eyes of her parents, she was actually a woman of experience, with no small insight into the ways of men. She knew, while watching Gantry and the deputy exchange words, that the deliverance she yearned for was about to happen. Her one hope was that it might be done without complications.

Fred and Erma Nesbeth, her parents, hadn't the faintest notion that Earl Gantry was her lover. She was a blonde tawny cat of a girl, with a sumptuous figure and a sultry manner. Her eyes were bold, large and expressive, yet bright with intelligence, and provocative. She lacked orthodox beauty, but her short impudent nose and her wide smiling mouth did nothing to lessen her impact on men. She was a stunning woman, and though her parents believed her to be naïve, she thought of herself as an enchantress. She liked the way men looked at her, and she had never once regretted her loss of innocence.

She deeply regretted, however, that her innocence had been wasted on Earl Gantry. In the beginning, she wanted only to escape the tedium and meager existence of her parents' world. She thought Gantry was her ticket to a life of excitement and forbidden comfort. A year ago, with a calculation that belied her age, she had allowed him to seduce her. Afterwards, when it was too late, she discovered he was a brutal man, vindictive and sometimes cruel. Because he was a braggart, forever attempting to impress her, she also discovered he was a thief. By then, her illusion of a new life shattered, she understood she had made a mistake. She could control him with feminine wile, and her body, but there seemed little hope she would ever escape him. Until today.

And now, helping her mother clear the supper dishes, her thoughts centered on that possibility. She was not a mean or spiteful person. While she connived, often manipulating those around her, there was no intent to hurt anyone. But tonight all that had changed. Her most fervent wish was that Earl Gantry would be arrested and sent to prison. The idea loomed before her like salvation itself. She saw it as her only chance, perhaps her last chance.

Yet, for all her wishful thinking, she was a realist. However much she wanted Gantry out of her life, she would do nothing to speed his downfall. She believed him capable of any act, not excluding cold-blooded murder. And anyone who betrayed him would do so at their own peril. She hoped the chief deputy—the one with the hard features and the measured voice—would expose Gantry, and take him off to jail. But she had thought it out quite clearly, and if asked, she would utter no word of condemnation against Earl Gantry. Death was not the escape she had envisioned for herself.

A knock broke the thread of her reverie. Her father, who was seated beside a pot-bellied stove, rose and crossed the kitchen. Even before he opened the door, some dark complex of intuition and dread told her it was the chief deputy. Then the door swung open, and he stood revealed in a spill of light.

"Evening."

"Evenin', Deputy." Fred Nesbeth stepped aside. "Come in out of the cold."

"Thanks."

Starbuck entered the kitchen, removing his hat. Nesbeth introduced his wife and daughter, and Starbuck nodded politely. His eyes touched on Ellen, and she sensed he was a good deal more clever than he appeared. With Gantry in town, he obviously meant to make the most of opportunity. Then her father offered him a chair, and the two men took seats before the stove.

"Well, now, Deputy," Nesbeth said affably. "What can we do for you?"

"If you don't mind, I'd like to ask you a few questions."

Ellen felt a sudden stab of alarm. Her father was a slender man, with the look of a rumpled sparrow, and altogether too trusting for his own good. He had eager brown eyes, a warm smile, and an almost compulsive need to please. To her knowledge, he had never told a lie in his life, and his simple-hearted honesty often worked to his own misfortune. She waited with mounting apprehension.

"Ask away," Nesbeth said agreeably. "I don't know as I'll be able to help you, but I'll sure give'er a try."

"Oh, it's just routine."

Starbuck took a stub pencil and a tally book from his coat pocket. He flipped to a clean page in the tally book and wet the tip of the pencil on his tongue. Watching him, Ellen was almost taken in by his artless performance. She moved closer to her father.

"Now, let's see, Mr. Nesbeth. The boys down at the bunkhouse tell me you're sort of the jack-of-all-trades around here. Would that pretty much describe your job?"

"Sure would!" Nesbeth chortled. "Fix anything, that's my line of work. Wagons, windmills, implements, you name it and I'll figger out what makes it tick. Pretty fair blacksmith, too. Always had the gift for workin' with my hands."

"And Mrs. Nesbeth?" Starbuck made another entry in the tally book. "I understand she looks after the main house, and does the cooking for Gantry and Mr. Coghlin."

"Yep, that's right, housekeeper and cook. Makes the choicest sourdough biscuits you ever popped in your mouth, don't you, Erma?"

Erma Nesbeth was a small woman, tending to middle-age spread, her skin prematurely lined by the plains sun. The crow's feet around her eyes gave her a perpetually worried expression, and she seldom smiled. She glanced up from the basin, nodding to her husband's question. Then she went on washing dishes.

"Anyone else live here?" Starbuck inquired easily. "Besides you folks and your daughter?"

"Well, Gantry's not married, and Mr. Coghlin's a widower, so that about does it."

"How about guests? Mr. Coghlin entertain a lot, does he?"

"No, not much. Few folks from town, now and then."

"Jack Dobson? Judge Hough? His business associates?"

"Oh, sure, they've stayed to supper a time or two."

Starbuck studied his tally book. "How about Billy Bonney?"

"The Kid?" Nesbeth laughed, shook his head. "No, the Kid never stayed to supper."

"But he's been here, hasn't he? Some of the hands told me they've seen him around the place lots of times."

"Why, sure, he's—"

"No!" Ellen Nesbeth hurried to her father. "Daddy, he's trying to trap you! No one told him anything. They wouldn't dare!"

Starbuck had to admire the girl's spunk. She spoke with a firmness that surprised him, and she had also read his hand perfectly. He was bluffing like a penny-ante cardsharp. The boys in the bunkhouse hadn't given him the time of day.

"Miss Nesbeth," he addressed her with a stern look, "it doesn't matter what anybody else told me. You've just confirmed that the Kid has been a guest in this house. The guest of Joe Coghlin."

"I did not!" She bridled. "You're putting words in my mouth!"

"I don't understand," Nesbeth said vaguely. "What's all the to-do about the Kid? He never made no trouble here."

"Oh, Daddy!" Ellen cried. "Hush up! Just hush up! You're only making it worse."

"No, ma'am, you're wrong," Starbuck said in a deliberate voice. "It couldn't get any worse."

She stared at him with shocked round eyes. "What do you mean?"

"I mean you and your folks are in bad trouble. You're accessories before the fact to the crimes of rustling and murder. That makes you as guilty as Coghlin and Gantry, and the Kid, too."

He saw anger, confusion, and a trace of fear in her eyes. She glared at him. "You're lying! You can't prove a thing!"

"Oh, I've got the proof," Starbuck lied, deadpan. "Why do you think Gantry hightailed it into town? No, it's not a matter of proof, Miss Nesbeth. From now on, we're just choosing up sides to see who stays out of jail."

"Jail?" Nesbeth asked in a hoarse whisper. "Mister, what in tarnation are you talkin' about?"

Starbuck leaned forward, his tone earnest. "I'm saying your boss is a thief, Mr. Nesbeth. He hired the Kid to do his rustling, and the Kid killed some people in the process, and that makes everybody who works here answerable to the law. Now, maybe you weren't in on it—"

"Of course he wasn't!" Ellen said fiercely. "He never knew a thing! You just have to look at him to tell that."

"Maybe so." Starbuck's face suddenly turned hard, as though cast in metal. "But the law don't make exceptions. Unless you folks come forward and agree to testify, then you're open to the same charges as Coghlin and everybody else."

"Testify!" Ellen flared. "Don't listen to him, Daddy! He's trying to scare you. We're not guilty of anything!"

Words appeared to fail Nesbeth. He looked from his daughter to Starbuck, completely undone by the thought of jail. There was a prolonged silence, broken only by the hiss of flames in the stove. Then, turning from the wash basin, Erma Nesbeth spoke for the first time.

"Fred, you do what the man says. We been living in a nest of vipers and we all knew it. No sense fooling yourself any longer."

"Oh God, Mama!" Ellen stared at her, aghast. "Are you crazy? Do you know what you're doing?"

"I know lots of things." Mrs. Nesbeth looked her up and down. "Things that shamed me, and sometimes made me wish you wasn't my own flesh and blood." She paused, tears welling up in her eyes. "It's time we got out of here. Way past time."

Ellen turned away, her face livid. For a moment no one spoke, and then, glancing at his wife, Nesbeth seemed to pull himself together. He cleared his throat, swallowed hard.

"Just exactly what is it you're askin', Mr. Starbuck?"

"I want you to make a deposition. Tell everything you know, get it down in writing, and sign it."

"And my womenfolk, nothin' will happen to them?"

"Not to them or you, Mr. Nesbeth. You have my word on it."

"Awright, Deputy, you got yourself a witness."

John Poe brought a buckboard and team to the house an hour after sunup. Starbuck stood outside the kitchen door, waiting on the Nesbeths to appear. To avoid trouble, he had delayed their departure until the bunkhouse emptied and the hands went off about their daily chores. He walked forward as Poe climbed down from the buckboard.

Late last night, he had explained the situation to Poe and the men. He believed it essential that the Nesbeths be removed from the ranch as quickly as possible. One reason was precautionary, a matter of their personal safety. Another was the girl, who from all indications had fallen under Gantry's influence. Once he had them safely in Lincoln, and had taken a deposition, he would return to the ranch. Poe and the men, meanwhile, were to continue combing Coghlin's herds. He wanted the rustled stock gathered and ready for inspection no later than tomorrow afternoon.

Starbuck halted where he could keep an eye on the house. He nodded to Poe. "Any trouble?"

"Nope." Poe shifted his quid and spat. "Most everybody had cleared out when I went to hitch up the team. Course, I had a little starin' contest with Gantry at breakfast."

"He was in the cook shack?"

"Bigger'n life," Poe noted. "For what it's worth, he looked like he'd just swallowed a couple of dozen canaries. You reckon he got some fresh orders in Lincoln last night?"

"We'll see," Starbuck said, glancing toward the cook shack. "Here he comes now."

Earl Gantry hurried across the compound. He moved with a determined stride, his expression one of sharp annoyance. Halting in front of Starbuck, he indicated the buckboard.

"What's the idea?"

"Borrowing your buckboard," Starbuck remarked. "I'll drop it off with Coghlin when I'm done."

"Why do you need a buckboard?"

Starbuck ignored the question. "I'm leaving Deputy Poe in charge. Him and the boys know what to do, and I'd suggest you stay out of their way."

"That still don't tell me why—"

Gantry stopped, his eyes suddenly hooded. He stared toward the house, watching with disbelief as the Nesbeths appeared at the kitchen door. Ellen carried a small valise, and her father struggled along with two heavy carpetbags. Mrs. Nesbeth, clutching an ancient mantle cloak to her bosom, brought up the rear.

"Gantry," Starbuck said quietly, "I'm taking the Nesbeths into custody. I'd advise you not to make any trouble."

"You're not takin' nobody unless you've got a warrant."

"I won't say it again—"

"Back inside!" Gantry shouted. He jerked his thumb at the house, and took a step toward the Nesbeths. "You heard me! Get the hell—"

Starbuck lashed out in a fast shadowy movement. He exploded two splintering punches on the jaw, a left hook followed by a clubbing right cross. Gantry went down as though his legs had been chopped from beneath him. He struck the ground and lay still, out cold.

Hardly winded, Starbuck motioned the Nesbeths to the buckboard and got them seated. He walked to the hitchrack, where his horse was tied, and mounted. Gathering the reins, he shifted in the saddle and looked back at Poe.

"John," he said in a low voice, "if our friend wants to argue about it when he wakes up, you give him some more of the same."

"I'll do'er, Luke," Poe grinned. "You watch out for yourself, you hear me?"

"I always do."

Starbuck nodded to Fred Nesbeth, and reined his horse around. With the buckboard trundling along behind, he rode toward Lincoln.

A chill winter haze obscured the sun. Starbuck consulted his pocketwatch, estimating time and distance. By rough reckoning, he figured they were halfway to Lincoln. Ahead, the road snaked past a boulder-strewn butte, descending gradually to a level plain. At the latest, he judged they would reach town by the noon hour.

Since departing the ranch, Starbuck hadn't exchanged a dozen words with the Nesbeths. Crowded into the lone buckboard seat, they looked solemn as molting owls. The girl was especially somber. She kept her eyes turned away from him, and he sensed she had been shaken by the way he'd manhandled Gantry. He felt some vague need to explain himself, the necessity to strike first and strike hard when confronted by a troublemaker. But he suppressed the urge. The Nesbeths and their daughter would never understand that violence was a part of his trade. When words failed, he used his fists. Or in the last resort, he used a gun. Certain men, unpersuaded by reason, left him no alternative. Only a fool allowed the other man the first blow.

Starbuck had ridden most of the morning beside

the buckboard. But now, as the road narrowed through a rocky defile, he waved Nesbeth on and drifted to the rear. His thoughts turned to details. He wondered if the county would pay to quarter the Nesbeths at the hotel. If not, then he would have to work out some arrangement with Chisum. There was also the question of round-the-clock guards. He didn't fool himself on that score, though he'd said nothing to the Nesbeths. Their lives were in jeopardy, and in the days to come, there would be no substitute for vigilance. He grunted softly to himself, struck by an unpleasant thought. He wondered if Garrett could be entrusted with the guard detail. It was no job for a tyro, and the sheriff was very definitely—

His saddlehorn suddenly blew apart.

A split second later he heard the gunshot, and then another. A slug fried the air past his left ear, and he saw a puff of smoke in the boulders directly ahead. All in an instant he realized he was trapped between two bushwhackers. One was to the front, and the other was on his immediate right, hidden in the rocks. He spurred his horse into a gallop, aware that Nesbeth was whipping the team. Slugs were pocking the earth all around him, and the blast of rifle fire quickened to an earsplitting drumroll. He knew then he had no chance of outrunning the ambush. His only choice was to stand and fight.

Yanking his carbine from its scabbard, he hauled back on the reins with savage force. His horse skidded to a halt, almost squatting on its haunches, and he jumped from the saddle. The sudden stop caught the bushwhackers by surprise; their fire slackened, and he blocked off the one on his right flank by crouching beside his horse. He jacked a shell into the carbine, and centered the sights on the spot where he'd seen a puff of smoke. A rifle muzzle was laid over the boulder, then the crown of a hat appeared and a man rose slightly to shift his aim. For an instant, bobbing up for a better look, his head was visible. Starbuck shot him between the eyes.

Whirling around, Starbuck stepped past his horse, and in the same motion, dropped to one knee. A slug whistled over his head, and on the rocky knoll to the right, he saw the second bushwhacker. Working the lever, he triggered a half dozen rounds into the rocks. The spang of ricochets spread across the knoll like a swarm of bees. Then, before he could steady his sights, a man leaped from behind a rock and dove headfirst over the knoll. He touched off another shot for good measure and rose to his feet, waiting. A moment later he heard the faint sound of hoofbeats, then nothing.

Starbuck caught a stirrup and scrambled into the saddle. Some distance ahead, he saw the buckboard jouncing down the road. He roweled his horse in the ribs and took off at a dead lope. Once clear of the defile, he jammed his carbine into the saddle scabbard.

In the heat of the fight, he'd had no time to think things through. But as he pounded after the buckboard all the pieces began falling into place. He realized the ambush had been arranged as a warning to the Nesbeths. Though they were sitting ducks in the buckboard, all the gunfire had been directed at him. Which meant Gantry had ordered the ambush only after he'd departed the ranch with the Nesbeths in custody. It made perfect sense. By cutting cross-country, the bushwhackers had easily gotten ahead of the slow-moving buckboard. Had Gantry selected cooler men—and better shots—he would now be dead.

Yet, for all that, there was an element of still greater consequence. Gantry would never have ordered the ambush on his own. Coghlin and Dobson, perhaps even Judge Hough, had met with the ranch foreman last night. One or all of them had clearly authorized him to take whatever steps he considered necessary. Killing a law officer was serious business, and the repercussions would have been felt all the way to Santa Fe. They were desperate men, willing to resort to desperate measures, and the conclusion was inescapable. Having failed to kill him, they wouldn't hesitate to kill the Nesbeths. The next try would be better planned and more skillfully executed. Unless he found sanctuary of some sort, there was no doubt as to the outcome. All the Nesbeths, the girl included, would be murdered.

When Starbuck overtook the buckboard, he signaled a change in direction. He turned east, across the plains, on a course that would bypass Lincoln entirely. He led the Nesbeths toward the Pecos, and the Jinglebob. To the man who more than any other needed them alive.

CHAPTER 10

"Politics be damned!"

"Easy to say," Chisum commented. "But politics are a hard fact of life. You can kick up all the dust you want, and it won't change a thing."

"That's about the lamest excuse I ever heard."

"Luke, I don't make the rules. If I had my choice, we'd go back to the way it was in the old days. Things was a damnsight easier when we didn't have so much law, and nobody knows it better than me."

"Over in the Panhandle we've got our own law. Anyone steps out of line and he gets what's coming to him—pronto."

"I don't doubt it for a minute. Dog-eat-dog and devil take the hindmost, ain't that about it?"

"Why not?" Starbuck said harshly. "Skip all the legal hocus-pocus, and keep it simple. That's the only kind of law most folks understand anyway."

Chisum marked again that the younger man was something of a cynic. "Well, Luke, I guess that's the price we pay for civilization. The law gets more and more complicated, and common folks wind up not havin' a helluva lot to say about the way things are run. Course, when you core the apple, it's all politics. A few people call the tune, and the rest of us spend our lives tryin' to keep time with the music."

"Politics or not, I still say we've got a case."

"And I repeat," Chisum emphasized, "where politics are involved, it has to be airtight and wrapped in a red ribbon."

"Jesus!" Starbuck muttered. "We've got the stolen cows and we've got the Nesbeths. What more do you want?"

"It's all circumstantial, Luke! Even the Nesbeths admit they never really heard anything. They saw Coghlin and the Kid together, and they saw money exchange hands a couple of times. So what's that prove?"

"How many times do I have to tell you? It ties Coghlin to the Kid and the rustled cows."

"Sure it does," Chisum nodded, "so far as you and me are concerned. But any grand jury impaneled in Lincoln won't be impartial about it. Lots of people are politically aligned with Dobson and Coghlin, and they're not gonna return an indictment unless we show 'em some rock-hard evidence." He paused, reflective a moment. "Besides, we ain't got nothin' on Owen Hough, and he's the one joker I don't aim to let slip past. Without him, we're just dealin' in small fry, and there ain't no way that'll put an end to it."

"The rustling," Starbuck asked, one eyebrow lifted, "or the politics?"

"Both," Chisum said firmly. "There ain't no way to separate one from the other. That's what I've been tryin' to get through your head since we started talkin'."

Starbuck scrubbed his face with his palms. Last night, when he'd delivered the Nesbeths to the Jinglebob, there seemed to him no loose ends. He had their testimony, and along with the rustled stock, that made the case against Coghlin. Today, all the loose ends had come unraveled.

The problem was John Chisum. The cattleman had readily agreed that the Nesbeths were a valuable, and unexpected, asset. He had them quartered in the main house, and assigned men to guard them night and day. No less than the Nesbeths, uncovering the stolen cows also drew his praise. A messenger was dispatched ordering Poe to drive the cows into Lincoln; there an inspector from the Stockgrowers' Association would verify that the brands had been altered. All last evening, in fact, Chisum had been in fine spirits. He marveled that so much had been accomplished in three days, and commended Starbuck on a remarkable piece of detective work. But this morning, completely reversing himself, he had argued against pressing charges. Politics, like war, demanded total victory. He wanted Owen Hough—or nothing.

Oddly enough, Starbuck had undergone a change himself. After retiring last night, he'd been unable to sleep for a long while. Something about the ambush bothered him, and his thoughts slowly turned to Coghlin and Dobson. Over the past four years, any number of men had tried to kill him; the attempts were viewed impersonally, for he understood it was the nature of outlaws to fight when cornered. An assassination, however, was an altogether different matter. For the first time, someone had ordered his murder, authorized his death by *name*. That seemed to him very personal, and not to be tolerated.

The Kid still had priority. Events of the last few days had in no way affected the determination to see him hung. Yet the more Starbuck pondered it, the more he realized the Kid was merely the tool of ambitious men. And those men were by far the greater evil. Their use of corruption and murder to achieve power was on a scale incomprehensible to anyone not personally touched by it. Lying awake, struck by this new perspective of things, Starbuck gradually became intrigued with the Santa Fe Ring. As a detective, the thought of bringing them to justice was irresistible, a professional challenge. On the personal side of the ledger, he needed no excuse. These men had ordered him killed. *By name!* Which was reason enough to follow the trail wherever it might lead. To Coghlin and Dobson, and then, without question, to Judge Hough. And perhaps beyond, to the men in Santa Fe.

Thinking on it now, he wondered why he was resisting Chisum. The logical next step was to go after Dobson, and before sleep had claimed him last night, he'd come to the same conclusion himself.

Perhaps it was nothing more than stubborn pride. He had an aversion to taking orders, and Chisum wasn't the most tactful man he'd run across. Whatever the cause, he suddenly realized he was being not only bullheaded, but short-sighted as well. He stared at the rancher a moment longer, then shrugged.

"Go ahead," he said without expression, "I'm all ears. What's your idea?"

Chisum sensed a change in attitude. He hitched forward in his chair, watching the younger man closely. "The Kid's the key to everything. With his testimony, we'd have Coghlin by the short hairs, and more'n likely that would open the door to Dobson. Do you agree?"

"Let's say I do," Starbuck allowed. "How do we get the Kid to talk?"

"Well, for the moment, we just sit tight. We keep the Nesbeths under wraps, and we don't say nothin' more about the rustled stock. Coghlin won't know what the hell we've got in mind, and that'll make him sweat all the more. So we let him sweat, and meantime, we wait for the Kid to be sentenced to hang. At that point—"

"Hold on," Starbuck interrupted. "You told me there's no chance of commutation."

"No chance at all," Chisum affirmed. "Course, we'll let him think we're still tryin', and at the same time we'll convince him his friends ain't turned a hand to save him. Which won't be no lie. I've got a hunch Coghlin and Dobson want to see him swing more'n we do."

"So we tell him he's been betrayed, turn him against Coghlin."

"And once he talks, we use that to turn Coghlin against Dobson."

"Then we offer Dobson a deal to spill the beans on Judge Hough."

"And one by one, we work our way up the line. Even if all of 'em don't crack, somebody's bound to lead us to the boys in Santa Fe. That's the payoff, and I say the odds favor us blowin' the whole mess wide apart."

A smile tugged at the corner of Starbuck's mouth. "Anybody ever tell you you're a devious old bastard?"

Chisum laughed. "I don't reckon you'd be the first."

"Probably won't be the last, either."

"By God, I hope not, Luke. I shorely do!"

There was a knock at the door. Sallie Chisum entered the den, and moved toward them. Her lips were set in a thin line, and she seemed attenuated, somehow on edge. She halted, looking from her father to Starbuck.

"We seem to have a problem with Miss Nesbeth."

"Oh?" Starbuck asked. "What's the trouble?"

Sallie flushed. "I'm afraid her language doesn't bear repeating. But to give you a loose translation, she refuses to stay cooped up in the house and she insists on being allowed to go for a ride."

"On horseback?"

"Yes," Sallie replied, her tone waspish. "And she had the nerve to ask if she could borrow a riding outfit. Honestly, some people! We're nowhere near the same size."

Starbuck had a strong suspicion they were nowhere near on anything. Sallie Chisum was a lady, with the genteel manner and refined air of someone accustomed to wealth. He had known only a few such women in his lifetime, and none of them intimately. But he had known hundreds of women like Ellen Nesbeth. Young hellions, they yearned for excitement and adventure, and one way or another, they always found it. Some made their way to the cowtowns, where they worked as dance hall girls, or chose a more lucrative profession in the parlor houses. The others, unable to escape home and family, devoted themselves to tantalizing the local farm boys or cowhands. These were the women who provoked fights at Saturday night dances, and thought themselves utter failures unless they had a string of admirers hanging on their every word. Their morals were questionable, and more often than not their bodies were used as instruments of emotional blackmail. Yet he understood them and, surprisingly, he enjoyed their company. Always a battle of wits, taming them was a spirited contest, never dull. To his way of thinking, it was not unlike skinning a faro dealer at a crooked table.

"I'll handle it," Starbuck said, rising from his

chair. "We have to keep Nesbeth happy, and like it or not, I suppose that means catering to his daughter."

He nodded to them, and walked from the room. Sallie's face reddened to the hairline. She avoided her father's eyes, seemingly struck speechless, her expression none too ladylike. Chisum suppressed a smile, and began fussing with his pipe.

Ellen Nesbeth wore a split riding skirt and a fleece-lined winter jacket. The outfit, borrowed from Sallie Chisum, was at least a size too small. Her breasts stood perfectly molded against the jacket, and the skirt stretched skin-tight across her buttocks. Walking down from the main house, she seemed oblivious to the stares of several Jinglebob hands loafing around the corral.

A grulla mare, one of Sallie Chisum's favorite mounts, had been saddled and brought from the stables. Starbuck waited beside his gelding, holding the reins to both horses. With a defiant look, Ellen ignored his greeting and snatched the mare's reins from his hand. When he offered to help her mount, she caught the stirrup with a practiced step and swung aboard the mare. For an instant, as her leg cleared the cantle, her fruity buttocks were outlined through the skirt. All eyes, the cowhands drew a breath in unison, their mouths ajar. She reined the mare around and rode off at a canter.

Starbuck mounted, laughing softly to himself,

and followed her south from the compound. He knew she had purposely put on a show for the men at the corral. She clearly delighted in flaunting her body, and an audience of leering cowhands added spice to the game. He thought it entirely likely that Sallie Chisum had lost her skirt for good.

When he rode up alongside her, Ellen slowed the mare to a walk. Surprised, he glanced at her, but she refused to meet his gaze. Her hair was drawn sleekly to the nape of her neck, tied with a ribbon, accentuating the smooth contours of her profile. She was a woman of surpassing beauty, with the bawdy eyes and sensuous mouth that certain men found compelling. Yet something in her carriage, the way her head tilted, brought to mind the old adage about vain women. He wondered if she got chapped lips from kissing cold mirrors.

A few miles from the house, Ellen reined to a halt on a slight rise. Before them, framed against the panorama of the Quadalupe Mountains, lay the Valley of Seven Rivers. She still hadn't spoken, and now, her eyes fixed upon distance, she studied the snowcapped spires beyond the valley. Starbuck hooked a leg around his saddlehorn, and rolled himself a smoke. He lit the cigarette, aware she could scarcely contain herself, but quite content to wait her out. Sooner or later they were bound to have words; and he knew the one thing she couldn't tolerate from any man was indifference. He provoked her with quiet disinterest.

"If I weren't a lady," she said at length, "you

117

would get your ears scorched six ways to Sunday."

"In that case," Starbuck exhaled a lazy stream of smoke, "let'er rip. I'm no gent and you're no lady, so why playact any different?"

"Bastard!" She invested the word with scorn. "You're the sorriest excuse for a man I've ever met."

"That and a nickel beer will get you a free lunch."

She was glaring at him now, face masked by anger. "You must be real proud of yourself. You lied to my folks—and scared them half out of their wits!—and then very nearly got them killed. Why couldn't you just leave well enough alone?"

"White lies don't count." Starbuck inspected the tip of his cigarette, flicked an ash. "Besides, those backshooters weren't after your folks anyway. Their orders were to get me."

"So what?" she said stiffly, her lips white. "Do you think I'm a fool? Next time they'll come after my folks—and me—and they won't miss. We're the targets now, not you."

"There won't be a next time. You're in protective custody, and you've got my word, no harm will come to you."

"Oh my God!" She laughed a tinny sound. "That's the biggest joke yet! What good is your word against bullets? Go on, Mr. Starbuck—tell me that!"

"Well, it's pretty simple from where I stand. Without your testimony, I'd never make a case. So

I don't aim to let anything happen to you."

"Really?" she said, lifting her chin. "And doesn't it bother you that a couple of people who never harmed anyone in their lives might end up dead? Do you sleep good at night, thinking about that?"

"I think about it," Starbuck said slowly, "but I don't lose any sleep. It's my job, and I do it the best way I know how."

"Your job!" She tossed her head. "Why, you're no better than the Kid! I weaseled it out of those dimwits guarding our rooms. You're a paid killer, Mr. Starbuck! A bounty hunter!"

Silence thickened between them. Starbuck assessed her with a cold, objective look. He was not a man who revealed his innermost feelings easily. His emotions were held under tight rein, and he was more apt to cover anything of a personal nature with an offhand remark. But her accusation stung, and there was a swiftly felt need to justify himself. He couldn't explain it, nor did he pause to think it through. He only knew it was important that Ellen Nesbeth not believe him to be a hired gun.

"I'm a manhunter," he said quietly, "but I don't take bounty. If the boys guarding your room told the whole story, then they must have told you I'm a range detective."

"I fail to see what difference that makes."

"In this case," Starbuck assured her, "it makes all the difference in the world. A few weeks ago the Kid murdered a man over in the Panhandle. His name was Ben Langham, and he was the best friend

I ever had. That's what brought me to New Mexico, that and nothing else."

"But the Kid's in jail! You caught him!"

"Yeah, but I've raised my sights since then. I want the man that hired the Kid, and the man that hired him. Coghlin and Dobson, and anybody else that had a hand in it. The whole bunch, top to bottom."

"You're crazy!" she said wildly. "You'll get yourself killed! You'll get us all killed!"

"No," Starbuck corrected her. "If there's any kill ing to be done, then I'm the one that'll do it."

Ellen Nesbeth stared at him, on the verge of saying something. Then she shook her head, her eyes suddenly sad and strangely bemused. She whirled the mare around with a sharp snap of the reins, and rode off. Starbuck kept her in sight all the way back to the ranch, but he made no attempt to overtake her. His mood was reflective, and he found himself troubled.

There was more to the girl than he'd expected, and her eyes told him things even she might not know. It was a disquieting thought.

CHAPTER 11

On the afternoon of April 12, William Bonney was led into the courtroom. An overflow crowd packed the benches, and several spectators shouted encouragement to the young outlaw. He waved, even though he was manacled hand and foot, and hobbled to the defense table. There, flanked by Garrett and Starbuck, he took a chair beside his attorney.

An air of tense expectation hung over the courtroom. The jury had retired late that morning, and now, after less than three hours' debate, they had reached a verdict. Opinion was divided among the onlookers; some thought a quick verdict would favor the Kid, while others believed it meant almost certain conviction. Either way, the sheriff of Dona Ana County was taking no chances with such a large crowd. Garrett and Starbuck had been assigned to guard the Kid, and local deputies were stationed at every door leading into the courtroom. Their orders were to move swiftly and decisively at the first sign of a demonstration.

The Kid, looking very cocksure, was perhaps the calmest person in the courtroom. Talking quietly with his attorney, Arthur Fountain, he appeared unconcerned about the verdict. Under the circumstances, many of those watching him thought it a fine display of bravado. But it was no act, and his bold manner was not meant to impress the spectators. He was, instead, utterly confident of acquittal.

To the Kid's way of thinking, the danger of a guilty verdict had diminished step by step. Some three months past he had been granted a change of venue, with the trial scheduled to be held in the town of Mesilla. Only a half day's ride from the border, Mesilla was populated largely by Mexicans. The people there had scarcely heard of the Lincoln County War, and they cared even less about political vendettas. One gringo killing another was simply a matter of no consequence. Americans, in their view, were all crazy.

All the more important, the process of jury selection had resulted in twelve Mexicans sitting in the jurors' box. The Kid could hardly credit his own luck. Throughout the territory, Mexicans looked upon him with respect and affection. He was known to them as *El Chivato*, and wherever he rode, he'd always been warmly welcomed into their homes. Their attitude was influenced to no small degree by his lukewarm manner toward Anglo women. He much preferred dark-haired señoritas, and in that, he was considered wise beyond his years. Quite clearly, as he had demonstrated many times, he trusted Mexicans more than he did his own people. And they in turn counted it a mark of honor to have shared a humble supper or a bottle of tequila with the young *bandido*.

The trial, begun only yesterday, had nonetheless given the Kid a few bad moments. Four eyewitnesses told essentially the same story. On a spring day in 1878 they had watched, horror-stricken, as the Kid and five members of his gang assassinated Sheriff William Brady. Crouched beside a building, the killers had caught the lawman on Lincoln's main street, and gunned him down without warning. Then, leaving nothing to chance, the Kid had coolly walked into the street and fired a final shot into the sheriff's head. The savagery of the act had been described in detail, and under cross-examination Arthur Fountain had done nothing to shake the witnesses' testimony. By late yesterday, when court had recessed, there seemed only one possible conclusion. William Bonney, with grisly premeditation, had murdered an officer of the law.

Earlier this morning, after closing arguments, the judge had charged the jury. When the twelve men filed out of the courtroom, there was little doubt, based on the evidence, as to their verdict. Yet now, waiting on them to return, the Kid appeared almost nonchalant. He simply couldn't believe an all-Mexican jury would convict him of anything.

"All rise!"

The bailiff's command brought everyone in the courtroom to his feet. Judge Walter Bristol emerged from the door to his chambers, and walked quickly to the bench. There was a moment of shuffling while the spectators resumed their seats, then the bailiff moved to a door behind the jury box. One by one, the jurors filed into the courtroom and took their chairs. None of them looked at the Kid.

Judge Bristol swiveled in their direction. "Gentlemen of the jury, have you reached a verdict?"

The jury foreman rose. "*Sí* . . . we have, Your Honor."

"Defendant will rise." The judge waited for the Kid and his attorney to stand, then glanced back at the foreman. "How do you find?"

"Guilty."

The foreman's mouth continued to move, but his words were lost in an outcry from the spectators. Garrett and Starbuck edged closer to the Kid, and the deputies posted around the room stood tensed, hands poised over their guns. Then the judge, banging his gavel, hammered the crowd into silence.

"Sentence will be pronounced at ten o'clock tomorrow morning. Court stands adjourned."

With a nod to the bailiff, Judge Bristol stepped down from the bench and disappeared into his chambers. The doors were thrown open, and at a signal from the sheriff, the deputies began clearing the courtroom. The crowd appeared unruly, darting sympathetic glances at the Kid and muttering among themselves. But the deputies, alert for trouble, herded them outside with a minimum of commotion.

The Kid looked as though he'd had the wind knocked out of him. His features were twisted in a grimace, and his eyes were vacant. He stared at the jury, watching with stunned bewilderment as they filed through the rear door. Once again, none of them met his gaze.

Arthur Fountain, who appeared somewhat sheepish, exchanged a few words with his client. Then, stuffing papers into his briefcase, the attorney hurried from the courtroom. Garrett and Starbuck fell in beside the Kid. The county jail was on the upper floor of the courthouse, and they walked him toward a door which led to the stairway.

"What's the matter, Billy?" Starbuck said as they moved through the door. "You look a little surprised."

"Go to hell."

"No need to get touchy. It wasn't me that let you down."

"What's that supposed to mean?"

"Why, it's simple enough," Starbuck observed. "Your friends got you a change of venue, and then let you sink or swim on your own. Isn't that about the size of it?"

"You're so smart, you tell me."

The Kid fell silent. The deal he'd struck while in the Santa Fe jail suddenly seemed shortsighted, and very unfair. He hadn't talked, and for that he had been spared a trial in Lincoln. But now, having been convicted, he knew there would be no further contact. He was on his own, with not the slightest hope of commutation. He felt alone and bitter, and he had a fleeting impression of the gallows. He sensed it was time to play his hole card.

On the second-story landing he turned to Starbuck. "Let's suppose I was ready to talk a deal. Your offer still open?"

"Depends on what you've got to trade."

"Joe Coghlin," the Kid said slowly. "And maybe enough to swing Dobson with him."

"Well—" Starbuck pursed his lips, thoughtful. "I reckon I could have a talk with Judge Bristol."

"Bristol?" The Kid's face congealed into a scowl. "What about the governor?"

"Waste of time," Starbuck remarked. "He couldn't do anything unless you'd already been sentenced. We're better off to take a crack at the judge." He paused, eyes narrowed in a squint. "Let's understand each other, Billy. I'll approach the judge; but whichever way it goes, I've got to have your word you'll still testify against Coghlin. Otherwise it's no deal."

"No monkey business," the Kid said sharply. "You make an honest try, and I'll hold up my end. But you try pullin' a fast one and all bets are off."

"Hell, Billy!" Starbuck mugged, hands outstretched. "You've got to learn to trust people. We're on the same side, now."

"Yeah, and bird dogs fly, too."

Garrett was silent throughout the exchange. Even after locking the Kid in his cell, the lawman seemed unusually thoughtful. But as they left the jail and approached the stairs, he looked at Starbuck.

"I understood Chisum had changed his mind about offerin' the Kid a deal."

"The way it worked out," Starbuck noted dryly, "he's the one that changed my mind."

"Oh?" Garrett asked. "How so?"

"He convinced me Coghlin and Dobson are more important than the Kid."

"How come I never heard nothin' about it?"

"Maybe you ought to ask Chisum."

Garret flushed. "Well, for my money, he should've left well enough alone. I never agreed with the idea in the first place. What the territory needs is an object lesson, and believe you me, it'd do lots of folks a world of good to see the Kid strung up."

"I don't know about that"—Starbuck gave him a quick sidewise glance—"but it'd sure be a feather in your cap, wouldn't it, Pat?"

Garrett sputtered something under his breath and stalked off down the stairs. Watching him, Starbuck was amused by the lawman's artless and rather heavy-handed ambition. But privately, he had to admit he was in complete agreement. He too would have enjoyed seeing the Kid strung up.

Judge Walter Bristol was a man of stern visage and inflexible temperament. His head was leonine, with a shock of wavy white hair, and his eyes were unwavering behind thick spectacles. He gazed across the desk at Starbuck and Garrett.

"Let me understand you, Deputy." He laced his fingers together, peering over his glasses. "You're asking me to grant clemency as an inducement to make William Bonney testify against certain men alleged to be operating a rustling ring. Is that correct?"

"Yes, sir, it is," Starbuck acknowledged. "All the evidence we've turned up so far is circumstantial. Without Bonney's testimony, we'll probably never make a case."

"And that's all there is to it?" the judge demanded. "A gang of rustlers?"

"That's all, Your Honor," Starbuck lied, straight-faced. "Of course, I'd ask you to keep in mind, it's not just the rustling. These men are indirectly responsible for several of the murders committed by the Kid."

"I see." Judge Bristol eyed him, considering. "To be frank, Deputy, I'm not convinced. At bottom, everything in Lincoln County revolves around politics. I find it incredible that you would ask clemency for William Bonney—the worst desperado in the history of New Mexico Territory!—merely to convict a band of rustlers. I detect a nigger in the woodpile. One, quite probably, by the name of John Chisum."

"Chisum would benefit," Starbuck conceded, "but I don't think it's altogether politics. The Jinglebob makes a mighty inviting target for cow thieves."

"Indeed." The judge turned slowly to look at

Garrett. "Sheriff, you've had little to say on the matter, but I feel obligated to pose a question. Do you believe any form of clemency—even a life sentence in prison—would reform Billy the Kid?"

Garrett thought it over, and spoke carefully. "Judge, anything's possible. The Kid's young, and life on the rockpile might just straighten him out. But if you want my honest opinion, it ain't very likely."

Judge Bristol rose. "Thank you, Sheriff. I appreciate your candor. Now, if you gentlemen will excuse me, I have work to do." He gave Starbuck an owlish frown. "Deputy, you can tell John Chisum you made a game effort. That, at least, will be no lie."

Outside the judge's chambers, Garrett kept his eyes averted. As they walked through the courtroom, Starbuck thought it wholly in character that the lawman, forced to a choice, hadn't allowed loyalty to stand in the way of ambition. But he decided just as quickly that his story would be the same for both John Chisum and the Kid. He had made a game effort. And failed.

The following morning, precisely on the stroke of ten, Judge Bristol rapped his gavel and brought the court to order. The Kid, heavily manacled, stood before the bench. Adjusting his glasses, Judge Bristol studied the execution warrant a moment, and then set it aside. He looked down at the young out-law.

"Before I pass sentence, have you anything you wish to say?"

"Damn right!" the Kid declared sullenly. "A whole bunch of fellows did just as much killin' as me up in Lincoln County. But they're walkin' around free as you please and no worries. How come I'm the only one that gets sent to the gallows?"

"Mr. Bonney, I believe it's common knowledge you violated the terms of the governor's amnesty proclamation. However, that falls outside the purview of this court. Have you anything else to say?"

"No, nothin' that'd interest you."

"William Bonney," the judge intoned, "you have been found guilty of the wanton and premeditated act of murder. It is the judgment of this court that on May 13, 1881, between the hours of sunrise and noon, in the County of Lincoln, New Mexico Territory, you be hanged by the neck until dead. May God have mercy on your soul."

There was a moment of oppressive silence, then Judge Bristol hammered his gavel. "The prisoner is hereby remanded to the custody of the Lincoln County sheriff. This court stands adjourned."

Garrett and Starbuck hustled the Kid out of the courtroom. In the corridor, bypassing the stairs to the jail, they walked directly to a door at the rear of the building. Outside, three mounted deputies waited with a wagon and team. The Kid was unceremoniously lifted into the back of the wagon, and Starbuck scrambled into the driver's seat. Garrett stepped aboard his own mount, and led the way north from Mesilla. Less than sixty seconds had elapsed since the reading of the death warrant.

A short distance outside town, Starbuck glanced around at the Kid. The wagon was loaded with supplies for the three-day ride to Lincoln, and the Kid had made himself comfortable on a pile of bedrolls. He returned Starbuck's look with a disgruntled stare.

"You sure fixed things up with the judge, didn't you?"

"I tried," Starbuck said firmly. "That's all I promised, and I did my best. But he had his mind set."

"Yeah, well," the Kid muttered. "You can forget our deal. Way it looks, you didn't try near hard enough."

"I thought I had your word."

"Hell, my word don't mean do-diddly squat! Besides, I ain't about to help somebody while he's fittin' a noose around my neck."

"Suppose we petition the governor? Would you agree to talk, then?"

"Won't nothin' make me talk except gettin' that death sentence lifted. You arrange it and you've got yourself a witness. You don't, then you might as well crap in one hand and wish in the other."

"You're a hard customer, Billy." Starbuck reflected a moment, then shrugged. "Well, I reckon time's on our side, anyway. We've got a month to make the governor see the light. Might just be enough to turn the trick."

"A month." The Kid gave him a strange crooked smile. "Hell, I hadn't thought about that. Goddamn near anything could happen in a month!"

"You sound awful chipper all of a sudden."

"Well, like the Good Book says, Starbuck: it's always darkest before the dawn. Thirty days and thirty nights, and only the last sunrise counts. Yessir, I like them odds!"

Starbuck merely nodded, and twisted around in his seat. He made a mental note to have a talk with Garrett. Any thought of the governor, or commutation, was now a secondary consideration. The Kid was thinking of those thirty days and thirty nights. And escape.

CHAPTER 12

The door to Garrett's office was locked. Starbuck knocked, waiting a moment, then turned away when there was no response. The county jail, where the Kid was being held, was on the upper floor of the courthouse. He crossed the corridor and mounted the stairs.

Almost two weeks had passed since he and Garrett had delivered the Kid to Lincoln. In that time, he hadn't spoken with the Kid, nor had he communicated any messages through Garrett. Instead, he'd let the young outlaw wonder what was happening, allowing the time to work its own pressure. With each passing day, he knew the uncertainty would have a corrosive effect on the Kid's nerves.

Climbing the stairs, he marveled that their scheme had gone so well. Apparently the Kid still believed they were working on his behalf, trying to secure a commutation of the death sentence. It seemed the only reasonable explanation, for there had been no jailbreak attempts, and according to reports, the Kid was a model prisoner. Yet the truth was poles apart from what the Kid had been led to believe.

There was no chance of commutation. John Chisum had made no overtures toward the governor, and the execution date remained unchanged. On May 13, as scheduled, the Kid would be marched to the gallows.

Biding his time, Starbuck had spent the past ten days at the Jinglebob. Aside from Ellen Nesbeth, whose company he found increasingly pleasant, his thoughts had centered on the Kid. In discussions with Chisum he had explored endless approaches to the final gambit in their plan. The more they talked, the more apparent it became that the simplest approach would also prove the most credible. Privately, Starbuck questioned that anything, short of executive clemency, would persuade the Kid. But he was fully committed to the idea, determined to see it through. And now, walking along the second-floor hallway, he marked once again that the means were always justified when dealing with killers. He steeled himself to lie like a Chinese bandit.

The Lincoln County jail always reminded Starbuck of a circus arena. The lone cell, located in the center of a large room, resembled a wild animal cage. It was essentially a holding pen, constructed of steel bars on the sides and interlaced steel strips on the top. For added security, all other prisoners had been released on bail or transferred to Santa Fe. The Kid had the cell to himself.

Jim Bell and Bob Ollinger, the regular deputies,

were on duty. The night shift, two of Starbuck's men, relieved them every evening at sundown. Bell was an amiable sort, too easygoing in Starbuck's opinion, but nonetheless an efficient officer. Ollinger was his exact opposite, loudmouthed and surly, with a thinly disguised streak of cruelty. Starbuck thought he had all the qualities of a mean dog.

The deputies were seated at a table, playing dominoes, when Starbuck entered the room. Bell rose, greeting him affably. But Ollinger merely looked around, his expression stolid. A double-barrel shotgun, which he always kept close at hand, was propped against the table. Starbuck ignored him, nodding to Bell.

"How's it going?"

"Jim Dandy," Bell said, smiling. "Little boring, but no problems otherwise."

"The Kid's behaving himself, then?"

"Hasn't give us a minute's trouble, and that's a fact."

"Wish to hell he would!"

Ollinger laid the shotgun across his lap. He stared toward the cell, where the Kid was stretched out in a bunk. He patted the shotgun, his voice sullen.

"Scared shitless, ain't you, Billy boy?"

No response.

"Knows he'll get a quart of buckshot up his gizzard if he tries anything funny. Ain't that right, badass? Go on, tell us it ain't so!"

"Ollinger." Starbuck's tone was commanding.

"You and Bell get back to your game. I want to have a word with the Kid."

Ollinger gave him a dirty look, but the baiting subsided. Moving past the table, Starbuck approached the cell. The Kid rolled out of his bunk and walked to the door. His mouth curled in a wide peg-toothed grin.

"Long time no see."

"Billy," Starbuck said pleasantly. "How're things?"

"Awright, except for ol' tough-turd Ollinger. Spends half his day wavin' that scattergun under my nose."

"I wouldn't pay him any attention."

"I don't." The Kid paused, regarding him with a lazy expression. "So where you been keepin' yourself?"

"Santa Fe, mostly," Starbuck lied. "Chisum asked me to sit in on the meetings between the Stockgrowers' Association and the governor."

"Well, don't keep it a secret! What's the news?"

"All bad." Starbuck shook his head, frowning. "The governor won't go for it. He thinks you'd welch on the deal once he commuted your sentence."

"Bullshit!" the Kid exploded. "It worked the other way round last time. He's the one that broke his word, not me!"

Starbuck shrugged. "Maybe he figures tit for tat. At any rate, he says you'll have to show good faith before he'd even consider a deal."

"Good faith?" the Kid repeated. "What the hell's that supposed to mean?"

"A deposition," Starbuck said without expression. "He wants a signed statement with everything you know about Coghlin and Dobson."

"Aww for Chrissakes! He must think I've got mush between my ears. If you had a deposition, then you wouldn't need me!"

"No, you're wrong, Billy. A deposition might get them indicted, but we need you on the witness stand to get a conviction."

"C'mon, Starbuck! That's a crock of applesauce and we both know it."

"I don't follow you."

"Like hell!" The Kid grimaced, flashing a mouthful of brownish teeth. "With a deposition, all you've got to do is wait for me to be hung. Then you bring Dobson and Coghlin to trial, and there ain't no way they could cross-examine a dead man's statement. A jury would convict 'em one, two, three!"

"You're off the mark," Starbuck said earnestly. "A judge wouldn't allow that kind of statement to be entered into evidence. He'd rule it inadmissible, and the jury would never hear it."

"Says you! I got a hunch it'd work just fine. So you trot on back and tell Chisum he can't have his cake and eat it too."

"You care to spell that out?"

"Goddamn, Starbuck, don't play dumb! You aim to let me swing, and you're tryin' to rig it so I'll pull the rest of 'em into the grave with me. Pretty slick thinkin', I'll hand you that. But it ain't gonna work."

"Well, Billy," Starbuck said, watching him carefully, "that sort of puts you between a rock and a hard place. The governor says it's no soap without a deposition, and the way I count, time's running out. You've got fifteen days, and unless you come through, that's all she wrote."

"You lousy bastard!" the Kid raged, glowering at him. "You're worse'n me! You'd sucker a man and then string him up without battin' an eye. You're just mighty goddamn lucky I ain't on the outside. You'd get yours quick, mister! Pronto!"

Starbuck looked solemn. "You've got me wrong, and I'm sorry you feel that way, Billy. I'd advise you to think it over. It's the only chance you've got."

"Don't hold your breath!"

The Kid whirled away, stumping angrily across the cell, and flopped down on his bunk. Starbuck knew then he had lost the game. The outcome brought with it no great surprise; unlike Chisum, who constantly underestimated the opposition, he'd never really believed the Kid would cooperate on the strength of promises alone. But now, having failed, he realized an escape attempt was all the more imminent. With no hope of commutation, the Kid had nothing to lose. A jailbreak was the only alternative to hanging.

Starbuck moved directly to the table, addressing Bell. "Where's Sheriff Garrett?"

"Out collectin' taxes."

"Taxes?"

"Yeah," Bell smiled, bobbing his head, "delinquent taxes. Lots of folks won't pay up till the wolf comes knockin' on their door."

Starbuck hesitated, wondering if he should warn the deputies personally. Then, reluctant to overstep himself further, he decided to wait and speak with Garrett. He nodded absently to Bell, and walked toward the hallway.

On the ground floor, he found the sheriff's office still locked. He pondered a moment, disturbed by the prospect of delay, when Garrett suddenly appeared through the main entrance. After they exchanged greetings, Garrett unlocked his office door and led the way inside.

"Pat," Starbuck said without preliminaries, "we've got big trouble. The Kid's all primed to try a breakout. I'd judge it'll be sometime within the next few days."

"That's what you told me the day we left Mesilla. So far, I haven't seen no indication of it."

"Things have changed," Starbuck noted. "He waited around thinking we might get his sentence commuted. The reason's not important, but he knows different now. He'll make his play for the first chance he gets."

"Maybe he will," Garrett said importantly, "maybe he won't. I'm not especially worried about it one way or the other."

Garrett had taken on grand airs since the Kid's

conviction. Newspaper reporters were hounding him for interviews, and an article in the *Police Gazette* had transformed him into a minor celebrity. Starbuck briefly considered deflating his balloon, then thought better of it. No useful purpose would be served, and it might adversely affect the job at hand.

"Any particular reason," he asked, "why you're not worried?"

"Bob Ollinger," Garrett said, grinning. "He hates the Kid worse'n the devil hates holy water. If the Kid tries to bust out, Bob will dose him with that shotgun and save us the trouble of hangin' him. Either way, though, the Kid winds up in a box. So it's six of one and half a dozen of another."

"If I were you," Starbuck advised, "I'd play it safe. The Kid's tricky as they come, and Ollinger's not exactly a mental wizard."

"Luke, you're a worrywart." Garrett laughed, and slapped him across the shoulder. "You just look after the Nesbeths and leave the Kid to me. Only one way he'll get out of here, and that's feet first."

Outside the courthouse, Starbuck paused to roll a cigarette. His nerves were gritty and restless, and he felt oddly unassured. For all Garrett's confidence, there were still fifteen days until the execution. And the Kid, given the least opportunity, would be long gone before that last sunrise. Yet there was little to be done that hadn't already been done. Somehow, though he couldn't say precisely why, that thought was what worried him the most.

His instinct told him something had been left undone.

Over the next couple of days Starbuck gradually put his mind at ease. The Jinglebob seemed a world apart from Lincoln and the Kid, and he decided it was senseless to brood on things that might—or might not—happen. He rode with Ellen Nesbeth every morning, and after supper, they took walks along the river. She was lively, filled with warmth and spontaneous laughter, and he found himself drawn to her bawdy good humor. More than anything else, she was a pleasant, and very attractive, diversion. She made him forget the Kid.

Then, on his second morning back at the ranch, the outside world once more intruded. Ellen, mounted on a fleet little mare, always insisted that they race the last mile to the corral. A fiery competitor, she considered herself any man's equal on a horse, and she loved to win. Starbuck understood that it was important to her, but he never made allowances for the fact she was a woman. He drove his gelding hard, and forced her to win legitimately, or not at all. Today, running neck and neck, they galloped into the compound in a dead heat. She nosed him out only within the last few yards.

As she dismounted, she was laughing, her eyes bright with excitement. But Starbuck was distracted by one of the hands, who ran forward to meet him. The look on the man's face told him there was trouble, and he prepared himself for the worst. He stepped down from the saddle with a sense of cold fatalism.

"Luke, the old man wants you up at the house!"

"Any idea what it's about?"

"The Kid escaped! Killed a couple of deputies and hightailed it out of Lincoln."

Starbuck excused himself, leaving Ellen looking dazed and suddenly somber. He hurried toward the house, aware he'd forgotten to ask which deputies had been killed. His pace quickened.

Some moments later he entered the study. Chisum was seated in his usual chair, and turned as he came through the door. One of his own men, Frank Miller, rose from the other chair. He breathed a sigh of relief, ignoring Miller's hangdog expression. He halted, his eyes hard.

"What happened?"

"The Kid busted out. Killed Bell and Ollinger."

"How?"

Miller told a fragmented story. Yesterday at noon Ollinger had stepped across the street for dinner. Somehow, though it was still a mystery, the Kid had managed to get hold of Bell's pistol. When Bell made a break for the stairs, the Kid shot and killed him. Upon hearing gunfire, Ollinger left his meal and started back across the street. The Kid, perched in an upstairs window of the courthouse, called out to him. Ollinger glanced up to find himself staring into the muzzle of his own shotgun. Onlookers said the Kid laughed, and then gave Ollinger both barrels in the chest. Terrified, the witnesses to the shooting scattered and took cover. The Kid, by then heavily armed, calmly left the courthouse and commandeered a horse. He rode out of Lincoln unchallenged.

"Me and Cole," Miller concluded, "was asleep at the hotel. We didn't hear the shootin', and it all happened so fast, nobody thought to come get us. By the time we was woke up, it was too late. The Kid had skedaddled."

"Where was Garrett?"

"Out collectin' taxes." Miller paused, studying the floor. "He's broke up bad, Luke. Took it real hard. He told me to hump it, and get you back to town straightaway."

A quietness fell over Starbuck. He dismissed Miller, who had ridden all night, ordering him to get some rest. When the door closed, he turned slowly to Chisum. His features were grim, and his mouth was set in a thin line.

"I'll leave soon as I get my gear together."

"Sorry, Luke." Chisum's expression was downcast. "I know that ain't much consolation, what with you havin' to start all over from scratch." He shifted uncomfortably in his chair. "Anything I can do to help?"

"One thing," Starbuck told him. "I'm taking John Poe with me, but I'll leave the rest of the boys here to guard the Nesbeths. They'll have their orders, so I'd appreciate it if you wouldn't get in their way."

"Hell, Luke, that ain't necessary! Go on and take

them boys along; you might need 'em. We'll look after the Nesbeths just fine."

"No," Starbuck said flatly. "I'm the one that got the Nesbeths behind the eight ball, and with the Kid loose, it makes things worse. From here on out, I want my own men on the job."

Chisum lifted an eyebrow in question. "Why would the Kid make a try for the Nesbeths?"

"He won't," Starbuck countered. "But Coghlin and his bunch might get some bright ideas. They'd like nothing better than to do away with the Nesbeths and let everybody blame it on the Kid. That way they'd be off the hook all the way round."

"Yeah," Chisum said, troubled, "you've got a point there. Specially since they'll know you're off huntin' the Kid."

Starbuck eyed him a moment, considering. "I reckon you ought to know something. I aim to get the Kid and I aim to keep the Nesbeths alive, but that's all. From now on anything else is your lookout. I don't want nothing more to do with your politics."

"You're sore 'cause the Kid got away, ain't you?"

"No, John, I'm not sore. I'm plumb pissed off."

Starbuck turned and crossed the study. He opened the door, moving into the hallway, and closed it behind him. The chime of his spurs slowly faded as he walked from the house.

An hour later, with Poe at his side, he rode toward Lincoln.

CHAPTER 13

There was a light in Garrett's office. Farther down the street, a crowd of men were gathered outside the largest of the town's saloons. The sound of loud talk and drunken laughter was intensified by the late-night stillness.

Starbuck and Poe reined to a halt before the courthouse. The commotion outside the saloon, unusual at any time in Lincoln, held their attention. They sat for a moment, listening and watching, struck by the raucous tone of the crowd. Though neither of them spoke, they exchanged a puzzled glance. With the Kid escaped, and two lawmen dead, there seemed little for the townspeople to celebrate. Finally, somewhat at a loss, they dismounted and tied their horses to the hitch rack.

John Poe slapped trail dust off his clothes, and fell in beside Starbuck. They had ridden straight through from the Jinglebob, scarcely talking the entire time. He took Starbuck's quiet mood as an ominous sign, much like a thunderhead darkening the skies before a storm. All the way into town one thought kept recurring, and now, as they walked toward the courthouse steps, he silently underscored the sentiment to himself. He was quite happy not to be standing in Pat Garrett's boots. Not tonight.

When they entered the office, Garrett looked up from behind his desk. He was hunched over a territorial map, unfurled across the desk top, and his features appeared haggard in the glow of lamplight. He rose, smiling weakly, and extended his hand.

"Been expectin' you, Luke. You made good time."

"Not good enough." Starbuck pointedly ignored the handshake. "I'd say we're about a day late, wouldn't you, Pat?"

Garrett flushed, quickly dropped his hand. "Awright, goddammit, you was right and I was wrong. You told me and I should've listened to you, and I wish to hell I had. So just don't rub it in, Luke! I've been kickin' my ass ever since it happened."

"Tell me about that," Starbuck said with a flat stare. "Miller wasn't too clear on details. Exactly how'd it happen?"

"Well, it's only a guess, but I've got an idea the Kid talked Bell into takin' him to the privy. He'd come down with a case of the trots—"

"The trots!" Starbuck interrupted. "He looked plenty healthy when I was here the day before."

"Yeah, I know," Garrett said glumly. "Course, hindsight's no better than hind tit."

"So he faked it and got Bell to let him out of the lockup to go to the outhouse. Then what?"

"Why, he must've jumped Bell somehow. He had

it planned out pretty slick, the way he waited till Ollinger went to dinner. So Bell got careless, what with the Kid bellyachin' and carrying on. It all fits."

"And nobody—" Starbuck paused, a knot throbbing in his jaw. "He just rode out of town and nobody lifted a finger to stop him."

"Not then," Garrett said defensively. "Hell, everyone that seen it like to wet their drawers. He damn near blew Bob Ollinger half in two with that scattergun!"

Starbuck squinted, watching him. "What do you mean, 'Not then'? That sounds like things have changed somehow."

"I'll say they have!" Garrett crowed, squaring his shoulders. "I put out a call for a posse and just about had to beat 'em off with a switch. Every sonovabitch and his dog volunteered!"

"A posse." Starbuck looked genuinely surprised. "You're talking about that bunch down at the saloon, aren't you?"

"Yep!" Garrett beamed, thumbs hooked in his vest. "Took the pick of the litter! Twenty men, already sworn in and ready to ride at daylight."

"Twenty drunks would be more like it. In case you haven't checked lately, they're tanked up on rotgut and going strong."

"Oh, don't pay that no nevermind. A couple of hours in the saddle and they'll sober up quick enough."

"What's holding you?" Starbuck asked. "You've had since yesterday noon to take the trail."

"Why, hell, Luke!" Garrett said affably. "I was waitin' on you to get here. Wouldn't hardly seem fair to go off without you."

"Then I reckon you just wasted a day."

"Wasted—" Garrett stopped, no longer grinning. "I don't get it."

"You'll have to handle this one by yourself, Pat. I don't care much for crowds, and I damn sure don't want any part of a wild-goose chase."

"C'mon, now, you got no call to say that."

"No?" Starbuck studied him a moment, frowning. "You take a posse out and you might as well telegraph ahead and let the Kid know you're coming. I'd rate your chances of catching him at about zero. Maybe less."

"I suppose you know a better way?"

"Yeah," Starbuck nodded, "I do. A couple of men, working real quiet, could run him down before he ever got wind they were tracking him."

"Lemme guess," Garrett said sourly. "You had yourself and Poe in mind, didn't you? I sit here on my thumb, and you two take off on your lonesome. Wasn't that about the size of it?"

"You want the Kid, don't you?"

"Hell, yes!" Garrett flared. "But the Kid's only part of it! Him breakin' jail made me look like a fool. So I've got to make a show of huntin' him down. A damn big show! Otherwise, I'm in a heap of trouble."

"And if I'm right?" Starbuck demanded. "If it turns out to be a wild-goose chase? What then?"

"I can't let that happen, Luke. I've got to catch him—got to, goddammit!—or else I'm a dead duck come election time."

Starbuck was silent for a long while. At last, with a look of weary resignation, he shrugged. "Where did you aim to start?"

Garrett turned the map on the desk. Starbuck and Poe moved closer, and he began a quick explanation of the search he'd planned. His finger traced a path west through the mountains, then across the Carrizozo Plains and along the slopes of the Oscuros. From there, he indicated the Three Rivers country, then the Organ Mountains, and, finally, a sweep through the border. When he finished, he stood back, awaiting Starbuck's verdict.

"That pretty well covers it," Starbuck allowed, "except for Fort Sumner."

"Oh, hell, Luke, he'd never go back there. Not in a month of Sundays! The Kid's too smart for that."

"Well, it's your show, Pat. You run it whichever way suits you best. I'll leave Poe with you—"

"Hold on! You mean you're not comin' along?"

"No." Starbuck shook his head. "You don't need me. I'll just stick close to the Jinglebob and keep an eye on the Nesbeths. Wouldn't pay to take any more chances with them."

Garrett looked relieved. "I suspect you're right, Luke. Makes damn good sense all the way round."

Starbuck purposely avoided any further discussion. He noted it had been a long day, commenting he would spend the night at the hotel, and left the office. Poe, after agreeing to meet Garrett and the posse at dawn, went along. Outside, walking toward their horses, Starbuck appeared thoughtful. When the silence held, Poe's curiosity finally got the better of him.

"You really headed back to the Jinglebob," he asked quietly, "or have you got some notion of trailin' the Kid on your own?"

"I considered that," Starbuck admitted, "but it'd just be wasted effort. I figure the Kid will stay on the move, leastways till Garrett gets tired of chasing around the territory. If I was him, I wouldn't spend two nights running in the same place."

"What's the sense in me taggin' along with Garrett, then?"

"Hold his hand," Starbuck remarked. "Keep him from making too big a fool of himself. He'll call it quits soon enough, and once the dust settles, that's when we'll make our move."

"How you aim to go about it?"

Starbuck smiled. "I'll be thinking on it, John. There's ways and there's ways, and it'll come to me by the time the Kid goes to roost. You just let me know when Garrett's got his fill."

Poe merely nodded. He was accustomed to Starbuck's cryptic manner, and as they mounted their horses and rode toward the livery stable, he knew he'd been told the one thing that mattered. Sometime soon, quietly and on his own, Starbuck meant to stalk the Kid and kill him. No quarter asked, none given.

Across town, in the home of Judge Owen Hough, another meeting was under way. Jack Dobson and Joe Coghlin were seated in the study. The sliding doors were closed, and the judge sat behind a walnut desk, assessing the two men with a cool look. His features were immobile, revealing nothing.

Since January, the strategy outlined by Warren Mitchell had proved almost infallible. Their monthly meetings were amicable, and according to Mitchell, their associates in Santa Fe were pleased by the gradual progression of affairs. John Chisum's health continued to deteriorate, and there was every reason to believe he wouldn't last out the year. The kid had been convicted and sentenced, and exactly as predicted, he hadn't cooperated with the authorities. The single fly in the ointment was the range detective, Luke Starbuck. Somehow, possibly through the Kid, he had uncovered information of an incriminating nature. In turn, he'd been led to Coghlin's ranch and the Nesbeths, and had developed what appeared to be a fairly strong circumstantial case. Still, despite all he'd learned, no charges had been filed. Which meant the Nesbeths were being held in reserve until some future time. The threat, then, was real, though hardly insurmountable. Witnesses were of no value unless they lived to testify.

For his part, Owen Hough had earned the praise of the men in Santa Fe. By one device or another, he had kept Dobson and Coghlin in line, and no hint of the political ramifications had been allowed to surface. He had the Lincoln operation under control and proceeding smoothly on schedule.

Then, yesterday at noon, all that had changed. With the Kid's escape, Hough was suddenly forced to assume full responsibility for the Pecos Valley venture. There was no way he could safely telegraph Warren Mitchell for instructions, and their next meeting was not scheduled until the latter part of the month. The situation dictated immediate action, and there was nowhere he could turn for advice. He was on his own.

The problem was compounded by Dobson and Coghlin. Their nerves were of the caliber he associated with small-time grifters; they lacked the strength of character necessary to a time of adversity. Watching them now, he knew tonight's meeting represented a critical juncture. Unless he calmed their fears, and somehow restored their confidence, they might very well crack under pressure. Which would spell disaster for him as well.

His voice dispassionate, he addressed them with a look of easy candor. "Gentlemen, let me assure you there's no cause for alarm. Even with the sheriff out of town, William Bonney wouldn't dare set foot in Lincoln."

"What's to stop him?" Coghlin insisted. "Once Garrett and that posse are gone, he could ride in here and do anything he damn well pleased."

"Perhaps," Hough conceded. "But believe me, he won't. You're assuming he has some grudge to settle, and that simply isn't the case."

"I don't agree," Dobson said nervously. "Granted, we got him a change of venue and all that. But I'm convinced he expected something more from us."

"Such as?"

"God only knows! The Kid's crazy as a loon! He probably thought we'd spring him somehow, maybe a commutation. Why else would he wait till two weeks before the hanging to bust out? He sure as hell didn't stick around because he liked jail cooking."

"Perhaps yesterday was the first opportunity he had. You're reading a great deal into it, Jack. I daresay, much more than exists."

"I know the Kid," Dobson countered, "and you don't! He's a vengeful little backshooter, and I'd bet money he thinks we sold him down the river. I told you all along we weren't doing enough! Not to his way of thinking, anyhow."

"Anything more was impossible," Hough said firmly. "We couldn't risk being connected to a common murderer, not this late in the game."

"We?" Dobson echoed. "Hell, it's not we you're talking about. It's that bunch in Santa Fe! The whole idea was to protect their hides, and no way on God's green earth you'll ever convince me otherwise."

"Yeah," Coghlin muttered. "We told you from the start what the Kid was like. You should've listened to us, judge! If we'd only fooled him into believing we was tryin' to help out, then none of this would've happened."

Hough brushed aside the objection. "I don't care to argue the matter any further. You two have your minds made up, so we'll let it rest there. But I direct your attention to certain advantages you've quite obviously overlooked. Has it ever occurred to you that we've been handed a remarkable opportunity?"

Dobson and Coghlin exchanged a quizzical look. When neither of them replied, he went on. "I refer to the fact that Pat Garrett is the laughingstock of Lincoln County. Unless he redeems himself, then he's through in politics. And that, gentlemen, means he will not attempt to recapture Mr. Bonney."

"What?" Dobson scowled. "What the hell are you saying, Owen?"

"I'm saying"—Hough paused for effect, "Garrett will kill the Kid. He needs something to capture the public's imagination, and nothing does it like a shootout. You can take my word on it—the Kid's as good as dead."

"Christ!" Coghlin mumbled. "Wouldn't that be sweet? It'd sure get us off the hook, wouldn't it?"

"It would indeed," Hough said, smiling. "But only halfway, I'm afraid."

Dobson gave him an odd look. "Now you're talking about the Nesbeths, aren't you?"

"Very perceptive, Jack. And, of course, you're

right. We have a chance to wipe the slate clean. No links to the past and nothing to hinder our plans for the future."

"I don't get it," Coughlin said, glancing from one to the other. "What's the big deal about killin' them now?"

"The big deal," Dobson informed him, "is that the Kid's on the loose. Isn't that what you had in mind, judge?"

"Precisely," Hough nodded. "The timing couldn't be more perfect. Chisum and his crowd will naturally jump to the conclusion that the Kid killed them. We couldn't ask for a better opportunity."

"Two birds with one stone," Coghlin laughed. "The Kid gets the Nesbeths, and Garrett gets the Kid. Goddamn!"

"There's one problem," Hough added. "We have to get the Nesbeths before Garrett gets the Kid. Otherwise it won't work."

"Why, hell," Coghlin grunted, "that's simple enough. I'll just tell Gantry to get on it muy pronto. The way he feels about the Nesbeths, he'd count it a pleasure."

There was a long moment of silence. Owen Hough studied the men across from him with a speculative gaze. Then, almost as though thinking aloud, he spoke directly to Coghlin.

"Tell him not to miss. I have a feeling we won't get a second chance."

CHAPTER 14

In the dark, fireflies darted among the trees. Starbuck and the girl were seated under a willowy cottonwood, talking quietly. Their voices were muted by the purl of the river, and they were only dimly visible beneath the moonless sky. She was close enough to touch, and her nearness seemed to him an invitation. She smelled sweet and alluring.

These evening walks had become something of a ritual. Following supper, whenever Starbuck was at the ranch, they excused themselves early and strolled off toward their favorite spot overlooking the river. Understandably, though the matter had never been discussed openly, everyone assumed they were lovers. Sallie Chisum, scarcely civil at times, made no effort to hide her disgust. Her father, who thought she was secretly jealous, looked on the whole affair with rueful good humor. The Nesbeths, on the other hand, knew their daughter and therefore surmised the worst. They accepted, as a matter of form, that she had seduced Starbuck. Their attitude was one of humiliation and shame, and disgruntled silence.

Starbuck, oddly enough, hadn't laid a hand on the girl. He was a confirmed womanizer, with all the instincts of a randy tomcat. His string of conquests included several ranchers' daughters—none of whom had gotten him anywhere near an altar— and he was on intimate terms with dance hall girls in every cowtown within riding distance of the Panhandle. Yet his feelings about Ellen Nesbeth veered wildly.

Over the past few months, the safety of the Jinglebob had brought about a marked change in her attitude. As her fears diminished, the friction between them dwindled as well, and she gradually warmed to Starbuck. Whenever they were together she seemed poised for laughter, filled with verve and gaiety. She no longer treated him like an unwanted protector; her manner was flirtatious and teasing, and she gave the impression an advance would not be unwelcome. Still, though the temptation was difficult to resist, he had kept her at arm's length. He was wary of involvement, fearful her parents would believe he had betrayed a trust, and taken advantage of the situation. Then too, he genuinely liked the girl, and found himself reluctant to test the depth of his own emotions. He avoided physical contact, and tried to ignore her broader hints. He also slept badly.

Tonight, evidencing a new vein of curiosity, she had turned the conversation to his personal life. Under normal circumstances, her questions would have been met with blunt reserve. But he was distracted by thoughts of Garrett—whose search for the Kid had begun only three days ago—and her opening question had caught him off guard. He was uncomfortable talking about himself, but there seemed no easy way to change the subject. For her part, Ellen was playfully amused by his discomfort. She was intrigued as well by that part of himself he kept hidden.

"Do you like your job?" she asked pleasantly. "I mean . . . well, you know . . . most people think a range detective doesn't do anything but go around hanging cow thieves."

"I've never put much store in what people think."

"It doesn't bother you, then—hanging men?"

"Some," Starbuck admitted. "But I've never hung a man that wasn't caught red-handed. Unless I had the goods on them, then they got off with a warning to stay clear of the Panhandle."

She looked at him with impudent eyes. "That's a little like playing God, isn't it?"

"Maybe." Starbuck was gruffly defensive. "Somebody's got to do it, though. Otherwise nothing would be safe, including a man's home and family. I suppose it's all a matter of where you draw the line."

"How many men have you hung?"

"God A'mighty! Hasn't anyone ever told you there are some questions you just don't ask?"

She cocked her head in a funny little smile. "They say you have killed a dozen men in gunfights, maybe more."

"Who says?"

"People," she said mischievously. "Everyone on the Jinglebob gossips about you. To hear them talk, you're sort of a cross between Wild Bill Hickok and a man-eating tiger."

"Well—" Starbuck broke off, chuckling softly. "You sure got yourself an earful, didn't you?"

"Nooo," she said slowly. "I only heard enough to make me curious."

"Oh, how so?"

She searched his face in the dim starlight. "If you like your work so much, why haven't you become a peace officer? Wouldn't a badge make the job easier?"

"Chisum made a good argument for that the day I rode in here. So I listened to him and agreed to let Garrett deputize me. The way it turned out, it made things tougher, not easier."

"I don't understand."

Starbuck pondered a moment. "You remember the fellow I told you about, Ben Langham?" She nodded and he went on. "The Kid killed him and there's no whichaway about it. If I hadn't been wearing a star, we would've hung him when we caught him. But we went by the book—played it straight and gave him his day in court—and you see what happened. He's loose and we're right back where we started."

"Are you saying he shouldn't have had a trial?"

"I'm saying all the legal delays kept him alive past his time. As a result, he's killed two more men and escaped and Christ Himself couldn't guarantee where it'll end."

"Would you have hung them all? Coghlin and Dobson and Gantry, all without a trial?"

"Every last one," Starbuck said gravely. "They're accessories to murder, and except for them, none of this would've happened. I figure they deserve whatever they get, and the faster the better."

"I couldn't agree more! But isn't that for a jury to decide? I mean, after all, that's why we have laws, isn't it?"

"Justice and the law aren't always the same thing. There's times when a man has to choose between them in order to get the job done."

"The terrible swift sword, with no legal tomfoolery?"

"It's a damnsight more certain than the courts! Especially for people like the Kid."

A hot rush of awareness swept over Ellen. Something in the timbre of his voice—the danger and deadly intensity of the man—evoked responses that left her weak in the knees and short of breath. She was drawn to him in some way she couldn't define, and each time they were together her fascination became all the more compelling. Yet she warned herself to beware of any emotional attachment. Behind that hard exterior was a hard man, and if not altogether insensitive, he nonetheless displayed little tolerance for weakness in others. She wanted him, but she felt very much like a small girl playing with matches. She told herself to go slow and hold to a light vein, for she sensed there was nothing beyond the moment, no tomorrow. Abruptly, heeding her own advice, she switched topics with a disingenuous air and a fetching smile.

"Why is it you have never married?"

Starbuck looked at her with some surprise. "Wrong line of work, I guess. Fellow in my trade doesn't run across many women who want to jump the broom with him."

"Fiddlesticks!" she said brightly. "Sallie Chisum is so sweet on you she goes tongue-tied every time you walk into the room."

"You're pulling my leg."

"I certainly am not!" Her throaty laughter floated across the still night. "All you need to do is snap your fingers! Sallie would jump the broom, and the old man would hand you the Jinglebob on a silver platter."

"No, you're wrong," Starbuck said in a low voice. "Even if you weren't, that'd be a poor reason to marry somebody."

"Poor, my eye! The Jinglebob will make someone a very handsome wedding present. Are you sure you won't think it over, Luke? You could do lots worse."

"Wouldn't doubt it. But don't you see, it'd just be another headache on top of the old one."

"What would?"

"The Jinglebob."

"What are you talking about?"

"My ranch."

"Your ranch!" She stared at him, astounded. "You own a ranch?"

"Yeah," Starbuck said, not cracking a smile. "The LX, over in the Panhandle. Course, it's only about half the size of the Jinglebob, but it's a nice little spread."

"You—!" She tossed her head, pouting. "You just let me run on and make a fool of myself. That's cruel."

"I didn't hardly see any way to stop you."

She sniffed. "It's probably a big fib, anyhow! Are you sure you own a ranch?"

"Cross my heart."

"And it's really half the size of the Jinglebob?"

"Close enough, give or take a few thousand acres."

She eyed him suspiciously. "Where did a range detective get an outfit that big?"

Starbuck looked away, suddenly somber. "Ben Langham willed it to me."

"The man the Kid—?"

"Yeah," Starbuck said quietly. "You might say the Kid made me a rich man."

"Oh, Luke." She touched his arm. "I'm sorry, I had no idea . . ."

Her voice trailed off. The warmth of her hand triggered something within him. All restraint dispelled, he took her in his arms. Whatever he'd guessed about her past, he was not prepared for the depth of her ardor, her sensual eagerness. Her lips were moist and inviting, and she greedily darted his mouth with her tongue. Her arms circled his neck with desperate urgency, and she pulled him down on the ground. He stretched out beside her on the grassy riverbank, and she snuggled closer, moaning softly. Her breasts were firm and swollen, her nipples pressed hard through his shirt, and he felt himself growing aroused by the feverish movement of her hips. His hand slipped beneath her skirt, touched yielding flesh, then quickly moved upward, caressing the warmth of her thigh. She began to tremble, her body wracked by convulsions, and her legs parted. Her nails dug into his shoulders, fierce talons holding him tighter, and he rolled on top of her. One hand clutching her buttocks, he began fumbling with the buttons on his pants. Her legs went around him, urging him.

A gunshot split the night. Too quick to count, the roar of a rifle hammered out several more shots in a staccato burst.

Starbuck scrambled to his feet. Cursing savagely, he ordered her not to move, and hurried off into the darkness. Once clear of the trees, he sprinted hard, running toward the main house. Ahead, he heard shouting and saw dim figures dashing across the compound. He flipped the leather thong off the hammer of his Colt, jerking and cocking the pistol in one smooth motion. His stride lengthened to a dead lope.

Outside the house, a clot of men stood jammed together before the veranda. Their voices swelled in a confused murmur, and several cowhands toward the front seemed to be shouting questions. Then the door opened and a spill of lamplight flooded the yard. John Chisum, with his daughter at his side, hobbled across the veranda.

Starbuck bulled a path through the crowd. He saw one of his own men, Jessie Tuttle, separate from the cowhands and approach the veranda. He recalled Tuttle had pulled the early watch tonight, guarding the perimeter of the house, and he grasped the situation immediately. It was Tuttle, still carrying his saddle carbine, who had fired the shots.

Chisum spotted him as he moved into the silty glow of lamplight. Tuttle turned, nodding soberly, and he halted before them. He felt Sallie Chisum's eyes on him, but he directed his attention to Tuttle.

"Let's have it, Jessie," he said, catching his breath from the run. "What happened?"

"Three men," Tuttle replied crisply, "maybe four. Sorta hard to tell in the dark. I was posted out back of the house and—well, you know how it is at night—all I caught was movement, more like shadows than anything else. I sung out real loud, and they took off like scalded dogs. That's when I cut loose."

"You were the only one that fired?"

"Yep," Tuttle grinned. "I sprayed 'em good! Black as pitch out there, so I just let go and hoped I'd get lucky."

"Any idea what they had in mind?"

"Not rightly. But the way they was headed put 'em on a beeline for the Nesbeths' bedroom window. I reckoned that was reason enough to stop 'em right where they was."

"You reckoned right," Starbuck acknowledged. "Any chance you winged one of them?"

"Nope," Tuttle said bitterly. "I heard a bunch of horses all take off at once. Figures they would've been slowed down some if anybody had caught a slug."

"Where were the horses, which direction?"

"North, over by that stand of trees where the crick runs into the river. Good hunnert yards away, but they made it lickety-split when I started dustin' their heels."

"Get some lanterns," Starbuck ordered, jerking a thumb at the throng of cowhands. "Take these boys and search that area foot by foot. If you spot any blood sign, give me a yell real quick."

The men trooped off into the night, and Starbuck quickly assessed the situation. Someone, intent on killing the Nesbeths, had been thwarted only at the last moment. A worm of doubt gnawed at him as he considered moving the Nesbeths to a safer location. Then, with bleak irony, he reminded himself there was no place safer than the Jinglebob. It would be necessary to double the guard and maintain constant vigilance. And he saw, too, that he could no longer afford to wait on Garrett. His own plan, complicated further by tonight's attack, must be put into effect without delay. At length, he turned to Chisum.

"I'm going after the Kid first thing tomorrow."

"Alone?"

"Alone," Starbuck told him. "We're running short on time, and one way or another, it's got to end."

"This business tonight," Chisum asked tentatively, "you think it was the Kid?"

"Maybe," Starbuck said without conviction. "Or maybe somebody that wanted us to think it was the Kid. Either way, it won't be settled until he's hung out to dry."

"Then you intend to kill him?"

Starbuck's eyes were angry, commanding. "Just as sure as God made little green apples."

Sallie Chisum suddenly drew a sharp breath. She stared past him a mere instant, then wheeled around, skirts flying, and marched into the house. He turned and saw Ellen walking toward them. Her clothes were disheveled and a long strand of hair hung loose on her neck. She stopped, her gaze fixed on him with a look of dulled terror.

"Were my folks . . . hurt?"

"No, they're fine." He gently touched her arm. "Why don't you go tell them there's nothing to worry about? I'll come by when I get things squared away."

She nodded, glancing absently at Chisum, and crossed the veranda. There was a moment of silence until she went through the door and disappeared down the hallway. Then Chisum grunted, his mouth curled in a wry smile.

"You'll likely find it a mite safer off huntin' the

Kid. There's gonna be lots of fireworks around here after tonight."

"Jesus!" Starbuck muttered. "Women sure do complicate things."

"Why, son, you ain't seen the half of it! Wait'll the fight really starts!"

Starbuck shook his head, and walked off toward the creek. Watching him, Chisum was struck by a whimsical notion, and suddenly chuckled. He wondered how it felt to be a manhunter and a lady-killer—all rolled into one!

CHAPTER 15

Starbuck's disguise was convincing though not elaborate. A brushy mustache covered his upper lip and a carefully cultivated stubble shadowed his features from chin to jawbone. He looked grimy and trail-worn, and his clothes were a regular rainbow of foul odors. Which was a normal condition for any man who rode the owlhoot. After a close inspection, even a diehard skeptic found it easy to believe he was only one step ahead of the law.

For the past two months, he had scoured the better part of New Mexico Territory. His route was roughly opposite to the path taken by Pat Garrett, who had long since abandoned the search and retired to Lincoln to await word of the Kid's whereabouts. On the move constantly, he had begun the hunt along the border. A week of discreet inquiry, pausing briefly in villages on both sides of the line, left him convinced the Kid had not sought refuge in Old Mexico. From there he had turned north, criss-crossing back and forth on wide sweeps that covered the central half of the territory. Every couple of weeks he returned to the Jinglebob, stopping overnight to exchange information with Chisum. Then, expecting no word of the Kid and receiving none, he quickly resumed the search. He drifted from towns to outlying ranches to rugged mountainous camps. And he found nothing.

At the outset, his plan had been based on a simple premise. He believed, with some conviction, that the Kid would go to ground once Garrett called it quits and stopped chasing around the countryside. Long ago he had mastered the trick common to game hunters: a man who consistently put meat on the table learned to think like his prey. In the Kid's place, he would have avoided Garrett's posse, then retreated to a secure hideout and laid low until the furor subsided. Yet it was not enough for a manhunter to merely think like an outlaw. Much the same as a wilderness hunter, he used that knowledge to cut sign and shorten the chase, and ultimately bring his quarry to bay. To date, the Kid had left no spoor, not the slightest trace.

Starbuck's cover story, like his physical disguise, was a work of credible simplicity. He posed as a friend of Dave Rudabaugh's, one of the outlaws captured at Stinking Springs with the Kid. Along with the rest of the gang, Rudabaugh had been convicted on a variety of charges and sentenced to a long term in prison. After exhausting all appeals, the conviction had been upheld and the gang members were to be transferred from the Santa Fe jail to federal prison on July 15. By weaving known fact with plausible invention, Starbuck was able to fabricate a tale that had the ring of truth. Dave Ruda-baugh had put out a call for help, requesting that the Kid arrange a jailbreak before the gang was transferred to federal prison. Passing himself off as a go-between, Starbuck told the same story everywhere he went. He desperately needed to make contact with the Kid, and deliver Rudabaugh's message. Otherwise the men who had loyally stuck by *El Chivato* would spend the rest of their days on a federal rockpile.

His tale drew sympathy from bartenders and wide-eyed peons and an assortment of hardcases who frequented back alley cantinas all across the territory. But no leads surfaced, and the trail proved cold as a demon winter wind. To all intents and purposes, the Kid had disappeared from the face of the earth.

At last, on the morning of July 10, Starbuck admitted he'd reached an impasse. His quest had consumed two wearying months and taken him on a corkscrew odyssey of nearly a thousand miles. Always on guard, constantly in the saddle, his bones ached as though he'd been run through an ore crusher. Even worse, the long, futile weeks of searching had sapped his will, left him emotionally drained. He saw no reason to punish himself further.

Outside Santa Fe, he paused at a crossroads. To the south lay Lincoln and the Jinglebob, and an end to a grueling journey. But with that end, having come full circle, he would be forced to swallow the bitter pill of defeat. It grated on him to think he'd fared no better than Pat Garrett. A matter of professional pride was involved, and he suddenly cursed himself as a quitter.

His gaze turned east, along a road that crossed the Manzano Mountains and led ultimately to Fort Sumner. There was little to be gained in that direction; he believed, like Garrett, that the Kid would avoid old haunts and known friends. Still, it was the one spot he hadn't covered, and perhaps his last chance to unearth a lead. Pete Maxwell, the rancher headquartered there, was a staunch defender of the Kid, and a longtime friend. While the odds dictated otherwise, it was always possible he'd heard from the Kid, or at least had some knowledge as to the outlaw's general whereabouts. If there was nothing to be gained in talking with Maxwell, there was certainly nothing to be lost.

Starbuck reined his horse eastward, toward Fort Sumner. He told himself it was just slightly out of the way, and therefore no real waste of time. And it delayed, if only by a day, his inevitable return to the Jinglebob.

Shortly after noontime the next day, Starbuck dismounted before Maxwell's house. He left his horse ground-reined and proceeded up the stone walkway. A middle-aged man with dark hair and a bulge around his beltline stepped through the door. He moved to the edge of the porch and stood digging at his teeth with a toothpick as Starbuck approached. His expression was neutral.

"Howdy."

"Afternoon," Starbuck responded. "Hope I didn't interrupt your dinner."

"No, I just now got up from the table. What can I do for you?"

"Thought maybe you could point me in the direction of Pete Maxwell."

"Who might you be?"

"Name's Bob Brown," Starbuck said in a weary tone. "I've got a message for Maxwell."

"No need to look no further, Mr. Brown. I'm Pete Maxwell."

"Then you'd know the feller that sent me, Dave Rudabaugh."

Maxwell stopped picking his teeth. "Yeah, I used to be on speakin' terms with Rudabaugh."

"I reckon you heard him and the rest of the boys pulled a long stretch?"

"Word gets around."

"Maybe you heard they're gonna be shipped off to the federal pen come next Monday?"

"Suppose I had?" Maxwell said, frowning. "What's that got to do with me?"

"Dave needs help." Starbuck took out the makings and sprinkled tobacco into a rolling paper. "He ain't exactly hankerin' to take that trip."

"I wouldn't be surprised."

Starbuck licked, sealing the paper, and twisted the ends. He struck a match, glancing up at Maxwell as he lit the cigarette. "Dave figures to bust out of jail. But he's gonna need someone on the outside to lend a hand."

"That a fact?" Maxwell studied him a moment. "You sayin' he had some idea I'd help spring him?"

"Nope," Starbuck said, exhaling a thin streamer of smoke. "But he thought you might get word to the Kid. He figures Bonney owes him one, for old-times' sake."

"Bob Brown." Maxwell underscored the words with a slow drawl. "I don't recall hearin' that name before. Who're you to Dave Rudabaugh?"

"A friend." Starbuck met his look squarely. "Let's get something straight, Mr. Maxwell. Dave got me out of a scrape once and I'm returnin' the favor. But I'm just a messenger boy in this here deal, nothin' more. I quit the owlhoot a long time ago, and I don't aim to get bollixed up in no jail-break."

"Ain't likely you will," Maxwell said coolly. "The way things stack up, you rode out here for nothin'."

"How so?"

"The Kid lit out for Mexico when he busted jail. Last I heard, he was holed up somewheres down in Sonora."

"Sonora!" Starbuck appeared distressed, took a couple of quick puffs on his cigarette. "Jesus, that don't give me much time! Any idea where I might find him?"

"Even if I knew—which I don't—it wouldn't do

no good. You only got four days till Rudabaugh's shipped out, and it'd take you damn near that long to locate the Kid. You might as well ride on back and tell Rudabaugh it just didn't pan out."

"Yeah," Starbuck grunted, "luck of the draw, ain't it?"

"Wish I could've been more help. Tell Rudabaugh and the rest of the boys I was askin' after them."

"I'll do that, Mr. Maxwell. Much obliged for your time."

Starbuck turned and plodded wearily back to his horse. He wasn't at all sure Maxwell had told him the truth; but there was no sign of tension, and no reason to believe the rancher knew anything of value. Then too, it was entirely possible the Kid had avoided the border towns and crossed into Mexico without leaving a trace. He ground his cigarette into the dirt, suddenly disgusted. *To hell with it!*

Pete Maxwell stood sucking on his toothpick. He watched Starbuck mount and ride west from the settlement. Only when horse and rider were dimly visible in the distance did he turn away. He entered the house and stopped just inside a bedroom which overlooked the veranda.

The Kid was positioned beside a window. His gaze was fixed on the western road, and a moment elapsed before he glanced around. His expression was grim.

"What do you think?" Maxwell asked. "Was he on the level?"

"Pete, it's a damn good thing you've got a poker face. The jasper you been talkin' with was Luke Starbuck."

"Starbuck!" Maxwell parroted. "The range detective?"

"Big as life." The Kid scowled, shook his head. "Sonovabitch just don't give up! I wasn't never worried about Garrett, but I was sure as hell hopin' we'd seen the last of that hardass."

"You think he bought my story?"

"Sounded like it." The Kid paused, considering. "Course, that ain't no guarantee he won't be back. I got a hunch it's time to be movin' on."

"Mexico?"

"Why not?" The Kid shrugged, a hint of mockery in his eyes. "Somewheres down around Sonora, wasn't that what you said?"

"You'll need money," Maxwell noted somberly. "I only got a couple of hundred here in the house, but I could send along some more later."

"No, you done too much already, Pete. Besides, I'll need enough dinero to last me awhile. Think I know where I can get it, too."

"Coghlin?" Maxwell growled. "Goddamn, Billy, him and Dobson ain't to be trusted! You don't want to risk that."

"Who they gonna tell?" The Kid gave him a grotesque smile. One side of his mouth curled upward, while the other side remained fixed and hard. "Don't worry, Pete. When they hear I'm headed south of the border, they'll come through and glad to oblige. Probably wet their drawers with relief."

"They'd a sight rather see you dead, and that ain't no lie."

"Won't happen, Pete. Them fellers know I'd talk a blue streak if they ever crossed me. You'll see! All I got to do is send one of your boys into town and they'll pony up so fast it'll make your head swim."

"You always was too goddamn nervy for your own good, Billy."

The Kid roared laughter. "Well, old man, there ain't nobody punched my ticket yet, have they?"

"Oh, Luke, for heaven's sake!"

Ellen Nesbeth looked at him, her eyes full of dark amusement. They were seated on the porch swing, shadowy figures in the early evening twilight. A cool breeze drifted in from the river, and with it the strains of a guitar. The sound of laughter and voices carried clearly from the bunkhouse quadrangle.

"Honestly, you did your best! What more could anyone ask?"

"That won't cut it," Starbuck muttered. "Not by half."

"Don't be silly." She sighed, then straightened her shoulders. "Sometimes I think you are the most exasperating man I ever met. You've done everything humanly possible. Even Mr. Chisum says so! You heard him yourself."

"Then I reckon humanly possible isn't enough.

Not where the Kid's concerned, anyway."

Starbuck had returned to the Jinglebob late last night. A shave and a hot bath, along with a change of clothes, had restored his outward appearance. But inwardly he was gripped by a deep melancholy. All day he had brooded around the house, withdrawn and miserable, and clearly in no mood to talk. Only after supper, at Ellen's insistence, had he agreed to venture outside. He gave the impression of a man who had looked within and found himself wanting.

"Let me ask you something, Luke. Have you ever failed at anything before? Anything at all in your entire life!"

Starbuck caught her eye for an instant, looked quickly away. "What's that got to do with the price of tea?"

"You haven't, have you?"

"No, by God, I haven't! So what?"

"Well, just look around you sometime. The world is full of men who haven't done anything but fail! If this is your first time, then count your lucky stars. You've been keeping very special company!"

"I don't give three hoots—"

The sound of hoofbeats silenced him, then a horse suddenly loomed out of the night. John Poe sawed at the reins, skidding to a dust-smothered halt, and leaped from the saddle. He ran toward the house.

Starbuck rose and went to meet him. "What's up? I thought we agreed you'd wet-nurse Garrett."

"Luke—" Poe caught his breath, started over.

"Garrett got a tip on the Kid! I made him swear he'd wait till we got back, then I rode like a bat out of hell. Figgered that was the only way we'd keep him from messin' it up the way he done before."

"Slow down." Starbuck stopped him with an upraised palm. "Now, let's begin at the beginning. What kind of tip?"

"A note under the office door. Garrett found it this morning. Wasn't signed, but it's the genuine article."

"What makes you think so?"

"Was you at Fort Sumner early yesterday?"

Starbuck stared at him, astounded. "How did you know that?"

"From the note," Poe said evenly. "Whoever wrote it said that would prove it's on the level. I got no idea who's behind it, but evidently the Kid was there and you showin' up somehow flushed him."

"The Kid—" Starbuck suddenly grinned. "The Kid's at Fort Sumner?"

"What the hell you think I'm tryin' to tell you? Somebody went to a lot of trouble to make us believe it's gospel truth."

"No, John," Starbuck corrected him. "Somebody went to a lot of trouble to get the Kid killed."

"Well, one thing's for damn sure. We got no time to argue about it! Garrett ain't gonna wait forever."

"Have somebody saddle my horse, and get yourself a fresh one while you're about it. I'll be with you directly."

Poe hurried off toward the corral, leading his horse. Starbuck turned and walked back across the porch. Ellen was still sitting in the swing, her hands folded in her lap. She smiled, something merry lurking in her eyes.

"Apparently you only thought you'd failed."

"We'll see," Starbuck remarked. "I haven't got him yet."

"You will." Her voice trembled slightly. "Just look after yourself and don't get . . . careless . . . Come back safe."

"Count on it." Starbuck hesitated, looking directly into her eyes, then nodded. "You're mighty pretty when you cry."

He stepped off the veranda, and a moment later vanished into the night. A tear rolled down her cheek, but she sat perfectly still, listening. She heard, somewhere far in the darkness, the faint chime of his spurs.

CHAPTER 16

Nightfall settled swiftly over Fort Sumner. A dog barked in the distance, and the murmur of voices carried distinctly from the saloon. The rest of the settlement lay quiet and still under an indigo sky.

Across the parade ground, now overgrown with weeds, were several abandoned buildings. One of them, an old and decaying barracks, afforded a perfect vantage point opposite the saloon. Crouched inside the barracks door, Starbuck and Garrett maintained a silent vigil. Neither man spoke, and a strained, almost palpable air of tension hung between them. Their eyes were fixed on the saloon; they watched the shadowy figures visible through the lamp-lit windows. Their wait, prolonged beyond anything they'd expected, seemed unendurable.

Shortly before sundown, accompanied by John Poe, they had halted a mile south of Fort Sumner. There, leaving their horses tied in a grove of trees, they had begun a cautious approach on foot. As dusk fell, and the supper hour slipped past, they stealthily made their way through the settlement. Once inside the barracks, they had mounted watch on the saloon, where Pete Maxwell's vaqueros normally congregated following the evening meal. Their plan, agreed upon earlier, was based on what seemed a reasonable assumption. If the Kid was hiding out at Fort Sumner, he would almost certainly be drawn to the saloon. Never one to drink alone, he preferred the coarse good humor of rough men. And with Maxwell's vaqueros there was no need for vigilance. He was among friends.

For an hour or more, the lawman had quietly observed as vaqueros began gathering in the saloon. Arriving singly and in small groups, none of those who entered the saloon bore any apparent resemblance to the Kid. But as twilight faded and the night sky grew darker, it became increasingly difficult to distinguish one form from another. The vaqueros tended to be short and slight of build, as was the Kid; from across the parade ground, particularly in the poor light, everyone looked very much alike. Finally, when full night descended, Starbuck began wondering if they hadn't somehow missed spotting the Kid. Troubled by the thought, he'd sent Poe to scout the saloon from the outside. Under the circumstances, it had seemed the only sensible course of action.

Yet now, awaiting Poe's return, all he could think of was a smoke. He hadn't had a cigarette since before sundown, and the interminable passage of time had whetted his craving minute by minute. Then too, he'd been in the saddle almost twenty-four hours straight, with little to eat and no rest.

Supper last night at the Jinglebob seemed a lifetime ago; his stomach growled in protest, and hunger merely aggravated his need for a cigarette. He suddenly envied Poe, and wished he had a taste for chewing tobacco. A jaw stuffed with Red Devil seemed a comforting thought. Or at the very least a distraction. He had a hunch they were in for a long night.

A burst of laughter from the saloon caught his attention. Voices were raised in a volley of Spanish, most of which he found unintelligible, and the commotion slowly subsided. Then, seemingly from nowhere, John Poe materialized out of the night and stepped through the doorway.

"Any luck?" Garrett demanded anxiously. "Was he there?"

"Nope," Poe replied. "All Mex, except the barkeep. No sign of the Kid."

"Damn!"

Garrett stumped away, halting by a window, and stood glowering out across the parade ground. Starbuck and Poe exchanged a worried look. All day, like a man nursing a toothache, Garrett had been crabby and on edge. The protracted wait had further frayed his nerves, and they were reminded that he hadn't the temperament necessary for a manhunt. His patience was clearly exhausted, and worse, there was a smell of fear about him. He seemed terrified that the Kid would elude them, and his spooky behavior was definite cause for alarm. A case of the jitters often got the wrong man killed.

With an oath, he turned and walked back to them. He halted, scowling at Starbuck. "I'm done waitin'! We could sit here all night and not know anything more than we do now."

"What do you suggest?"

"I say we go have a talk with Pete Maxwell. If the Kid's here, he could tell us exactly where to look."

"What makes you think Maxwell will talk? He wouldn't give me the time of day when I was here before."

"He'll talk or I'll bust him upside the goddamn head!"

"You figure that'll turn the trick, do you?"

"It might," Garrett said gruffly. "If it don't, then we ain't lost nothin'. We can keep watch from his house just as easy as we can here."

Starbuck studied him a moment. "All right, Pat, we'll give it a try. But you've got to promise me one thing."

"What's that?"

"Stick a pillow in his mouth before you bust him upside the head. Otherwise you're liable to raise just enough racket to scare the Kid off."

Garrett agreed, and Starbuck led the way out of the barracks. Walking single file, they ghosted from building to building, hugging the shadows. There were no lights in Pete Maxwell's home.

* * *

Saval Gutierrez and his wife, Maria, went to bed
around nine. A man of rigid habits, Gutierrez always retired early, for his workday began at the first
light of dawn. He was Maxwell's *caporal*, responsible for the entire cattle operation, and he allowed
nothing to interfere with his normal routine. That
included his friend and houseguest, *El Chivato*.

Bonney was seated at the kitchen table. The
lamp-wick was turned low and he idly stirred a cup
of coffee, now grown cold. His lopsided features
were glum and his expression was vaguely abstracted. He stared at a fly crawling across the
rough-hewn wooden table.

Nearly two days had passed since he'd sent the
message to Joe Coghlin. The reply, brought back by
the vaquero who had ridden into Lincoln, was af-
firmative and seemingly reasonable. Coghlin promised a large sum—at least $5,000—but pleaded a
momentary shortage of cash. He asked for time, no
more than a day or so, and gave every assurance
that the money would be forthcoming. He indicated
that Earl Gantry would personally make the delivery, using Maxwell as a go-between. All within a
couple of days.

At first heartened, Bonney had congratulated
himself on his assessment of Coghlin and Dobson.
Much as he'd suspected, they were willing to pay
quite handsomely to see the last of him. Moreover,
with $5,000 in his kick, he could live high on the
hog in Mexico. In a land where a thousand pesos
was considered a fortune, he would be filthy rich,

without a care in the world. His mind turned to visions of sloe-eyed señoritas and long nights of revelry, and an end to running from the law.

Except for Starbuck, he might have stayed on at Fort Sumner indefinitely. The game of cat-and-mouse he'd played with Garrett was almost laughable, little more than a diversion. There was an ironic twist about it that also appealed to his warped humor. For the past two months he had been an honored guest in the home of Pat Garrett's brother-in-law. Saval Gutierrez, who was married to the older sister of Garrett's wife, detested the lawman. Like everyone else at the settlement, he believed Garrett had sold out to the *gringo politicos*, and he took pride in harboring the territory's most wanted outlaw. A simple man, Gutierrez considered it both an act of defiance and a grand joke. One day he planned to tell his upstart brother-in-law that it was he who had provided sanctuary for *El Chivato*.

Yet now, seated alone in the kitchen, Bonney no longer found it a jesting matter. Since late afternoon, he'd begun to have second thoughts about Coghlin. It seemed to him suspicious that the money hadn't been delivered; he could think of no reason for Coghlin to stall, unless the purpose was to hold him at Fort Sumner. That went against his judgment of Coghlin—who had a great deal to lose by betraying him—but he could hardly afford to discount the possibility. He had survived by trusting no one who might profit from his death. And tonight, all his instincts told him the time had come and gone for trusting Joe Coghlin.

Pondering on it, a sudden image of Starbuck fleeted through his mind. He feared no man; but he respected Starbuck's dogged determination to kill him; and the odds of that happening had increased greatly over the last three days. The money Coghlin had promised abruptly ceased to be a factor in the scheme of things. He would borrow whatever he could from Maxwell, and put Fort Sumner behind him long before dawn. A few days in the saddle, careful to watch his backtrail, and then . . .

Adios and goodbye. Hello, Mexico!

Bonney grinned, satisfied he'd made the right decision. And having made it, he saw no reason to delay a moment longer. He stood, moving to the back door, and stepped outside. He walked toward Pete Maxwell's house.

On the porch, Starbuck and Poe stood gazing at the distant lights of the saloon. Neither of them had spoken since Garrett entered the house. Only a few minutes had elapsed, but they assumed Maxwell was undergoing some rough and heavy-handed form of interrogation. Given Garrett's mood, it seemed the most likely prospect.

A figure suddenly rounded the corner of the house and stepped onto the porch. They turned, startled by the sound, but he saw them an instant before they could collect themselves. His hand moved, and they heard the metallic whirr of a Colt hammer thumbed to full-cock. He stared at them, unable to distinguish their features in the pitch dark.

"¿*Quién es?*"

Starbuck thought he recognized the voice, but he hesitated. Spanish somehow changed the inflection, and he wasn't certain enough to risk killing one of Maxwell's vaqueros. Nor was he anxious to get himself killed. The shadowy figure had the drop on them, and he willed Poe not to make any sudden moves.

"¿*Quién es?*"

The tone was harsher now, more demanding. Starbuck squinted hard, trying desperately to identify the face behind the voice. Only a blurred shape was visible, however, and he forced himself to remain quiet. Poe once more followed his lead.

With the gun trained on them, the figure moved sideways across the porch. No one spoke, and as in some strange ritual dance, the lawmen froze still as statues while the figure scuttled crablike past them. Then, before they realized his intent, the door opened and closed. He was inside the house.

The voice was distinct and unmistakable to the men in the bedroom. Pete Maxwell lay immobile, propped up against his pillow and scared witless. The snout of a pistol barrel was pressed firmly to his temple, and the hand behind it was shaking. Garrett, round-eyed and scarcely daring to breathe, sat in a wooden chair beside the bed. He watched as the figure sidled through the door and stopped. The voice he knew better than his own spoke.

"*¿Quienes son esos hombres afuera, Pete?*"

Garrett swung the pistol around. His hand was trembling violently, and he felt a warm trickle running down his leg. He fired, hurling himself sideways out of the chair. He struck the floor, frantically thumbing the hammer back, and triggered a second shot. A streak of flame exploded from the muzzle, and in the flash of light he saw a figure slumping forward, knees buckled. An instant later he heard the soft thud of a body hitting the floor.

Starbuck and Poe had entered the house at the sound of gunfire. Flattened against the wall outside the bedroom, they waited in a void of eerie black silence. At last, hearing nothing, Starbuck edged closer to the door.

"Pat! You all right?"

A muffled voice answered. "I think the Kid's down."

"Maxwell!" Starbuck rapped out. "Can you hear me?"

"Yeah," Maxwell replied softly. "I hear you."

"Light a lamp! Pronto!"

A long moment passed. Then a match flared in the darkness. The cider glow of a lamp slowly lighted the bedroom. Starbuck took a quick look, scanning the room in one swift glance. Maxwell cowered against the headboard, the burnt match still clutched in his hand. Hugging the floor, Garrett lay prone beside the bed. His eyes were wild and his pistol was pointed across the room. A still form was sprawled face down near the opposite wall.

Starbuck entered the room. He kept his pistol trained on the fallen man, approaching step by step while Poe covered him from the door. He scooped a Colt Lightning off the floor, then hooked a toe under the dead man's arm and rolled him onto his back. A bright red splotch was centered on the Kid's chest. His eyes were open, sightless.

"Is he dead?"

Garrett climbed to his feet, took a shaky step forward. Starbuck turned, watching him, then nodded. "He won't get any deader, Pat."

"Jesus." Garrett righted the overturned chair, and sat down heavily. "I knew it was him the minute I heard his voice. Then he busted in here and I figured my time had come sure as hell."

"Was that when he fired?"

"No." Garrett looked puzzled. "What're you talkin' about? The Kid never got off a shot."

Starbuck holstered his own gun and smelled the muzzle of the Colt Lightning. "You're right." He glanced up, one eye cocked in a sardonic squint. "It hasn't been fired. Guess he never knew what hit him."

"So what?" Garrett muttered, slightly shame-faced. "He wouldn't have give me no better chance. I had to get him before he got me!"

"Don't get touchy, Pat. In your place, I suppose I would've done it exactly the same way."

"Bet your sweet ass you would! One peep out of me and he'd have let go without blinkin' an eye."

Starbuck looked at the body without expression. He reflected a moment, then turned and handed Garrett the unfired gun. "Well, Pat, I reckon the Kid's worries are over. Wish to hell I could say the same for us."

"What's that supposed to mean?"

Starbuck stared past him at Maxwell. "Billy contacted someone in Lincoln, didn't he?" When Maxwell nodded, he went on in a cold voice. "Whoever it was informed on him slipped a note under the sheriff's door. That's what brought us here and that's what got him killed. You care to give me a name?"

"Joe Coghlin," Maxwell said vindictively. "Billy was set to hightail it for Mexico. He asked Coghlin for money, and Coghlin promised to send it along by Earl Gantry. Looks like he sent you instead."

"It figures." He glanced quickly at Garrett. "There's your answer, Pat. They got the Kid and now they'll try for the Nesbeths. A clean sweep."

"How you aim to stop 'em?"

A ghost of a smile touched Starbuck's mouth. "The same way you stopped the Kid. Only a little different."

CHAPTER 17

Everyone gathered in the parlor. Their manner was somber, and they sat down as if assembling for a last supper. Starbuck had expected a lighter mood, but apparently the Kid's death struck them as a bad omen. He walked to the fireplace and began rolling a smoke.

Chisum took a rocker, his pipe clamped between his teeth like a bone. Fred and Erma Nesbeth huddled together on the settee, their eyes darting nervously around the room. The two girls looked daggers at each other. Sallie was stiffly proper, her ankles crossed beneath her skirt and her hands folded demurely in her lap. Ellen, by contrast, appeared ready for battle, with the icy stare of a vixen defending her den. An oppressive air of uncertainty and tension hung over the group, like strangers brought together to witness a beheading.

Starbuck twisted the ends on the cigarette and stuck it in his mouth. With Poe, he had ridden straight through from Fort Sumner, and he was still covered with a grimy layer of trail dust. Last night, listening to the women of the settlement mourn *El*

Chivato's death, he had slept badly. And tonight, watching the Nesbeths fidget on the settee, he was filled with a sense of misgiving. He wondered if any man had the right to toy with other people's lives, and the thought itself, alien to his very character, further compounded his apprehension. So long as his own purpose was served, he had never before considered the hardship it might impose on others. He found this new concern troublesome, almost impossible to believe of himself. He saw it as a weakness, and yet he was not a weak man. The sensation gave him a moment's pause.

At length, with no real idea how it would end, he lit his cigarette and began talking. He briefly related the events leading to those last moments in Pete Maxwell's bedroom. He told them how the Kid had died, and noted that Garrett had given permission for the young outlaw to be buried at Fort Sumner. Then, stressing the words, he repeated Maxwell's statement regarding Joe Coghlin. There was no doubt whatever that Coghlin and Dobson, in league with Judge Owen Hough, had arranged the Kid's death.

"Of course," he concluded, "the only new evidence we've got is the vaquero that delivered the message to Coghlin. Anything the Kid said to Maxwell would be ruled hearsay. So it's not much, maybe nothing."

"Nothing!" Chisum rumbled. "Why, it's—uh—cor—cor—aww hell, Sallie, what's the word I'm searchin' for?"

"Corroboration," Sallie said brightly. "Testimony that tends to substantiate previous testimony."

"Damn right!" Chisum affirmed. "That vaquero can back up everything the Nesbeths testify to. We've got a link between Coghlin and the Kid, and we've got it in spades!"

"I don't know," Starbuck said doubtfully. "Granted, it'll help, but it's still pretty circumstantial. Coghlin will deny it, so it'll boil down to a matter of their word against his."

"Judas Priest!" Chisum yelled. "You should've thought of that before you and Garrett killed our best witness."

"The Kid called the tune," Starbuck observed. "Besides, his lips were sewed shut long before that, and we all know it."

There was a time of stony silence. Chisum puffed on his pipe, eyes slitted against the smoke. He was clearly disgruntled, but Starbuck held his gaze, waiting him out. After a long while Chisum gestured with his pipe, as though dismissing a matter of no consequence. His eyes softened and his features assumed a visage aged by tolerance. His gaze shuttled around the room, then settled on the Nesbeths. He smiled, and regarded them with a look of benign wisdom.

"Luke and me seem to be at loggerheads, but don't you folks let that fool you. We both want them fellers in Lincoln. Want 'em so bad it makes our teeth hurt! Course mine are store bought, so that kind of gives Luke the worst of it."

Everyone smiled dutifully at the joke. He chuckled, eyes still fixed on the settee, then resumed. "Now, Fred, Mrs. Nesbeth"—he suddenly remembered the girl—"you too, Ellen! Here's the way I see things. The Kid would've strengthened our case, but we're still in good shape without him. Your testimony—added to the rustled cows we found and the testimony of Maxwell's vaquero—all of that wouldn't leave a jury no choice but to bring in a guilty verdict. Course, we got an ace in the hole I ain't even mentioned yet."

He gave the Nesbeths a slow, conspiratorial nod. "You've heard the sayin' about rats deserting a sinking ship. Well, that's exactly what'll happen! Once we jail them fellers—Coghlin and Dobson, especially Gantry!—one of 'em will start talkin'. Pretty soon they'll all be out to save their own skins, and we'll have 'em beggin' us to make a deal. See, contrary to what you've always heard, there really ain't no honor among thieves. You folks can take my word on it."

Fred and Erma Nesbeth shifted uncomfortably on the settee. They were aware Chisum was awaiting a response, but they avoided his gaze. Finally, Fred Nesbeth coughed, clearing his throat, and looked at Starbuck.

"Luke, you've always treated us square, and I'd like to hear what you got to say. Do you go along with Mr. Chisum?"

Starbuck was torn between conscience and expediency. He took a long pull on his cigarette, exhaled slowly. "A couple of days ago I figured to get the Kid and call it quits. But now that he's dead, it turns out that wasn't enough. I want the men behind him—for personal reasons—so I'm not sure I could give you a straight answer."

"You just did," Nesbeth said evenly. "We knowed all along you had a personal score to settle, but we trust you, Luke. So go on and tell us how it looks to you. That's all we're askin'."

"Well, first off," Starbuck said in a deliberate voice, "there're no guarantees. You've got to understand your lives will be in danger from start to finish. There's nothing they won't do to keep you from testifying."

"I reckon we done figured that out, Luke."

"All right." Starbuck paused, choosing his words. "The next thing you ought to consider is whether or not we'll get a conviction. I'd say the odds are fifty-fifty, strictly a toss-up. Everything we've got is circumstantial, no hard evidence." He flipped his hand back and forth. "A jury might buy it, and then again, they might not. We wouldn't know till they brought in a verdict. It'd be just that close."

"Go on," Nesbeth prompted. "We're still listenin'."

Starbuck flicked an ash off his cigarette, thoughtful. "I'd have to say you can't count on that bunch turning against one another. Coghlin's the weak link, but we would have to run a mighty good bluff before he'd crack. All depends on the breaks and how we handle it. Like I said, no guarantees."

"No guarantees," Nesbeth repeated hollowly. "Anything else?"

"One more thing. Whether you go ahead or pull out, I'll stick by you right down the line. Anybody gets to you, they'll have to get past me first. That's the one thing I'll give you my word on."

Ellen Nesbeth looked startled. In all the time she'd known him, she had never once suspected that Starbuck could feel compassion for anyone. His emotions were buried so deep—sealed off by a hard stoicism—that he appeared immune to all forms of sentiment. Yet now, to her profound shock, he had actually taken pity on her parents. By telling the truth, he risked dissuading them from the very thing he wanted. And still, he had offered them a way out. She marveled at the change, and wondered if perhaps she hadn't misjudged him all along. She felt a sudden outpouring of affection. Her heartbeat quickened and she sensed there was no turning away.

"Listen to him, Daddy." She looked directly at her father. "Luke won't let us down. He never has and he never will."

"Ellen's right," Erma Nesbeth said firmly. "We've trusted him this far, and there's no call to back out now. You do like she says, Fred."

Nesbeth grinned weakly and threw up his hands. "Well, Luke, what's a feller to do? You got my womenfolk convinced, and I reckon that's good enough for me. We'll play along till you tell us different."

"You're sure?" Starbuck pressed him. "I wouldn't want to think I'd talked you into it."

"We're sure," Nesbeth said, glancing at his wife and daughter. "Learned a long time ago not to go against female intuition. Gets a man in a passel of trouble every time he tries it."

"Well now!" Chisum beamed, giving them a nut-cracker grin. "That's dandy, just dandy. We'll teach them fellers in Lincoln a thing or two they won't never forget!"

Starbuck took a last drag on his cigarette and tossed it into the fireplace. He felt Ellen's gaze on him, but he avoided her eyes. His misgiving, suddenly stronger than before, gave him an uncomfortable moment. He wasn't at all certain he'd done the right thing.

A short while later he met with Poe and Chisum in the cattleman's study. Chisum was in high spirits, his features ruddy with excitement. Seated in his usual chair, he appraised Starbuck with a shrewd glance.

"That was pretty slick the way you let them talk themselves into it. Yessir, Luke—pretty damn slick!"

"Let's get something straight." There was a hard edge to Starbuck's tone. "If the Nesbeths had backed out, I was ready to get them the hell and gone from here right now. And if things start going wrong, I aim to do just that."

"What the hell are you talkin' about?"

"I'm saying it better go smooth as silk. Otherwise I'll get them out of the territory so fast you won't have time to pucker up and whistle."

"Bullfeathers!" Chisum admonished him. "There ain't nothin' gonna happen, Luke. With you and the boys guardin' them, nobody would have the nerve to try!"

"Well, I guess we'll just have to wait and see, won't we?"

Starbuck didn't relish the thought of taking the Nesbeths into Lincoln. The idea was studded with danger, and he knew their lives would be in jeopardy the entire time. But there was no way around it, no alternative. To bring criminal charges, the Nesbeths had to appear in court. The only choice was when, and under what circumstances. Which gave him a chance, however slim, to stack the deck in their favor.

He turned to Poe. "I want you to ride into town tonight. Tell Garrett to arrest Coghlin and Gantry tomorrow. You bird-dog him, and make sure he gets them locked up by sundown."

Poe appeared skeptical. "What's the rush?"

"Surprise," Starbuck said bluntly. "With the Kid dead, they won't expect us to move so fast. I want them jailed no later than dark tomorrow night. Understand?"

"Whatever you say, Luke."

"Don't let me down. I plan on slipping the Nesbeths into town sometime after dark. We'll put them up at the hotel and keep them surrounded with guards."

He reflected a moment, massaging his jaw. When he spoke, his voice was low and urgent. "John, it's got to come off like clockwork. One mistake and the Nesbeths will wind up in a funeral parlor. So tell Garrett to arrange a court appearance for early the next morning. I want that preliminary hearing over and done with before anyone's the wiser."

"Sounds good to me," Poe acknowledged. "What happens after the hearing?"

"We separate Coghlin and Gantry, and start working on them one at a time. By then, they'll have a fair case of the jitters, and we ought to be able to run a decent bluff. Assuming one of them breaks, we'll arrest Dobson and Hough on conspiracy charges. Then we'll start offering deals and see who talks the loudest."

Starbuck took a moment to repeat his instructions, stressing the need for speed and secrecy. Poe left the room immediately afterwards, and went to prepare for the ride into Lincoln. When he was gone, Chisum fired up his pipe, puffing thoughtfully. He regarded Starbuck with a speculative look.

"I didn't hear nothin' about what happens if Coghlin don't break. You got any ideas on that score?"

Starbuck's eyes narrowed. "If he won't talk, then I reckon we'll stop playing rough and start playing dirty."

"I ain't sure I follow you."

"Why, it's simple enough. I'll forget the rules and do it my own way."

"Quit talkin' riddles! What way is that?"

"Judge Colt and the jury of six. Verdict guaranteed."

She was waiting for him by the river. Her legs were drawn up and her chin rested on her knees. He sat down, saying nothing, and for a long while they stared out across the water. Presently, with a contented sigh, she turned her head and looked at him. Her eyes appeared misty in the dim starlight.

"You had me fooled until tonight."

"How so?"

"I thought you didn't have a drop of mercy in you. But I was wrong. Underneath that tough act, you're really a softy, aren't you?"

He smiled. "What makes you say that?"

"You gave my folks a chance to change their minds. That wasn't the Luke Starbuck I thought I knew."

"What makes you think tonight wasn't an act?"

"I don't understand."

"Well, the way it works out, I'll be taking you and your folks into Lincoln tomorrow. Maybe I rigged things tonight just to keep everybody on the string. That'd mean I fooled you into thinking you'd been fooled. Wouldn't it?"

She laughed happily. "You aren't fooling me

now, either! But don't worry, I won't tell anyone.
Your secret's safe with me."

"Cross your heart?"

She crossed her heart. Then she lay back on the
grassy river bank, her eyes laving him with a look
of tenderness. When she spoke, her voice was almost inaudible, entreating him with a shy, virginal
innocence.

"Luke, make love to me; let me love you."

He took her in his arms and embraced her. She
helped him with the buttons and stays, and he
slowly undressed her. When she lay naked before
him, he dropped his gunbelt on the ground and
quickly removed his clothes. Then he stretched out
beside her, gathering her once more in his arms.

Her mouth opened and she pulled his head down.
Their tongues met and dueled, then he took one of
her breasts in his mouth and sucked the nipple erect.
Her hand grasped his manhood, now hard and
gorged with blood, and she stroked it with a gentle
caressing motion. He probed the moist bog between
her legs, teasing the cleft where it parted within an
abundant swell of flesh. She exhaled a hoarse gasp
and they came together in an agonized clash of
loins. Her legs spidered around him and he slipped
into her, found his motion. His strokes quickened
and he thrust deeper and she jolted upward to meet
him. Her hips moved faster and faster, lunging and
insistent, until at last she could hold back no longer.
She clutched his flanks, ramming him to the very
core of herself, and together they exploded in a mol-

ten rush, blinded and feverishly holding tighter in that last instant. Forever passed, then he rolled away one arm around her waist, her head pillowed on his shoulder. She shuddered and he hugged her and they lay entwined, silently joined by the warmth of a quenched flame.

He thought no thoughts of tomorrow.

CHAPTER 18

Starbuck led the way into town. The Nesbeths, seated in a buckboard, trailed him by several yards. His men flanked the buckboard, two at the front and two at the rear. They were positioned to shield the Nesbeths, and their eyes were constantly on the move.

Only moments before, the last rays of dusk had been leeched from the sky. Nightfall lay over Lincoln, and the town's few streetlamps were now lighted. The stores were closed, and aside from the saloons, the business district was quiet. Several passersby, hurrying home to supper, glanced at the strange caravan as it proceeded uptown. The only sound was the muffled thud of hoofbeats on the dusty street.

At the hotel, Ellen and Mrs. Nesbeth were assisted from the buckboard. Then, with the guards formed in a tight phalanx, they trooped into the lobby. Starbuck motioned them to wait by the stairs and walked toward the front desk. Through a doorway on the opposite side of the lobby, he noted the dining room was doing a lively supper trade. Halting at the desk, he nodded to the night clerk.

"I'd like four rooms on the second floor."

"Yes, sir, Mr. Starbuck." The clerk darted a glance at the Nesbeths. "Any special room order . . . for the ladies?"

"No," Starbuck said without elaboration. "But the rooms have to be off the street side of the hotel, and I want them all in a row, next door to each other."

The clerk took a minute to produce the keys. He laid them on the desk. "There you are, Mr. Starbuck. Upstairs and down the hall on the left."

"Is there a back entrance on the second floor?"

"Upstairs—?" The clerk gave him an odd look. "No, sir, not upstairs. The only other entrance is the back door to the kitchen."

Starbuck spun the room ledger and scrawled his name. "We'll stay the night, maybe longer. Anybody asks, you just tell them the rooms are in my name."

He turned and crossed the lobby. Handing the keys to Frank Miller, he pointed to the staircase. "Hike upstairs and check out these rooms. While you're there, make sure there's no way to get into the building from the rear."

Without waiting for a reply, he jerked his chin at Jessie Tuttle and moved off to one side. "Here's the way we'll work it, Jessie. Take the Nesbeths to supper"—he indicated the dining room—"then get them upstairs and locked in their rooms. I want two guards in the hall at all times, no more than four-hour shifts. Put the Nesbeths in the center rooms, and you boys split up in the rooms on either side of them. One man sleeps while his partner stands watch, one on and one off, all night. Got it?"

Tuttle bobbed his head. "You ain't stickin' around for supper?"

"I'll eat after I get things squared away over at the jail. Might take a while, so you boys keep your eyes open and brace anybody that comes near those rooms. Act polite, but don't take any chances. Unless they're registered in the hotel, they've got no business up there."

Ellen Nesbeth approached, halting beside them. Starbuck nodded to Tuttle, who quickly rejoined the others near the stairway. She waited until he was out of earshot before she spoke.

"Are you expecting trouble?"

"No," Starbuck assured her. "Not tonight anyway. With Coghlin and Gantry in jail, it'll take Judge Hough a while to get things sorted out."

"Then why so serious?"

"Well, it impresses the boys, keeps them on their toes. I've got to have a talk with Garrett, and I'm liable to be gone—"

"Not too late, I hope?"

"All depends." Starbuck caught something in her voice. "What makes you ask?"

"You did get me a separate room, didn't you?"

"Yeah—"

"Good!" A slow smile warmed her face. "Then you can come tuck me in when you get back."

"How do you suggest I get past the boys? They'll be standing guard outside your door."

"You'll think of something!" Her eyes suddenly shone, and she laughed. "After last night, I'll be very insulted if you don't!"

Starbuck had given a good deal of thought to last night. Their lovemaking had touched him in a way that left him unsettled, vaguely disturbed. Never before had he considered the possibility that one woman might satisfy him in all things. He was a loner by nature, and he'd always assumed he would live out his life footloose and unencumbered. Yet, there on the riverbank last night, he had realized there was something more between them than physical attraction. She was an unusually spirited woman, with the gamy wit and resolute manner to match his own. And like him, she cared nothing for convention or the social restraints others imposed on themselves. In that, as well as their general outlook on life, they were very much birds of a feather. He wasn't certain where it would lead them, nor was he entirely comfortable with wanting someone, the sensation of need. He only knew he wanted time, with her and with himself. Time to determine who she was. And what she meant to him.

"You're right," he said at length, grinning. "I'll think of something. One way or another—"

"Any way at all!" she interrupted, her voice low and vibrant. "I'll be waiting . . . all night."

Frank Miller appeared on the stairs. As he approached them, Ellen gave Starbuck a secretive wink and rejoined her parents. Miller's report required only a moment: he had inspected the upper floor thoroughly and found everything in order. Satisfied, Starbuck placed Tuttle in charge, and waited while the Nesbeths were escorted into the dining room. Then he turned and walked from the hotel.

Outside, he hurried toward the courthouse. As he moved along the boardwalk, his thoughts centered on Coghlin and Gantry. He briefly considered trying to bluff them into a confession on their first night in jail. But then, curbing his impatience, he decided to hold to to the original plan. Tomorrow, once they were formally charged, would be the time to offer them a deal. He crossed the street and moved along the walkway to the courthouse steps.

The door to the sheriff's office was open. The instant he entered the room, he sensed something had gone wrong. Poe was slouched down in a rickety armchair, and Garrett was seated behind the desk. Neither of them spoke, but they exchanged a quick hangdog look. His gaze settled on John Poe.

"All right, let's have it! What's the problem?"

"Earl Gantry," Poe said, painfully embarrassed. We arrested Coghlin this morning, but there's no sign of Gantry. The sonovabitch pulled a vanishing act."

"Tell me about it."

"Nothin' much to tell. By the time we got out to Coghlin's ranch, Gantry was long gone. We searched the place from one end to the other, but it didn't do no good. All the hands just dummied up and gave us the silent routine."

"Keep talking," Starbuck said sternly. "There's more to it than that."

"Don't blame him," Garrett interjected. "Word gets around damn quick, Luke. By the time we arrested Coghlin and got him locked up, the news was all over town."

"You're saying Gantry got wind of it somehow?"

"Hell, he must've!" Garrett blustered. "More'n likely Dobson sent a rider to warn him. We weren't exactly loafin' around, but all he needed was a few minutes' head start."

"Well, Pat," Starbuck said woodenly, "from what you say, he had time to spare and then—"

The dull roar of a shotgun sounded somewhere in the distance. A second blast followed almost instantaneously, then silence. Starbuck whirled toward the door, ordering Garrett to watch the jail. With Poe at his heels, he ran from the courthouse and turned uptown.

A few moments later they pounded into the hotel lobby. The door to the dining room was blocked with people, their faces stamped with a look of ghoulish absorption. From inside, someone moaned and another voice ripped out a savage curse. One of the onlookers suddenly backed away, gagging violently, and retched his supper on the lobby floor.

Starbuck shouldered a path through the crowd. In the doorway he slammed to an abrupt halt, momentarily undone by the grisly scene before him. His features colored, one moment ashen and the next dark with rage. His vision glazed and blood roared in his ears as he stared at the carnage.

Fred and Erma Nesbeth had been blown out of their chairs. They lay sprawled on the floor, their clothes splotched with dark stains. Ellen sat perfectly still, her eyes rolled back in her head and her arms dangling loosely at her sides. The front of her dress was pocked with small dots the color of wine. Frank Miller, seated beside her, was slumped across the table. A single ball had punched through his skull, splattering bone and brain matter over the checkered tablecloth. Another of the guards was down, blood pumping from his neck, and Tuttle had a napkin pressed to the wound. The last man, untouched, stood watching in a hollow-eyed daze.

Starbuck finally collected himself. He crossed the room, followed closely by Poe, careful to keep his gaze averted from the girl. They halted near the table as Jessie Tuttle rose and flung the bloody napkin aside. He looked at them, tears streaming down his face.

"Couldn't stop the bleeding. He's gone, Luke. Dead."

For a moment no one spoke. They stood in a tight circle, unable to look at each other or the gruesome shambles around them. Then, his voice calm but insistent, Starbuck grasped Tuttle's arm.

"Tell me what happened, Jessie. All of it, start to finish."

"We were havin' supper—" Tuttle's voice cracked and he swallowed hard.

"Go on, you were having supper. What happened next?"

Tuttle told it quickly, the details fragmented yet agonizingly clear. The Nesbeths and their guards were seated at a table near the front of the room. A window beside their table—which looked out on a passageway between the hotel and an adjoining building—suddenly blew apart. The first shotgun blast killed Nesbeth and his wife instantly. The second shot, meant for the girl, went wide and claimed two of the guards as well. There was no chance for Tuttle or the remaining guard to return fire. The window exploded in a hail of buckshot, and within the space of a heartbeat, five people lay dead or dying. The killer had done his work and gone before anyone realized he was there.

Starbuck asked several questions, waiting until he was certain Tuttle had control of himself. Then, anxious to have a look at the outside passageway, he left Tuttle and the other guard with the chore of summoning an undertaker. He walked from the hotel, accompanied by Poe, and proceeded directly to the side of the building. There, squatting down, he struck a match and searched the flintlike soil for footprints. Finding nothing, he rose and stood for a time staring through the shattered window. At length, his face a stony mask, he turned to Poe.

"How—?" He choked on his rage, slowly gathered himself, then tried again. "How did they know? No one was told about the Nesbeths."

"Not exactly." Poe looked wretched. "But I got an idea who might've guessed."

"Guessed?" Starbuck's eyes bored into him. "What the hell are you talking about?"

"Hough," Poe said hoarsely. "The circuit judge was called over to White Oaks late yesterday. If he ain't in town, then Hough handles all preliminary hearings. When Garrett told me about it—"

Starbuck spoke through clenched teeth. "You let him ask Hough to schedule a hearing?"

"I didn't see no harm," Poe explained sheepishly. "Coghlin was locked up, and you were already on your way into town. I figgered we'd surprise Hough and show up at the hearing with the Nesbeths. I never thought he'd put two and two together—"

"You should've, John." A vein in Starbuck's temple stood out like twisted cord. "You're too old a hand to underestimate the other fellow."

Poe nodded, his expression downcast. "The minute I saw 'em"—he made a lame gesture in the direction of the window—"the Nesbeths and the boys. Goddamn, Luke. I'd give anything if it'd been me instead of them! I just never figgered—"

He faltered, the words trailing away. Silence thickened between them, and for a moment the breach seemed irreparable. Then Starbuck stepped past him, walking toward the courthouse.

"Let's leave it there, John. We've got work to do."

*   *   *

Garrett looked up as they entered the office. Starbuck halted before the desk and slowly unpinned the badge from his shirt. He stared at it while Garrett and Poe in turn stared at him.

"Pat, I reckon I won't need this now."

"You mean . . . the Nesbeths . . . they got the Nesbeths?"

"Yeah." Starbuck tossed the badge. Garrett caught it, and in the same motion, Starbuck pulled his gun. "Stand up, Pat. Slow and easy, no sudden moves."

"Luke, you've gone off your—"

"Around here!" Starbuck commanded, wagging the gun barrel. "Keep your hands high and move around here. Now!"

Garrett obeyed. He stood, hands over his head, and walked around the desk. Starbuck stepped behind him and eased his pistol from the holster. Then, the snout of his own gun in the lawman's back, he nudged Garrett forward.

"Upstairs, Pat. No funny business or you're liable to spring a leak."

With Poe bringing up the rear, they left the office and mounted the stairs. On the second floor they proceeded to the jail room, pausing to collect the keys off a wall peg. Following Starbuck's instructions, Garrett then unlocked the cell and swung the door open. Joe Coghlin, watching them in stark terror, backed to the far side of the lockup.

"Inside!" Starbuck pushed the lawman through the door. His gaze quickly shifted to Coghlin. "All right, fat man, let's go."

"No, don't." Coghlin cringed against the bars. "I haven't done—"

"Outside!" Starbuck said furiously. "Move it!"

Coghlin warily crossed the cell and stepped through the door. Starbuck halted him there and dropped Garrett's pistol at his feet. Slowly, one click at a time, he thumbed the hammer on his Colt.

"You've got a choice, Coghlin. You can talk or you can be shot while trying to escape. What'll it be?"

"It won't wash!" Coghlin whined. "Nobody would believe that in a hundred years."

"Maybe, maybe not." Starbuck's tone was icy. "Unless you unbutton your lip, you won't be around to find out, will you?"

Coghlin blinked several times. He saw something pitiless and feral in Starbuck's eyes, and knew he was very close to death. He chose life. "I'll talk! Honest to God, the whole story. Everything!"

"One thing." Starbuck's mouth hardened. "One straight answer or you're a dead man. Who ordered the Nesbeths killed?"

"Hough!" Coghlin blurted. "He's the one that called the shots all along. Me and Dobson never had no sayso in nothin'. We just took orders! I swear—"

"Back in the cell."

Coghlin gave him a dumbfounded, doglike stare. "What?"

"I said back in the cell. Get the lead out!"

Coghlin backpedaled through the door. He moved quickly to the bunk and sat down. Starbuck lowered the hammer on his Colt, holstering it, then nodded to Poe. He turned and strode off toward the hall.

"C'mon, Pat! Lock him up, and don't forget your gun."

CHAPTER 19

John Poe recognized all the signs. The quiet manner and the impassive stare. The blunt, menacing cadence of speech, almost as though words were a barrier to be surmounted quickly. The deadly calm and iron determination of a man prepared to kill.

He was frankly amazed that Starbuck hadn't killed Coghlin. He had expected it, and he still had no ready explanation as to why the fat man had been spared. Over the years he had seen men grovel and beg, pleading for their lives, all to no avail. When it had gone that far, there was, to his recollection, no instance of mercy shown. But while Coghlin had escaped with his life, Poe knew he'd read the signs correctly. The Nesbeths' brutal slaying had triggered remorseless anger, and a quiet rage to kill. He could only surmise that Starbuck was after bigger game.

Starbuck stood by the window, rolling a smoke. He struck a match, lighting the cigarette, as the clump of footsteps sounded on the hallway stairs. Garrett stormed into the office, outrage twisting his features into a grimace. He stopped, his voice hectoring and curiously shrill.

"You've got your goddamn nerve! You hear me, Starbuck? You're the sorriest bastard I ever run across, and I've seen 'em all!"

Starbuck stared out the window a moment longer. When he turned, his face was pale and his eyes were grim. "I'm sorry, Pat. I had to make it look convincing, and I wasn't sure you'd go along with me."

"Why the hell didn't you ask? You got no call to humiliate me that way! And I won't stand for it no more! You hear me, Luke? No more!"

"I hear you." Starbuck exhaled smoke, watching him. "You've had your apology, so don't push it."

"Well, that's better!" Garrett muttered, suddenly leery of pressing the matter. "Just so we understand one another. Now, suppose you tell me what you've got up your sleeve. And after that fool stunt, it better be damn good."

"Coghlin just put a rope around Hough's neck. That's good enough for me."

"Aww for Chrissakes! You had a gun on him! You really expect him to come into court and spill his guts the same way?"

"He'll talk," Starbuck said without inflection. "Because if he doesn't, he knows I'll kill him."

Garrett looked surprised. "You weren't jokin', then?"

"No, Pat, I'm fresh out of jokes."

"Awright, let's assume he'll talk. What's next?"

"We need to arrest Dobson and Hough. I'd suggest we split up and do it quick. That way we'll have them both in jail before either one has a chance to run."

"Yeah, that sounds reasonable. Which one you want?"

Starbuck took a long pull on his cigarette. He glanced at Poe, shook his head in an almost imperceptible motion. Then, with a deadpan expression, he looked at Garrett.

"Why don't you take Dobson? I'd sort of like to bring in the judge myself."

"What about Gantry?"

"There's time," Starbuck observed. "Let's get the big dogs and worry about him later."

"Suits me," Garrett said easily. "Ought to be official, though. Suppose you pin that badge back on and we'll forget you ever took it off."

Starbuck hesitated only a moment. Then he crossed the room, took the badge off the desk, and pinned it on his shirt. When he looked around, there was a faint smile at the corners of his mouth.

"Thanks for reminding me, Pat. Wouldn't want it to be unofficial."

"What the hell, Luke, it's all in the line of duty, ain't it? No thanks needed."

Garrett grinned and led the way out of the courthouse. On the street, Starbuck and Poe turned in the direction of the residential district. Garrett, hitching up his gunbelt, walked toward the center of town.

* * *

North of the business district, Starbuck and Poe stopped before a large two-story frame house. The upper floor was dark, but the windows on one side of the ground floor blazed with lamplight. After studying the layout a moment, Starbuck sent Poe to cover the rear of the house. Then he walked to the front door and yanked the pull bell.

From somewhere within the house he heard footsteps. A few seconds elapsed, with the measured tread growing louder, then the door opened. Owen Hough stood framed against a backdrop of light.

"Evening, Judge."

"Deputy." Hough nodded amiably. "Something I can do for you?"

"Garrett thought you might be able to help us out. Have you got a minute?"

"Of course." Hough stepped aside. "Always glad to assist in any way I can."

Starbuck entered, removing his hat. A central hall ran the length of the house. On the left was a staircase to the upper floor, and on the right a door opened onto the parlor. Farther down the hall, a shaft of light spilled through another doorway. He quickly scanned the parlor, waiting until Hough closed the door.

"Anyone else in the house, Judge?"

"Why do you ask?"

"We've had some trouble downtown. I need to talk to you confidential."

"I see," Hough said equably. "As it happens,

we're quite alone. My wife has choir practice to-night."

"That a fact?" Starbuck seemed amused. "No offense, but I wouldn't have figured you for a deacon."

"Oh, why not?"

"Well, politics and God are sort of like trying to mix vinegar and honey. Leastways that's what a pretty smart fellow told me once."

"Indeed? Was he a minister?"

"A rancher," Starbuck said flatly. "The Kid killed him last fall, over in the Panhandle."

Hough stared at him a moment, then led the way down the hall. "Shall we talk in the study? If you care for a drink, perhaps you'll join me in a brandy."

"Thanks, but I make it a habit never to drink on duty."

"Very commendable."

Hough turned into the study, entering through wide sliding doors. Lamplight streamed across the hall, bathing a formal dining room in dim shadows. Starbuck, lagging behind a pace, gave the dining room a swift visual check. He noted a closed swinging door, directly opposite the entranceway, which he assumed led to the kitchen. He thought he detected the lingering odor of cigar smoke.

The study was paneled, with a fireplace along one wall and a gleaming walnut desk at the far end of the room. The wall opposite the fireplace, from floor to ceiling, was lined with English classics in red morocco bindings and row upon row of legal texts.

A matched pair of leather armchairs was positioned before the desk.

"Have a seat." Hough circled the desk, motioning him to a chair. "You mentioned something about trouble downtown. What kind of trouble?"

Starbuck remained standing. He pulled out the makings and began rolling a smoke. Hough was on the verge of sitting, then apparently changed his mind. He waited, one hand resting on the desk top, watching as the cigarette took shape. Starbuck struck a match on his thumbnail, glanced up quickly.

"The Nesbeths were killed about an hour ago."

"The Nesbeths?" Hough appeared bemused. "Are you talking about the couple who kept house for Joe Coghlin?"

"Them and their daughter." Starbuck snuffed the match and dropped it in an ashtray on the desk. A pile of cigar ashes caught his eye, but there was no cigar stub in the ashtray. He exhaled a wreath of smoke. "Somebody shotgunned the Nesbeths and a couple of deputies while they were having supper at the hotel."

"Good Lord." Hough shook his head with a rueful frown. "Does Garrett have any idea as to why they were killed?"

"Way it looks, somebody didn't want them testifying against Coghlin at the hearing tomorrow."

"Then you suspect Coghlin's behind it?"

Starbuck regarded him evenly. "Coghlin says you're behind it."

"I beg your pardon?"

"He says you could tell me who pulled the trigger on the Nesbeths."

"That's ridiculous!"

"He's also willing to swear that you're the one who ordered them killed."

"Am I to understand you're accusing me of murder?"

"Among other things."

Hough drew himself up to his full height. His sallow features appeared jaundiced in the lamplight, but his gaze was steady. He lifted his chin and stared across the desk at Starbuck.

"What other things?"

"How about conspiracy? Or cattle rustling? Maybe four or five counts of accessory to murder?"

"Completely unfounded! Not to mention the fact that you're relying solely on the word of an alleged cow thief."

"No," Starbuck said slowly. "Not altogether. You see, Garrett's out arresting Jack Dobson right now. I've got a hunch he can be persuaded to go along with Coghlin. That'll make it two against one."

"I think not! My only connection with Dobson is political. And as for Coghlin, I barely know the man. You're on a fishing expedition, Deputy, and if you'll pardon my saying so . . . you're not much of an angler."

"Well, for a man you hardly know, Coghlin sure knows a lot about you."

"Oh, such as?"

"Such as those monthly trips you take to Santa Fe."

"Those trips are certainly no secret. Everyone knows I have business interests in Santa Fe."

Starbuck took a chance. "In the back room of a feed store?"

Hough's eyes suddenly became guarded. "I don't believe I follow you."

"The Acme Grain and Feed. That's where you meet Warren Mitchell every month."

"Warren Mitchell is a business acquaintance, nothing more. From time to time, he advises me on matters pertaining to land investments."

"C'mon, Judge." Starbuck gave him a sardonic look. "Who're you trying to kid? Everybody knows Mitchell is the front man for the Santa Fe Ring."

"Allegations are cheap," Hough said blandly. "To my knowledge, Warren Mitchell is a man of integrity and high moral character. As for the Santa Fe Ring, I've always considered it a pipe dream concocted by a certain political element. A fairy tale designed to obscure the issues and smear the reputation of honorable men."

Starbuck laughed a bitter laugh. "You wouldn't admit anything if your life depended on it, would you, Judge?"

"That sounds vaguely like a threat, Mr. Starbuck."

"Take it any way you please."

"Am I to assume my life is in danger?"

Starbuck considered a moment. "All depends."

"Perhaps you could elaborate."

"I'm trying to decide which way suits me best. You'd suffer a lot more if I let them hang you. But the way the law works, that could drag out till who knows when."

"And the . . . alternative?"

"Well, after what happened tonight, I'm tempted to do the job myself. I'll have to say it would give me a world of pleasure, Judge. Lots more than seeing you hang."

"You mean here—now?"

"Better now than never, leastways from where I stand."

"An unfortunate choice on your—"

Starbuck heard the creak of a door an instant before Hough ducked behind the desk. He whirled, drawing as he turned, and peered across the hallway into the dining room. He leveled the Colt and drilled two fast shots through the kitchen door. Centered waist-high, the bullet holes were no more than a handspan apart. The door swung open, and Earl Gantry, clutching a sawed-off shotgun, stumbled into the dining room. Starbuck fired the instant he appeared, placing the third shot slightly below the breastbone. The scattergun flew out of Gantry's hands and he pitched forward across the dining room table. His legs collapsed and he toppled sideways to the floor.

All in a split second, Starbuck crouched and spun around. Owen Hough froze, his hand wedged inside the center drawer of the desk. Starbuck extended the Colt to arm's length.

"Don't get brave, Judge. Bring it out real slow."

Hough took a bulldog revolver from the drawer, holding it between his thumb and forefinger. He carefully laid it on the desk, each movement distinct and exaggerated. Then he dropped his arms at his sides.

"An impulsive act," he said weakly. "I'm really not a man of violence, Mr. Starbuck."

"You could've fooled me."

"Luke!"

Starbuck spoke over his shoulder. "In here, John. On your way by, check Gantry out."

There was a lull of several seconds, then John Poe moved through the dining room and advanced into the study. He halted beside Starbuck.

"Stone cold dead. You got him all three times."

"Guess I haven't lost my touch."

Poe grunted. "How'd you know it wasn't me? I could've slipped through the back door easy as not."

"You don't smoke cigars."

"What the hell's that got to do with anything?"

"A private joke," Starbuck said with a tight smile. "The judge thought he had me in a squeeze. I told him what he wanted to hear, and he gave Gantry the high sign. Worked out a little different than he expected."

"You set me up!" Hough flared. "You never meant to kill me."

"Oh?" Starbuck's eyes were cold; impassive. "I didn't say that, Judge."

Hough suddenly looked uncertain. "I have powerful friends in Santa Fe. Kill me and I promise you, you're a dead man, Starbuck! They'll hunt you down wherever you go."

"Yeah, they might," Starbuck said quietly. "But let's suppose you were arrested and brought to trial. Carry it a step further, and say Coghlin and Dobson talked enough to get you convicted. Do you think your powerful friends would let you swing, Judge?"

"I—" Hough stopped, his eyes filled with panic. "Yes, they would! I know they would!"

"No, they wouldn't, Judge. To keep you quiet, they'd arrange a commutation. Then in a few years, you'd get an executive pardon, and walk out a free man."

A quiet steel fury spilled over in Starbuck's voice. "I don't reckon that's an idea I could live with."

"I'll turn state's evidence! I'll give them to you, Starbuck! Mitchell and all the others—the Santa Fe Ring!"

"You should've thought of that before you had the Nesbeths killed."

"For the love of God—"

Starbuck shot him. The impact of the slug drove him backward into the wall. He hung there, his eyes distended and his lifeblood jetting a brilliant red starburst across his chest. Then he sagged at the knees, and like a limp concertina, folded slowly to the floor. His sphincter voided in death.

There was a moment of tomblike silence. Without speaking, Starbuck jacked empties out of his Colt and calmly reloaded. Then, his brow lifted in a saturnine squint, he glanced at Poe.

"John, we'll just act like all this happened while you were still outside. Anybody wants to argue about it, I'll deal with them myself. Understood?"

Poe muttered something under his breath. He walked to the desk, scooped up the bulldog revolver, and tossed it on the floor beside the body. Dusting his hands together, he turned to Starbuck, grinning.

"Crazy sonovabitch! Got himself killed resisting arrest."

Starbuck smiled. "Yeah, I guess he did at that."

CHAPTER 20

"We buried them yesterday."

"Nice service, was it?"

"Not bad," Starbuck replied, "if you like funerals."

Chisum nodded soberly. "Luke, at a time like this, there ain't a helluva lot that'll ease a man's misery. But I want you to know I'm sorry, most especially about Ellen. Her and her folks were good people."

"Well, all things considered, I guess they got a pretty fair send-off. Garrett arranged for a preacher, and about half the town turned out. Weren't exactly what you'd call mourners, but it was decent of them to make the effort."

"How about funeral expenses? I'd count it a privilege to look after that personal."

"Already covered," Starbuck told him. "I figured that was the least I could do . . . seeing as how . . ."

He left the thought unfinished, and Chisum eyed him in silence for a moment. "For whatever it's worth, it ain't gonna do no good to blame yourself, Luke. These things happen, and no one man ought

227

to hold himself responsible. Life's hard, but it ain't that hard."

"Maybe not." Starbuck paused, considering. "One time I heard a fellow say it's people that haunt our lives, not ghosts. I never really understood what he meant until now."

Chisum merely nodded. Neither of them were overly sentimental by nature. Nor were they comfortable with philosophical maunderings. Death was no stranger, and both of them had killed often enough that they had come to view it with a degree of pragmatism. Watching the younger man, Chisum sensed there was no need to dwell further on the dead. He put a match to his pipe, and turned the conversation to a happier note.

"So Owen Hough pulled a gun on you, did he?"

Starbuck smiled in spite of himself. "That's the official version. Course, looking at it the other way round, you might say he committed suicide."

"Queer, ain't it?" Chisum puffed his pipe, thoughtful. "Him tryin' a damn-fool stunt like that?"

"How so?"

"I just never pegged him as the type, that's all. His kind generally ain't got the stomach to do their own fightin'."

"Yeah, generally," Starbuck said, with a touch of irony. "I reckon it was a case of him having his back to the wall."

Chisum gave him an owlish look. "Sometimes a man gets stood up against the wall."

"It happens," Starbuck allowed. "Sometimes."

"Naturally, you wouldn't have done that to Hough, would you?"

"Why, aren't you satisfied with the way things worked out?"

"Suppose you tell me."

"Well, we've got Coghlin and Dobson in jail. Coghlin's talking a blue streak, and more than likely he'll manage to get Dobson hung. All the rest—Gantry and Hough, the Kid—they're dead. I'd say that pretty much squares the account."

"Not altogether," Chisum commented. "Hough was our only lead to the Santa Fe Ring. Or had you forgot that?"

"Tell you the truth"—Starbuck smiled, spread his hands—"when Hough pulled that gun on me, it plumb slipped my mind. I never gave a thought to that bunch in Santa Fe till it was too late. Hope I didn't spoil it for you, John."

Chisum reflected a moment. "You much of a reader?"

"No," Starbuck looked surprised. "Why do you ask?"

"Well, if you were, you'd understand why I ain't too bent out of shape. Not that I'm a scholar, or anything like that; but I've always had a taste for history books. Taught me stuff that's come in mighty handy over the years."

"What's that got to do with the Santa Fe Ring?"

"Funny thing about history, Luke. The true-blue scoundrels hardly ever get caught in the wringer.

I'm talkin' about the men behind the scenes—the ones with *real* power—like that bunch in Santa Fe. One way or another, they generally manage to slip loose. It's the kings and conquerors that get their heads lopped off. The men pullin' their strings are goddamn near invisible—and untouchable."

"Are you saying you never really expected to nail them?"

"I'm saying, I ain't all that disappointed. We fought 'em to a standstill, and they're gonna stay clear of the Pecos for a long time to come. I ain't greedy, Luke. I'll settle for that, and thankful to get it."

"Kings and conquerors," Starbuck mused aloud. "Don't know why, but that puts me in mind of Garrett. When I left Lincoln, he was holding court for a regular herd of reporters. To hear him tell it, he's brought law and order to the territory, and done it with one hand tied behind his back."

"Guess it figures," Chisum grumbled. "Course, men like Pat don't last long. A little fame goes to their heads, then the hullabaloo dies down, and before you know it, they're lost in the shuffle. I'd say Pat's had his day in the limelight. From here on out, he's got nowhere to go but down."

"Too bad he thinks so much of himself. With some experience under his belt, he could've made a good lawman."

"Yeah, like the sayin' goes, a man's just askin' for trouble when his reach exceeds his grasp. If I'm any judge, killin' the Kid was the worst thing that ever happened to Garrett."

Starbuck uncoiled from his chair and stood. "I reckon it's about that time, John. The boys are waiting on me, and we've got a fair piece to travel."

"Where you headed?"

"The Panhandle. What with one thing and another, it's been a spell since I looked after personal business."

"Jumpin' Jehoshaphat!" Chisum laughed. "I clean forgot you're a rancher now! Lemme be the first to welcome you to the club."

"Waste of time," Starbuck pointed out. "I don't aim to be a rancher very long."

"Why not?"

"Well, I suppose it's mainly a matter of being tied down. I've thought it through, and owning a cattle spread don't make sense for a man with itchy feet. Lucky for me, there's a group of fellows over there that want the LX real bad. I plan to sell while they're still keen to buy."

"Then what?" Chisum's rheumy eyes narrowed. "You're gonna have more money than you ever dreamt possible. You given any thought to that?"

"No, not a lot. I'll likely squirrel it away in a bank and just take things as they come."

"Sounds like you mean to retire from the detective business?"

Starbuck was silent for a time. "I've got a taste for it, and I'd only be fooling myself to say otherwise. One way or another, I guess I'll stick with it."

"Good!" Chisum hunched forward in his chair. "Now I'm gonna tell you a little secret. Come next spring, there'll be an organization called the International Range Association. It'll be headquartered in Denver, and the board of directors will be made up of men representing stockgrowers' associations from every territory and state in the West."

He paused, frowning. "I had a hand in puttin' it together, and I won't horse you around, Luke. One of the reasons was political; we need more clout in Washington, and the only way that'll happen is for us to get our own men elected to Congress. But the other reason is right up your alley. We're gonna put together the goddamnedest force of stock detectives there ever was! They won't be hogtied by state boundaries or the law or anything else. They'll go wherever they're needed, and their one purpose will be to put the fear of God in cattle rustlers and horse thieves."

Once again he stopped, and this time he fixed Starbuck with a penetrating gaze. "How would you like to be the head wolf of the detective squad?"

"I don't know." Starbuck sounded wary. "I'm used to operating pretty much on my own. An outfit the size you're talking about, it'd be hard to say."

"Will you think it over?" Chisum demanded. "You're made for the job, Luke! I'll write the people involved and tell 'em to give you a free hand, no strings attached. Hell, if you want it, I'll get you a guarantee chiseled in stone! How's that sound?"

Starbuck smiled, nodding. "I might be willing to talk about it."

"Fair enough! You get your ranch sold and keep your saddle handy. I'll let you know when to contact our people in Denver."

"I'm available," Starbuck assured him. "Leastways I will be once I've got the LX off my hands."

"Before you go," Chisum said, suddenly solemn, "there's one more thing. It ain't likely I'll be around this time next year, so it's best said now." His eyes glistened, but his voice was firm. "You fought my fight, and when I check out, I want you to know I'll do it with my mind at rest. You're a helluva man, Luke Starbuck."

The two men clasped hands, staring gravely into each other's eyes. Then Starbuck walked swiftly toward the door. He stopped, almost into the hallway, and turned to look once more at Chisum.

"I'll want to hear from you, John. Count on it."

The old man nodded, unable to meet his gaze. He gently closed the door and moved along the hall. Ahead, he saw Sallie Chisum waiting in the vestibule. She appeared cool and poised, remarkably self-possessed. Yet as he halted in front of her, a wistful smile played across her lips.

"You're leaving us, Luke?"

"For now," Starbuck said quietly. "Don't want to overstay my welcome."

"You will always be welcome on the Jinglebob."

"I'll keep it in mind, next time I'm over this way."

She went up on tiptoe and kissed him on the cheek. "For your sake, I wish it had worked out, Luke. She loved you very much. So very much."

There was a moment of silence. She stared at him with a look of tenderness and warmth. When he spoke, the timbre of his voice was charged with vitality.

"I'll hold on to the thought, Sallie. It's the kind that'll last a man a long ways."

Starbuck smiled, gently touching her arm. Then he stepped past her and went through the door. Outside, the men were waiting where he'd left them, near the hitchrack. He exchanged a look with Poe, unlooping the reins of his gelding. He stepped into the saddle.

"Let's ride."

"Where to?"

"Denver."

"Colorado!"

Starbuck smiled. "By way of the Panhandle."

INTO THE VALLEY OF DEATH

They topped a low rise and Starbuck hauled up hard on the reins. His jaw dropped open and his eyes went round as buttons. Struck speechless, he simply sat and stared.

A creek meandered through a stretch of grassland on the prairie below. Willowy cottonwoods lined the stream, and tendrils of smoke drifted skyward through the trees. At a quick glance, Starbuck estimated there were upward of twenty men camped beneath the cottonwoods. But it was the horses that transfixed him. There were three herds, guarded closely by outriders and bunched separately across the prairie. A nose count was unnecessary.

Each herd numbered at least fifty head—almost the same number being trailed by Chub Jones. Starbuck suddenly grasped the meaning, and his jaw dropped a notch lower.

He was gazing upon a trade fair of horse thieves.

"Matt Braun is one of the best!"
    — *Don Coldsmith, author of the Spanish Bit series*

"Braun tackles the big men, the complex personalities of those brave few who were pivotal figures in the settling of an untamed frontier."
    — *Jory Sherman, author of* Grass Kingdom

HANGMAN'S CREEK

Matt Braun

St. Martin's Paperbacks

This is a work of fiction. All of the characters, organizations and events portrayed in this novel are either products of the author's imagination or are used fictiously.

HANGMAN'S CREEK / JURY OF SIX

Jury of Six copyright © 1980 by Matthew Braun.
Hangman's Creek copyright © 1979 by Matthew Braun.

Cover photo © Steve Terrill/Corbis.

ISBN: 0-312-94780-1
EAN: 9780312-94780-4

Printed in the United States of America

Hangman's Creek Pinnacle Books edition / March 1985
Jury of Six Pocket Books edition / May 1980
St. Martin's Paperbacks edition / July 2002

St. Martin's Paperbacks are published by St. Martin's Press, 175 Fifth Avenue, New York, NY 10010.

10 9 8 7 6 5 4 3 2 1

To The Gang
All of Them Aces High
Doris & Dick
Betty & Otto
Diana & Ed

Author's Note

Throughout the period 1875–1895 outlaw gangs roamed the western frontier, preying relentlessly on ranchers, stagecoach lines, railroads and banks. While the Wild Bunch and the Daltons gained the most notoriety, there were other renegade bands led by men of cunning and equal deadliness. The law was often stymied by vast distances and poor communications; no sooner was one gang routed than another appeared to take its place. Cattlemen's Associations, railroads and mine operators quickly discovered the futility of relying on local law enforcement officers. Instead they commenced hiring men who were cold-blooded and fast with a gun, and set them to hunting the outlaws. These men were the first of a breed — range detectives— and they were hindered neither by state boundaries nor the law itself. Their orders were to run the outlaws to earth, wherever the trail might lead, and see justice done. More often than not justice came at the end of a gun, for western desperadoes seldom surrendered when cornered.

Luke Starbuck was one such detective, and HANGMAN'S CREEK is the story of his first manhunt. It is based on a true story.

CHAPTER ONE

Starbuck sat his roan gelding on a grassy knoll.

The sun was a fiery ball lodged in the sky and over the plains a shimmering haze hung like threads of spun glass. At noonday the heat was sweltering, and Starbuck's throat felt parched. He licked his lips, tasting salt, and took a swipe at his mustache. With one leg hooked around the saddlehorn, he watched the dusty melee of men and bawling calves on the prairie below. Spring roundup was under way, and several hundred cows had been gathered on a holding ground near the river. There the calves were roped, quickly separated from a herd of protesting mothers, and dragged to the branding fire. Working in teams, the cowhands swarmed over each calf after it was thrown. One man notched its ear with a knife, while another

stepped forward with a white-hot iron, and
moments later the calf scrambled away with
LX seared on its flank. Hazed back to the
herd by outriders, the calf was reunited with
its mother, and ropes snaked out again under
the broiling Texas sun.

The work was monotonous, a seemingly
endless procession of calves from sunrise to
sunset. Yet the cowhands never slackened
their pace, and despite the heat, the branding
went forward with smooth precision. For
Luke Starbuck, it was merely one of several
operations he would inspect in the course of
a day. From early spring to late fall, the LX
spread was a beehive of activity, and he was
in the saddle almost constantly. As foreman
of the largest ranch in the Panhandle, he was
responsible for the crew, which numbered
nearly a hundred men, and close to 50,000
cattle. Scattered around the ranch were a
dozen branding camps, all working feverishly
to tally and mark a fresh crop of spring
calves. At the same time, separate crews were
gathering grass-fattened steers and older
cows for the trail drive to Dodge City. Before
cold weather, at least ten herds, totaling more
than 20,000 head, would be driven to railhead and sold. To the LX, it meant upward
of $500,000 in the bank, and to Starbuck, it
meant one long, unremitting headache that
vanished only with the close of trailing
season. He wouldn't have traded it for a

rajah's palace and a harem of honey-tongued whores.

Since dawn, Starbuck had checked four branding camps and one of the trail herds. Altogether, he'd ridden better than fifty miles, twice swapping horses with remudas along the way, and he talked at length with each of the crew bosses. By sundown, when he reported to Ben Langham, the LX owner, he would have hit another four or five camps and have a pretty clear picture of the progress to date. All in all, he was satisfied with the way things were shaping up, and by rough estimate, he calculated it to be a very profitable season. Yet his report would be spotted with a touch of bad news, and the prospect dampened his mood. During the night, one of the branding camps had lost eight cow ponies out of its remuda, simply vanished without a trace. He'd given both the crew boss and the nighthawk a stiff reaming, and he would likly get a dose of the same himself later tonight— Ben Langham would be furious.

Still, he wasn't a man to dwell on problems, and it was a long way to sundown. He unhooked his leg from the saddlehorn and swung his boot into the stirrup. As he gathered the reins, about to ride down to the branding camp, a cowhand galloped over the knoll, spotting him at the last instant, and slid to a dust-smothered halt. Starbuck's roan shied away, dancing sideways across the slope, and he hauled back hard on the reins.

"What the hell's the rush?" he shouted through a curtain of dust. "Your pants on fire?"

"Damn near!" The rider was winded, and his horse lathered with sweat. He took a moment to catch his breath, then jerked a thumb over his shoulder. "The old man wants you—pronto!"

"What for?"

"Beats me, boss. He just come stormin' out of the house and I happened to be standin' in the way. Told me to light out damn quick, and not waste no time findin' you."

"How long ago?"

"Couple of hours. I missed you not more'n ten minutes over at the Blue Creek camp."

"Yeah, and goddamned near killed a horse in the bargain."

"Well hell's bells, boss, the old man said—"

"All right, you've found me. Now, get that horse cooled down, and do it right or you'll be walkin' home!"

Starbuck wheeled the roan away and rode east along the river. Slow to anger, he was nonetheless a stickler on certain things, and he wouldn't tolerate anyone who needlessly abused a horse. He made a mental note to have the cowhand draw his pay and clear out by morning. Then he put it from his mind, easing the roan into a steady lope, and turned his thoughts to Ben Langham.

Unless he read the sign wrong, the old man was on the warpath. Whatever it was apparently couldn't wait until nightfall, and if it was that urgent, then it figured to be trouble of one sort or another. Good news could always wait; bad news travels fast. Over the years, by simple observation, he'd learned to anticipate the old man, most especially when there was trouble brewing. It was one of the reasons they got along so well, for Langham had a short fuse and a temper to match. Starbuck acted as a buffer, taking the brunt of his anger and then calmly setting right whatever had his nose out of joint. It saved everyone a world of grief, and had earned the old man's esteem in a manner he himself considered highly uncommon. He took delight in the fact that Starbuck could get people to swallow his orders with hardly a murmur of protest. He thought it a damn fine trick, and one of life's better jokes.

For his part, Starbuck thought it remarkable that Langham had never lost either his determination or his sense of humor. Several years past, Starbuck had hired on as a trailhand with the LX. At the time, Langham's spread was located in Southern Texas, less than a day's ride from the Rio Grande. A drifter, wandering aimlessly since the war, Starbuck had intended to work the season and

then move on. But Langham saw qualities in
the young saddle tramp that he'd never seen
in himself. By the end of the season, Starbuck had been promoted to head wrangler,
and charged with a sense of responsibility
he'd never before experienced. The following
season, when the youngster was jumped to
trail boss and took a herd to Wichita, Langham's judgment was confirmed. Thereafter,
year by year, Starbuck had assumed ever
greater responsibility, until he was promoted
to segundo, second only to the LX foreman.

Then, during the summer of 1874, an outbreak of cholera struck the ranch. Before the
disease ran its course, Langham's wife and
three children, along with the foreman and a
score of cowhands, had fallen victim. The
tragedy was compounded when Mexican
bandidos, with jackal-like cunning, took advantage of the epidemic and intensified their
raids from south of the border. Devastated by
the loss of his family, and besieged by rustlers, Ben Langham sold out to the King
Ranch, which already controlled much of the
Rio Grande Valley. Yet, while he was determined to outdistance memories of the past,
his spirits were by no means broken. Looking
for a fresh start and a new land, he turned his
gaze north, to the Texas Panhandle.

There, on the banks of the Canadian River,
he established a new ranch. Luke Starbuck,
who had stuck by him through it all, became

foreman of the LX. Within a year's time, a
cattle herd had been trailed into the Panhandle, a main house and outbuildings were
raised, and Starbuck attracted top hands by
paying top wages. Though barely thirty when
he assumed the job, Starbuck had quickly
earned the respect of every man on the LX
payroll. His knowledge of the cow business
was sufficient in most cases, and those hands
foolish enough to test a young foreman were
soon persuaded by his fists. After a couple of
bunkhouse brawls, everybody decided he was
chain lightning in a slug fest, and an air of
harmony settled over the ranch. Once again,
Ben Langham's faith in Starbuck's ability to
handle men and events had been confirmed.

To the south of the LX, Colonel Charles
Goodnight had already established a ranch
along the eastern rim of Palo Duro Canyon.
With Langham's operation thriving, and
Goodnight running close to 100,000 head,
other cattlemen were shortly attracted to the
Panhandle. When the Plains Tribes were
herded onto reservations in Indian Territory,
thus removing the last obstacle, there was a
sudden influx of ranchers. Within the last
year, four cattlemen had settled around the
LX boundaries, and Langham had been in-
strumental in forming the Panhandle Cattlemen's Association. Charlie Goodnight, who
ruled his own spread like a medieval liege
lord, had declined to join. Far from being of-

fended, Langham thought it best for everyone concerned. He'd had enough of cattle barons, and their overbearing ways, along the Rio Grande. On the Canadian, with good neighbors and a spirit of cooperation, he was convinced all would prosper equally.

In that, Luke Starbuck concurred heartily. After the chaparral and mesquite thickets of southern Texas, the boundless plains of the Panhandle seemed a cattleman's Eden. There was sweet grass and clear water, vast prairies laced by streams feeding into the Canadian— everything western stockgrowers envisioned in their most fanciful daydreams. It was what all men searched for and few found—a land of milk and honey and sweet green grass.

Today, riding toward the LX headquarters, Starbuck was reminded that much had been accomplished in a brief span of time. Everywhere he looked there were cattle, standing hock-deep in lush graze, with a bountiful supply of water flowing endlessly eastward along the Canadian. It warmed him with pride, knowing that he and Ben Langham, working together, had created something substantial and enduring out of a raw wilderness. Truly, for the first time in his life, he felt a part of something, a nomad without family or ties who had at last taken root. He felt at home, and he felt a great debt to the man who had befriended a stray, turned a brash fiddle-footed saddle tramp into somebody—somebody who, in turn, had found himself.

All of which warmed his innards and gave him considerable pleasure. Yet fell short, now that he was approaching the ranch house, of quieting a curious sense of unease. Ben Langham was quick-tempered but hard as nails, not a man to be spooked. His summons today was all out of character, too urgent and somehow alarmed. It seemed to Starbuck an ominous sign. . . .

CHAPTER TWO

Ben Langham rose from his chair as Starbuck entered the study. Grouped around the desk were the four ranchers who, along with Langham, comprised the Panhandle Cattlemen's Association. The men turned but remained seated as Langham crossed the room. He paused before Starbuck, frowning, his voice lowered.

"Where the hell you been?"

"Tendin' cows."

"Well, you took your own sweet time gettin' here."

"Pushed right along," Starbuck informed him. "If you wanted me sooner, you should've sent for me sooner."

"Try mindin' your manners and don't give me any lip. I want these boys to think I'm still runnin' this outfit."

It was a standing joke between them. Age

had begun to thicken Langham's waistline,
but he still moved and spoke with vigor, and
he was still very much in command of the
LX. A bear of a man, he was an imposing
figure, with a great mane of white hair and
weathered features burned the dark mahogany
of old saddle leather. Beside him, the
young foreman appeared dwarfed in the
shadow of a giant. Yet Starbuck was built
along deceptive lines. He was corded and
lean, all rawboned muscle, with a square jaw
and faded blue eyes and lively chestnut hair.
At first, men were fooled by his appearance,
but not for long. Once they looked deeper
into his eyes and observed his lithe catlike
manner, their attitude changed. Life made
many men hard and tough, brutalized them,
but there was a greater difference, apparent
upon closer examination. Luke Starbuck was
dangerous.

After a moment, Langham turned, clapping
an arm over Starbuck's shoulders, and
walked forward with a broad grin. "Luke, say
howdy to the boys. No strangers here, so we
won't stand on ceremony. Grab yourself a
chair and take a load off your feet."

Starbuck sat down warily, the way a hawk
perches on a branch. The men nodded, greeting
him by name, but he was aware of an
undercurrent, something unspoken in their
manner. Will Rutledge and Vernon Pryor
were seated on his right, Oscar Gilchrist and

Earl Musgrave on the opposite side; his chair
was centered on the desk and he felt
crowded, acutely uncomfortable, almost as
though he were on display. Yet he never in-
dulged in small talk or encouraged it in others, and no one thought it unusual now that
he held his silence. While Langham circled
the desk, he took out the makings and started
building himself a smoke. As he finished rolling and licked the paper, there was a moment
of leaden stillness. Langham settled back in
his chair, the smile slowly fading, and stared
across the desk. Finally, with a heavy grunt,
he hitched forward.

"Luke, we've got a problem, helluva problem." Langham waved his hand at the ranchers. "Every one of these boys was hit by
horse thieves within the past week. Lost
more'n forty head between 'em."

Starbuck struck a match on his thumbnail,
lit the cigarette. "Guess that makes it unani-
mous." He snuffed the match, tossed it in an
ashtray. "We lost eight head over at the Blue
Creek camp last night."

"Last night! They hit us last night? Well,
why in the samhill didn't you tell me?"

"Never gave me a chance. Besides, I only
found out about it myself this morning."

"That settles it!" Langham's fist slammed
into the desk. "By God, boys, we'll nail those
bastards and hang 'em out to dry. Damned if
we won't."

"Sooner the better!" Will Rutledge added hotly. "Sonsabitches gotta be stopped or they're gonna ruin us certain."

The others murmured agreement, nodding among themselves, then turned their attention to Langham. He looked around, studying their faces a moment, before his gaze fell on Starbuck. His expression was grave, and very earnest.

"Luke, me and the boys have been in a powwow all mornin', and we've decided it's time we took things in our own hands. That's why I sent for you."

Starbuck took a long drag, watching him, and slowly exhaled smoke. "I've got an idea I won't like it, but go ahead . . . I'm listening."

"Well, you see, it's like this, we talked it out and we've agreed—"

"I haven't agreed to nothin'!" Earl Musgrave broke in. "Leastways, not yet."

"All right, Earl, duly noted. But we took a vote and it still stands."

"Vote?" Starbuck frowned. "What kind of vote?"

"Now, Luke, we've all been losin' horses, I don't have to tell you that. But it's gotten damn serious, 'specially when you consider all the time and money invested in a good cow pony. Way we calculate it, we've lost upward of three hundred head in the last six months, and that ain't chickenfeed. We're talkin' about better'n $50,000!"

"Yeah, I know, but let's get to the part about the vote."

"I'm comin' to that," Langham assured him. "I just want you to understand the problem. We're way the hell out here in the middle of nowhere—with no law closer'n a four-day ride—and somebody's stealin' our horses regular as clockwork. We've got to put a stop to it!"

"You're greasin' the chute, Ben. What's the point?"

Langham sighed, looked him straight in the eye. "We need a range detective, Luke, need one bad. I sort of volunteered you for the job."

Starbuck was genuinely surprised. "That's real thoughtful of you, but why me? Hell, I'm no lawman."

"See there!" Musgrave crowed. "Same thing I've been tryin' to tell you the whole damn day."

"Awww, for Chrissakes!" Langham groaned. "He's meaner'n tiger spit, and everybody knows it. There ain't a man within a hundred miles that'd tangle with him. Go on, answer me that if you're so damn smart . . . *is there?*"

"Maybe not," Musgrave conceded. "But that don't mean he's got a taste for raw meat.

What we need is a bounty hunter . . . a professional."

"You seem to have forgot he served with Rip Ford durin' the war. I reckon he's killed his share and then some. Ain't that right, Luke?"

"Yeah, a few," Starbuck agreed. "But I can't say I exactly developed a taste for it."

"Told you so!" Musgrave bobbed his head with a smug grin. "Fistfights are one thing. . . . Huntin' men down and hangin' them—that's a different ball of wax altogether."

"Goddamnit, Earl, why don't you leave well enough alone?"

Langham's brushy eyebrows drew together in a scowl. He leaned across the desk and stabbed at Musgrave with his finger. "We done decided, and that's that! So just button your lip and let's get on with it. Savvy?"

For a moment, the two men glared at each other, and an uneasy silence fell over the room. Then Vernon Pryor cleared his throat, broke the stalemate. He was a man of glacial calm, tall and bony with distinguished features. He seldom spoke, and as a result, the other men attached a certain weight to his opinion.

"I agree with Ben," Pryor told them. "We need a man of our own—not some outsider—and to my way of thinking, Luke fits the ticket."

"Hold off!" Starbuck interjected. "Before

we go too far, I'd still like an answer to my question. Why me?"

"Several reasons," Langham replied. "You've got the backbone for the job, and we know you'll see it through. But I reckon Vern hit the one that counts the most. You see, we trust you, Luke. It's as simple as that."

"What he's trying to say," Pryor added, "is that we don't want the law involved. We intend to deal with these thieves in our own way."

"Damn right!" Oscar Gilchrist growled. "Give 'em a stiff rope and a short drop!"

"In other words," Starbuck noted, "you're talkin' about Judge Lynch. No trial, no jury . . . no nothin'?"

"String 'em up," Rutledge flared, "and have done with it! We want it ended neat and tidy—ended permanent—and the law would only complicate things."

"It ain't pretty," Langham observed, "but he's right, Luke. The nearest court's in Fort Worth, and a jury of shopkeepers and ribbon clerks ain't about to look at horse thieves the way we do. You know it yourself; city folks just don't understand that when you steal a man's horse and put him afoot out here, you've the same as murdered him."

"Yeah, sometimes," Starbuck admitted. "But we're talkin' about herd stock, not a man's personal horse."

"Judas Priest!" Langham thundered. "You've got to draw the line! Besides which, we ain't got time to sit around a courtroom and wind up with a jury givin' 'em a couple of years in the pen. We need an object lesson, and we need it goddamn quick! Otherwise, we'll look like easy pickin's to every son-ovabitch with a long rope and a runnin' iron."

"Luke knows that," Pryor said in a reasonable tone. "Unless we deal harshly with horse thieves, then we're simply invitin' trouble from cattle rustlers, and we can't afford to let it get out of hand. Don't you agree, Luke?"

"No argument there, none at all."

Langham gave him a dour look. "Then suppose you tell us what the hell's botherin' you. I figgured you'd be keen for the job, or I wouldn't't've called you in here."

"Why, it's simple enough," Starbuck remarked. "You aim to hang whoever I point my finger at. That's a pretty heavy load, and to tell you the truth, I don't much like the idea of playin' God."

There was a moment of deliberation, then Langham shook his head. "Maybe I know you better'n you know yourself. Unless you was plumb goddamn certain, you'd wait till hell froze over before you pointed your finger. Now, ain't that a plain fact?"

Starbuck shrugged. "Yeah, I reckon you've got a point there."

"Then we're of a mind," Langham said

with assurance. "You take your time and don't worry about yellin' sic 'em until you're dead-sure satisfied. Sound fair?"

Starbuck took a long drag on his cigarette, thoughtful. At last, exhaling smoke, he leaned forward and stubbed out the butt in an ashtray.

"Who would you get to ramrod the ranch?"

"Don't trouble yourself about it. Jack Noonan's made you a good segundo, and I'll work close with him while you're gone."

"You're sayin' I'll come back as foreman . . . when it's finished?"

"Hell, it's yours as long as you want it." Langham paused, suddenly chuckled. " 'Course, you never know. Maybe you'll get to like bein' a manhunter."

"Maybe," Starbuck allowed. "Reckon we'll have to wait and see."

"You'll take the job, then?"

"Yeah, I'll give it a try." Starbuck cocked one eyebrow, squinted at him hard. "So long as we're agreed it's not permanent."

"You've got my word on it, straight down the line."

"All right, when do I start?"

"Now by God! We're already a day late and a dollar short."

Langham unfurled an oilskin map and spread it across his desk. "Have a look-see.

I'll explain what we've got in mind and you take it from there."

Starbuck rose and stepped forward, his gaze fixed on the map. The ranchers gathered around and Langham began talking. His finger jabbed at an X marked on the oilskin, then another and still another, tracing a line along the Red River. Starbuck smiled, nodding, not at all surprised by the old man's craft. It was a good plan, simple but tricky, and even a little appealing.

A plan tailored perfectly for a former saddle tramp.

CHAPTER THREE

After supper that evening, Starbuck stripped to the waist and stepped out to the washbasins in front of the bunkhouse. He lathered his face, peering into a faded mirror tacked to the wall, and shaved with a freshly stropped razor. Then he scrubbed his upper body with the soapy water, washing away an accumulation of sweat and grime, and toweled dry. Wetting his hair, he gave it a few licks with a comb and studied himself in the mirror. He had little vanity, but the inspection convinced him he'd done a passable job, considering his hard-planed features. He knuckled back his mustache, gathered his gear, and returned to the bunkhouse.

Several minutes later he emerged dressed in his good shirt and the hand-tooled boots generally reserved for dances and church socials. Some of the men were loafing out front,

and he took a bit of good-natured ribbing as
he walked toward the corral. Since he seldom
left the ranch on weeknights, their comments
were perhaps more ribald than usual. But
Starbuck wasn't offended, nor did he ac-
knowledge their remarks. He'd learned long
ago that most men, cowhands in particular,
only joked with someone they genuinely
liked. For his part, he knew it kept them uncertain and slightly off balance if he simply
ignored the jibes. That was his joke, and certain men thought him humorless, aloof. Yet,
in his quiet way, he was something of a
jester. He preferred to outwit them rather than
outtalk them.

By the time he was saddled, the sun had
gone down over the river in a great splash of
orange and gold. He mounted and rode north
into the gathering dusk. The main house was
already ablaze with lamplight, and it made
him laugh to think of the old man lecturing
Jack Noonan. Before morning, the entire
crew would know they had a new foreman,
and the thought prompted an even deeper
chuckle. Cowhands were inveterate grum-
blers, thrived on it. The sudden switchover
would set them rumbling like a flock of
scalded owls.

One thought triggered another, and the
smile slowly dissolved. Starbuck realized he
wasn't all that easy about the arrangement
himself. It was a challenge—the biggest of

his life!—and that part intrigued him. But it was a whole new world, far afield from bossing a cattle outfit. Though he hadn't admitted it to Langham or the others, he was bluntly honest with himself. He still had a few qualms about his prospects as a range detective. Or, to put the word on it that better fitted . . . a manhunter.

Not that the idea of a hanging bothered him. On that score, Langham had him pretty well pegged. He'd ridden with Colonel Rip Ford's volunteer cavalry all through the war. Scarcely seventeen when he joined up, he'd learned quick enough that killing was merely a peculiar sort of habit, easily cultivated. In the heat of battle, with Yankee troopers intent on killing him, he had experienced no difficulty whatever. At first, it was a matter of being scared and simply fighting for his life. Later, after he'd taught himself to master fear, it became a natural, and very elemental, form of anger. It just made him damned mad that anyone would try to douse his lights. Nor was his anger merely the anger of war, limited to Bluebellies. Once, in a dispute over cards, he'd killed a tinhorn in a Brownsville saloon. If anything, it was more satisfying than the men he had slain on the battlefield, for it was a very personal thing with the gambler, face-to-face across a poker table. By the summer of 1865, when Union troops officially occupied the Rio Grande, he was a seasoned veteran of the killing ground. Blooded himself, having been wounded in three separate engagements, he had grown somewhat fatalistic regarding the possibility of his own death. As for spilling blood, he'd long since lost the queasy sensation. Pulling the trigger on another man wasn't easy, but then neither was it difficult. It was an acquired habit, like tobacco or hard liquor.

Yet there was a vast difference between killing men and hunting them down. One required only the twitch of a finger; the other demanded skill and persistence and a certain amount of guile. Starbuck wasn't at all sure he had the flair for such work. Deception simply wasn't his strong suit, and he had no knack for turning the other cheek. If someone curried him the wrong way, he promptly dusted their skull and pondered the wisdom of it later. With outlaws, of course, that wouldn't work. He'd have to take it slow and easy, pick up their trail with no one the wiser. Then, once he found them, it would be necessary to worm his way into their confidence. All that would require some mighty convincing lies, and a tight grip on himself at all times. Even the simplest lapse, one unguarded moment, would expose his hand . . . and probably get him killed.

It was a dicey proposition. One with long odds and damned little room for error. A regular bear trap of a job, especially for a man unfamiliar with the tricks and dodges of those who rode the owlhoot. Still, Ben Langham thought he could pull it off, and the old man had never been wrong before. As a matter of fact, there in the meeting today, he'd actually touched a nerve. Perhaps more than he realized at the time.

Starbuck sort of liked the idea of turning manhunter. He hadn't yet put his thumb on the exact reason, and whether or not the feeling would last was anyone's guess. But tonight he had a hunch, a good hunch. He meant to follow it.

An hour later Starbuck dismounted in the yard of the Pryor ranch. On the porch, seated in rockers, were Vernon Pryor and his wife. Starbuck figured the younger children were already in bed, but he hadn't thought Janet would retire so early. He cursed under his breath, wondering if he'd ridden all that way for nothing. As he looped the reins around the hitch rack, Pryor rose and walked to the edge of the porch.

"Good evening, Luke."

"Evenin'." Starbuck moved to the steps, touching the brim of his hat as he glanced into the shadows. "Evenin', Mrs. Pryor. How are you tonight?"

"Tolerable, thank you. Just tolerable."

Agnes Pryor was a lumpy woman, with big slack breasts and widespread hips. Her husband looked almost skeletal by comparison, and Starbuck had always thought it a curious match: a bit like a greyhound and a brood sow. Yet it was revealing in other ways, especially where the Pryors' oldest daughter was concerned. He knew that Janet, given a few years, would turn out very much like her mother. He kept the image fresh in mind whenever he came calling.

Pryor knocked the dottle from his pipe, smiled. "Guess you're here to see Janet?"

Starbuck nodded. "Thought I'd say goodbye, unless it's too late. She still up?"

"Oh, don't worry about that. She's expecting you—has been since sundown."

"She knows I'm leavin', then?"

"I told her when I got home."

Pryor's smile widened. Watching him, Starbuck thought he appeared awfully pleased with himself. There had never been any discussion about Janet—or his intentions—but neither had he been made to feel welcome here. He got the sudden impression that Pryor wouldn't be unhappy to see him leave.

"Does she know I'm liable to be gone a while?"

"Yes. I told her that, too. She asked, and I saw no reason to shade the truth."

"No reason at all." Starbuck paused, considering. "How'd she take the news . . . about the job?"

"Why don't you ask me yourself?"

Janet Pryor emerged from the door, framed in a spill of light. She was a robust girl, with a wide mouth and apple cheeks and deep set dimples. Her hair was parted in the middle and drawn back in a bun, with a cluster of golden curls fluffed high on her forehead. Normally, she was engaging and eager to please, but tonight her eyes were flecked with greenfire. As she crossed the porch, Starbuck noted she was sulled up, the gingham gown stretched taut across her breasts.

"Evenin', Jan." Starbuck doffed his hat. "Thought I'd surprise you, but your dad tells me—"

"Daddy, Mama"—Janet stepped off the porch and walked past him—"would you excuse us? We have some talking to do."

Pryor gave him a cadaverous grin, and Starbuck hurried after the girl. When he caught up, she ignored him, looking straight ahead. At a quick pace, her stride determined, she crossed the yard. Without another word, they disappeared into the darkness.

A brisk walk brought them to a creek south of the house. Huge live oaks sheltered the grassy bank, and in months past, it had been their trysting place. But tonight there was no warmth in Janet's manner. She halted, arms folded at the waist, and stared into the water for several moments. At last, she turned on him, her face masked with anger.

"You've certainly got your nerve, Luke Starbuck!"

"Yeah, I thought you might be a little upset."

"A little upset!" she cried. "You think that's all it amounts to?"

"C'mon, it's only a job. No need to get yourself worried before I've even started."

"Worried? I'm not worried, Luke—I'm mad!"

"Oh." Starbuck looked puzzled. "I don't get it . . . mad about what?"

"Don't play the fool with me! We had an understanding, and now I find out you practically jumped at this job."

"Well, it's honest work and the pay's good. Nothing wrong with that."

"Stop it!" she demanded in an insistent voice. "You don't really think I intend to marry a . . . bounty hunter . . . do you?"

Starbuck thought it unlikely. Which was one of the reasons he'd accepted the job. Within the last few months, he had begun to feel trapped. She was making great plans for the future—their future—and he wasn't at all sure the arrangement suited him. Yet a man should be dead certain before entering into anything that permanent. He needed time to think things out, and the new job seemed somehow providential. Away from her, off on his own again, perhaps he'd find he couldn't do without her. On the other hand . . .

"Guess your mind's pretty well set, hmm?"

"No, it's not! I'm confused and hurt and I don't understand, Luke. I just don't understand why you're doing it!"

"Whatever my reasons, you're definite about not marrying a bounty hunter, aren't you?"

"Yes! I most certainly am, very definite!"

"Thought so." He deliberated a moment, then shrugged his shoulders and smiled. "Well, in that case, maybe you'd consider foolin' around with a range detective."

"Oh . . . you . . . you sneaky bastard!"

Janet turned away in a huff. But she made no attempt to leave, and after a moment Starbuck stepped forward. He took her arms and slowly pulled her around. Though she offered little resistance, she refused to look at him directly. He cupped her chin in his hand, gently lifted her mouth to his, and kissed her. Then he nuzzled her ear, his voice warm and husky.

"One thing I promise you—I'll come back."

"How nice!" she sniffed. "Am I supposed to sit around and pine while you're gone?"

"It won't take long, couple of weeks at the outside." Starbuck smiled, very earnest now. "That's what I've been tryin' to tell you, the job's not permanent. I've got Langham's word on it."

"Honestly?" Her eyes brightened. "You'll still be foreman of the LX . . . he told you that . . . agreed to it?"

"Anytime I want it. And you know the old man, his word's good as gold."

She glanced aside. "That's not what my father said, Luke. He told me wild horses couldn't have stopped you."

"Hell, him and Langham are the ones that talked me into it."

"Really and truly—you swear it, Luke—it was their idea?"

"For a fact!" Starbuck assured her. "Your dad wants to see me long gone . . . or haven't you figured that out yet?"

"I know," she murmured. "He thinks we're . . . well . . . that I like you too much."

"How about you?" Starbuck asked. "What do you think?"

Janet held his gaze for a long while. She scrutinized him openly, searching for any trace of guile, but his look was level, steadfast. Finally, she put her arms around his neck and smiled.

"I think I'm going to miss you every minute you're away."

Starbuck drew her into a close embrace. Her mouth met his greedily, and her tongue parted his lips, at once inviting and teasing. He lifted her in his arms, slowly lowered her

to the grassy bank and eased down beside
her. A tangle of arms and legs, breathing
hard, they came together in a frenzied clash.
His hand touched bare flesh, crept higher beneath her dress, and she moaned. Along the
creek the katydids fell silent. Then he levered
himself on top of her and she cried out and
the night sounds ceased altogether. Starlight
filtered dimly through the trees, and their
shapes were blurred, joined as one . . .

A long time.

CHAPTER FOUR

Starbuck rode into Tahlequah early in June.

The sky was like dull pewter, threatening rain, and the road leading into town was rutted iron. Directly ahead, across the town square, was the capitol building of the Cherokee Nation. It was a large, two-story brick structure, with a sweeping portico in front, and it dominated a thriving business district. There was an air of bustling efficiency about the place, and to Starbuck's amazement, a group of men gathered on the capitol steps were dressed in swallowtail coats and top hats. In contrast, his own clothes were caked with sweat and grime, and stubble covered his jaw. He'd been on the trail nearly three weeks, and he hadn't had a bath since the last time it rained.

The path that led him to Tahlequah had been long and frustrating, an odyssey of sorts. Upon departing the LX in late May, he had ridden directly to Fort Sumner, in New Mexico Territory. With Billy the Kid on the rampage—leading a gang of veteran rustlers— it seemed the most likely spot to look for stolen horses. But a few days' inquiry quickly convinced him it was a washout. The Kid was a cold-blooded killer, with a price on his head, and conducted will-o'-the-wisp raids whenever it struck his fancy. Still, for all his brash daring, the Kid had never been known as a horse thief. His specialty was cattle . . . and murder—not cow ponies.

Turning eastward, Starbuck had then followed a meandering course along the Red River. At Doan's Store and Red River Station, the main crossings for cattle drives to Kansas, he had paused briefly. Posing as a saddle tramp, he was able to make discreet inquiries, and soon satisfied himself that there was little commerce in stolen horses. Still holding to Ben Langham's plan, he'd next turned northeast into Indian Territory. Yet he uncovered nothing in either the Chickasaw Nation or the Choctaw Nation, and within the week, he'd headed due north toward Tahlequah. By then, his hopes were rapidly diminishing, and as he crossed the Cherokee Nation, his mood darkened. Altogether, he'd ridden better than a thousand miles, without unearthing so much as a single lead. It suddenly seemed futile, a damnedable waste of time. He was searching in the wrong direction.

Not that he wasn't enjoying himself. The old wanderlust of days past had once again taken hold, and he found it an exhilarating sensation. Since leaving the LX, he'd given only scant thought to Janet Pryor, and in all honesty, he simply hadn't missed her. Nor had he experienced any great yearning for the ranch itself. Curiously, it was as though an enormous burden had been lifted from his shoulders. Until he was away from it, he'd had no idea of how heavily the responsibility weighed. Over the years he had gradually convinced himself it was the kind of life he wanted; with Ben Langham as an image, and ever-greater responsibility the lodestar, he had been beguiled into accepting a role totally foreign to his character. With only a few weeks' freedom, out on his own again, he'd come to a sharp awakening. By nature, he was a loner, perfectly willing to answer for his own actions but uncomfortable when saddled with the responsibility of others. For the first time in almost twelve years, he felt unfettered and at ease deep within himself. He now had grave doubts about the life he'd led all that time. High on the list was the LX . . . and Janet Pryor.

Yet he wasn't a man to shirk obligation. He'd accepted a job and he meant to see it

through. Time enough to settle his personal
affairs—one way or another—once he'd run
the horse thieves to earth. All of which kindled a wry smile. Considering his luck to
date, that looked to be a long and lonely
chore.

Crossing the town square, Starbuck was
reminded that he was very much the outsider
here. A strange white man drew stares of suspicion and hostility anywhere in Indian Territory. The Five Civilized Tribes had suffered
grievously at the hands of whites, perhaps
none more so than the Cherokees. Except
through intermarriage, white men were not
allowed to own property within the Nations.
Nor were they welcome as visitors, unless the
courts had branded them outlaws. By some
twisted logic, a white businessman, however
scrupulous, was thought to be less trustworthy than a white desperado. All too often the
Cherokees connived with outlaws, offering
them asylum from federal marshals, and that
made Starbuck's task all the more difficult.
The Cherokees felt a bond of affinity with
anyone who flouted the white man's law, and
they resented nosy intruders. He had to be
careful about the questions he asked. Very
careful indeed.

On a side street, Starbuck dismounted in
front of a livestock dealer. Several mules
were bunched in a corral at one end of the
building, but there were no horses in sight.

As Starbuck walked forward, a man appeared in the doorway. He had a cured look, as though he'd been dipped in a tanning vat and left too long. His features were angular, with a hawk-like nose and high cheekbones, and his jaw was loaded solid with chewing tobacco. He worked his quid, eyes expressionless, offering no greeting.

"Howdy." Starbuck nodded. "Wonder if I could have a word with the owner?"

"You're looking at him."

"Well, good, glad to hear it. Thought maybe you could help me out."

"How so?"

"I'm a wrangler lookin' for work. Figured you might know somebody that needs a top hand."

The dealer shifted his cud and spat. A puff of dust exploded in the dirt. Then he jerked his head toward the corral. "You see any horses out there?"

"Nope, can't say as I do."

"Guess that answers your questions."

"Yeah, maybe it does." Starbuck pulled at his ear and studied the mules a moment. "'Course, it could be you've just sold off all your horses."

The dealer uttered a noncommittal grunt.

"Any outfit that buys lots of horses, you'd be doing them a favor. Like I told you, I'm a top hand, that's no brag."

"And I already told you, times are slow."

"Come on, you mean to say nobody's hirin' in these parts?"

There was a moment of deliberation, then the dealer fixed him with a hard look. "You ask a lot of questions . . . for a white man."

Starbuck met his gaze, eyes impersonal, but seething inside. Finally, with a tight grip on his temper, he turned and walked to his horse. As he stepped into the saddle, he glanced back at the dealer and smiled.

"Mister, you've been a real help, and I'm obliged. Won't forget your courtesy, that's for sure."

With a curt nod, Starbuck reined the gelding around and rode toward the square. He felt the dealer's eyes boring into his back, and congratulated himself on his restraint. A skulldusting would have done the man a world of good, perhaps taught him to watch his mouth. But it was better to leave peaceable, without drawing attention to himself. All the same, it was hard to swallow.

Entering the square, Starbuck proceeded west, past the capitol building. As he rode by, the group of men on the steps fell silent, watching him closely. From their dress, he assumed they were legislators, and it occurred to him that the Five Civilized Tribes were aptly named. The Cherokee Nation was, for all practical purposes, an independent republic. With slight variations, the tribe's form of government was patterned on that of

the white man. A tribal chief was elected
head of state, and the legislative body, called
the tribal council, was comprised of two
houses, similar in function to the U.S. Congress. It all appeared very democratic, and
highly civilized. Yet there remained a hard
core of hatred toward white men, and that
seemed to him a real puzzler. Folks seldom
aped their enemies . . . enlightened or otherwise.

Starbuck put it from mind and turned his
thoughts to business. Now, more than ever,
he was convinced the direction of his search
must shift westward. By pushing it, he could
reach Fort Supply in perhaps four days, and
that would be his last stop in Indian Territory.
Unless the army had evidence to the contrary,
he seriously doubted the Comanches were
conducting secret raids into the Panhandle.
That being the case, he meant to turn north,
toward Dodge City. If he drew a blank there,
then he'd have little choice but to write Ben
Langham and broaden the search into Colorado. Some inner hunch—strengthened by
his miserable luck thus far—told him Colorado was where he should have started in the
first place. But ahead lay Fort Supply and
Dodge. If not by deduction, then by process
of elimination he would gradually whittle
down the possibilities. As he rode out of
town, he wondered if real detectives went

about their work in a similar manner. He thought not.

Several miles west of Tahlequah, the Light Horse Police overtook him. There were five of them, led by a hard-eyed sergeant, and they came on at a gallop, surrounding him before he realized their intent. One look convinced him it wasn't routine, but he couldn't believe they meant to arrest him. Nonetheless, he kept his hands in plain sight, firmly anchored to the reins.

"What's your name?" the sergeant demanded. "Your real name?"

"Starbuck. Lucas Starbuck. Only name I've got."

"Where you from?"

"Texas, mostly, or leastways I was. Been driftin' around, lookin' for work."

"How come a top-hand wrangler can't find work in Texas?"

Starbuck warned himself to proceed cautiously. It was no accident he'd been pursued, that much was now apparent. The Light Horse Police were rough customers, known for dispensing summary justice at trailside. Whatever the reason, he was in a touchy spot, and it was no time to go off half-cocked. He shrugged.

"Got a case of itchy feet, simple as that. Work awhile, drift awhile, that's my motto."

"Why you ask so many questions about horses?"

"Say, look here, I never meant to rub that fellow back in town the wrong way. But, hell's bells, he wasn't very polite, and that's a fact."

"Don't talk, just gimme straight answers."

"Judas Priest, horses are my line of work! He must've told you that."

The sergeant eyed him a moment, then rapped out a sharp command. "The truth—don't lie—how long ago you leave Fort Smith?"

"Fort Smith?" Starbuck glanced around, found himself ringed by cold stares. "Wait a minute, boys, you've got me mixed up with somebody else. Hell, I've never been to Fort Smith."

"You lie! All Judge Parker's men lie! Got no business here!"

"Well, I'll be damned! You think I work for Parker, don't you? You actually think I'm a marshal!"

Starbuck's expression was one of genuine surprise. Along with it was a look of mild relief, and the combination left the sergeant momentarily confounded. Then he scowled, muddy brown eyes alive with hate.

"No more talk! You keep ridin' and don't bother Cherokees no more."

He paused, lips skinned back in an arrogant grin. "Or maybe the Judge lose himself a marshal."

Starbuck bristled, unaccustomed to threats.

But the odds were bad and the timing even worse. Better to let them think what they wanted and be on his way. Particularly since it wasn't his fight, anyway. He stared at the sergeant for a moment, then nodded and reined his gelding around. The Light Horse Police broke their ring, backing their mounts aside, and sat watching as he rode off along the rutted trail.

Some distance away, Starbuck suddenly chuckled to himself. It was ironic as hell! The Hanging Judge and his U.S. Marshals were considered pure poison in Indian Territory. All across the West, Judge Isaac Parker was celebrated for his love of hemp and his dispassionate attitude toward Indian lawbreakers. Only last year, with a thousand or more spectators looking on, he had hung six men with one spring of the trap. And three of them Cherokees! Small wonder that his very name raised hackles in Tahlequah. But Starbuck found it grimly amusing that he'd been mistaken for one of Parker's manhunters. Apparently, there was more to this detective business than he'd suspected. Had to be, for it was clear now that he had fooled the livestock dealer too well.

Almost too well for his own good.

CHAPTER FIVE

Under the brassy dome of a plains sky, Star-buck reined to a halt. After removing his hat, he pulled a filthy bandanna and mopped his face. The Kansas prairie shimmered with heat waves, a vast grassland that seemed to extend onward into eternity. He shaded his eyes with the hat and regarded the angle of the sun. Three o'clock, perhaps a bit later, and Dodge City still fifty miles up the trail. Unless he found a stream, it meant a dry camp tonight, even though his canteen was nearly full. The prospect did little to improve his mood.

Stuffing the bandanna into his hip pocket, he crammed the hat on his head. Then he gathered the reins, feathering the gelding with his spurs, and rode north. Behind him lay a week's hard riding, and the deep con-viction he'd wasted the past month on a wild-goose chase. So far as he could determine, horse-stealing was fast becoming a lost art in Indian Territory. Even the Comanches, once considered the supreme horse thieves of all the Plains tribes, were content with government handouts and the idleness of reservation life. It was a sorry state of affairs, and, for a tyro manhunter, downright discouraging.

Shortly before dawn that morning, he had left Fort Supply. A day there, spent in casual conversation with a grizzled master sergeant and several troopers, had merely confirmed what he already suspected. The Comanches and Kiowas, who traditionally raided into Texas, had become tame Indians, wholly dependent on the government for their subsistence. His hunch stronger than ever, he had turned north, skirting the Western Trail. It was the height of the cattle season, and the trail was choked with Texas longhorns; he avoided the dust and confusion, preferring to strike overland and make better time. By early afternoon, he had forded a dogleg in the Cimarron River, which placed him roughly ten miles above the Kansas border. While he was hot and weary, drenched in sweat from the blazing June sun, he felt a renewed surge of determination once across the Cimarron. Ahead lay Dodge City, one last stop before he ditched Langham's plan and headed for Colorado. It was a fresh start, almost as though he'd just begun the hunt.

Yet now, with the sun slipping westward,

his exuberant mood slowly faded. Though
he'd been up the Western Trail several times,
the open prairie was a complete mystery.
Boundless and parched, it swept on with an
undulating sameness that left a man mesmerized. He was by no means lost, for the cardinal points of the compass were like a sixth
sense, born of a lifetime spent in wilderness
terrain. But a dry camp, with one canteen to
be shared with his horse, promised an uncomfortable night. Worse, it meant no coffee
tomorrow morning, and perhaps a long,
thirsty ride to Dodge. He kneed the gelding
into a trot and began scanning the distance
for a treeline. Trees and creeks often went
together, and with several hours of daylight
left, anything was possible. Even morning
coffee.

Late that afternoon he topped a rise and
suddenly pulled up short. Below was a grove
of trees, bordered by a stream, and off to one
side stood a clapboard house and a barn with
a log corral. A wagon road snaked westward,
and to the north he saw a herd of cattle grazing on a level stretch of prairie. It looked to
be a small operation, perhaps a couple of
hundred head, but somebody had picked a
choice location. With water in sight, and
morning coffee assured, his spirits took a
sharp upturn. He tickled the gelding's ribs
and rode toward the house.

Several minutes later Starbuck crossed the

stream and spotted two men outside the corral. A horse was tied to the log fence and an enclosed wagon was parked nearby. While one man, obviously a farrier, worked on the horse's hooves, the other man lounged against the fence. As Starbuck rode closer, the men glanced around, regarding him with a speculative look. Then the blacksmith went back to fitting a shoe, and the other man pushed off the fence, walking forward. By his dress—worn boots and faded range clothes—he appeared to be a cowman. His legs, bowed like barrel staves, merely confirmed the impression. He nodded, eyes squinted and watchful, as Starbuck reined to a halt.

"Howdy."

"Afternoon."

Starbuck waited, allowing himself to be inspected. Since range etiquette required an invitation, he made no move to dismount. With a practiced eye, the man quickly scrutinized clothes and horse and trappings. At last, satisfied with what he saw, his manner thawed.

" 'Pears you've had a long ride."

"Long and thirsty," Starbuck replied. "Not a helluva lot of water between here and the Cimarron."

"That's a fact," the man agreed. " 'Course, you're a little off the track, leastways if I read your rig right. We don't see many Texans over in this direction."

Starbuck smiled. "Tell you the truth, I got

fired off a trail drive. Nothin' serious, you understand, but me and the ramrod sort of parted company." He shrugged. "Figured I'd have a look-see at Kansas on my way into Dodge."

"Been up the trail a few times myself. Finally got a gutful and married a widder woman. Her and her spread." He pursed his mouth, cocked one eye. "Ain't much, but it beats thirty a month and beans."

"Looks mighty good to me. Your wife wouldn't have a sister, would she?"

"Hah! Had your fill of eatin' dust, have you?"

"Enough for one day, no doubt about it."

"Well, light and tie, make yourself to home."

"Much obliged." Starbuck stepped down out of the saddle. "If you've got no objection, I wouldn't mind pitchin' camp on your stream for the night."

"Help yourself." He stuck out his hand. "Name's Clute Jordan."

"Luke Starbuck."

Jordan was a wiry man, with gnarled features and a beard so thick that his face resembled a good-humored cockleburr. He grinned and pumped Starbuck's hand.

"Whyn't you unsaddle and hobble your horse on that grassy stretch by the creek? I got some of mine gettin' shod, and the smith only gets out this way ever' couple of

months, so I'm sorta tied up. You're welcome to join us, though, if you're of a mind."

"Thanks, I'll do that."

A while later, after he'd watered the gelding and left him to graze, Starbuck walked
back to the corral. Jordan greeted him and
nodded at the farrier, who was toasting a
horseshoe in a steel-plated portable forge.

"This here's Sam Urschel. Best damn
smith in Kansas. Sam, meet Luke Starbuck."

Urschel was a large man, heavy through
the shoulders, and given to few words. He
grunted something unintelligible, then began
hammering the cherry-red shoe on an anvil
bolted to the rear of the wagon. Starbuck
watched a moment, then turned his attention
to the horse, a dun gelding standing hipshot
at the fence. Out of habit, he checked confirmation and weight, judging the dun at a hair
over fourteen hands. Small but with good
bottom, built for catlike turns and short bursts
of speed.

"Nice-lookin' cow pony."

"Damn sure oughta be," Jordan snorted,
"considerin' the price he fetched."

Starbuck moved around the gelding, running his hand over the hindquarters. On the
opposite side, he paused, staring at the brand.
It was a Circle B, unknown to him, and yet
somehow vaguely familiar. Still, he couldn't
place it, and after hesitating briefly, he turned
back to Jordan.

"Say he cost you top dollar, huh?"

"Bet your dusty butt, he did! Him and them three there"—Jordan jerked his chin at the corral—"set me back pretty near five hundred simoleons."

"Yeah, you're right, that's a little stiff."

Starbuck walked to the corral and leaned down, peering through the log rails. Inside were two sorrels and a chestnut, all built along the lines of western-bred cow ponies. He studied them with a horseman's eye and, unwittingly, found his attention drawn to one of the sorrels. A gelding, it had a blaze face, and for no particular reason, he was again gripped by a sense of familiarity. Yet he shrugged it off, chiding himself. Sorrel cow ponies with a blaze face were common as dirt. In his lifetime he'd seen hundreds of them, and nothing remarkable enough to distinguish one from the others. All the same, there was something about this particular sorrel . . . it nagged at him . . . something unusual . . .

Then his gaze drifted to the brand, and he stiffened. He stared at it intently—Box Double X—trying to find reason in a rush of instinctive certainty. In his mind's eye, he slowly took the brand apart, mentally shifted the pieces like a jigsaw puzzle and began refitting them in logical order. His mouth popped open, and understanding came so sudden he felt as though his ears had come unplugged. It was plain as a diamond in a goat's ass!

Someone handy with a running iron had altered the brand. And done it with a crafty eye for detail! The original LX had been converted into ⊠⊠—Box Double X—altered so deftly that no one would give it a second glance. The blaze-faced sorrel was one of Ben Langham's cow ponies! Probably one of the bunch stolen from the Blue Creek camp a month ago. The very day Langham had offered him the job of range detective. It all dovetailed, time and brand and . . .

Suddenly Starbuck remembered the brand on the dun gelding. Turning, he stepped to the horse and examined the brand more closely. Hardly discernible, but apparent upon critical inspection, was a faint difference in the mark. One section inside the Circle B appeared slightly fresher! An expert with a running iron had altered ℗ to a perfect Ⓑ. Whoever it was that had doctored the brands was an artist, much slicker than any run-of-the-mill rustler. His handiwork on Ben Langham's LX and Vernon Pryor's ℗ would have gone undetected by anyone unfamiliar with the brands. A man had to be looking for it to find it, and even then it was virtually impossible to spot. Starbuck felt a grudging sense of admiration for the phantom horse thief. With a running iron, the bastard was one-of-a-kind.

Yet the discovery immediately posed a regular briar patch of questions. How had these horses gotten from the Panhandle to Kansas? How many times had the animals changed hands? Who sold them to Clute Jordan? Or, if he hadn't bought them, was it possible he'd stolen—?

"Somethin' wrong?"

Jordan's voice brought Starbuck around. The rancher was standing at his shoulder, watching him with a quizzical expression. Before Starbuck could reply, the farrier approached with horseshoe and hammer and a mouthful of nails. Starbuck stepped aside, patting the dun on the rump and smiled at Jordan.

"Damn nice little cow pony. Wouldn't care to talk a swap, would you?"

"Not on your tintype! Hell, I just bought the critter."

"Never hurts to ask." Starbuck glanced at the dun, kept his voice casual. "Any more where he come from?"

"Christ A'mighty!" Jordan flashed a mouthful of brownish teeth. "You've got an eye for horseflesh, but you'll need more'n that before you start dickerin' with Ben Echhardt."

"Who's Ben Echhardt?"

"Feller what sold me them horses, that's who. Biggest livestock dealer in Dodge, and the goddamnedest crook this side of perdition."

"Pretty slick, is he?"

"Slick!" Jordan crowed. "Hell, that won't cut it, not by half. Sonovabitch could lie his way out of a locked safe, and that's a plain fact."

"Well, maybe I'll look him up. I'm headin' for Dodge, anyway, and it don't cost nothin' to talk."

"Says you!" Jordan countered. "You start jawbonin' with Echhardt, and before you know it, he's got his hand in your wallet. Take my word for it, where he's concerned . . . talk ain't cheap."

"Guess I'll just have to take my chances."

"Your funeral," Jordan said, one eyebrow lifted in mock concern. " 'Course, if you mean to tangle with Ol' Ben, you'll need to be in fightin' trim."

"Oh?" Starbuck remarked. "You got some ideas on how I'd go about punchin' his ticket?"

"Naw, hell, you already been broke of suckin' eggs. But you shore look like you could use a good feed. Bet you haven't had a home-cooked meal since way back when, have you?"

"Near as I recollect, the last time was mother's milk."

Jordan's beard parted in a whiskery grin. "Know the feelin', Luke! Know it well.

How'd you like to stay to supper?"

"You won't have to twist my arm," Starbuck told him, "if you're sure it won't put your wife out."

"Hell, don't fret none about her! 'Course, I oughta warn you aforehand—she's got her bad side."

"Yeah, how's that?"

"Well, she's a good cook, mighty good. But gawddamn, she's a powerful talker, Luke. Powerful! Talk the molars right out of your jawbone."

"Maybe she'll get me in practice for—what's his name?—Echhardt . . . the horse trader."

"Kee-rist! Ain't it the mortal truth. Sonovabitch won't stand a chance once my ol' woman's got you primed. No chance a'tall!"

"Then lead me to her, Clute. Wind her up and let 'er rip!"

Jordan laughed a braying laugh and flung a wave in the general direction of the blacksmith. Then he grabbed the younger man's arm and marched off briskly toward the house. As they walked away, Starbuck glanced over his shoulder, took a last look at the dun gelding. His mouth creased in a faint smile, and his mind raced ahead to Dodge and tomorrow.

To Ben Echhardt.

CHAPTER SIX

Dodge City sweltered under a late-afternoon sun as Starbuck rode into the South Side. It was the peak of the trailing season, and the vice district was jammed with Texans. Upward of a thousand trail-weary men were in town at any given time, and a carnival atmosphere permeated the streets. Saloons and whorehouses and gambling dives had sprouted like weeds in a berry patch, all catering to the rowdy nature of cowhands. A combination of wild women and popskull whiskey quickly separated most of them from a summer's wages.

Starbuck was in no way surprised by the crowds. Though he generally sent trail bosses north with the LX herds, he had come himself the first year Dodge captured the cattle trade. Hammered together out in the middle of nowhere, it had sprung, virtually over-

night, from a trading post for buffalo hunters
into the rawest boomtown on the western
plains. A sprawling, windswept hodgepodge
of buildings, the town was neatly divided by
the railroad tracks. The vice district, known
simply as the South Side, was woolly-booger
wild. There, the trailhands were allowed to
let off steam with no holds barred, gunplay
excepted. But at the railroad tracks, locally
dubbed the Deadline, all rowdiness ceased.
Anyone who attempted to hurrah the town
north of the tracks was guaranteed a stiff fine
and a night in jail.

The lawmen of Dodge City had always impressed Starbuck. Handy with their fists, and
sudden death with a gun, they rigidly en-
forced the Deadline. Upon crossing the
tracks, it was like passing from a three-ring
circus into a sedate churchyard. Along Front
Street, the dusty plaza gave every appearance
of a thriving little metropolis. Down at one
end, flanked by a mercantile and several smaller establishments, were the Dodge
House, Zimmerman's Hardware, and the
Long Branch. Up the other way were a couple of trading companies and the bank, bordered by cafés and shops and varied business
places. To the north was the residential section, and outside town vast herds of longhorns were being grazed along the Arkansas
River.

It was sort of eerie in a way. Everyone

along Front Street conducted themselves in
an orderly fashion, and acted as though the
South Side simply didn't exist. Starbuck
thought it a remarkable yet highly sensible
arrangement. The wages of sin on one side
of the tracks and the fruits of commerce on
the other. With a neutral ribbon of steel in
between. To the benefit of all concerned, it
worked uncommonly well.

Skirting the train station, Starbuck held the
gelding to a walk. His eyes scanned the row
of buildings, then suddenly paused. Toward
the end of town, near the cattle pens and
loading yard, was a livery stable. A sign, em-
blazoned across the top of the structure, also
identified the proprietor as a livestock dealer.
After a fifty-mile ride, there was no need for
hesitation. He'd thought it through, and he
knew exactly how he intended to approach
Echhardt. Still at a walk, he angled across the
plaza.

Several moments later he dismounted in
front of the livery stable and left his horse
tied to the hitch rack. Walking through the
broad double doors, he paused and inspected
the row of stalls on either side of the building. The place was immaculate, filled with a
regular rainbow of odors—old leather, hay
and fresh droppings—blended into a pleasant, musk-like aroma. Except for the stalled
horses, and a stablehand shoveling manure,
the livery appeared deserted. Then a door

opened, leading from an office on the left,
and a man hurried forward. By the cut of his
clothes, and the gold watch chain dangling
across his paunch, it seemed unlikely he'd be
caught tending stables. He stopped, nodding
amiably, thumbs hooked in his vest.

"Afternoon, friend. What can I do for
you?"

"I'm lookin' for Ben Echhardt."

"Look no farther," Echhardt beamed.
"You've found him."

"Glad to meet you," Starbuck replied. "I'm
in the market for a good cow pony. Clute
Jordan told me you're the man to see."

Echhardt gave him a keen, sidewise scrutiny. "That the Jordan with a little spread
north of the Cimarron?"

"Yeah, same one."

"And he told you to come see me?"

"Sure did, just last night. Why, aren't you
in the horse-tradin' business no more?"

"Oh, no, nothing like that! It's just . . .
well, Jordan's a real stemwinder . . . called
me all sorts of names last time he was here."

Starbuck shrugged. "Guess it come natural, him bein' so tight and all. But he told me
you had the best stock in Dodge."

"Now, that's no lie, friend. Anybody who
knows horseflesh deals with Ben Echhardt!
Sound horses and a square deal, that's my
motto."

Echhardt was a human wrinkle, stout and

full-bellied, but with a face like ancient ivory and a disarming smile. Yet there was something of the charlatan about him; his voice had the cadence and broad exaggeration of a man hawking snake-oil liniment from a torch-lit wagon. It was a disconcerting combination, which he used, with great aplomb, to his own advantage.

Starbuck's expression revealed nothing. "Jordan said you talk good, too. But I reckon horses kind of speak for themselves."

"A profound observation, friend! Very profound indeed. Are you buying or trading?"

"Figured on buyin'. Need something that can double up as a cow pony or a packhorse."

"I take it you're a traveling man?"

"Wrangler, by trade," Starbuck informed him. " 'Course, sometimes I catch on with a small outfit and have to punch cows. Never hurts your chances to have an extra pony along."

"Shrewd thinking." Echhardt nodded sagely. "Always admired a man that invests in himself."

"Think you've got somethin' that fits the ticket, do you?"

"Oh, you can depend on it, friend. I'm a little low at the moment, but like Jordan told you, Ben Echhardt has the finest livestock in town. Just follow me, corral's out back."

Echhardt led him through the stable to a

rear door. Outside there was a large stock
pen, built to hold fifty head or more. But today something less than twenty horses stood
munching hay scattered on the ground. With
an eloquent wave, Echhardt grinned and cast
a proud eye over the animals.

"There they are, friend! None better anywhere in Kansas, and you can mark my
word."

"Mind if I have a look for myself?"

"Not at all. They're sound as a dollar.
Every last one!"

Starbuck crawled through the fence and
slowly circled the horses. To all appearances,
he was checking confirmation and general
condition. Yet his eyes moved constantly,
studying brands for any sign of alteration.
After a time he reversed direction, completely puzzled. So far as he could determine,
there wasn't a horse in the bunch with a
brand similar to those used in the Panhandle.
Then, a few steps from the fence, something
caught his attention. He moved between a
blood bay and a roan, talking softly to gentle
them, and made a show of examining the
roan. All the while, he kept his head lowered,
darting hidden glances at the blood bay and
a chestnut standing nearby. One carried a
Forked Y and the other a Slash Diamond;
both brands had been doctored with the same
deft touch he'd seen at Clute Jordan's ranch.
Still, the original brands, probably a simple

Y and an open Diamond, were unknown to him. Though he had no doubt the horses were stolen, his certainty brought to light a whole new element, and complicated matters greatly. It was now apparent that the Panhandle wasn't alone; horses were being stolen from other areas, as well. Taking his time, inspecting the roan's hooves and teeth, he did some fast thinking. In terms of the plan he'd worked out, it really changed nothing. With a little improvising, perhaps he could still snooker Echhardt into a corner.

Walking back to the fence, Starbuck crawled through and stood for a moment studying the horses. Then he pulled out the makings and began rolling a smoke. "How much you askin' for that roan?"

"Fine animal," Echhardt said expansively. "Pick of the litter."

"How much?"

"Hundred and fifty, and worth every penny."

Starbuck struck a match on the fence and lit his cigarette. "Now that I've heard what you're askin', suppose you tell me what you'll take . . . rock bottom."

"Well, since you're a friend of Clute Jordan, I guess I might shave it some. Let's call it a hundred and a quarter, and shake hands on it."

"Too rich for my blood."

"You won't do any better, and that's a fact."

"Maybe." Starbuck nodded, turned to leave. "Been nice talkin' with you."

Echhardt threw up his hands. "Hold on a minute, friend! Let me ask you something—nothing personal, you understand, but it might change your mind. Whereabouts do you call home?"

"Texas." Starbuck took a long drag, exhaled smoke. "But I've rode for outfits all over, and I never heard tell of prices like that. Not for a common workin' horse."

"What about outfits up north—Montana and Wyoming? Ever rode up there?"

"Nope, got better sense. Way I hear it, them fellers get Injun haircuts real regular."

"There's your answer!" Echhardt trumpeted. "You just haven't got the news, have you?"

"What news is that?"

"Why, friend, the Sioux and the Cheyenne and all the rest of those rascals have been whipped! The army herded them onto reservations the year after Custer went under. There's a natural land boom up there, more ranches than you can shake a stick at!"

Starbuck glued a smile on his face. "You're joshin' me."

"No siree, not even a little bit. That's what I'm trying to tell you. Folks up there want good cow ponies, and they're willing to pay the price."

"So? What's that got to do with the price of your roan?"

"Supply and demand!" Echhardt countered. "Why, close to fifty thousand horses will be trailed to the High Plains this summer. *Fifty thousand!* That makes cow ponies scarce as hens' teeth. And it drives up the price everywhere, even Dodge." He gestured toward the horses. "There's your proof! I sell 'em faster than I can get 'em, and no way to keep the pens full."

"The hell you say." Starbuck regarded him evenly, still smiling. "Looks to me like Jordan just waltzed in here and bought himself the cream of the crop. 'Course, the roan's not bad, but the rest of them scrubs wouldn't last the day."

"Think so, huh?" Echhardt leveled a finger at the corral. "See the bay there, and the chestnut next to him?"

"Yeah." Starbuck felt his pulse quicken, took a casual glance at the horses with altered brands. "What about 'em?"

"I got 'em off the best damn trader in these parts, that's what! Fellow by the name of Chub Jones. Only deals in prime horseflesh! And for your information, he's the same one that sold me the bunch Clute Jordan bought."

"That a fact?"

"A mortal fact, friend! Sure as we're standing here."

"Well, I still think Jordan got the better stock. Maybe I'll just wait till this fellow—Jones—brings in another string."

"Don't hold your breath," Echhardt advised. "I won't see Jones for another month or so. He trades somewhere out in New Mexico, and he only brought this bunch in last week." Suddenly he smiled, shook his head. "You're a hard man, but I tell you what. Take your pick—the roan, the bay, whichever one you want—and I'll come down to a hundred and ten. Now, I ask you, is that fair, or is that fair?"

"Thanks all the same." Starbuck hesitated a moment, thoughtful. "You know, I was wonderin' . . . this trader fellow . . . Jones?"

"What about him?"

"You reckon he could use a wrangler?"

"A wrangler!" Echhardt glowered. "How the hell would I know?"

"Never hurts to ask."

"Then ask him yourself."

"Yessir, I would . . . do it in a minute . . . if I knew where to find him."

"Well, friend, I tell you what you do. Climb on board that horse of yours and head west along the Cimarron. Somewhere out around the Colorado line, you'll find Chub Jones's spread, and when you see him . . . tell him . . . just tell him Ben Echhardt thinks you're a prince of a fellow. Not too bright, but a real prince!"

Echhardt stormed off and quickly disappeared through the door of the livery stable. Starbuck ground his cigarette underfoot, then turned and walked to the corral. He leaned across the top of the fence, eyes fixed on the bay and the chestnut. A slow smile tugged at the corner of his mouth.

He had a name and a direction . . . a fresh trail.

CHAPTER SEVEN

The water was steamy-hot. Starbuck lounged back in the tub, submerged to his chin in suds. A cigar jutted from his mouth, and he stared at the ceiling, luxuriating while he considered the clever fellow he'd become. He was feeling peacock-proud, and immensely gratified by the day's events. All in all, he thought he'd at last gotten the hang of the detective business.

Earlier, after leaving the livery stable, Starbuck had taken a room in the Dodge House. The first priority was a bath, and he had ordered a tub and buckets of hot water brought to his room. Then, lolling about in the tub, he'd scalded off an accumulation of sweat and gritty trail dust. Altogether, with the aid of a hog-bristle brush and rank yellow soap, the cleansing process had consumed the better part of an hour. Afterward, the cigar clamped in his teeth, he surrendered himself to the steamy warmth and let his mind drift.

Upon reflection, he concluded that Ben Echhardt was both a disappointment and a veritable gold mine of information. Before reaching Dodge, he would have bet everything that Echhardt was somehow involved with the horse thieves. The notion had been quickly dispelled, however, by Echhardt's candor and garrulous manner. A thief simply didn't run off at the mouth that way!

Yet, with unwitting honesty, the livestock dealer had supplied all the right answers. At first, when Echhardt mentioned the High Plains, Starbuck thought he'd struck paydirt. It made perfect sense. With fifty thousand horses headed north—at sky-high prices— the logical places to look for stolen stock were Montana and Wyoming. Even now, the idea couldn't be written off entirely. Not with great numbers of Panhandle stock still unaccounted for . . . at least in Dodge.

All the same, the place to look was west, along the Cimarron. The instant Echhardt mentioned Chub Jones, the connection was obvious. One man tied to two different strings of stolen horses pretty much spoke for itself. Like Echhardt, he might very well have bought the horses off someone else. But the connection made him a damned fine suspect. The best yet!

With all he'd learned, however, Starbuck

was still stumped. The numbers wouldn't jibe, no matter how many times he sorted them out. The best he could calculate, Chub Jones had sold Echhardt between eight and ten head of Panhandle stock. That was nearly a month ago—at a time when more than fifty head had been stolen—which left a lot of horses unaccounted for. Maybe Jones had sold them off piecemeal, in small bunches. On the other hand, maybe he'd bought only a few head—in good faith—from the real thief. It was possible, but somehow it didn't square with the facts. Jones apparently had an eye for livestock, and a slick horse trader didn't buy a few good cow ponies when he could just as easily buy the whole herd. Then there was the matter of the bay and the chestnut, carrying unkown brands but clearly stolen. A new piece to the puzzle, and one that raised even broader questions. Somebody was stealing horses across a wide area, stealing them hand over fist, and it all seemed linked to one man. Chub Jones.

If nothing else was clear, that much, at least, was chiseled in stone. Chub Jones was the man with the answers. The linchpin that would bring it all together.

On the personal side, Starbuck was immensely pleased with himself. The major questions remained unresolved, at least for the moment. But deep down he knew he'd put on a humdinger of a performance for Ben

Echhardt. Compared to the way he'd botched
things in the Cherokee Nation, it was an absolute masterpiece. Even his interrogation of
Clute Jordan—despite a great effort at hood-
winking the rancher—had caused raised
eyebrows and lingering suspicion. With Echhardt, however, he'd played a cool hand
straight down the line. Apparently practice
made perfect, and with a little experience under his belt, he had learned to assume whatever role the situation demanded. Somewhere
along the way, he'd also uncovered a taste
for guile and craft and the illusion of mas-
querade. He actually enjoyed it!

Then too, apart from the excitement itself,
there was an element he'd sensed only today.
Somewhere between Jordan's ranch and Echhardt's livery stable, he had acquired a touch
of expertise. Perhaps he wasn't a professional—not yet—but he'd come damn close
that afternoon. A Pinkerton couldn't have
done any better, and for a homegrown detective, he knew he'd conducted himself with
passing skill. He was alert, relying heavily on
logic and deduction, and his instinct had
never been sharper. The end result was information and leads, the stuff of investigation
and hard-nosed detective work. He was proud
as punch. Damned if he wasn't!

Puffing on his cigar, Starbuck abruptly
warned himself to go slow. There was nothing wrong with pride, in moderate doses. But

he'd known fellows who'd gotten chapped lips from kissing cold mirrors. And he realized he was on the verge of it himself. That wouldn't do when it came time to match wits with Chub Jones. Not by a damnsight! Cocky had got more than one man killed, and out in the wilds of Cimarron country, he'd have to watch his step. One miscue would get him snuffed out faster than a firefly in a sleet storm. Which was a thought worth remembering . . . all the time.

Still, there was no need to let it put a damper on his spirits. He'd earned a celebration, and he meant to treat himself in style. Tonight he would see the elephant . . . tour the South Side, have a few drinks, then maybe a few more. Once his tonsils were oiled, he might even visit a cathouse. Now that he studied on it, he realized it'd been nearly five weeks since he'd had his pole greased. The thought made his teeth hurt, and removed any trace of doubt.

Tonight he'd get his juices jitterated! Let the ladies of negotiable virtue anoint him with love and sap his log and send him off tomorrow with a limber twig and fond memories of warm things in the dark. Jesus Crucified Christ! It sounded too good to wait.

Starbuck bolted out of the tub and doused his cigar in the bathwater. He grabbed a towel and dried himself with a sort of sensual urgency. Then he stepped into a fresh pair of pants, shrugged on a clean shirt and rammed his feet barefoot into his boots. After hitting his hair a few licks, he cinched his gunbelt tight and gathered his hat.

He was whistling when he went out the door.

The South Side was wide open and running wild. As Starbuck crossed the tracks, nightfall was descending on Dodge, and the boardwalks were already packed with carousing trailhands. Directly ahead lay the Lady Gay and the Comique, the favorite watering holes of Texas cowmen. Within easy walking distance, drunk or sober, was a thriving infestation of gaming dens, dance halls, and parlor houses. A rough-and-ready form of free enterprise prevailed in the vice district, perfected to a near science. The idea was to send the Texans back down the trail with sore heads and empty pockets, and the sporting element supplied all the temptation necessary. Wicked women, pandemic games of chance and enough sneaky pete to ossify even the strongest man's gizzard. It was a bizarre and ribald circus, irresistible.

Starbuck bulled a path across the boardwalk and pushed through the batwing doors of the Comique. A band was blaring away on the upper balcony, and shouting cowhands whirled girls around the dance floor like a gang of acrobatic wrestlers. The bar was lined three deep, with an even more dazzling array of girls mingled among the drinkers. All fluffy curls and heaving breasts, they resembled kewpie dolls decked out in spangles and war paint. The back bar was a gaudy clutch of bottles, and as Starbuck elbowed his way through the crowd, a lard-gutted Texan keeled over, glass in hand, and toppled to the floor. Stepping across him, Starbuck quickly filled the hole and whacked the counter with the flat of his hand.

"Barkeep! A shot of the good stuff. Without the snake heads!"

One of the bartenders hustled forward with a shot glass and a bottle of rye. He set the glass in front of Starbuck and filled it to the brim. Corking the bottle, he tapped the counter with his finger.

"Dollar a shot; pay as you go."

"Dollar!"

"You said the good stuff."

"Well, it damn sure better be!"

"Best whiskey west of Kansas City."

Starbuck dug in his pocket and pulled out a handful of double eagles. "Not that it matters, but what d'you get for rotgut?"

"Two bits." The barkeep smiled. "Guaranteed to clean your pipes and melt the wax in your ears."

"I believe you!" Starbuck dropped a gold piece on the counter, nodding at the bottle.

"Stick to the good stuff, and keep it comin'
till I tell you different."

"You're the boss."

The barkeep collected the double eagle and
left the bottle. As he walked off, his gaze
shifted to a girl standing with a couple of
trailhands. He flipped the coin with his
thumb, deftly plucked it out of midair and
jerked his chin at Starbuck. The girl glanced
along the bar, then gave him a faint nod.
With a bright smile, she disengaged herself
from the Texans, kissing one and patting the
other on the cheek. She strolled off to a chorus of drunken protests.

Starbuck caught the byplay out of the corner of his eye. He jammed the coins into his
pocket, ignoring the girl, and hooked one
boot over the brass rail. Holding the glass to
the light, he studied the amber liquid with a
look of constrained eagerness. Then he lowered the glass and took a long sip, savoring
the whiskey a moment before he swallowed.
His mouth creased in a slow smile.

The girl stopped beside him, placed a hand
on his arm. Her lips were muted crimson,
eyelids shadowed with kohl, and her cheeks
were tinted coral. She dimpled and flashed a
gleaming smile.

"Welcome to Dodge, honey! Buy a girl a
drink?"

"Not tonight." Starbuck stared into his
glass. "Maybe another time."

"What's the matter, cowboy?" Her fingers trickled across his neck. "Got something against girls?"

Starbuck turned, slowly looked her up and down. She wore a skimpy peek-a-boo gown, which accentuated her breasts and long, lissome legs. She was dark and vivacious, with black ringlets piled atop her head, and her eyes held a certain bawdy wisdom. She ran the tip of her tongue across her lips, staring straight at him while he finished the inspection. Starbuck was impressed, tempted, and she knew the look.

"Satisfied with the goods, honeybun?"

"Yeah, real nice . . . but I'm still not buyin' drinks."

"Oooo, c'mon, be a sport!" Her lips curved in a teasing smile. "We could have ourselves some laughs."

"Sure could, and the joke'd be on me."

"On you . . . a joke on you . . . how so?"

"I saw the barkeep give you the nod"— Starbuck shrugged, watching her—"a dollar a shot makes for pretty expensive conversation."

"Well, you're no dimdot, are you?" She simpered, batted her lashes. "But what the hell, honey? A girl's got to make a living!"

"I suppose." Starbuck took a sip of whiskey, considering all the bare flesh spilling out of her peek-a-boo gown. His mouth suddenly went dry, and he cleared his throat. "You

know, somethin' occurs to me, if you
wouldn't take offense."

"Try me and see."

"After work . . . when you leave here . . .
you run right home, do you?"

"You guessed it!" Her voice rippled with
laughter. "Home's right upstairs, honey."

"Shucks!" Starbuck feigned a hangdog
look. "Wouldn't you know it! And me all set
to ask if I could walk you home."

The girl fell silent, still smiling but sub-
jecting him to a frank examination. He was
neat, freshly shaven and smelled of soap. A
rarity among men who reeked of cow dung
and sweat. Not exactly handsome, but by no
means ugly, and he had a sense of humor.
Even the way he'd propositioned her was
quietly offhanded, and she somehow knew he
would treat her gently in bed. All in all, there
were worse ways to fill a lonesome night.
She'd slept with them, lots of times.

"I guess we could talk about it"—she gave
him a minxish smile—"if you don't mind
sneaking up the back stairs."

"Just call me Johnny Lightfoot!"

"Well, Johnny, I haven't said yes, not yet,
anyway. All I said was . . . we could talk
about it."

"I reckon that'll do for openers."

"No, for openers you'll have to buy a bottle of champagne."

"Oh?" Starbuck frowned. "How's that?"

"Because you were right, honey. Conversation is damned expensive in this joint. Either you buy the champagne—and we talk—or I have to keep circulating and hustling drinks. It's a house rule."

She lowered one eyelid in a naughty wink. "A bottle of bubbly and you get me all to yourself."

Starbuck held her gaze a moment. He found something of the imp lurking there, but her look was steadfast, without guile. His mustache lifted in a wide grin, and he nodded. Then he turned and slapped the counter with lightning-like report.

"Bartender! A bottle of bubbly!"

Lamplight spilled over the bed in a cider glow. She lay curled against his body, her head nestled in the hollow of his shoulder. There was little talk, and they lay quietly, drifting on a quenched flame. Her hair, now uncoiled, was like the wings of a raven fanned darkly across the pillow. Her skin, soft and silky-smooth, tingled as his fingers gently stroked her buttocks. After a long while she sighed, twisting around, and looked at him.

"That's not your real name . . . is it?"

"What name?"

"Johnny." She giggled and punched him in the ribs. "Forget the Lightfoot and just tell me about Johnny."

He smiled. "It's Luke . . . Luke Starbuck."

She repeated the name several times to herself. "That's nice. I think it . . . well, somehow . . . it fits you."

"Now that you brought it up, you never told me your name."

"Lisa." She watched his expression. "Lisa Blalock."

"Same song, second verse. Is it real?"

"Well, it's really Elizabeth, but I don't like to be called Betty. So I fudged a little and picked Lisa."

"Pretty name." He paused, straight-faced. "Fits you, too."

"You're a tease! You really are!"

"Guess we're birds of a feather. You just about teased me to death with that little thing of yours."

"The same for me." She uttered a low gloating laugh. "Only yours isn't so little."

"The way I recollect, you had a lot to do with that."

"Luke?" Her voice was husky velvet. "It was good, wasn't it . . . special?"

"Extra special, and that's no lie."

"Maybe we can do it again sometime, hmm?"

"You can bank on it, and that's no lie, either."

"You wouldn't kid an old kidder, would you?"

"No, ma'am, not you." He deliberated a moment. "I've got some business to tend to, but it won't take too long."

"Hah! I'll bet it's business . . . monkey business!"

"Yeah, you might say that—'specially if you're talkin' about the right kind of monkeys."

"Sorry, lover, you lost me."

"It'll keep, just a private joke."

"You're full of private jokes . . . and secrets . . . aren't you?"

He stroked her buttocks and smiled a cryptic smile. After a time, when he remained silent, she snuggled closer and let her fingers trickle down his belly. Then she grasped him, gently fondling and caressing, and felt him grow within her hand. Suddenly his arms lifted her and swung her kneeling astraddle him, centered on his hardness. She impaled herself with a whimpering cry of urgency.

CHAPTER EIGHT

The day was bright as new brass, without a cloud in sight. Overhead a hawk floated past on smothered wings, then slowly veered windward of man and horse. A shallow trickle of water ran listlessly through the riverbed, and the flintlike soil, baked hard and yellow by the sun, was spotted with clumps of withered grass. To the west, near the river, were a couple of buildings and a corral. There was no sign of life.

Screened by a cluster of trees, Starbuck squatted on his heels, staring at the buildings. Since early afternoon, he had watched and waited, scouting the ranch of Chub Jones. Now, with sundown approaching, he had a mental inventory of the operation. All the pieces seemed to fit, and the more he'd observed, the greater became his certainty. The search ended here.

The buildings were crude log structures, with a ramshackle look of impermanence. The smaller one, Starbuck had concluded, was Chub Jones's personal dwelling. It was occupied by a lone man, who had appeared briefly not long after the noon hour. The larger building, clearly a bunkhouse, was occupied by four men. Except for trips to the privy, they had remained indoors throughout the afternoon. The corral held fifteen head of horses, exactly two mounts per man, with five spares in reserve, which was adequate for a small working ranch.

Yet this was no working ranch. Grazing south of the river was a herd of slat-ribbed longhorns, numbering scarcely a hundred head. In this parched land, the cows had to rustle to survive, and from their scrawny condition, it seemed obvious Chub Jones was no cattleman. All the more revealing were the loafers in the bunkhouse. A crew of four hands was about three too many for the size of the operation. The cattle were apparently window dressing—meant to create the illusion of a small outfit—which unquestionably placed the men in another line of work. The stark isolation of the ranch merely confirmed the thought. A hundred miles from Dodge, out in the wilds of Cimarron country, it was a desolate land of no value to anyone—except to a man with something to hide.

Still, for all its barren solitude, the ranch

had a strategic value of no small consequence. To the south, across a lawless strip called No Man's Land, lay the Texas Panhandle. A day and a night of hard riding, roughly a hundred miles as the crow flies, would strike the very heart of Ben Langham's spread. In between, there was virtually no human habitation, nor were there any lawmen. It all seemed fashioned by the hand of God for the benefit of horse thieves.

Starbuck found it ironic that he'd come very near full circle. If he was right about Chub Jones—and deep in his gut he knew it was so—then he had ridden not on a search, but on a fool's errand. The man he sought was practically within spitting distance . . . the whole time . . . the whole damned time!

Starbuck waited until sundown, then rose and stretched his legs. In the distance, there was activity in front of the bunkhouse, and he knew the men were washing up for supper. Unless he was mistaken, Chub Jones would join them shortly, and from where Starbuck stood, he estimated it was a tenminute walk to the ranch yard. With nightfall approaching and supper on the table, he figured the timing was damn near perfect. All he had to do was act the part.

Before leaving Dodge, he had changed back into the clothes he'd worn for almost six weeks. Three days on the trail had added stubble to his jawline, and earlier in the af-

ternoon he had dabbed a little cow dung
under his armpits. He looked grungy and
trailworn, and smelled ripe as a billy goat.
Which was a normal condition for any diehard saddle tramp. All that remained was his
horse.

It was a trick widely known among cowhands, especially the lazy ones. He jerked a
hair from the gelding's mane, then knelt beside the near front leg and took a couple of
turns around the small pastern bone. He
pulled the horsehair tight, tied it off in a
square knot and clipped the loose ends with
his pocketknife. Undetectable, it would do no
harm, yet it made any animal appear lame.
When he gathered the reins and moved off a
few steps, the gelding limped along, gingerly
favoring the leg. Satisfied, he led the horse
out of the trees and proceeded toward the
buildings at a slow walk.

Dusk had fallen when Starbuck angled
away from the river and skirted the corral.
There were now five men gathered outside
the bunkhouse, and they watched with
wooden expressions, eyes like bullets, as he
crossed the yard. When he halted, the gelding
hobbled a couple of steps closer and stopped,
standing with the game leg crooked, slightly
off the ground. None of the men moved or
spoke, and after a moment he nodded.

"Evenin'. The boss around?"

A chunky man, squat as a beer keg, separated from the others. He had the look of a bright pig, with wide nostrils, pudgy jowls and small, beady eyes. In the dim light he squinted, mouth hooked in a frown.

"Do somethin' for you?"

"All depends. You the boss?"

"I own the land, whichever direction you care to spit. That good enough?"

"Yessir, it shore is Mr.——?"

"Jones." The beady eyes examined him as though he were something that had fallen out of a tree. "L. C. Jones."

"Well, Mr. Jones, I've plumb walked my butt off, and I don't mind tellin' you"—Starbuck gestured toward a spill of lamplight from the doorway—"I was tickled pink when I saw this place all lit up. What with dark comin' on, and a stove-up horse, it shore was a pretty sight."

Jones ignored the hint. "How long's he been favorin' that leg?"

"Since about noontime. I figure he got himself a stone bruise, but hell's bells, I wasn't partial to stoppin' the night. See, all I'm packin' is a little cornmeal and some coffee."

A swarm of flies buzzed around Starbuck's armpits, looking interested. Jones fixed him with a dour stare, and when he spoke, his voice was rough, insistent.

"Mister, we're sorta off the beaten path. How'd you know where to find this place?"

"I asked." Starbuck kept his gaze level, and cool. "Last place I stopped—maybe twenty miles downriver—fellow's name was McKittrick. Never hurts to ask—not when you're headed into strange country."

"Get a lot of handouts that way, do you?"

"Every cripple does his own dance, Mr. Jones."

Jones's laugh was scratchy, abrasive. "You're an obligin' sort of jasper, ain't you?"

"Just try to go along and get along, that's all."

"Whereabouts you headed, exactly?"

Starbuck sensed a sudden alertness in the other men. The question was bluntly asked, but nonetheless loaded, and there was no leeway for mistakes. The wrong answer would get him killed.

"Well, it's this way," he said evenly, "I'm a wrangler by trade. But I'm sick to death of trail drives in the summer and the Rio Grande in the winter. All I've ever seen is flatlands and flies, and I figure I'm due for a change. Thought I'd try Colorado, have a look-see at them mountains. Hear tell they're mighty pretty."

"Who'd you wrangle for?"

"*Ere Flecha*," Starbuck replied without hesitation. "Cap'n King's spread. Tightfisted old bastard works you like a greaser and pays you like one, too."

"You got a name?"

"Starbuck. Luke Starbuck."

There was a moment of silence, then Jones gave him a slow nod. "Awright, Starbuck, you can stay the night. But come mornin', you be on your way—mounted or afoot!—don't make no nevermind to me, you understand?"

"Shore, do, and I'm obliged, Mr. Jones. *Mucho gracias.*"

"Cut the Mex talk and get unsaddled." Jones turned and walked toward the bunkhouse. "Grub's on the table."

The bunkroom smelled like a wolf den. But its sparse comforts were no less than Starbuck had expected. On the left, just inside the door, was a commode with a faded mirror, and strewn on the floor was a jumble of warbags, filthy clothes and weathered gear. A set of double bunks stood end to end along the opposite wall, and a rough-hewn table, flanked by a potbelly stove, occupied the central living area. Beyond the table, at the far end of the room, was a wood cooking stove and shelves packed with canned goods. Since there was no spare bunk, Starbuck had tossed his bedroll in a corner beside the firewood.

Supper was typically overcooked and tasteless. A platter of charred beefsteak, accompanied by beans and spotted-pup rice, had been washed down with coffee thick as

mud. The men devoured everything in sight,
grunting and belching like a pack of carni-
vores gorging themselves on a fresh kill. All
through the meal they kept one eye on Starbuck, apparently taking their lead from Jones,
who ate in ravenous silence at one end of the
table. At the other end, with Starbuck seated
on his right, the largest man in the crew occasionally paused and wrinkled his nose, as
though testing the wind. He was tall and
sledge-shouldered, with the lean flanks of a
horseman. His features were hard, all rough
planes set off by splayed cheekbones and an
undershot jaw. He had taken the choice seat
with an air of ownership, and when the other
men offered no protest, Starbuck had immediately pegged him as the bunkhouse bully.
It looked to be an interesting night.

After the table was cleared, someone produced a deck of cards. Apparently a poker
game had been in progress throughout the afternoon, and from their remarks, the men
were anxious to resume play. The big man,
addressed by the others as Tate, was heavy
winner for the day, and they jokingly threat-
ened to bust his lucky streak. Starbuck tilted
back in his chair, rolling himself a smoke,
and watched as the men dug greenbacks and
coins from their pockets. So far, no one had
spoken to him or acknowledged his presence
at the table. Yet he had a hunch it wouldn't
be long.

"What say, Chub?" Tate stared the length of the table with a crooked grin. "You gonna rathole or take the plunge?"

"Well, I'll tell you, Sam"—Jones fished a wad of bills from his pocket—"I think I'll just sit in and show the boys how to clean your plow."

"Fat chance!" Tate laughed. "Comes to cards, you'll wind up suckin' hind tit like ever'body else."

"Ain't but one way to find out. Quit runnin' your tongue and deal 'em."

Starbuck sensed a rivalry between the two men. Tate probably kept the crew in line and performed Jones's dirty work, but the fat man clearly had a tiger by the tail. It appeared to be a case of brains needing brawn—and vice versa—with ill-concealed antagonism on both sides. A glimmer of an idea popped into Starbuck's head, one ripe with possibilities. Before he could pursue it further, Tate's voice intruded and he looked up to find himself riveted by a churlish stare.

"How about it, shitkicker? Wanna take a hand?"

Starbuck regarded him with great calmness. "You talkin' to me?"

"Ain't nobody else in here that smells like bearbait! Jesus, I like to puked my supper just sittin' aside you."

"The way you wolfed it down, I never

would've guessed you had a sensitive sniffer."

"Don't push your luck," Tate muttered. "You wanna sit in or not?"

Starbuck studied his cigarette as though he'd never seen one. A moment passed, and some inner voice told him to follow his instinct. It might very well turn the trick, but if he was wrong . . .

"You know, my daddy taught me a couple of lessons about the game of poker. First off, he said a man oughn't to never play with a light poke, and right now, mine's flatter'n a pancake. Then he told me a Gospel truth, regular commandment. Only a damn fool plays with strangers."

The statement froze everyone at the table. Tate glared at him with a bulldog scowl, jaws knotted tight. Then he gently placed the cards on the table, and when he spoke, his lips barely moved.

"You tryin' to say this ain't a straight game?"

"I reckon it was more on the order of an observation."

"Cut the bullshit! Was you or wasn't you?"

Starbuck smiled. "Take it any way you please."

Tate kicked his chair back and stood. "On your feet, peckerhead!" He spat on his hands and briskly rubbed them together. "I'm gonna stunt your growth and stomp all over you."

Starbuck flipped his cigarette. The big man dodged sideways, and before he could recover, Starbuck was on his feet. Tate uncorked a haymaker, and Starbuck ducked low, belted him in the gut. It felt like he'd hit a sack of wet sand, and out of nowhere, Tate laid one upside his jaw. The brassy taste of blood filled his mouth, and pinwheeling lights exploded in his head. A left hook sent him reeling backward, his eyebrow split to the bone, and he crashed over the chair. Tate launched a kick and he skittered away, rolling to his knees. On his feet again, he circled, feinted with his shoulder, caught his wind and gave his head time to clear. Then he bobbed, lowering his guard and suckered Tate into a sweeping roundhouse. Slipping inside the blow, he struck two splintering punches to the chin. Tate staggered, shook his head like a man who had walked into cobwebs and Starbuck landed a hard, clubbing right squarely between the eyes. The impact buckled Tate and he rocketed across the room, slammed upright into one of the bunks. He wavered a moment, then his eyes glazed and he slid to the floor. His nose looked like a rotten apple and blood seeped down over his jaws. He was out cold.

"Well I'll be jiggered!"

One of the men at the table rose for a better look and Starbuck's reaction was sheer

reflex. He spun, crouched low, and the Colt
appeared in his hand. The men went still as
stone, eyes like saucers. An instant of tomblike silence slipped past. Then he wiggled the
tip of the barrel.

"You're the unfriendliest bunch of bastards
I ever run across. Now just shuck them guns
over here—one at a time!—and I'll be on my
way."

"Hold on a minute!"

Jones started out of his chair, quickly sat
down when the pistol snout swung in his direction. Starbuck smiled without warmth.

"Mr. Jones, I'll have to borrow one of your
horses. All things considered, I figure it's an
even swap."

"Look here, whyn't you simmer down and
let's talk? You got no fight with me."

"Yeah, and I got nothin' to talk about either."

"Never know." Jones gave him a crafty
smile. "You're ridin' the grubline and I got
use of an extra hand. Might just make ourselves a deal."

Starbuck regarded him with a cool look of
appraisal. "Why would you offer me work?"

"You said you was a wrangler, didn't
you?"

"Hell, you haven't got horses enough for
a wrangler, and we both know it."

"Forget the horses! There's other reasons."

"Try me."

"I like a man that's sudden, and you're fast
... damned fast!"

"Hold 'er right there." Starbuck jerked his
chin toward the bunks. "Are you talkin'
about that pile of dog meat?"

"Damn right!" Jones grinned. "Anybody
that can haul Sam Tate's ashes is my kinda
man. Havin' you around might keep him on
his toes. Ain't that right, boys?"

The other men bobbed their heads in unison, beaming wide smiles. Jones sensed a
weakening in Starbuck's look, and quickly
resumed.

"C'mon, what've you got to lose? Sit
down and let's talk! No harm in that, is
there?"

Starbuck hesitated a long while. Then he
straddled a chair backward still covering
them with the Colt. He nodded.

"All right, talk. But no sudden moves! I'll
drill the first sonovabitch that takes his hands
off that table. Savvy?"

Everyone savvied, and Jones began to talk.

CHAPTER NINE

"Queens bet a dollar."

"Have to raise you five."

"Too rich for my blood."

"Count me out. Somebody else'll have to keep him honest."

"Not me! I'll fold 'em and watch."

"Luke, you shore as hell ain't gonna buy it! There's your five and another five on the queens. I think you're runnin' a sandy."

"Cost you another five to find out."

"By God, I'll take the last raise! Five more says you ain't got beans."

"Forced to call you, Tom."

"Hot damn!" Tom flipped his hole cards. "Read 'em and weep, pardner. Queens and nines!"

"Not enough." Starbuck turned a pair of fours. "Caught a couple in the hole to go with the one on top . . . three fours."

"Jesus Pesus Christ! Ain't there no way to beat you?"

"Outhouse luck, Tom. Caught the case four on the last card."

"Like shit! I'll bet'cha had 'em wired the whole gawddamn time."

Starbuck smiled and raked in the pot. Across the table, Sam Tate gave him a glance that could have drawn blood. The other men merely shook their heads in wonder, watching as he added to the neatly stacked piles of coins and greenbacks. Then Tom, who had lost the pot but won the deal, riffled the cards and called for a cut. Everyone anted a dollar.

For the past week, night and day, a marathon poker game had been in progress. Almost from the outset, Starbuck had enjoyed sporadic winning streaks. When the cards turned sour, he bluffed occasionally but only enough to keep the other men guessing. He was ahead nearly three hundred dollars.

Yet he felt like a man marking time in quicksand. For all his luck at cards, he had gleaned not the slightest scrap of information regarding stolen horses. Instead, he had been subjected to a heavy-handed grilling by the men and Chub Jones, and told so many lies he'd long ago lost track of the truth. It was scarcely the way he'd planned it.

The night he whipped Sam Tate everything had seemed so simple. With a great show of skepticism, he had finally holstered his six-gun and allowed Jones to hire him on as wrangler. The story Jones told was reasonably plausible. The ranch dealt mainly in horses; the cattle were a mere sideline. Periodic buying trips were made to New Mexico; the idea was to buy cheap and sell high after trailing the stock to Dodge. All the men shared in the profits, and except for light chores around the ranch, there was little to do in slack periods. It paid good and the hours were short. A square deal all the way round!

To anyone with common sense—especially horse sense—it was a farfetched tale. Nonetheless, Starbuck appeared to swallow it whole, and even offered a lame apology for pulling a gun. At the time, he thought he'd given a jim-dandy performance, and figured he had everyone convinced. But in short order, it became apparent he had underestimated Chub Jones.

The tip-off was one of attitude. The men shared cooking chores, tended to their own mounts and occasionally someone remembered to check on the small herd of longhorns. Yet there was never any mention of horse trading. Almost as though it were a forbidden subject, neither Jones nor the men alluded to it after that first night. Instead, they invited him to join the poker game and spent the next few days asking veiled questions about his past. Later, in casual conversation,

chance remarks were dropped to verify details. It was a test, plain and simple, and none
too tactfully done. Jones apparently liked his
style but wasn't wholly convinced he could
be trusted.

Starbuck stuck to his original story, em-
bellishing it with a string of fabrications
about the Rio Grande and the King Ranch.
Within a few days, the questions ceased and
he assumed he'd come through with flying
colors. Still, despite the abrupt turnabout,
there was no mention of horse trading. The
men settled down to serious poker—bitching
incessantly about Starbuck's winning streak—
and he was left in a quandary. To all appearances, there were no immediate plans for
a raid. He speculated on the reasons, wondering if Jones worked on some erratic
schedule or simply waited for the urge to
strike. There was no way to know—or find
out—and trying to second-guess a horse thief
was like trying to catch smoke. At last, resigned to wait it out, he joined in the spirit
of things and began playing cutthroat poker.
The bitching rose by several decibels.

On the average, Starbuck folded three
hands out of five. Unless the cards showed
early promise, he got out; the end result,
whenever he stayed the limit, was that the
other players never knew if he'd filled a hand
or was simply bluffing. The one exception
was Sam Tate. If only he and Tate were left

in a game, he raised like a wild man and bluffed on anything . . . and usually won.

Since the night of their fight, Tate had gone out of his way to avoid trouble. He seldom spoke, and though his hostility simmered beneath the surface, he even treated the other men with a certain gruff tolerance. Yet Starbuck wasn't fooled. A bully never forgot or forgave, and one whipping rarely got the job done. To rule the bunkhouse— and enhance himself in Jones's eyes—he had to squash Tate at every opportunity. He accomplished it at the poker table; with stinging regularity, he browbeat Tate into folding whenever they met head-to-head. Oddly enough, a chance presented itself late that afternoon on Tate's deal. The game was stud poker, with two cards dealt. Tate had an ace showing and bet the limit, five dollars. The next man folded, and Starbuck, who had a king on board, immediately raised. The others dropped in turn, and that made it a two-man game. Tate glowered across the table, studying the king for a moment. Then he grunted a coarse laugh.

"Another five says you ain't got 'em wired!"

"Once more," Starbuck observed, peeling off greenbacks. "You stick around and chase another ace and it'll cost you, Tate."

Before Tate could reply, the bunkhouse door opened. Chub Jones stepped through

and walked to the table. There was a peculiar
glint in his eyes, and his mouth was set in a
crooked smile. He looked around the table,
then chuckled and jerked his thumb toward
the door.

"Get your gear and get saddled! We ride
at sundown."

Without a word, the men began gathering
their money, grinning and exchanging quick
glances as they trooped out the door. But
Tate held his seat, glaring at Jones, hands
spread wide on the table.

"Chub, I mean to finish this hand. He's
tryin' to buy it, and I've got him beat!"

"Whose bet?"

"Mine," Tate answered. "He just raised."

Jones took in the cards at a glance. "Then
call him or fold . . . on the cards you got."

"Wait a goddamn—"

"That's it! Play it like it lays, or you don't
play it at all."

"Suits me," Starbuck noted. "Put up or
shut up, huh, Tate?"

"There's your raise!" Tate slammed a bill
on the table and turned his hole card. "Ace
with a ten kicker. Got'cha high-carded!"

"Other way round." Starbuck turned an
ace. "I've got one too . . . with a king kicker."

Tate stared at the cards for a long while,
then shoved his chair aside and lumbered toward the door. At the last moment, he turned,
face wreathed in anger, and scowled at Jones.

"You take him along and you've got mush between your ears! You hear me, Chub?"

"That's up to me, ain't it? You just get saddled and be ready to ride."

Tate stormed out the door, and there was a lengthy silence before Jones looked around. He shook his head, eyeing Starbuck with mild wonder. "You believe in pushin' a man to the wall, don't you?"

"Hell!" Starbuck gave him a brash smile and stood. "You put Tate's brains in a jaybird and the sonovabitch would fly backward."

"Maybe he ain't so bright, but he's mean. You keep on pushin' and he's liable to back-shoot you some night."

"I sleep real light." Starbuck grinned. "Anybody tries that and I'll put a leak in his ticker."

"Yeah, I reckon you would at that."

There was a moment of deliberation while Jones studied him. Then the fat man pursed his lips, thumbs hooked in his belt. "Guess it's time you and me had ourselves a little talk."

"You're the boss."

Jones nodded, went on. "Been watchin' you, and I like the way you handle yourself. Seems to me you'd fit in real well with our operation."

"Funny thing, I had the notion you'd already hired me."

"Let's just say you've been on trial the last week."

"Well, I guess I must've passed muster, huh?"

"So far," Jones agreed. " 'Course, if you're of a mind, you can still walk."

Starbuck shrugged. "Why would I walk?"

"Some men would." Jones paused, watching him carefully. "See, things ain't exactly the way I told you. We're in what some folks might call a risky business."

"Oh, what's that?"

"Stealin' horses."

The words were bluntly spoken, almost a challenge. Starbuck stared at him blank-eyed, aware that his reaction was yet another test. A lightning calculation warned him not to play the fool. At length, with a canny look of regard, he laughed.

"Had a hunch you were stringin' me!"

"That a fact?"

"Yessir, the whole damn time I kept tellin' myself it smelled fishy. That's gospel fact."

"But you stuck around anyway?"

"Say, look here, there's no angel wings waitin' on me!"

"Then you've got no bones about horse-stealin', that it?"

"Not to speak of." Starbuck abruptly turned sober. "Naturally, it'd depend on the dinero. I damn sure wouldn't risk gettin' hung for wages."

"Naturally." Jones appeared to relax. "We split it half for me and even shares for the crew. How's that sound?"

"Beats the buckwheat out of thirty a month and food!"

"Good!" Jones bobbed his head. "Thought I had you pegged right."

"Lucky for me, too, wasn't it?"

"How's that?"

Starbuck lifted one eyebrow. "How far would I've got if I'd walked?"

Jones glanced at the door. His expression was thoughtful, almost as though he were estimating distance. Then he looked around and his jowls widened in a jovially menacing smile.

"I judge about ten feet. What d'you think?"

"Chub, I'm thinkin' it would've been a mighty long walk."

"Yeah, it would've, for a fact—all the way to hell!"

CHAPTER TEN

The plains were still under a darkened sky. A gentle breeze whispered through the night and dim starlight bathed the land in an inky haze. Within sight of the house, the horses grazed in a fenced pasture.

Joe Sixkiller ghosted through the tall grass. His movements were deliberate, all sound cushioned by the lush graze, and he stayed downwind of the horses. His approach was agonizingly slow, but necessary. Working so close to the house, he assumed there were dogs. Even a faint whicker from the horses would set off howling and barking, and ruin an entire night's work. He took his time.

As he neared the herd, Joe Sixkiller grunted deep in his chest and began making horse talk. The horses eyed him warily, but held their ground, listening. He stooped, talking softly all the while, and gathered a handful of clover. Crushing it between his fingers, he rose, careful of making any sudden moves, and extended his hand to a roan gelding. The sweet scent brought the horse closer, until it stood before him, nibbling clover as he lulled it with low, muted grunts. His hand stroked the velvety muzzle. Then he leaned forward and breathed softly into the roan's nostrils. The horse snuffled, eyelids fluttering, thoroughly bewitched. Slowly, with gentle hands, he slipped a hackamore over the gelding's head. Then he turned, holding the halter, and walked away. The roan followed, still in a daze, nuzzling his hand.

Along the western edge of the pasture, a section of wire had been cut and removed. Chub Jones and Sam Tate, both armed with shotguns, were stationed beside the fence posts. As Sixkiller led the roan through the opening, they kept their eyes trained on the ranchhouse. Some distance to the rear, Starbuck waited with Tom Webb and Frank Tucker. Starbuck had been assigned to hold the gang's horses; Tucker and Webb were to hold the rustled stock. By the time Sixkiller reached them, the roan was gentled and calm, offering no trouble. Webb attached a lead rope to the halter, then began soothing the horse in a low voice. Without a word, Sixkiller turned and walked back toward the fence.

Off to one side, Starbuck watched with

mounting respect for Chub Jones. Every man in the gang handled his assignment with practiced skill, and their teamwork was flawless. It was a professional operation, and small wonder that none of the Panhandle ranchers had ever caught Jones and his men in the act. Joe Sixkiller, a renegade half-breed, had descended from generations of Comanche horse thieves. His craft with animals had been handed down from tribal ancients, and he understood the ways of horses to a degree few white men could comprehend. Among his own people, where horse-stealing was considered a form of commerce, he would have been accorded great honor. But while the old days were gone, his wizardry was nonetheless in demand. Chub Jones had given him work, and restored his pride, and it was all very much to the fat man's credit. With Joe Sixkiller, he had built himself an incomparable band of horse thieves.

Yet there was one element of tonight's job that had Starbuck troubled. The ranch being raided was in Kansas—southwest of Dodge— nowhere near the Texas Panhandle. In terms of gathering proof about past raids, it was a complete washout. All the more baffling was how Jones intended to dispose of the stolen horses. Even with altered brands, it would be foolhardy to sell them anywhere in Kansas, most especially in Dodge. The alternative, of course, was to sell them elsewhere. But that led to a guessing game, and Starbuck had no taste for conjecture. He decided to leave it for the moment. Time would tell, and meanwhile, he was spectator to a master horse thief at work.

Joe Sixkiller took less than two hours to complete the job. Altogether, he made ten trips into the pasture, without once spooking the horses. Every animal he selected was a gelding, and in prime condition. As he came through the fence for the last time, Jones and Tate followed him to the rear. After everyone was mounted, with each of the men leading two stolen horses, Jones led them due south across the prairie. By false dawn, they struck the Cimarron and rode west for several miles in midstream. At a junction, where three creeks flowed into the river, Jones chose the southerly stream and continued on for another mile. There, almost at the water's edge, he led them onto an old buffalo trail. Ahead lay a wilderness of blackjack thickets and rolling hills.

Waving the other men on, Jones waited and fell in beside Starbuck. He was grinning, and with an eloquent gesture, he indicated the stolen horses.

"Not bad for a night's work, huh?"

"Slickest thing I've ever seen, and that's no lie."

"Hell, you ain't seen nothin' yet!"

"I don't get you."

"We've just started!" Jones said grandly. "We'll hit four spreads before the week's out and wind up with better'n fifty head. What d'you think of that?"

"Tell you the truth, I think it's damn risky raidin' so close to home."

"Well, don't start lookin' over your shoulder. Nobody'll pick up our tracks . . . not the way we come."

"Maybe not, but where the devil you figure on hidin' fifty head? That's a fair bunch of horses!"

"See that rise?" Jones pointed south. "There's a little valley over there, hills on every side. Natural holding ground, and unless you know where it's at, you wouldn't find it in a hundred years."

Starbuck gave him a puzzled look. "Chub, I'm not exactly dense, but I must've missed something. So you stole fifty head—and managed to hide 'em—what the hell you aim to do with 'em? We sure as Christ can't trail 'em back to Kansas!"

Jones smiled. "All in good time. There's ways and there's ways, and, like I said . . . you ain't seen nothin' yet."

"By God, it must be a beaut! It surely must!"

"Pop your eyes out, Luke. Pop 'em clean out of your head!"

Jones laughed and gigged his horse. Several minutes later, once more at the head of

the column, he topped the hill and led them
into the valley.

Over the next fortnight Starbuck grew increasingly bewildered. After the fourth raid
in southern Kansas, the gang had assembled
a herd of fifty-two stolen horses. A couple of
days were spent in camp, with the men loafing about while the horses grazed across the
small valley. Then Jones ordered camp broken one morning at dawn, and the horses
were gathered in a trail herd. He led them
west, along the Beaver River, into a forgotten
land.

No Man's Land.

To Starbuck, it was an unexpected and per-
plexing turn of events. He kept thinking back
to his conversation with Ben Echhardt, the
livestock dealer. Echhardt had told him Chub
Jones always traded in Dodge City, where
cow ponies commanded top price. Then too,
Echhardt had indicated that Jones was regular
as clockwork, trailing a herd into town once
a month, every month. Yet Jones was headed
away from Dodge!

In one way, of course, it made perfect
sense. Starbuck had suspected all along that
these particular horses would never be sold
in Kansas. The risk was simply too great. On
the other hand, the alternative made no sense
whatever. Echhardt had mentioned that Jones
traded for horses in New Mexico, and the

Beaver River led in that direction. But why
would he trail horses to New Mexico and
trade them there for another herd? To come
out on the deal, he would have to trail the
new herd all the way back to Dodge. Considering the time and effort involved—not to
mention a butt-busting ride of almost a thousand miles—it was a rough way to make a
few extra bucks. Since the original herd was
stolen, it was all clear profit, anyway. Why
not go ahead and sell them in New Mexico?
Why not indeed!

There seemed no reasonable answer. It was
like a puzzle with pieces missing, somehow
incomplete. Echhardt's statements in no way
squared with Jones's actions, yet Starbuck
never for an instant believed their destination
was New Mexico. That being the case, he
was drawn inevitably to a dread, and even
more astounding, conclusion. Chub Jones
had been aiming all along for No Man's
Land.

Starbuck's misgivings were wholly justified. No Man's Land literally belonged to no
one. Through a maze of obscure treaties, it
was an expanse of raw wilderness forgotten
by God and government alike. Separated by
Texas and Kansas for a depth of some thirty-
five miles, it extended in a narrow strip
nearly two hundred miles long. Indian Territory marked its eastern boundary, and its
western reaches touched the borders of Col-

orado and New Mexico. In time, this remote
and lawless land had become a sanctuary for
killers and renegades of every stripe. Not
even U.S. Marshals dared venture into the
outlaw stronghold, and in a very real sense,
it was a place where Judge Colt ruled supreme. A man on the dodge could find no
safer haven, and those who rode the owlhoot
retreated there with no fear of pursuit. Yet it
was a land to be avoided, for it was a land
where predators preyed on their own kind. A
land where none survived without a finely
whetted instinct for the jugular.

For three days now, Jones had led them
ever deeper into the wilds of No Man's Land.
Dawn of the fourth day found them camped
at the headwaters of a tributary running
northwest from the Beaver. Starbuck estimated they were within a day's ride of the
New Mexico border. But the last leg of their
journey had proved his hunch correct. New
Mexico lay due west, and the course Jones
had set angled away, toward a point where
the Cimarron River joined No Man's Land to
Colorado. While they were breaking camp, it
occurred to him that Ben Langham's spread
lay on a beeline scarcely a hundred miles to
the southeast. By now, he told himself, Langham had probably given him up for dead. Almost ten weeks had passed since he rode out,
and in many ways it seemed longer, more
like a lifetime. As he saddled his horse,

glancing around at Jones and Tate and the others, he had a sudden urge to see the LX, to sleep a whole night without one eye open and his nerves on edge. Instead, he mounted and took a position on the flank as the gang hazed the horses toward the Cimarron.

Sometime around noon, Starbuck sensed a change in the men. At first, he thought his mind was playing tricks on him; then he listened closer and knew there was no mistake. A bantering tone had entered their voices, and Jones was even trading barbed quips with Sam Tate. He hadn't the faintest notion as to what prompted the change, but it grew more apparent by the minute. They were laughing and joking, swapping jibes, suddenly frisky as a bunch of colts.

Then they topped a low rise and Chub Jones's prediction almost came true. Starbuck hauled up hard on the reins, slid to a halt. His jaw dropped open and his eyes went round as buttons. Struck speechless, he simply sat and stared.

A creek meandered through a stretch of grassland on the prairie below. Willowy cottonwoods lined the stream, and tendrils of smoke drifted skyward through the trees. At a quick glance, Starbuck estimated there were upward of twenty men camped beneath the cottonwoods. But it was the horses that transfixed him. There were three herds, guarded closely by outriders and bunched separately across the prairie. A nose count was unnecessary.

All three herds were uniform in size, each numbering at least fifty head. By no mere coincidence, it was almost the exact number being trailed into camp by Chub Jones. Starbuck suddenly grasped the meaning, and his jaw dropped a notch lower.

He was gazing upon a trade fair of horse thieves.

CHAPTER ELEVEN

"Luke, this here's Monty Hall."

"Howdy."

Hall ignored them. He sat, puffing on his pipe, propped up against the base of a cottonwood. The other men merely watched, their eyes flicking from Chub Jones to Hall. Upon entering camp, Jones had been greeted with catcalls and crude humor from the outlaws. Waving them off, he'd laughed and shaken hands with a couple of men. But while Starbuck was at his side, he hadn't introduced anyone until they stopped before Monty Hall. Now, with an air of suppressed amusement, the men waited as the silence stretched and Hall continued to puff his pipe. Jones shifted to the other foot.

"Goddamn, Monty, you ain't being very sociable."

"Hey, lardass!" one of the men called.

"Pucker up and give him a big kiss. Maybe that'll help."

"Yeah, Chub!" another yelled. "Sweet-talk the ole fart! Tell him you're sorry and it won't never happen again."

Starbuck was still in a mild state of shock. His expression betrayed nothing, but he was growing more confused by the moment. The men were a rough lot, and despite their noisy vitality, he knew he'd stumbled upon a pack of hardcases and killers. Yet he couldn't figure Monty Hall. On the sundown side of fifty, Hall was a boozy husk of a man. He was toothless, with rheumy eyes and the constipated look of an oldster past his prime. He seemed totally out of place among these men—a lame dog running with hungry wolves.

Nor could Starbuck figure Jones. The fat man appeared sheepish, almost apologetic. Which was not only damned strange, but curiously out of character. At length, shifting from foot to foot, Jones sighed heavily.

"C'mon now, Monty! You got no call to stiff me that way."

"Humph!" Hall fixed him with a waspish look. "Took yore own sweet time gettin' here, didn't you?"

"Hell, we ain't all that—"

"Says you! Damn me if you ain't the last one ever' time, ever' goddamn time!"

"Look here, Monty, you know good and

well we got a one-day leeway. Always have
had!"

"Save yore breath and just tell me how
many horses you got."

"Fifty-two head, on the button."

"Jumpin' Jesus! It'll take me till dark to
get you done."

"Well, we'll get a quick bite—"

"Pot's empty!" Hall gestured at the cooking fires with his pipe. "You'll just have to
wait till supper."

"Hold it right—"

"Godalmightybingo! You act like you forgot what'll happen if we ain't done by mornin'!"

Jones frowned. "No, I ain't forgot."

"Then I'd advise you to get the lead outta
yore ass. Nuff said?"

The rebuff brought a chorus of laughter
from the watching men. Jones turned away,
muttering to himself, and walked toward the
edge of the trees. Starbuck followed along, now
thoroughly confounded. When they reached
the picket line, where their horses were tied, he
ducked his chin back at the camp.

"Who the hell's that old coot, anyway?"

"Best goddamn brand artist there is, that's
who!"

"Does good work, does he?"

"If he didn't, I would've shot him a long
time ago. Shot him deader'n hell!"

Jones mounted and rode off. Some distance away the rest of the gang had milled the stolen horses, holding them on a stretch of prairie. Starbuck swung aboard his gelding and reined sharply around, smiling to himself. The day suddenly seemed filled with promise.

Monty Hall was in a class all by himself. Starbuck realized that the moment they led the first horse to the branding fire. Thick stakes were driven into the ground several feet apart, and laid out beside the fire were lengths of heavy-gauge wire and a lip twist. A wooden bucket, with a rag dauber fastened to a stick, was positioned away from the heat of the fire. After studying the horse's brand— Bar S—Hall selected a piece of wire. His hands worked the metal the way a sculptor fashions clay; with a twist here and a curl there, he shaped one end of the wire into a graceful, but oddly patterned, design. A quick measurement against the old brand apparently satisfied him, and he gave the signal.

The horse was thrown and the men swarmed over him. Within seconds, his legs, front and rear, were lashed to the stakes. Tate held his head eared down, while Webb and Tucker kept his hindquarters from thrashing. Then Sixkiller stepped in with the twist. He attached the rope loop to the horse's lower lip, then began turning the handle like a tourniquet. The pain, intensifying with every turn, quickly distracted the horse from all else.

Hall pulled the length of wire, now cherry-red, out of the fire and stepped forward. With a critical eye, he positioned the wire and laid it over the old brand. The smell of burnt hair and scorched flesh filled the air, and an instant later he moved back, inspecting his handiwork. As if by magic, a simple S had been transformed into an ⟨brand mark⟩.

Grunting to himself, Hall laid the wire aside and collected the bucket. He stirred the contents, which appeared thick as axle grease and had the faint odor of liniment, then returned to the horse. With a quick stroke of the dauber, he spread a dark, pasty layer across the new brand. Finished, he nodded to the men, and walked away. The entire operation had taken less than five minutes.

Off to one side, Jones and Starbuck had watched quietly. There was no second chance when altering a brand, and Jones wanted him to observe a while before lending a hand. As the horse was released, and choused back to the herd, another was being roped and led toward the fire. Jones smiled and nudged him in the ribs with an elbow.

"What'd I tell you? Just blink your eyes and the old bastard's done give us a perfect Anchor Eight!"

"Damned if he didn't!" Starbuck shook his

head in wonder. "That's some trick with the wire. Only way I ever saw it done was with a runnin' iron."

"Hell, I told you he's an artist! All the time I been at this business, I've never had nobody question his work. Goddamn horses look like they was foaled with a brand!"

"What's that dope he uses, the stuff in the bucket?"

"Secret recipe," Jones chuckled. "Sonova-bitch won't tell nobody the mix! But it's pure magic, and that ain't no bullshit. Heals the brand in a couple of days, and Christ Hisself couldn't tell it'd ever been touched."

Starbuck nodded, kept his voice casual. "Guess that's a real comfort when it comes time to sell 'em."

"Luke, I thought you was swifter'n that. Ain't you caught on yet?"

"Caught on to what?"

"Why, Christ A'mighty, we ain't gonna sell the same horses we stole! We're gonna switch with these other fellers."

"Switch herds?" Starbuck frowned, thoughtful a moment. "What's the idea, you draw straws, do you . . . to see who goes where?"

"Naw, hell!" Jones groaned. "It ain't that simple. You pay attention now, and lemme explain how it works."

The operation, according to Jones, was similar to a game of checkers. Several dozen livestock dealers, spread throughout four states, represented the squares on the board. Once a month, the gangs met with horses stolen from Kansas and Colorado, New Mexico and Texas. After the brands were altered, the herds were switched, but always in a rotating order. In that manner, horses stolen in Kansas were never sold in Colorado twice in a row; with four gangs, operating out of four states, there was a constant mix of rustled stock. To muddy the water further, the order of the raids was also rotated. A gang raided within its own territory every fourth time out, and as a result, local ranchers could never establish any pattern to the raids. Seemingly, the rustlers struck at random, always from a different direction. Yet it was all very methodical, and virtually impossible to defend against.

Warming to the subject, Jones next explained how the checkers game was played out. Upon leaving No Man's Land, each gang was trailing livestock stolen from another state. Upon arriving home, the horses were then split into smaller herds, generally numbering ten head or less. Afterward, these herds were sold to livestock dealers over a widespread area. There were never enough horses in any given bunch to arouse suspicion, and as an added precaution, each of the small herds contained a mix of altered brands. To all appearances, the stock had been acquired by an itinerant horse trader who operated on a shoestring and bought only a few head at a time. In the end, the original four herds, numbering more than two hundred horses, had been split into nearly thirty small bunches and sold across the breadth of four states. The checkerboard effect was complete.

By its very complexity, their method of operation virtually eliminated any chance of being detected. With cow ponies in demand, and livestock dealers crooked as a barrel of snakes, there were no questions asked.

"Hell, it's foolproof!" Jones concluded. "Not one chance in a thousand of gettin' caught."

"You know something, Chub? I'd say the odds were better than that, lots better."

"Told you it'd pop the eyes clean out of your head, didn't I?"

"Yeah, and you weren't lyin', either. I thought I'd seen 'em all, but this one wins hands down."

"Guess you're sort of glad you tied in with us, ain't you?"

"Chub, I wouldn't have missed it for the world. That's a mortal fact!"

Late that night, Starbuck lay in his bedroll, staring at the sky. Several of the outlaws were still gathered around the campfire, playing cards and spinning windy tales. Off by themselves, Chub Jones and three men were huddled around a bottle of whiskey, talking in low tones. To Starbuck, they had the look of generals hatching a battle plan, and he knew it wasn't far from the mark. Earlier in the evening, by listening more than he talked, he'd learned that the men commanded the other three gangs. He assumed, though it was sheer speculation, that plans were now being laid for the next rendezvous in No Man's Land.

Yet all speculation ceased there. He was certain, beyond any vestige of doubt, that Jones and his three cohorts were merely gang leaders. Not the ringleader!

Since noon, Starbuck had sustained one shock after another. There was scarcely any need to conceal his surprise, for Jones had been at some pains to impress him with the magnitude of the operation. But in the process, however unwittingly, Jones had also convinced him of something else. The operation was a marvel of planning and coordination. Even the logistics of it—moving hundreds of horses back and forth throughout four states—fairly boggled the mind. Someone with a genius for organization had brought the concept and the men together. And only because that same genius guided the operation could it have functioned so smoothly, with no hint of its existence, for so long. All of that took brains and audacity,

a type of vision not found among ordinary
men. Which eliminated Jones and the other
gang leaders.

At first, upon riding into camp, Starbuck
had been flabbergasted by the sight of so
many outlaws and stolen horses gathered together in one spot. Yet it was a chance remark from Monty Hall—a remark that
visibly rattled Chub Jones—which had left
him thoroughly stumped.

*You act like you forgot what'll happen if
we ain't done by mornin'!*

Jones's troubled reaction was no longer a
mystery. Simple observation, combined with
all he'd learned, had given Starbuck the last
piece to the puzzle. Every outlaw in camp,
Jones included, was a hired hand. Somehow,
in a way not yet revealed, the entire operation
was directed from a distance. By a mastermind of some sort! A man with cunning
enough to stay clear until the dirty work was
done. A man who took no chances and still
managed to walk away with all the marbles.

A man everyone in camp expected tomorrow morning.

CHAPTER TWELVE

A red ball of fire slowly rimmed the horizon. Since dawn, when the men were rousted out of their blankets, the camp had swarmed with activity. A hearty meal was wolfed down—bacon, biscuits and beans, with strong black coffee—which indicated a hard day's ride lay ahead. Then the bedrolls and camp gear were stowed away, and the cooking fires doused. Afterward, the men began drifting toward the picket line, and now, at the crack of sunrise, everyone was busily engaged saddling horses. Camp was struck, and the outlaws were preparing to ride.

Starbuck had spent a restless night. Long before dawn he was awake and alert, waiting. By all logic, he told himself, today had to be the day. Before the sun was high, the gangs would have scattered to the winds, not to regroup for another month. Whoever ran this

outfit—the mastermind—wasn't fool enough
to allow the likes of Chub Jones to operate
without orders and guidance. Then too, there
was the money. Somehow the loot had to be
split, and there was no safer spot than a remote creek in the wilds of No Man's Land.
Considering the amount of money involved,
it seemed unlikely the four gang leaders
would be trusted to deliver it in another manner. A personal accounting was the only way
that made sense, and that meant here and
now, today. Apart from the logic of it, there
was a gut instinct that wasn't to be discounted. For all the scurry and rush, a sense
of waiting hung over the camp. Someone was
expected.

Yet, as Starbuck threw a saddle blanket
across his horse, he began to have second
thoughts. Unless that *someone* appeared
pretty damn quick, everyone else would be
gone. By the look of things, it was only a
matter of minutes before the men would be
ordered to mount. Allow another five
minutes—ten at the outside—to get the herds
on the trail, and that would end it. So it had
to happen soon, or it wouldn't happen at all.
Which meant his fancy theory would prove
to be so much whiffledust.

Goddamn!

Turning to gather his saddle, Starbuck bent
down, one hand on the cantle, the other
grasping the horn. Then he halted, listening,

struck by an almost oppressive silence. All talk among the men, the early morning grumbling and cursing, abruptly ceased. The jangle and creak of saddle gear went still, and a deadened lull fell over the camp. Out of the corner of his eyes, he caught a flicker of movement, and as he turned, Chub Jones and the other gang leaders hurried back to the campsite. Looking past them, he spotted a horse and rider, coming on at a walk through the cottonwoods. He smiled, nodded once to himself.

The horse was a steel-dust gelding, bright as ivory in the morning sun. The rider wore a slouch hat, features indistinguishable at a distance, and sat his mount as though he'd been frozen in place and nailed to the saddle. Still at a walk, he rode into the campsite and stepped down. Jones and the others were waiting, and he shook hands all around. There was a moment of conversation, with all the men along the picket line watching. Then the three gang leaders turned away, moving swiftly in the direction of their horses. Jones hung back talking earnestly in a low voice, but the stranger interrupted him with an abrupt gesture. Bobbing his head, Jones smiled and moved off a couple of steps, looking toward the picket line. He lifted his hand, motioning, and yelled out in a commanding tone.

"Hey, there . . . one of you boys . . . Luke!

Grab my saddlebags! Get 'em up here, and make it quick!"

Starbuck walked down the line to Jones's horse and collected the saddlebags. The weight in no way surprised him, and he slung them over his shoulder. Then he sauntered off, taking his time, aware that he had the attention of everyone in camp. Common gang members, it seemed, were rarely summoned into the presence of the top dog. He determined to make the most of the opportunity.

As he drew closer, a sudden chill settled over him, left a residue of uneasiness. All his life he'd lived by hunches, and the icy feeling along his spine told him he was looking into the face of death itself. The man beside Jones was tall and strongly built, with a huge head and craggy features and a mouth like the slit of a razor. There was no sign of warmth in his wide, dour face, and the fearsome impact was lessened not at all by the menace in his eyes. Almost chalk-blue, his eyes touched quickly, seemed to leave a man stripped and vulnerable, his secrets laid bare. It was an odd sensation, spooky.

Starbuck halted, unslung the saddlebags from his shoulder. Jones snatched them out of his hand and waved him off, on the verge of turning away. But he held his ground, hopeful of forcing an introduction, and Jones dismissed him with a curt nod.

"That's all, Luke. Thanks."

"Who we got here, Chub?" The pale eyes fixed on Starbuck. "Thought I knew all your men."

"Hell, I'm sorry, Dutch! Clean forgot you two hadn't met."

Jones beamed like a trained bear. "This here's Luke Starbuck. Luke, meet the boss, Dutch Henry Horn."

"Howdy." Starbuck extended his hand. "Pleased to meet you, Mr. Horn."

Horn ignored the hand. "How long you been with Chub?"

"Couple of weeks, maybe a little longer."

"Closer to three," Jones noted quickly. "Good man, Dutch! Took to it like a duck to water."

Horn gave him a short look. "Your memory must be slippin', Chub. Near as I recall, we agreed not to hire any new men."

There was a quiet undercurrent of authority to his words. Jones fidgeted a moment, eyes averted, then offered a lame smile.

"Yeah, you're right, Dutch. Hundred percent right! But men like Luke don't come along ever' day." Jones paused, got no response, then rapidly went on. "I'm tellin' you straight, Dutch. No whichaway about it! He's double wolf on guts and got lots of horse savvy too."

"How so?"

"Well, for one thing, he's a wrangler. Got

a natural-born gift with horses, and that ain't no lie."

"What else?"

"He's tough, Dutch. Tougher'n boiled owl!" Jones laughed a nervous laugh. "Goddamn, I wish you could've seen it! Him and Sam Tate got into it, and he come unwound like a buzzsaw. Laid ol' Sam out colder'n a wedge!"

"Figures," Horn observed. "You never could handle Tate, could you?"

"Awww c'mon, Dutch, it ain't that. I just know a good man when I spot one. Hell, you oughta see him with a gun. Talk about sudden!"

"That good, huh?"

"Good as I ever seen," Jones assured him. "Plenty cool, too! Got no more nerves than an undertaker."

"What about it, Starbuck?" Horn looked him over in a mild, abstracted way. "You piss ice water, do you?"

Starbuck regarded him with a level gaze. "I generally manage . . . one way or another."

"Why don't you tell me about it?"

"What's to tell?"

"Pick a peg and go from there. Just for starters, how'd you get so handy with a gun?"

"Shootin' people."

"No bones about it, huh?"

"I sleep pretty good."

"How many men you reckon you've shot?"

"Not includin' Mex and Injuns?"

"Why, do you kill one different than another?"

"No, I guess not. Any man that's worth shootin' is worth killin'."

"Regular widow-maker, aren't you?"

"I never pulled on a man that wasn't askin' for it."

"Seems like lots of folks must've rubbed your fur the wrong way."

"I don't get you."

"Well, Chub says you're a wrangler by trade."

"Yeah?"

"So how come a wrangler's been puttin' leaks in all them people?"

Starbuck smiled. "I suppose that depends on who he's ridin' for."

"You ride for anybody I ever heard of?"

"Cap'n King, mostly. Down on the Rio Grande."

"When he hires the man, he hires the man's gun, that it?"

"Let's just say workin' on the border's not for greenhorns."

"You talkin' about *bandidos*?"

"White or Mex, I guess horse thieves and rustlers all pretty much fit the same pigeon-hole."

"You've killed your share, I take it?"

"Enough."

"Doesn't bother you, then . . . switchin' sides?"

"Chub says stealin' horses pays good. All I ever got the other way was a sore butt and holes in my pockets."

"Sounds reasonable." Horn suddenly riveted him with a stare. "How'd you come to drift so far north?"

"Got a case of itchy feet." Starbuck hesitated a moment, then shrugged. "Got fired off a trail drive, too. Had a little trouble with the ramrod."

"Killed him?"

"No, just busted him up pretty bad."

"Let's see, the King spread? That'd be the Broken Arrow R, wouldn't it?"

"Ere Flecha," Starbuck corrected him. "The Cap'n always brands with the arrow straight through the letter. Goddamn near impossible to monkey with it."

"So I've heard."

"Yeah, every now and then some dimdot takes a stab at it. But most of the stock he loses gets sold off down in Old Mexico."

The shadow of a question touched Horn's eyes, then moved on. He nodded with chill dignity.

"I think Chub's right. You've got the makings of a first-class horse thief."

"Don't worry, I'll hold up my end, Mr. Horn."

"See that you do," Horn remarked. "Now, if you don't mind, me and the boys have got a little business to wrap up."

Starbuck turned and saw the other gang leaders waiting several paces away. Chub Jones gave him a hidden wink, and with a brief nod in Horn's direction, he walked off toward the picket line. For the first time, he realized his hands were clammy and a trickle of sweat was running down his backbone. Suddenly he understood why there was an odor of fear about Jones and the other gang leaders.

Dutch Henry Horn was a slick piece of work!

Glancing back, he saw that someone had thrown a saddle blanket on the ground. The men were kneeling down, transferring money from their saddlebags to the blanket, while Horn looked on without expression. Starbuck pondered the name a moment, then decided it was an alias. The "Dutch" part was fitting enough, for the man clearly had German blood in him. Stolid and cold, with a merciless set to his jaw and no trace of compassion in his manner. But the name was too easily bandied about to be real. On the other hand, he was one tricky gent. So perhaps it was the straight goods, after all. Wherever he called home—and where the hell was that?—perhaps he went by an alias there. It was a toss-up, and a whole new puzzle to be considered with care.

One thing, though, was certain. To run Dutch Henry Horn to earth would be no simple task. The interrogation just completed was merely a sample of the man's quick wits and guile. The trap he'd laid about the King Ranch brand had been a lulu. It was smooth as butter and cleverly staged, the work of a man who was one step ahead at every turn. All the more apparent, it indicated the extreme caution he employed in every phase of the operation. His tracks were well covered, there could be no doubt of that. Even the way he'd ridden in at sunrise—after very likely watching the camp all night—showed a foxlike cunning that commanded respect. To track him down and take him off guard was probably an option not even worth considering. But if not that . . . then what?

Chub Jones and his gang presented no great problem. There were several ways they could be nailed and put out of action. The most expedient, of course, was simply to notify the Panhandle ranchers and take Jones unaware at his home base. As for the other gangs, Starbuck already had a glimmer of an idea. It would require planning and stealth, and a rather healthy dose of luck. Nonetheless, it had promise, and given time to arrange the details, he thought it might very well work. But the ringleader himself was another ball of wax entirely. So far as he could determine, the man never left anything to chance. All the pitfalls had been anticipated and eliminated, and that posed a bitch-kitty of a question. A real headscratcher.

How the hell to sucker Dutch Henry Horn?

CHAPTER THIRTEEN

A week later the gang fanned out across Kansas. Chub Jones, accompanied by Starbuck and Tate, drove twelve head into Dodge City. The balance of the herd, trailed farther north by the other men, would be split and sold to livestock dealers in towns along the Smoky Hill River. Everyone was to meet back at the ranch within ten days.

At that time, with the herd sold and a final tally on the proceeds, the men would be paid. In conversation along the trail, Jones estimated Starbuck's share would exceed two hundred fifty dollars. The figure was roughly ten times the monthly wage of a cowhand, and it underscored the point that horse-stealing paid very well, indeed. By simple calculation, Starbuck estimated in turn that Jones's share would reach upward of twelve hundred dollars. Carried a step further, it appeared Dutch Henry Horn would clear double that amount. With four gangs in operation, the ringleader's overall monthly take jumped to ten thousand dollars or more.

To Starbuck, it was a staggering figure. There were scores of cattlemen who seldom cleared that much in a year. One of them was his boss, Ben Langham.

Yet the amount of money involved was merely an offshoot of the central problem. All the way into Dodge, Starbuck had pondered his next step. Slowly, it had become apparent that he would have to risk everything on a single stroke. There was no practical way to separate the four gangs and eliminate them piecemeal. Nor was it reasonable to believe Dutch Henry Horn could be hunted down and taken by himself. Even now, after puzzling on it for a week, Starbuck was still at a loss as to how he might uncover further information about Horn. The man's name had never once been mentioned; it was almost as though the gang members were leery of raising the topic. So any questions directed to Jones—however tactfully couched—would immediately arouse suspicion . . . which was a danger he simply couldn't chance, not at this point.

All things considered, then, he had no choice. The only workable plan was to lay a trap in No Man's Land. To somehow surprise all four gangs—and Dutch Henry Horn—at next month's rendezvous. It was a bold gamble, but one dictated by the odds. An all-or-nothing proposition, with secrecy the key element. An ambush of sorts.

Having settled on a plan, Starbuck was now confronted with more immediate problems. Approaching Dodge, he was reminded that he had to avoid Ben Echhardt, or risk being exposed. Not quite a month ago, he had obtained Jones's name from the livestock dealer; if he suddenly appeared with Jones and a string of horses, Echhardt was certain to make the connection. Any comment, no matter how casual, would alert Jones and lead to questions about his previous meeting with Echhardt. Questions that would inevitably tip his hand.

To complicate matters further, there was the problem of getting a message to Ben Langham. A letter wouldn't do the job; the nearest post office was three days' ride from the ranch, and all mail was collected on monthly supply trips to town. Yet, somehow, Langham and the other Panhandle ranchers had to be advised of the situation. Only then could they organize, and stand prepared to meet him, in secret, at some designated spot in No Man's Land. The problem, then, was one of hiring someone to act as courier. Someone not only trustworthy, but with experience enough to chart a course across open plains. It was a large order, a matter to be approached quietly, without haste.

On the outskirts of Dodge, Starbuck decided he had to get free of Jones and Tate. He needed time to locate a courier—which would require discreet inquiry—and he also couldn't chance an encounter with Echhardt. All the way around, it was necessary that he shed his companions, for at least a couple of hours. After mulling it over, he concluded the best way was the simplest way. As they circled eastward, toward Echhardt's stock pen, he rode up alongside Jones. With a wave of his hand, he indicated the horses.

"Now that we got 'em here, you don't need me anymore, do you?"

"What d'you mean?"

"Well, I just figured you and Tate could handle it from here."

"We ain't got 'em sold yet!" Jones grumbled. "Don't you wanna see how I dicker for top dollar?"

"Say, listen, I've got faith in you, Chub! Whatever suits you is fair by me."

"Seems like you'd take a little more interest in things. What the hell's your rush, anyway?"

"Oh, let's just say I'm green and full of sap."

Jones frowned. "You ain't talkin' about women, are you?"

"Chub, I haven't been thinkin' about nothing else for the last twenty miles."

"Maybe so, but we're here on business. Time enough for dippin' your wick later."

"Later might be too late! Come sundown, the South Side'll be crawlin' with cowhands."

"So what?"

"So I met this gal last time I was in Dodge. She's a regular wildcat, and if you don't get her early, you don't get her at all."

"Goddamn, you must have some case of stiff pecker."

Starbuck laughed. "Tell you the truth, it's a wonder I made it this far. I'm so horny I'm liable to swell up and burst!"

"Where's this gal of yours hang out?"

"The Comique."

Jones hesitated, finally nodded. "Awright, go ahead and take off. I'll meet you there when I'm done at Echhardt's."

"Chub, you're a real sport. First drink's on me!"

Starbuck gigged his horse and rode off toward the South Side. Jones watched him a moment, then shook his head and glanced around. On the opposite side of the herd, Sam Tate quickly looked away, his mouth set in a dark scowl.

Lisa spotted him the instant he came through the door. She laughed and clapped her hands like an exuberant child. Hurrying forward, she fended off a group of Texans

seated at a table and rushed to meet him. Her
cheeks were flushed and she took his hands,
eyes bright with excitement.

"Luke, you kept your promise!"

"Told you I was a man of my word."

"I know"—her breasts rose and fell with a
sigh—"but you've been gone so long I almost gave you up for lost."

"Well, it took a little longer than I figured.
Went into business with a couple of horse
traders."

"And I'll bet you made scads and scads of
money."

"Enough to keep you all to myself for the
night."

"Oh good!" She hugged him and slipped
her arm around his waist. "I was hoping
you'd say that."

Starbuck gave her a squeeze, and signaled
a passing waiter. "A bottle of bubbly for the
lady! And make it quick!"

Lisa led him to a table at the rear of the
room. The saloon was in the midst of an afternoon lull, and they had a corner to themselves. After the champagne was served, and
they had toasted his return, she began plying
him with questions. Her curiosity was genuine, seemingly limitless, and she wanted to
know everything about his business affairs.
Starbuck found it necessary to shade the
truth, but he nonetheless told a convincing
tale of wandering the western territories in

search of horses. All the while, with one arm draped around her chair, he was aware of her hand resting lightly on his leg and the touch of her knee. Finally, when he'd answered all her questions, there was a moment's silence. She took a sip of champagne, eyelashes lowered, then glanced at him over the rim of her glass.

"I guess you won't be staying long?"

"Longer than last time." Starbuck watched her eyes. "Couple of nights, anyway."

She held his gaze. "I hear the hotel's pretty crowded."

"Tell you the truth, I was hopin' to get a better offer."

"Oh?"

"Thought maybe you could put me up . . . if it's no bother."

"You mean it, Luke? Honestly?"

"Bet your bottom dollar! I'll even square it with your boss, make it worth his while. How's that sound?"

She squealed and hugged him around the neck.

"Oooo, Sugar, it sounds marvelous! Sweet enough to eat!"

Starbuck detected a note of vulnerability in her voice. It was a cry of loneliness, even more apparent than when he'd seen her last, and he suspected it stemmed from her work. Every night was like the night before, with rough-mannered cowhands squeezing

and pawing, exacting their drunken demands
for the price of a drink. A saloon girl's life
was hard and vulgar, and for those like Lisa,
the sensitive ones, it was a bleak existence.
Any act of kindness, the slightest consideration, touched deeply and left its imprint. The
moment and the man were a bright memory,
never forgotten.

Yet, however genuine his own feelings,
Starbuck was toying with a new idea. Upon
entering the Comique, he'd meant to have a
quick drink and then get on about his business. All that was changed by the warmth of
her greeting and the look in her eyes. He
sensed he could trust her—he knew it with
gut certainty—and a sudden thought flashed
through his mind. There were few secrets in
a town the size of Dodge, and his inquiry
regarding a courier was certain to raise speculation. By far, it would be better to enlist a
go-between and keep his name out of it altogether. Lisa seemed to him the perfect con-
federate, all the more so because of their
personal arrangement. With her as a buffer,
his chances were vastly improved, and any
qualms he'd had at first were now dispelled.
He was convinced she wouldn't betray him.

All that remained was to sound her out.
But there was time for that later, when they
were alone. For now, he would enjoy himself
and continue ordering champagne and per-
suading everyone he was out to paint the

town red. It fit perfectly with the yarn he'd
fed Chub Jones, and so far as Lisa was concerned, no pretense was needed. He remembered the last time, and perhaps fresher still
was the surprise he'd felt afterward. He had
missed her.

An hour or so later, Jones and Sam Tate
entered the Comique. Walking to the rear of
the saloon, they found Starbuck in a mellow
mood and Lisa giggly, well into their second
bottle of champagne. After a round of intro-
ductions, Jones and Tate seated themselves at
the table. Starbuck was expansive, calling for
extra glasses, but the men declined, ordering
whiskey, instead.

"By golly, Luke!" Jones cocked one eye at
the champagne bottle. "You believe in whole
hog or nothin', don't you?"

"Easy come, easy go, Chub. Wine,
women"—Starbuck waved toward the brass
band on the balcony—"and song! Told you
I meant to tie one on!"

"You weren't kiddin', either." Jones lifted
his whiskey glass to the girl. " 'Specially
about your lady friend! She's a real looker,
and then some."

Lisa dimpled. "Why, thank you, Mr.
Jones."

"My friends call me Chub."

"Like hell!" Starbuck laughed. "Some of

the things they call you aren't fit for a cat to hear."

Jones wagged his head. "Luke, you oughta get pickled more often. Brings out your sense of humor, does for a fact! Ain't that right, Sam?"

Sam Tate flicked a baleful glance at Starbuck. Within him the effects of the bunkhouse whipping had smoldered for nearly a month, shadowing his every thought. He feared Jones was slowly easing him out as second-in-command of the gang. Far worse, he feared the man who had humiliated him was being groomed to take his place. Now, with his face set in an oxlike expression, he downed his whiskey neat and placed the glass on the table. His gaze shifted to Lisa.

"How 'bout you and me havin' a dance?"

There was a strained silence, then Starbuck smiled. "Sam, I'm afraid you'll have to look elsewhere. She's taken for the night . . . all of it."

"Says you!" Tate grunted. "She works here, don't she?"

"Yeah, she works here all right. No dispute on that score."

"Well, I reckon you'd better just climb down off your high horse, then. 'Cause that means she's gotta dance with any sonovabitch that asks her!"

"Wrong." Starbuck fixed him with a gallows grin. "The only sonovabitch she's got to dance with is the one that gets past me. You feelin' nervy enough to try?"

"I might be!" Tate replied hotly. "You got lucky once, but I figure I can still take the kinks outta your tail!"

"No, you figure I'm drunk enough that you might just get lucky. That's more like it, isn't it?"

"Drunk or sober, you can still be took!"

"Don't bet your life on it," Starbuck told him. "Or if you do, take a deep breath! It'll have to last a long time."

A moment elapsed while the two men stared at one another. Tate's face went ocherous, and little knots bunched tight along his jawbone. Suddenly he stood, kicking his chair away, and walked toward the bar. Lisa let out her breath, and Starbuck smiled, patting her hand.

"Goddamn!" Jones chuckled. "Looked like he had a mouthful of hornets and couldn't find a place to spit!"

"I don't know, Chub," Starbuck said amiably. "Since he's all mouth, he'd be spittin' the rest of his life."

Jones pounded the table, laughing so hard his jowls quivered. Starbuck poured champagne, looking immensely pleased with himself, and Lisa gave him a wan smile. She took the glass, holding it in both hands while she sipped, and her eyes went across the table to Jones. Her smile slowly faded.

*   *   *

Starbuck closed the door to her room and turned the key. It was past midnight, and his head buzzed from the effects of too much champagne. But he was reasonably sober, still quite aware that he had to talk with the girl. Wondering on the best approach, it suddenly occurred to him that the morning might be better. She was no slouch with champagne herself, and it was vital that she have a clear head before they talked. He decided to let it wait until morning.

When he turned, Lisa was standing beside the window. In profile, she appeared distracted, staring without expression into the darkness. He crossed the room, halting behind her, and placed his hands on her shoulders. She lowered her head, nuzzling his hand with her cheek, but continued staring out the window. Her manner left him bemused, and after a long silence, he leaned closer.

"Something wrong?"

She kissed his hand, kept her eyes averted. "Luke, are you in trouble . . . with the law?"

"Where'd you get an idea like that?"

"Your friend—Jones—he's no horse trader."

"What makes you think so?"

"I've seen his kind before, lots of them."

"Sounds like female intuition to me."

"Maybe." She turned, her eyes darkly intense. "But it's true, isn't it?"

"And if it was . . . what then?"

"Oh Luke—damnit!—it's you! Can't you see that? I don't care who you are or what you've done or anything else! It's your friends, Jones and that other animal—!"

"I wouldn't exactly call them friends."

"But they've gotten you mixed up in something dirty, haven't they? Please, Luke . . . trust me . . . don't lie to me! They're outlaws, both of them, aren't they?"

"Yeah, I reckon they are." He paused, underscoring his next words in a low voice. "But I'm not."

"You're not?" She shook her head. "I don't understand."

"You asked me to trust you." He lifted her chin, gave her a searching look. "Let's say I needed help. Would you be willing?"

"Anything, Luke! Anything at all!"

"Suppose I had to get a letter to someone— a long ways off—would you be willing to find me a rider on the q.t. and hire him to deliver it?"

"Yes, of course, you know I would."

"Even if you had to keep my name out of it? All hush-hush and no questions asked?"

"If that's the way you want it . . . yes!"

"Do you know anyone that fits the ticket? Somebody you'd trust to keep his mouth shut?"

"Well, I'm not . . ." She suddenly smiled, eyes bright. "Yes, there's an old buffalo hunter! Everybody calls him Gimpy, because he has a game leg and stinks to high heaven. The other girls tease him a lot, but I've always felt sorry for him. All he wants is a drink and a little conversation . . . and . . . well, you know . . . he's sort of sweet on me."

"You think he'd do it, if I made it worthwhile?"

"He would for me. I know he would! And he'd never breathe a word to anyone."

Several moments slipped past while he studied her face. At length, taking her hand, he led her across the room and seated her on the edge of the bed. Pulling up a chair, he straddled it and sat facing her. Then he took out the makings and began rolling a cigarette.

"You ever hear of a range detective?"

"I've heard talk . . . stories."

"It's a story, all right! Damned long one, leastways where I'm concerned."

She smiled. "We've got all night, Luke."

"Yeah, I guess we do at that."

He lit his cigarette and took a long drag, exhaling slowly. Then he told her everything.

CHAPTER FOURTEEN

A gray shroud lighted the sky at dawn. Chub Jones crested a hill and reined to a halt, briefly surveying the small valley south of the Cimarron. Below, grazing near the far tree-line, was a herd of some forty horses. Behind him, hazed along by the gang, were another eight head stolen during the night. He waved the men forward and turned his horse down the slope.

Off to the side, riding flank, Starbuck was grim-eyed and thoughtful. For the past week, ranging as far south as Palo Duro Canyon, the gang had struck several outfits in the Panhandle. The Goodnight spread had been hit hardest, with smaller ranchers contributing less than twenty head. One of those was Earl Musgrave, whose land bordered Goodnight's eastern line camps. But the other members of the Cattlemen's Association, including Ben

Langham, had been bypassed this time out. While pleased by that aspect of the raids, Starbuck had experienced a sense of frustration throughout the week. To be so close to LX headquarters—at times within an hour's ride—had tempted him greatly. Upon reflection, however, he had decided against contacting Langham. Any attempt to sneak off from the gang, especially during a raid, would have jeopardized the entire operation. With no small effort, he'd stuck to his original plan.

As he rode down the slope, he reminded himself that today was the day for the next step. Some three weeks ago, before he left Dodge, Lisa had arranged for delivery of the first letter to Langham. But now, with the raids completed and the rendezvous forthcoming, it was time for his second message. Based on the schedule Jones had followed last month, he knew the gangs would gather in No Man's Land within the next five or six days. Langham and the Panhandle ranchers had to be alerted, and the timing was critical. If they were to meet him as prearranged, then his letter had to leave Dodge by late tonight. Which meant he'd have to bluff like a bastard before the sun was high.

Once the new bunch of horses was mixed with the herd, the men rode to the campsite and began unsaddling their own mounts. Everyone was tired and hungry, their thoughts on breakfast, and no one noticed that Starbuck merely loosened the cinch on his gelding. A fire was kindled, and within a few minutes coffee had boiled. Starbuck poured himself a cup, then rolled a smoke and watched quietly while the others went about their cooking chores. When he finished his cigarette, he drained the last sip of coffee and tossed the cup beside the fire. Walking to his bedroll, he stripped off his shirt and dropped it on the ground. Then he dug a clean shirt out of his saddlebags and put it on. As he finished buttoning and began stuffing the shirttail into his pants, Jones looked around.

"What's with the fresh duds?"

"Aww, you know how ladies are, Chub. They're partial to a man with a scrubbed look!"

"Ladies?" Jones frowned, eyes narrowed. "What the hell you talkin' about?"

"Women—ring-dang-doo!—what else?"

"Talk sense! There ain't no women around here."

"No, guess not." Starbuck walked back to the fire. "But there's one in Dodge just waitin' for the sight of me."

"You tryin' to pull my leg?"

"Wouldn't think of it."

"Well, if you're thinkin' about going into Dodge, then you'd better think again."

"How's that?"

" 'Cause you ain't!" Jones exploded. "Judas Priest, in case you forgot, we ain't done tendin' to business yet!"

"I haven't forgot," Starbuck informed him. "Thing is, you don't aim to leave till day after tomorrow, do you?"

"What the samhill's that got to do with anything?"

"Plenty, the way I figure it. No sense sittin' around on my butt when there's better things to do. I'll whip on into Dodge and be back no later than tomorrow night. Where's the harm?"

"We don't work that way, Luke. Ever'-body stays on the job till it's done, and then we go to town. Not the other way round."

"Chub, I didn't sign on to be a monk. Once a month might suit you and the boys, but it sort of cramps my style."

"Now, look here"—Jones gave him a lop-sided smile—"that gal of yours won't mind waitin'! Whatever you've got, she likes it a lot. I seen that for myself."

"It's me, not her!" Starbuck countered. "Hell, it'll be close to two weeks before we get back, and I just don't see any sense in waitin' that long."

"By God, you stay, Luke! That's that, and let's not hear any more guff about it!"

"Maybe you'd rather I draw my time, Chub."

A stillness settled over the men around the

fire. For a time, no one moved, waiting on Chub Jones to react to the challenge. At length, scowling heavily, he shook his head.

"Nobody quits my outfit! You included, Luke."

Starbuck shrugged. "Then I reckon you'll have to bend your rules a little. Like it or lump it, Chub, I aim to go into town."

"You push it and we're just liable to stop you."

"Yeah, I suppose you could try. But I wouldn't if I was you, Chub. It'd sure spoil a beautiful friendship . . . spoil it clean to hell."

Jones watched him carefully, weighing the threat. The silence grew, stretched longer, and for a moment it could have gone either way. Then, spreading his hands, Jones nodded and gave him a wintry smile.

"You're a contrary sonovabitch, ain't you?"

Starbuck laughed. "Only when somebody gets between me and my ring-dang-doo."

"Awright, get the hell outta here! Go on and hump yourself blind in both eyes. But, goddamnit, you be back here no later'n tomorrow night, and I mean it, Luke! You hear me?"

"Screwed, blued and tattooed, Chub. You can count on it."

Several minutes later Starbuck rode out of camp. As he topped the hill, headed north,

Jones pursed his lips, thoughtful. Then he glanced across the fire, met Sam Tate's gaze and nodded.

"Get saddled! I got an errand for you."

Early that evening Starbuck dismounted in front of the Comique. He looped the reins around the hitch rack and slowly inspected the street in both directions. The feeling of being watched was almost palpable, and he knew his instinct hadn't played him false. He'd been followed! Quite likely by Joe Sixkiller, for Jones wouldn't have chanced a miscue, and the Indian was practically invisible day or night. The street appeared normal enough, but the crowds of trailhands would only make Sixkiller's job easier. He cautioned himself to keep a close lookout, and with a last glance around, walked toward the saloon.

Inside, Starbuck moved directly to a clear spot at the end of the bar. Lisa was standing with a Texan at the opposite end, and a moment passed before she happened to look his way. Her eyes widened with surprise, and he crooked a finger, wiggled it in her direction. By the time she detached herself from the cowhand, he'd ordered two drinks and had them waiting on the counter. She stopped beside him, her smile tentative, and touched his arm.

"This isn't a social visit, is it?"

Starbuck beamed a wide grin and put his arm around her waist. "I want you to laugh and act like you're tickled pink to see me. We're probably being watched, so make it good."

"Oh, Luke you're a real sport!" She flashed a dazzling smile and hugged him, lowering her voice. "What's wrong? Are they on to you?"

"No, but we've got to play it damn cagey. Jones got his nose bent out of shape about me comin' into town."

"I'll just follow your lead, then, all right?"

"Good enough." Starbuck toasted her, still grinning, and waited until she'd sipped her drink. "Things are movin' faster than I thought. Any chance you can get hold of your friend tonight?"

"Gimpy?" She cut her eyes to the side. "That's him down there, the one with the beard. He came in a few minutes before you did."

Starbuck took a casual look. Halfway down the bar, he saw a man in his late forties, with a brushy salt-and-pepper beard and battered features. The man was drinking alone, elbows hooked over the counter. Sipping his own whiskey, Starbuck leaned closer, nuzzled Lisa's ear.

"Here's the way we work it. I can't wait till you get off, and I can't risk anybody seein' you slip him a letter in here. So you'll have to arrange for him to meet me somewhere."

Lisa blinked. "You mean he has to leave tonight?"

"The quicker the better, and even then we'll be cuttin' it mighty close."

"Where should he meet you?"

Starbuck considered it. "Tell you what . . . there's some sort of warehouse at the edge of town—"

"Thompson's Wine and Liquors."

"That's the one . . . we'll meet there . . . in the alley."

"When?"

"Now we've got to get tricky, do a little playacting. You up to it?"

"Mama always said I belonged on the stage."

"Tonight's your chance," Starbuck said, nodding toward a staircase at the rear of the saloon. "I'll go up to your room and get the letter written. You wait a while . . . act like you're pushin' drinks . . . that'll give you a chance to slip the word to Gimpy. Then pretend you're sneakin' off to meet me."

"You want me to come to the room?"

"Yeah, come there and wait. Shouldn't take more than fifteen minutes for me to duck out the back stairs and get Gimpy squared away. Then we'll come back down here together, and whoever's watching me will think we had ourselves a quickie."

"You know"—Lisa fluttered her lashes—"that's not a bad idea."

"Why rush things? After Gimpy's on the trail, we'll have lots of time . . . the whole night."

"You mean it, Luke? Honest and truly!"

"Yes, ma'am, I surely do. You just put on a convincing performance for whoever's watchin' . . . and later tonight I'll turn you every way but loose!"

"Sugar, the bastard will think he's watching Sarah Bernhardt. I guarantee it!"

Starbuck laughed and swatted her on the rump. She gave him a bawdy wink as he stepped away from the bar and walked toward the rear of the room. She waited until he mounted the stairs, then strolled down the bar flirting with trailhands. With no apparent rush, she moved steadily closer to the bearded man.

Some while later, Starbuck paused at the bottom of the stairs behind the Comique. He glanced quickly in both directions, then turned south along the alley. A few minutes' walk brought him to the edge of town, and the warehouse. The alley was dimly lit by the glow of lamplights from the street, and a man waited in the shadows beside the loading platform. He moved closer, halting when he recognized the whiskery face.

"Thanks for comin'." Starbuck put out his hand. "I'm Luke Starbuck."

"Jack Martin." The man shook his hand, smiled. "Folks call me Gimpy, but that's only 'cause they ain't got sense enough to lick grease off a spoon."

"Well, Jack, you're all right in my book. I'm much obliged for that little trip you made down to the Panhandle."

"Weren't nothin'," Martin replied. "Besides, that rancher fella—Langham—he treated me like a king, damed if he didn't! 'Course, he was fit to be tied wonderin' where in tarnation you'd got off to."

"How would you like to visit him again?"

"You got another letter you want carried?"

Starbuck unbuttoned his shirt and extracted an envelope. "Jack, it's worth double what Lisa paid you last time . . . if you can leave tonight."

"No problem," Martin observed. "All I gotta do is bag up some grub and saddle my horse. Be on the trail in a couple of shakes."

"That's the ticket!" Starbuck smiled and handed him the envelope. "Just make sure you get it there by sundown day after tomorrow, agreed?"

"Hell, I'll make it long 'fore that."

"Both you bastards get 'em up—*now goddamnit!*"

Sam Tate stepped around the corner of the warehouse. He eared back the hammer on his pistol and waggled it in their direction. Approaching a few steps closer, he halted and looked them over with a crooked grin.

"Starbuck, you're cute—I'll give you that. But you ain't near cute enough, not by a damnsight!"

"What the hell's the idea of buttin' in, Tate? This here's private business, and you're out of line!"

"Cut the horseshit!" Tate rumbled. "We'll just let Chub decide who's out of line. Now, pass me that envelope . . . nice and easy."

Starbuck wasted no time on alternatives. The decision to kill Tate was made quickly, and without regret. The consequences could be dealt with later, but for now . . .

"You're making a mistake, Tate."

"Close your flytrap and lemme have that goddamn envelope!"

"All right, Jack," Starbuck said with a note of resignation, "give him the letter."

Martin extended the envelope, and Starbuck laughed a bitter laugh, then shook his head. "Honest to Christ, Tate! When Chub hears about this, he'll flat skin your—"

Starbuck's arm moved in mid-sentence. The Colt appeared in his hand and exploded in a streak of flame. The heavy slug sent Tate reeling in a strange, nerveless dance. His knees buckled, the pistol dropped from his hand and he collapsed in a heap on the ground. A faint stench filled the alley as his bowels voided in death.

Holstering his gun, Starbuck turned. "Jack, I haven't got time to explain. Are you still with me or not?"

"Hell, I'm game! Lisa says you're square, and that's good enough—"

"Then hit the trail! Make dust and don't look back!"

Jack Martin took off at a fast limp and vanished around the corner of the warehouse. Working swiftly, Starbuck manhandled the corpse off the ground and stuffed it underneath the loading platform. A gleam of metal caught his eye and he kicked the dead man's gun into a patch of weeds. One last look satisfied him that all appeared in order. He dusted his hands and set off at a brisk pace toward the Comique.

CHAPTER FIFTEEN

Starbuck forded the Cimarron late the next afternoon. His expression was solemn, and his thoughts were hardened to indrawn bleakness, focused on the task ahead. He figured it was even money he wouldn't live to see the sun go down.

Once in camp, he knew he would face a kangaroo court. Chub Jones would sit in judgment, with the men drafted as jurors. If the verdict went the wrong way, he had no doubt they would also serve as his executioners. Whipping Sam Tate in a fistfight was one thing. The men could applaud that with brutish amusement. Killing a member of the gang was an altogether different matter. One that struck too close to home. An act that would arouse fear and uncertainty, perhaps vengeance.

At first, Starbuck had considered not men-

tioning Tate at all. Simply ride into camp and
act as though nothing had happened. But he'd
quickly discarded the idea. Jones would be
all the more suspicious if he appeared, pre-
tending ignorance, and Tate failed to return.
Once the doubt was instilled, it would fester
and cause even greater suspicion. Which
could very easily hamper his freedom of
movement when they reached No Man's
Land. Far better to get it out into the open,
somehow absolve himself of blame. Confront
them with rage and indignation—bluster his
way through—and convince them he'd killed
for no other reason than to save himself.
Killed because Sam Tate had forced him to
kill . . . in self-defense.

It sounded good, but he wasn't at all sure
they would be persuaded. Sundown suddenly
seemed ominously near.

A vagrant thought surfaced. As he gained
the south bank of the Cimarron, he wondered
if he'd seen Lisa for the last time. He hadn't
told her about Tate, for fear it would upset
her and spoil their night together. In that
sense, it had proved a wise decision. Thrilled
by their success, she had taken him to bed
with a fire and passion that seemed un-
quenchable, left him sated. Yet now, on the
verge of a showdown with Jones, it struck
him as odd that she intruded on his thoughts.
He questioned the wisdom of dwelling on the
future—and Lisa Blalock—at a time when

the future itself seemed questionable.

A still greater paradox was why he chose to face Jones at all. Why not simply say the hell with it and cut a beeline for the safety of the LX? Under the circumstances, it made a great deal more sense. The only explanation he could offer himself was one of pride. Stubborn pride and bulldog contempt for quitters. Which seemed the poorest excuse imaginable for getting himself killed. But it was the only one he had, and apparently excuse enough for seeing it through. A man stuck until the job was done.

No alibis accepted.

The sun was low, sheeting the valley with rays of fire, when Starbuck rode into camp. The men fell silent as he dismounted, and he felt their eyes boring into him while he unsaddled. With no word or gesture, he went about his business, ignoring them. Only after he'd hobbled his horse, and left it to graze, did he turn in their direction. Walking to the campfire, he halted across from Jones, and still no one spoke. He hauled out the makings, built himself a smoke, and struck a match on his thumbnail. Then he lit up, took a couple of puffs, and at last fixed Jones with a hard look.

"Sam Tate sends his regrets."

Jones's eyes were flat and guarded. "What's that supposed to mean?"

"It means he won't be ridin' with us any-more."

"Why not?"

"Because I killed him"—Starbuck flicked an ash off his cigarette—"Killed him deader'n a doornail."

Jones exchanged a glance with the men and something unspoken passed among them. Sixkiller shifted to the rear, and the other two held their positions, covering Starbuck from all sides. Several moments elapsed before Jones pursed his lips, nodding.

"I suppose you had your reasons?"

"All the reason I needed."

"Which was?"

"The sonovabitch tried to bushwhack me!"

"No, I don't think so, Luke. I think you killed him for reasons all your own."

Starbuck blinked, as though surprised by the accusation. "Where'd you get a damnfool notion like that?"

"Little bird told me."

"Chub, I don't want you to take it personal, but you're full of shit."

"You callin' me a liar?"

"I'm sayin' you'd better check your paintpots again. Tate braced me out back of the Comique and he had a gun in his hand. Any man does that, he's just plain askin' for it."

"Why would he draw down on you with no reason?"

"No reason!" Starbuck laughed in his face.

"Jesus H. Christ! You're the one that told me to watch out for him. You said it yourself . . . he hated my guts . . . he was lookin' to even the score!"

Jones returned his gaze steadily. "What were you doin' out back of the Comique?"

"In case you forgot, Lisa's boss don't like folks to think he's runnin' a whorehouse. Even with an invite, you've got to use the back stairs."

"I don't believe a word of it, Luke. Looks to me like Sam caught you—up to something—and you had to kill him to keep him quiet."

"Listen, fat man"—Starbuck's tone was icy—"you keep on crowdin' me and I'll make your asshole wink."

"Think you could take all of us, do you?"

"No, wouldn't even try. But I'll dust you on both sides before these boys ever clear leather. You know I can do it, Chub, so you'd best think on it before you start the ball rollin'."

Jones regarded him thoughtfully, then shrugged. "One time's good as another. No way, nohow you're gonna walk away clean, Luke! Not after what you done!"

"Bullshit!" Starbuck invested the word with scorn. "If anyone's to blame, it's you!"

"Me!" Jones was astounded. "Just how in the billy hell you figure that?"

"Because, goddamnit . . . you're the one that sicced Tate on me!"

"In a pig's ass!"

"Yeah?" Starbuck jerked his thumb at the men. "Well, let's see if the boys here will bear me out. Tate wouldn't have come into Dodge unless you sent him, would he?"

"Now you hold it right there! I told Sam to keep an eye on you, and by God, that's all I told him!"

"C'mon, that don't make sense! Why would you set him to spy on me?"

Jones gave him a hangdog look. " 'Cause I didn't buy your story about seein' that gal. You gotta admit, it's a helluva long ride for a little poontang!"

"Why would I lie about the girl? Or Tate, for that matter! I could've waltzed in here and told you I never even saw him, and you wouldn't have known the difference, would you?"

"Guess not," Jones conceded. "But it still seems damn funny."

"Well, Chub, you and your double-dealing are what got Tate killed. Christ A'mighty, it was made to order! You should've known he'd try to put me under."

"Awright, so I made a mistake! So what?" Jones suddenly flushed, spread his hands in a lame gesture. "Come right down to it, I reckon there wasn't no love lost between none of us and Tate anyway."

"Maybe so," Starbuck replied grimly, "but you pretty near got me killed, and I don't appreciate it one damn bit."

"It's spilt milk now." Jones averted his eyes, tried to collect himself. "What'd you do with him . . . you know . . . afterward?"

"I lugged him down the alley and hid him out behind a warehouse. Things happened so quick, it was all I could think of to get him away from the Comique."

"Hope nobody puts two and two together. Lots of folks seen him with me the times we was in Dodge."

"Hell, one dead man more or less don't mean nothin' in that town. The law will chalk him off for another juiced-up cowhand that got himself killed. Happens all the time."

"Guess you're right," Jones agreed. "All the same, I think we'll steer clear of Dodge when we go to sell this next bunch."

With the situation reversed, and Jones on the defensive, the other men relaxed. Looking everywhere but at Starbuck, they traded sheepish glances and hunkered down by the fire. Jones seemed at a loss himself, fidgeting uncomfortably under Starbuck's level stare. Finally, when the men busied themselves pouring coffee, Starbuck dismissed the incident with a brusque wave of his hand.

"Chub, I'm willin' to let bygones be bygones, but it seems to me I ought to get something in return for my trouble."

"Yeah, like what?"

"A bigger slice of the pie."

"Listen here, Luke"—Jones shook a finger at him—"You just back off! I made a mistake and I ain't tryin' to weasel out of it, but that don't give you no leave to sandbag me. The split's fair and that's all there is to it!"

"Suppose I wasn't talkin' about our split?"

Jones eyed him warily. "You wanna spell that out?"

"Let's say—just for the sake of argument— I was talkin' about the split with Dutch Henry."

"I'd say somebody must've rung your bell. With a goddamn sledgehammer!"

"Why don't you wait and hear me out? You've got nothin' to lose by listenin', have you?"

"Hell, talk away!" Jones gave him an indulgent smile. "Tell you the truth, I could use a good laugh right about now."

"Well, it's like this," Starbuck began. "All the way into Dodge I had my thinkin' cap on. I kept rememberin' you and them other three jaybirds squatted around that horse blanket countin' out money with both hands. And there was ol' Dutch Henry—all by his lonesome—waitin' to scoop it up and run on back to wherever the hell he came from."

"You just beatin' your gums or have you got a point?"

"Oh, the point's real simple. Unless I'm

off the mark, I calculate Dutch Henry got about half the divvy. That left a quarter-share for you, and a quarter to be split up amongst the rest of us."

"So you can count! The split ain't exactly no secret."

"No, I reckon the only secret is where Dutch Henry skedaddles off with half the gravy."

Starbuck's tone was deliberately casual. He'd seen an opening and taken it on the spur of the moment. The reaction he drew was little more than he had expected.

Jones gave him a sharp sidelong look. "Lemme tell you something, Luke. You're a bright fella and you're a handy man to have around. But you're gonna wind up stiff as a board if you start askin' the wrong questions. Dutch Henry don't take kindly to people that get curious about him and his ways."

Starbuck brushed away the warning with a quick gesture. "Forget I asked! Him and his big dark secrets aren't important anyway. The thing I was drivin' at's the split . . . the money."

"Then you make your point, for Chrissakes!"

"Suppose we got our heads together—all four gangs—before Dutch Henry shows at the meet. Take it a step further, and suppose we agreed to hold out for sixty-forty—or maybe even seventy-thirty—in our favor!

Hell, he wouldn't have any choice! He's only one man, and without us the whole shebang goes up the flume. He'd have to see it our way!"

"Goddamn!" Jones roared. "You're crazy as a loon!"

"Why?"

" 'Cause me and them other three jaybirds you was talkin' about go back a long way with Dutch. He's the one that put this horse-stealin' operation together, and without him we'd still be robbin' penny-ante banks. Or rustlin' cows and workin' ten times as hard for the same money!"

"That's my point!" Starbuck said earnestly. "You're doin' all the work now, you and your men. Why settle for half?"

"Now look here, Luke! I'm as partial to money as the next man. But I ain't stupid! If I ever raised that idea with them other boys, they'd drill me so full of holes I'd never get the leaks plugged up."

"For a man that's never tried, you sound awful damn sure."

"You just take my word for it. I know them boys, and they don't mess around. Anybody tries to cross Dutch Henry and they'll feed him to the crows. In little pieces!"

"How about you, Chub? Those your sentiments, too?"

"Never mind me! You just stick to business and let me do the talkin'. That way, we'll all live a lot longer."

The exchange proved revealing for both men. In the silence that followed, Chub Jones decided he'd sadly misjudged the younger man, and he congratulated himself on having picked a suitable, if somewhat headstrong, replacement for Sam Tate. For Starbuck, it was a matter of having turned adversity to advantage. Aside from learning details about the gang leaders themselves, he had wormed his way further into Jones's confidence. It was an edge that might very well tip the scales in the days ahead. Jones finally broke the silence, glancing around with a wry look.

"Luke, lemme ask you something. Did you shoot ol' Sam, or did you talk the sonovabitch to death?"

Starbuck laughed. "Chub, I reckon it was a little of both. See, he was listenin' so hard, he never heard the gun go off."

CHAPTER SIXTEEN

"Yessir, boys, it's a mortal fact," Jones told them. "Luke's what you might call *real sudden* with a gun. Ain't that right, Joe?"

Sixkiller nodded solemnly. "Strike like snake."

"Snake, my ass!" Tom Webb hooted. "He's faster'n greased lightnin'! *Zip! Bam!* And it's all over but the prayin'."

The men were sprawled out around the campfire. All four gangs had gathered after supper for the usual session of yarn-spinning and tall tales. It was the highlight of the No Man's Land rendezvous, by now something of a ritual. Normally, the stories centered on some prodigious feat of horse-stealing, and were related with a grand air of braggadocio. But tonight it was Chub Jones and his crew who were doing the bragging. The death of Sam Tate was the talk of the camp, and Starbuck a morbid curiosity that piqued the out-laws' interest. Jones and his older hands were treating it as the stuff of legend, and basking in Starbuck's reflected glory. A glory they themselves were at great pains to extoll with much exaggeration.

"Well, if you wasn't there"—one of the outlaws eyed Jones with a skeptical frown—"it beats me how you're so sure he's all that sudden."

"You questionin' my word?"

"Nope, never said that. But you done told us Tate had the drop on him."

"Shore as hell did! Had him cold!"

"Then suppose you just explain how he did it. Case you forgot, Tate weren't no slouch with a gun hisself."

"The hand's quicker'n the eye!" Jones chortled. "All you gotta do is blink, and ol' Luke, he'll turn you into dog meat!"

"You make him sound like some sorta ma-gician."

"Bet your balls, he is! Christ, I seen him in action once myself! Ain't that so, Luke?"

Starbuck was seated off to one side, smok-ing quietly in the shadows. Until now, he hadn't joined in the conversation; all the bragging made him feel uncomfortable, and worse, drew attention to him. Which was per-haps the last thing he wanted tonight. Yet there was no way to avoid Jones's question. All the men were watching him, intent at last on hearing his version of the shootout. He decided to play it for laughs.

"Yeah, Chub's right." A pause for effect, then Starbuck went on. "The night he hired me, we had ourselves a few words, and I felt obliged to put a gun on him. Near as I recollect, he lost about twenty pounds of that lard when he shit his drawers."

Jones's sputtering objection was drowned out by laughter. The men thought it a real knee-slapper, and ridiculed him with a chorus of vulgar jibes. But the one outlaw still wasn't satisfied, and waited until the tomfoolery slacked off.

"I ain't heard nothin' yet," he persisted, "that tells me what happened. How the hell'd you walk away clean when Tate had you dead to rights?"

Starbuck smiled. "Only two men at a time knows the trick, and one of 'em always ends up with a new belly button."

"I don't get you."

"Well, the way it works out, one fella does the trick and the other watches. That's the only way to learn."

"But the one watchin' gets hisself killed!"

"That's exactly what Tate said," Starbuck noted, deadpan. "Pissed him off some proper, too."

Jones roared, stabbing a finger at the outlaw. "You sorry bastard, that'll shut you up!

Or would you like him to show you the trick
personal?"

Starbuck rose, ground his cigarette underfoot. "Chub, I make it a practice never to
show off in public. 'Specially when the big
talker in the crowd aims to step aside and
hold my coat." He grinned, glancing around
the fire. "Think I'll catch some shut-eye. See
you gents in the mornin'."

As Starbuck turned and walked toward his
bedroll, the outlaws began ribbing Jones. So
far as he was concerned, the man had made
a fool of himself, and deserved the mockery.
He thought it ironic that Jones's attitude had
undergone such a pronounced change. Apparently, in the end, might made right, and
despite the circumstances of the killing, only
the survivor commanded respect. All the
more outlandish was the intent behind
Jones's bragging. The gang leader sought to
boost his own stature—now that Sam Tate
was dead—by heaping kudos on the one who
had done the killing. It was comic, almost
laughable. A dog rolling in the droppings of
another simply to fortify the potency of his
own smell.

Once in his bedroll, Starbuck closed his
mind to the men around the fire. His thoughts
turned to the night ahead, and tomorrow
morning. It was the second day of the rendezvous, and late that afternoon Monty Hall
had altered the brands on the last of the stolen

stock. At sunrise, the herds would be switched, and as the gangs prepared to scatter, Dutch Henry Horn would appear to collect his share of the loot. Between now and then, Starbuck had to make contact with the Panhandle ranchers, arrange the details and precise timing of the attack. All of which involved sneaking out of camp during the night and somehow returning undetected. No small order given the wary nature of men who slept light and kept their pistols close at hand.

Still, for all the risks entailed, sneaking out of camp was perhaps the least of Starbuck's worries. As he closed his eyes, willing himself to catch a brief nap, his last thought was disquieting. He wondered if Ben Langham was actually there . . . waiting downstream . . . *tonight*.

The sky was purest indigo when Starbuck rose from his blankets. All around him were men snoring, tossing in their slumber, bedrolls scattered helter-skelter around the camp. The glow of a waning moon filtered through the cottonwoods, and the fire was by now a simmering bed of ashes. Without a sound, he cat-footed through the camp and vanished deeper into the darkness.

A shadow, moving from tree to tree, he worked his way downstream. There were five night guards, one stationed somewhere below camp and the others riding watch on the horse herds. Nearing the picket line, where the outlaws' personal mounts were tied, he paused behind the base of a cottonwood. It was essential that he not spook the horses, and all the more imperative that he pinpoint the guards' position before moving farther. He waited, scanning the darkness, the thud of his heart like a drumbeat in his ears. After what seemed an interminable length of time, he saw a spark of light on the opposite side of the creek. A man's face appeared in the flare of a match, quickly snuffed. Then the fiery dot of a cigarette winked orange in the night.

Quiet as a drifting hawk, Starbuck faded north through the trees. Circling wide around the picket line, he again intersected the creek some hundred yards below the guard. There he stopped, listening a moment for any sign of alarm, then hurried on.

An hour later, he rounded a bend in the stream and halted. A massive boulder stood sentinel in the night, marking the spot where he was to meet Ben Langham. Yet there was only silence, the inky stillness of trees bordering the creek. Nothing.

"Don't move or you're dead!"

Several men stepped out of the trees, and Starbuck's heart skipped a beat. Walking forward, their carbines leveled on him, the men approached on a line. Suddenly he recognized one of them, the ambling gait and the massive frame. He laughed.

"Call 'em off, Ben! I'll come peaceable."

"Luke? Is that you, Luke?"

"It sure as hell ain't Santy Claus!"

Langham splashed across the creek and embraced him in a great bear hug. "Goddamn, you're a sight for sore eyes! Where the hell you been, anyway? We been waitin' here since sundown. Are them bastards camped upstream, where you said they'd be?"

"Hold off!" Starbuck freed himself, grinning. "Give me a chance to get a word in edgewise."

"Christ A'mighty, boy, talk all you want! It's almost like you come back from the dead. I don't mind tellin' you, though, them letters of yours has kept me on pins and needles." Langham laughed, smote him across the back. "All the same, you're one helluva fine mapmaker! We just followed your drawin' and come here like we had the place tied to a string. Damned if we didn't!"

"Ben, would you just close your mouth for—"

Suddenly there were men swarming all around him. Vernon Pryor began pumping his arm, crowded closely by Oscar Gilchrist, Will Rutledge and Earl Musgrave. Upward of fifty cowhands, many of them from the LX crew, emerged from the trees to watch the reunion. Starbuck was touched by the warmth of their greeting, but he felt pressed for time, his nerves on edge. The night was short, with much still to be accomplished, and a long hike back to the outlaw camp. Finally, when they continued to pepper him with questions, he fended them off, palms upraised.

"Everybody hold it right there!"

The men fell silent, and he nodded. "That's better! Now, I don't mean to cut you short, but I've only got about ten minutes before I have to head back. So let's save the jabber for later and get down to business."

"He's right, boys," Langham added quickly. "We're here to get a job done, and Luke's the only one that knows the layout. Let's tie it off and give him a chance to call the shots."

The other ranchers mumbled agreement, and Starbuck motioned them to a patch of ground lighted by the moon. He knelt, then began scratching in the dirt with a stick. Langham and the others gathered around, watching intently. A pattern took shape in the dirt, and they saw he had drawn a crude sketch of the terrain upstream.

"Here we are." Starbuck jabbed with the stick. "Now, from this point, I judge it to be a couple of miles, maybe a little more, to the camp."

"How do we recognize it," Pryor asked, "without stumbling in blind?"

"By this dogleg." Starbuck tapped the diagram farther upstream. "You come around a sharp bend, then the trees start to get heavier, and you're less than a quarter-mile away."

Langham grunted. "You're figgerin' we ought to come afoot?"

"Only way," Starbuck noted. "Otherwise, they'll hear you and we'll lose any chance of surprise."

"What time you want us there?"

"A little before sunrise. The one I wrote you about—the head dog—that's when he rides into camp. Him and the four gang leaders will get together in the center of the camp"—the stick marked a spot, then moved eastward—"and all the men will be down here at the picket line. That's when we hit 'em."

"What about this?" Rutledge proposed. "Suppose we swing one bunch around to the west and the rest of us come straight up the creek? That way we got 'em boxed between us."

"Too risky, Will. Last time, Dutch Henry rode in from the west, and we've got to assume he'll do it the same way this time out. If you try circlin' the camp, he's liable to spot you and make tracks before we even know he's there."

"That lets that out!" Langham told them. "If there's one sonovabitch I want, it's this Dutch Henry Horn."

"No two ways about it," Starbuck agreed.

"We've got to get Horn and the gang leaders, all of 'em. That's the only way we'll end it permanent."

"How, just exactly?" Pryor interjected. "Since you're the only one that knows Horn by sight, we'll need a signal of some sort."

"Yeah, I was comin' to that." Starbuck again poked the diagram. "Vern and Will, you bring most of the boys up the south bank of the creek. Everyone will be saddlin' their horses, and when you open fire, that'll cause a diversion." The stick leaped the creek. "Ben, you and Oscar come up the north side with about ten men. When the shootin' starts, you bust right into the center of camp and let fly. Nobody will see you till it's too late."

"But what about the signal?" Gilchrist demanded. "How'll we know Horn's actually there?"

"Keep your eye on me." Starbuck studied the diagram a moment, looked up. "I'll be down at the picket line with the men. When Horn rides into camp, I'll walk up to meet him. That's your signal."

"Jesus Christ!" Langham exploded. "You'll be out there all by your lonesome! I'd rather see you get clear before the shootin' commences."

Starbuck smiled. "I've worked it all out in my head, Ben, and this is the only way that makes sense. Besides, if I haven't told you before, I want Horn as bad as you do . . . maybe worse."

Several minutes were spent rehashing the plan. Starbuck drilled them until they were letter-perfect, satisfying himself there would be no mishap at the crucial moment. Then he shook hands all around and trudged off upstream. The men watched in silence, and at last, when he disappeared into the darkness, Ben Langham found his voice.

"Boys, he's aces high and all guts. Goddamn if he's not!"

CHAPTER SEVENTEEN

Dawn broke over the cottonwoods and limned the camp in a dusky blue halo. Sunrise was still an hour away, and the night damp, strongest at first light, filled the air with a crisp earthen smell. As the bleak sky slowly brightened, the camp stirred to the sounds of men awakening.

Starbuck lay still, listening and alert, but feigning sleep. Since ghosting back into camp, scarcely an hour past, he'd had no trouble staying awake. In his mind's eye, he saw Langham and the others creeping through the trees, cautiously working their way upstream. He waited, stomach knotted with dread, listening for a shout from the night guard. Any sudden commotion, or a warning gunshot, would sound the alarm and alert the camp to danger. But there was nothing, merely another dawn filled with the fart-

ing and grumbling of men roused from a
weary sleep.

Presently, when he heard the clatter of a
coffeepot, Starbuck sat up in his blankets,
stretching his arms wide and yawning.
Across the way, he saw the night guard feeding sticks to the fire, a galvanized coffeepot
balanced on rocks near the flames. From the
direction of the picket line, the four horse
guards, their vigil over the herds completed,
trooped toward the fire. Nearby, Jones rose
from his bedroll, buckling on his gunbelt, and
nodded.

"Mornin'."

"Mornin', Chub. Sleep good?"

Jones grunted something unintelligible and
stepped off into the trees, unbuttoning his
pants. He relieved himself, splattering the
ground with a steamy spray, and sighed heavily. As he turned, tucking himself away, he
suddenly stopped and peered intently through
the woods. To the north, obscured by the tree
line, a horse and rider moved steadily closer
to camp. In the dim light, the rider was indistinguishable, dressed in a dark frock coat
and a slouch hat. But the horse, snorting little
puffs of smoke, was unmistakable. It was the
steel-dust gelding of Dutch Henry Horn.

"Goddamn!" Jones whirled away, fumbling with the buttons on his pants. Hurrying
toward the clearing, he motioned to the other
gang leaders. "Look sharp, boys! Dutch

Henry's here! He's ridin' in right now!"

Starbuck spun around, ignoring the flurry of activity near the campfire. For an instant, he felt a profound sense of admiration. Dutch Henry had completely reversed the pattern of last month, approaching from the north rather than the west, and appearing at dawn instead of full sunrise. It was a cunning stratagem! The mark of a man who kept everyone else off balance, forever stayed a step . . .

With a jolt, Starbuck realized his own plans were now in jeopardy. He'd told Langham and the ranchers to expect Dutch Henry at sunrise! Yet it was barely dawn—an hour earlier than he'd anticipated—and he questioned whether they were even in position to attack. All the more worrisome, his diversionary tactics were now out the window. The outlaws had only begun gathering around the cookfire—not at the picket line saddling horses—which eliminated any chance of separating Horn and the gang leaders from their men. The situation was suddenly topsy-turvy, bassackward to what he'd planned.

Still another problem confronted him. As Horn rode into the clearing, Starbuck realized the ranchers would have no way of identifying the ringleader. There were simply too many men milling about camp to single out one from the others. From a distance, Horn

would appear to be one of the crowd, just
another horse thief.

His nerves jangled, Starbuck watched as
Horn dismounted several yards from the fire.
Jones and the other gang leaders, lugging
their saddlebags, went to meet him. After a
few minutes' conversation, a blanket was
spread on the ground and the men began
counting out money. Pondering the turn of
events, Starbuck knew he had to devise a new
plan, and do it quickly. Everything hinged on
two elements, vital to the success of any attack. Somehow he must stall for time, delay
Horn's departure until the ranchers were in
position. Then, at the very last minute, he
must somehow identify Horn in a manner unmistakable to Langham and the men north of
the creek. Only one way occurred to him, and
he swiftly calculated the risk involved. By no
means the best of schemes, he nonetheless
decided it would have to do. Walking to the
fire, he rolled a cigarette, poured himself a
cup of coffee and settled down to wait.

A short time later, Horn and the gang leaders seemed to have concluded their business.
The men stepped back, talking among themselves, while Horn knelt and began stuffing
the money into his own saddlebags. Starbuck
waited until the very last moment, when
Horn had the saddlebags strapped in place
and turned for a final word with the men.
Then he rose, resigned to what he must do,

and moved toward them at a deliberate pace.

As he approached, Horn and the men stopped talking. Jones frowned, and the others studied him with a mixture of surprise and irritation. He ignored them, halting a few feet away, staring directly at Horn.

"Dutch Henry, I'd like to have a word with you."

Horn fixed him with a curious look. "What's on your mind?"

"Money." Starbuck dismissed the gang leaders with a wave. "Nothin' against these fellas, but the split's sort of lopsided, and I figured it was time somebody spoke up."

"Holy Jumpin' Jesus!" Jones erupted. "You crazy sonovabitch, you get your ass down there and start saddlin'! I mean right now!"

"Hold it!" Horn ordered. "Let him have his say."

"Dutch, I swear to God I didn't have nothin' to do with this! Whatever he's after, he cooked it up all by hisself. Honest to Christ!"

"It's all right, Chub." Horn turned a cold eye on Starbuck. "You elected yourself to do the talkin' for everybody, that it?"

"Well, it shore didn't appear nobody else would do it."

"Why's that, you reckon?"

" 'Cause they're all scared shitless of you, that's why."

"And you're not?"

"Oh, I'm a little nervy, but I don't scare as easy as some."

"So you took it on yourself to brace me . . . just like that?"

"Only way I know, straight out and get to it!"

"Starbuck," Horn said with wintry malice, "it appears to me you're gettin' too big for your britches."

On the north side of the creek, Ben Langham paused some fifty yards below the camp. Behind him were Oscar Gilchrist and ten cowhands, all armed with carbines. He motioned them to the ground and dropped to one knee beside a cottonwood. Scanning the area ahead, he spotted the picket line, and a short distance upstream, the campsite itself. Smoke drifted skyward from the cooking fire, and through the dusky light it appeared the outlaws were preparing to break camp. He smiled, nodding to himself. Everything was right on schedule, exactly as Starbuck had described it. Perfect.

Then he squinted, looking closer. Off to one side, Starbuck stood facing a small group of men. The discussion appeared heated, and oddly enough, Starbuck and one other man were doing all the talking. Even more puzzling, the man was standing beside a saddled horse, steel-dust in color. It was almost as though Starbuck had caught him before he could mount and ride out of camp.

Or maybe he'd just now ridden into camp!

Langham frowned, considering the only possibility that made sense. The man was Dutch Henry Horn—had to be!—and the other four were the gang leaders. For whatever reason, Horn had arrived in camp before sunrise, upsetting the timetable Starbuck had laid out. Which led to a fearful conclusion. Starbuck was holding him there, stalling for time. To all appearances, he'd provoked an argument with Horn to identify him, single him out from the crowd. But it was a perilous dodge, and it wouldn't last long. Starbuck was playing with dynamite, and he'd already lit the fuse. Time was running out.

Langham rose and signaled his men. He waved his arms, spreading them on a line abreast of him, then motioned toward the camp. At a measured pace, their carbines cocked and ready, they advanced through the trees.

Vernon Pryor and Will Rutledge were huddled behind a tree on the opposite side of the creek. They watched, thoroughly astounded, as Langham led his men forward. From their position, directly opposite the picket line, Starbuck was nowhere in sight. All they could make out was a throng of men milling about the campsite. Yet Langham was moving to attack—long before sunrise!

After a hurried conference, they could only surmise that Langham had received the signal from Starbuck. Nothing else made sense. Whether or not Dutch Henry Horn had arrived in camp was a moot question. But there seemed no doubt that Starbuck, for reasons all his own, had signaled an early attack. Otherwise, Ben Langham would never have jumped the gun.

A long moment ensued as they deliberated their own course of action. The outlaws were even now breaking camp, but it was clear very few of them would reach the picket line before Langham struck from the north. Their choice, then, was to hold their position, taking potshots from a distance, or advance on the camp. With Langham already on the move, it was no choice at all. If the outlaws wouldn't come to them, then they must go to the outlaws.

Pryor climbed to his feet, with Rutledge at his side, and raised his arm. Some forty cowhands emerged from the trees, their carbines at the ready, and stood waiting. Pryor dropped his arm and led them splashing across the creek. On the opposite bank they fanned out, walking softly through the murk of the fading dawn. A horse whickered as they neared the picket line.

*　　*　　*

"Seems to me," Starbuck observed, "you're a mite too stingy for your own good."

"If that's a threat," Horn said with a trace of amusement, "you're got some chore on your hands. In case you haven't looked around, it's you against us . . . all of us."

"Maybe, maybe not." Starbuck smiled. "If we was to put it to a vote, I've got an idea you'd be the one that comes out on the short end of the stick."

"Got it all figured out, have you?"

"Well, let's just say I think most of the boys would go along with me."

"Forget it! There's only one vote that counts in this outfit, and that's the way she stays."

"Hell, Dutch Henry, nothin' stays the same forever. Sometimes you gotta bend with the wind."

"I don't hear no wind, but I'm sure gettin' tired of listenin' to a blowhard."

"I'll be damned! You think I'm tryin' to run a sandy, don't you?"

"No, you're done tryin'," Horn countered. "You've shot your wad, and all you bought yourself is a peck of trouble."

"Wanna bet?"

Starbuck turned away, sensing he'd pushed it to the limit. Horn was through talking, and if he hoped to stall any longer, it would require a switch in tactics. Walking off several paces, he halted and raised his voice in a blustering shout.

"Hey, there! You boys give a listen! Dutch Henry wants a word with you!"

Chub Jones and the gang leaders stared at him with slack-jawed amazement. The men themselves, arms loaded with gear as they trooped toward the picket line, wheeled around in surprise. Even Dutch Henry Horn was taken aback, but the shock lasted a mere instant. His eyes hooded and he pulled his gun. Thumbing the hammer, he took deliberate aim, sights centered on Starbuck's shoulder blades.

The metallic whirr of the hammer caught Starbuck unprepared, his arm raised to summon the men. All in a motion, acting on sheer reflex, he threw himself sideways and drew his Colt. But as he hit the ground and rolled, a rifle cracked from the tree line north of the camp. A slug plucked the lapel of Horn's coat, and, whistling past, fried the air around his horse's ears. The horse reared, and Horn grabbed the reins, momentarily shielded from Starbuck's view. Then the gunfire became general, a dozen carbines spitting lead from the cottonwoods.

As though struck by a scythe, the three gang leaders went down in a bunch, dark stains spotting their clothes. Chub Jones, miraculously untouched, had already drawn on Starbuck and snapped a hurried shot. Dirt exploded in Starbuck's face, and he quickly shifted aim, touching off the trigger. Jones was jerked off his feet, hogsheads of blood spurting from his kneecap, and pitched rag-like to the ground. Swinging around, Starbuck saw Horn mounted and spurring hard, draped low over his horse's neck. Cursing with rage, Starbuck thumbed off shot after shot, blazing away until the hammer fell on an empty chamber. By then, Horn was deep in the trees, pounding west at a hard gallop.

Starbuck's immediate reaction was to find a horse and give chase. But as he scrambled to his feet, he suddenly became aware of a raging battle to his rear. At the opening shot, the outlaws had flung their gear aside and commenced firing on Langham's men. Then, with devastating volley, the force led by Pryor and Rutledge struck them from the flank. Within a matter of seconds, nearly half the outlaw band was killed outright. Several more were mortally wounded, winnowed to earth by a rolling barrage that swept the clearing. The survivors, outgunned and out-flanked, quickly called it quits. Tossing their guns to the ground, they raised their arms, and as suddenly as it began, the fight ended.

Langham's men, and the larger group led by Pryor, stepped from the trees and slowly converged on the clearing. Of the original band, numbering upward of twenty outlaws, only five remained standing. The others lay dead or dying, literally cut to shreds by the murderous cross fire. Later Langham would estimate that nearly three hundred rifle slugs had crisscrossed the clearing in less than thirty seconds, and marvel that anyone had lived through the holocaust. But, for now, he motioned his men to take charge of the survivors, and walked toward Starbuck.

After shucking empties from his pistol, Starbuck had reloaded and approached the fallen gang leaders. Three were dead and Chub Jones lay writhing in agony, clutching his shattered kneecap. Starbuck's expression was stoic, and he stood watching blood seep through Jones's fingers, vaguely noting that it puddled a rich chocolate-brown on the earth. As Langham halted beside him, Starbuck holstered his gun and nodded.

"Thanks."

"For what?"

"For gettin' here in time. Somebody saved my bacon with that first shot."

"Some shot!" Langham grumbled. "Clean missed the sonovabitch! I must be gettin' old."

"Close enough to count," Starbuck remarked. "You nicked his coat front, threw him off. I saw the dust fly."

"Close don't count, 'cept in horseshoes. I should've drilled him straight through the lights! Think I'll get myself some specs."

"I'm still obliged. Bastard had me cold, and no two ways about it."

Langham grunted, wiggled his rifle barrel at Jones. "Who we got here?"

"Chub Jones, the one I've been ridin' with."

"You shoot him?"

"Yeah." Starbuck studied on it a moment. "Guess we ought to do somethin' about his leg before he bleeds to death."

"Waste of time!" Langham said curtly. "He ain't gonna live long enough for it to matter."

"You still plannin' to string 'em up?"

"Why, you got a better idea?"

"No, reckon not."

For a time, each man lost in his own thoughts, they fell silent, watching Jones bleed. Then Starbuck turned away and stood gazing west along the creek. His eyes were distant, as though fixed on something visible only to himself, and his mouth was set in a hard line. Langham kicked at the dirt, frowning thoughtfully, and gave him a sidelong glance.

"You thinkin' the same thing I'm thinkin'?"

"Wouldn't be surprised."

"Got any idea where he's headed?"

"No, but I've got a hunch who's gonna tell us."

"Yeah, who's that?"

Starbuck turned just far enough to rivet Jones with a cold look. "Three guesses, and the first two don't count."

CHAPTER EIGHTEEN

The buzzards dropped lower as a mid-
morning sun beat down on the cottonwoods.
Quartering a sector of sky, the scavengers
slowly wheeled and circled over the clearing
below. With mindless patience, they waited
for the living to relinquish the dead.

Corpses littered the campsite, and a warm
breeze was ripe with the stench of death. The
outlaws lay where they had fallen, sprawled
and grotesque, their bodies stiffening in a
welter of dried blood. Under a huge cottonwood, Chub Jones and the five survivors, one
of them Joe Sixkiller, sat staring blankly at
the carnage. Sixkiller and the others were
bound, arms behind their backs, their wrists
cinched tight. Jones was unbound but ashen-
faced, gritting his teeth against the pain. A
tourniquet had staunched the flow of blood
from his kneecap, and his leg was stretched

flat on the ground. There was no conversation among the men, and for the past couple of hours, like the buzzards overhead, they had waited with grim patience. All of them understood how it would end.

The delay, rather than humane, was strictly a practical measure. After a long night, capped by a savage minute of bloodletting, the attackers needed time to regroup and collect themselves. To their surprise, the cowhands had discovered that killing was hard work and, oddly enough, increased a man's appetite. Once their horses were brought upstream, at Langham's order, the men replenished themselves with cold rations and several gallons of hot coffee. A few were bothered by the corpse-strewn campsite, but for the most part they ate with gusto and swapped grisly recollections of the shootout. While several of them were nursing wounds, only three of their number had been killed, and that alone was cause for celebration. The meal was a welcome respite, and their laughter the quiet laughter of men who had closed with death and emerged alive. Toward the end, however, lingering over a final cup of coffee, their mood turned somber. With the sun high, and the buzzards circling lower, they were reminded of the distasteful part. The job yet to be done.

Off to one side, Starbuck huddled in conversation with Langham and the other ranchers. Their talk centered on Chub Jones, and for once they were in total agreement. Starbuck had proposed a plan, and now, as they nodded approval, he concluded in a flat voice.

"That's the way we'll play it, then. You gents just act natural—like it'd all been settled beforehand—and leave Jones to Ben and me."

"Let's hope to hell it works," Musgrave said earnestly. "One way or another, we gotta make that bastard spill his guts."

"It'll work," Starbuck assured him, "if everybody acts like good little soldiers and keeps their mouths shut. But we've got to convince him Ben's word is law! Once he believes that, he'll talk and keep right on talkin'."

"And if he don't?" Rutledge inquired. "What then?"

"Then we're no worse off than we are now."

"What bothers me," Vernon Pryor observed, "is that he might not have all the answers. It's just possible he doesn't know any more than we do."

"In that case," Starbuck said, without irony, "Chub Jones is in for a rough mornin'."

"Suppose we quit jawbonin'," Langham told them, "and find out for ourselves. I figger he's had plenty of time to think about meetin' his maker. You of a mind, Luke?"

"Sooner the better, Ben. Remember what I said, though . . . lots of fire and brimstone."

"Gawddamn, that won't be no trick a'tall!"

Walking away, Langham began thundering orders in a stern, commanding voice. The tree, under which the outlaws waited, suddenly became charged with activity. Several cowhands gathered lariats from the gear strewn about camp, then tossed the ropes over a stout limb and snubbed them firmly around the base of the cottonwood. Other men, meanwhile, saddled five horses and led them forward, halting below the limb. Within a matter of minutes, everything was arranged to Langham's satisfaction, and he nodded toward the outlaws.

"Get 'em mounted!"

Rutledge and Pryor, assisted by a number of the men, jumped to obey. The five outlaws were hoisted aboard the horses, then positioned beneath the dangling ropes. All the while, no one paid the slightest attention to Chub Jones. His eyes glittered like broken glass, and he waited, with a sort of terrified wonderment, for the sixth rope to appear. But he was left, alone and petrified, cowering against the trunk of the cottonwood.

A mounted cowhand rode forward, and one by one the outlaws had a noose fitted around their necks. Then the four ranchers and Starbuck moved to the rear of the horses, carrying freshly cut switches. Langham held his position, to the front and slightly to one side. He fixed the doomed men with a look of God-like wrath.

"If you boys are prayin' men, you got about ten seconds."

Behind him, formed in a semicircle at the edge of the limb, the cowhands gathered to watch. Their faces were like bronze masks, and they stared at the outlaws in rapt silence. Joe Sixkiller turned in the saddle, pinning Starbuck with a look of cold black hatred, then shifted around and gazed stolidly into the distance. The men on either side of him seemed resigned, their eyes dull and empty. The outlaw nearest the tree wet his pants, tears streaming down his face, and his lips moved in a monotone chant.

"Ooo Jesus, Jesus! Lord God Jesus! Ooo God!"

The last man, somewhat older than the others, laughed. His eyes settled on Langham with a hard stare of contempt. "Mister, you're the sorriest shitheel I ever seen. Hangin' us is lots worse than what we done to you."

"That all you got to say?"

"Yeah, reckon so. 'Cept I shore hope we meet in hell."

"If we do, don't let me catch you stealin' horses."

Langham raised his arm, hesitating a moment, then dropped it. Almost simultaneously,

five switches cracked across the horses'
rumps, and the animals bolted forward. The
outlaws were jerked clear of their saddles,
then swung back as the ropes hauled them
up short. When the nooses snapped tight,
their eyes seemed to burst from the sockets,
growing huge and distended, streaked fiery-
red with engorged blood vessels. The men
thrashed and kicked, dancing frantically on
air, as though they were trying to gain a foot-
hold. Slowly, their faces purpled, then grew
darker, turned a ghastly shade of blackish
amber. Their gyrations spun them in frenzied
circles, and one by one their mouths opened,
swollen tongues darting and flopping like
onyx snakes. A full three minutes passed
while they vainly fought the ropes.

Chub Jones, flattened against the tree
trunk, stared up as though mesmerized. His
face blanched, eyes round as saucers, and he
felt his own throat constrict as the outlaws'
struggles grew weaker. Even after the men
had slowly strangled to death, he couldn't
force himself to look away. Their bodies
hung limp, necks crooked, swaying gently in
the breeze. He clung tighter to the tree, par-
alyzed with terror, watching.

Langham's voice, harsh and cutting, suddenly broke the stillness. "Awright, boys, one
more to go! Get him on his feet!"

Jones cringed away as the four ranchers

walked toward him. His eyes fastened on
Starbuck, imploring mercy. Then the men
pried his hands loose from the tree and
roughly jerked him off the ground. A rope
whistled over the limb as they carried him
forward and held him upright. Someone
slipped the noose around his neck, snugged
it tight, and the ranchers stepped clear. His
wounded knee buckled, but the rope snapped
taut and left him teetering on one leg. Behind
him, the ranchers relieved a cowhand who
was holding the rope, and to his front, Starbuck halted beside Langham. Struck dumb,
his face rigid with fear, he saw Langham's
arm rise and fall.

The ranchers hauled back on the rope and
he was snatched high in the air. Clawing at
the noose with his hands, he found himself
face-to-face with one of the hanged outlaws.
His eyes bulged, lungs afire, and he gasped
for breath, felt his tongue thicken against his
teeth. Then, with a sense of deliverance, the
rope slackened and he was slowly lowered to
the ground. He ripped the noose clear of his
throat, sucking great draughts of air, and
struggled to hold himself erect on his one
good leg. A buzzing in his ears gradually
subsided, and he heard his name spoken.

"Are you listenin', Jones?"

Jones took a deep breath, blew it out heavily, took another. His eyes shuttled around,
found Langham, and he nodded. His throat

was clogged, but he forced himself to answer. "I hear . . . you . . . listenin'."

"By God!" Langham intoned. "You listen good and pay attention! What you just got was only a sample. Next time, you go up and you stay up! Savvy?"

"No." Jones blinked, shook his head. "What're you sayin'—?"

"Why, it's simple, Jones. I'm sayin' you talk or you swing . . . your choice!"

"Talk?" Jones asked hoarsely. "Talk about what?"

"Dutch Henry Horn."

"What about him?"

"Here's the deal," Langham said woodenly. "You tell us where to find Dutch Henry, and you ride out of here a free man. You don't tell us, and we'll stretch your neck like a turkey gobbler. Now you savvy?"

"Dutch never told us nothin'—I swear it! None of us ever knew where he come from or where he went . . . never!"

A harsh bark of laughter. "You're wastin' your breath, Jones. Try again!"

"Honest to God, I'm tellin' you—"

Langham glanced past him and nodded. The rope went taut and Jones was lifted up on tiptoe. He grabbed at the noose, only to be hoisted a few inches higher and left dangling. Langham let him struggle for several seconds, then nodded, and he was once more lowered to the ground.

"Now let's understand each other, Jones. You try to bullshit me again and that's all she wrote! End of the line!"

"I wasn't," Jones gagged. "Don't you see—"

"I see a dead man, unless you start talkin' pretty damn quick."

"You really mean it?" Jones whispered, desperation in his voice. "You'll let me go?"

"You can chisel it in stone," Langham prompted him. "Hell, man, it's Horn we're after, not you! Figger it out for yourself."

Jones threw a quick, guarded glance at Starbuck. "Is he on the level, Luke?"

"Chub, do yourself a favor and spill it. Otherwise, he'll string you up and leave you—"

"Jesus Christ, Luke, you owe me one! I treated you right, and all the time you was foolin' me! So just tell me—straight out— will he let me go?"

"I've known him a long time," Starbuck remarked, "and I've never known him to break his word. I'd advise you to go along, Chub. It's the only chance you've got."

"Awright." Jones bobbed his head. "I'll tell you! But it ain't much, so you gotta gimme your word you'll stick to the deal."

"Goddamn!" Langham scoffed. "You ain't in no position to make demands. Talk up or get strung up, there's your deal!"

Jones swallowed nervously. "Well, first

off, you gotta understand Horn's close-mouthed as they come. All I ever learned was what I picked up in bits and pieces."

"Get on with it!"

"Pueblo," Jones said softly. "He's got a hideout somewhere around Pueblo. That's it, all I know."

"Awwww for Chrissakes!" Langham muttered. "You and him was thick as fleas! You expect us to believe he never told you anything except Pueblo?"

"He never even told me that! I just put it together from little things he let slip now and then."

"C'mon now, Jones—somewheres around Pueblo?—hell's fire, that'd take in about half of Colorado. You'll have to do better'n that, lots better."

"I wouldn't shit you!" Jones's eyes filled with panic. "I swear to God . . . that's it . . . everything!"

Langham pursed his lips. "What do you think, Luke? Figger he's tellin' the truth?"

"Wouldn't surprise me," Starbuck observed. "Horn's the kind that plays it close to the vest, real skittish."

"Guess that's it, then." Langham studied the fat man a moment, then shrugged. "Hang him."

Jones's protest ended in a gurgled cry as the rope jerked him off the ground. His face contorted in a rictus of agony, and he began the slow dance on thin air. The ranchers snubbed the rope around the tree, then walked back to join Langham and Starbuck. Heavier than the other outlaws, Jones strangled quicker, and within a couple of minutes he hung slack from the limb. When it was over, Langham stood silent for a time, then turned to Gilchrist.

"Oscar, you was always pretty handy at whittlin' "—he paused, nodded at the cottonwood—"I want you to carve me somethin' on that tree."

"Awright," Gilchrist replied. "What do you want carved?"

"Well, since this place ain't got no name, we might as well give it one that's fittin'. So take your knife and do the honors on that tree. We'll call it Hangman's Creek."

Everyone agreed it was a fitting name, and Gilchrist went to work on the tree. The men watched, suddenly sobered by the gravity of all they'd done, and no one spoke for a while. At last, Langham cleared his throat.

"Luke, I reckon it's finished, all except for Horn."

"Funny thing, Ben"—Starbuck knuckled his mustache, thoughtful—"you make that sound like a question."

"Well, the reason I asked," Langham explained, "is because you've done your share and then some. If you'd sooner come on back to the ranch—and take over as foreman

again—we'll figger out another way to take
care of Horn. Seems to me that's only fair."

"Nooo," Starbuck said slowly. "I guess I'll
play out the hand. Always like to finish what
I start."

"You're sure now, plumb certain?"

Starbuck nodded, glancing around the
campsite. "Hell, it's me that's leavin' you
with the dirty chore. Won't be much fun dig-
gin' graves for this bunch."

"We ain't gonna bury 'em!" Langham an-
nounced. "We're gonna let the buzzards pick
'em clean and leave the sun to bleach their
bones. That'll let their kind know they ain't
safe no more ... not even in No Man's
Land!"

Starbuck smiled. "Yeah, I reckon a half-
dozen skeletons hangin' from a tree oughta
be message enough for anybody."

"If it ain't, we'll damn sure accommodate
'em with a tree of their own."

The men were silent a moment. Then Starbuck regarded the angle of the sun. "Gettin'
on toward noon. If I was to leave now, I expect I'd be pretty near the Colorado line before dark."

Langham hawked and spat. "Ain't much to
go on. How do you figger your chances?"

"Ask me the next time you see me."

"When'll that be?"

"After I've fixed Dutch Henry's wagon."

"Watch out he don't fix yours first."

"I'll keep my nose to the wind, don't worry."

Starbuck shook hands all around and went to saddle his horse. A while later, leading the gelding, he returned to find Langham supervising as Oscar Gilchrist put the finishing touches on his carving. Everyone else was mounted and preparing to take the trail; on the grasslands to the south, the men were gathering the stolen horses into a single herd. Starbuck paused beside the tree and Langham joined him. There was concern in the older man's eyes, and Starbuck avoided his gaze, nodding instead at Gilchrist's handiwork.

HANGMAN'S CREEK

"Pretty well tells the story, doesn't it?"

"Yeah, reckon it does."

A moment slipped past. "Guess I better head out. Got a fair piece to travel."

"Don't forget your way home, you hear me?"

"I won't, Ben. You can bank on it."

Starbuck stepped into the saddle and rode west along the creek. When he looked back, Langham was still standing there, watching him. On the verge of waving, he suddenly changed his mind. There was something final about a wave—a gesture of farewell rather than a promise of the future—and the old man was concerned enough already on that score. For his part, Starbuck gave little thought to what the future held. His vision was limited to Colorado and Dutch Henry Horn, and beyond that all else was without substance. A thing of conjecture until they'd met one last time.

He tugged his hat down and kneed the gelding into a lope.

CHAPTER NINETEEN

Seated at the desk in his study, Dutch Henry Horn pondered the vicissitudes of life. He was an orderly man, with the discipline of mind and iron will to shape events to suit his own ends. Yet his certainty of purpose was now in disarray, and these days he felt some deep-rooted need to snatch tranquility from the jaws of turmoil.

All morning he'd sat there, abstracted and listless, staring at an opened ledger book. It was the end of the month, time to reconcile his accounts and take stock of the month ahead. But thus far he hadn't touched a pen or made a single entry in the ledger. A stack of bills, along with memos of credit from his bank in Pueblo, lay where he had placed them earlier that morning. Correspondence from the slaughterhouse in Denver and a purchase request from the quartermaster at Fort

Lyon also demanded his attention. Still, for all the pressing matters before him, he'd been unable to shake his sluggish mood. His thoughts were elsewhere, on another business venture. The one he'd fled so ingloriously in No Man's Land.

A knock at the door brought him upright in his chair. He took a bill off the top of the stack, dipped his pen in the inkwell, and hunched over the ledger. With a precise stroke, legible as a draftsman's lettering, he began the entry.

"Come in."

The door opened, and Harry Birdwell entered the study. A large, beefy man, with the girth to match his shoulders, Birdwell had served as foreman of Horn's ranch for the past year. Holding a battered Stetson in one hand, he crossed the room and halted in front of the desk.

"Mornin', Mr. Miller."

Horn nodded brusquely. "What is it, Harry?"

"Thought as how I oughta ask you about the payroll."

"What about it?"

"Tomorrow's the first of the month," Birdwell reminded him. "The hands'll be wantin' their pay."

"Goddamn!" Horn glowered. "Why haven't you said something before this?"

"Ain't my place, Mr. Miller. Besides, I never had to say nothin' before."

Birdwell knew next to nothing about the man who called himself Frank Miller. So far as he could determine, Miller had neither family nor past. From his manner of speech, Birdwell pegged him as a Texan; but he volunteered nothing, and his cold attitude hardly encouraged questions. Still, there were many things, bits and pieces gleaned from observation, that told Birdwell all he wanted to know. Frank Miller had a seemingly inexhaustible supply of money; he was a knowledgeable cattleman; and within the last year he had transformed the old Diamond X spread into a topnotch outfit. He was a harsh taskmaster, aloof and demanding, and apparently considered idleness the cardinal sin. Yet he readily delegated responsibility, once a man had earned his trust, and he gave his foreman a free hand with the crew. For Harry Birdwell, that was enough, and he was satisfied to leave certain questions unanswered.

All the same, Birdwell had noted a pronounced change in the Diamond X owner within the last month. He seemed withdrawn, even more distant than usual, and he'd allowed business matters to slide drastically. That was wholly out of character, and it left Birdwell in an uncomfortable position. Today, faced with Miller's churlish attitude, he decided to force the issue. The ranch was suffering, through no fault of his own, and he wasn't about to accept the blame. It was time for a little straight talk.

"Mr. Miller, we got ourselves some problems, and I'm thinkin' it's time we laid 'em out on the table."

"Birdwell—" Horn started, then stopped, took a grip on his temper. "What sort of problems?"

"Just for openers," Birdwell commented, "the beef contracts. We're way past due on both of 'em, and you still haven't give me the go-ahead."

"Why the hell haven't you brought it up before now?"

"I have, and all I got was a deaf ear. Nothin' personal, Mr. Miller, but it's like I told you a minute ago. I'm only the foreman around here."

"The way you're talkin," Horn said with heavy sarcasm, "maybe you figure you ought to be sittin' behind this desk."

"No, sir, never said nothin' of the kind. All I said was, I'm accustomed to your givin' the orders, and lately, I ain't been gettin' any."

Horn gave him a dour look. "Watch your step, or you're liable to find yourself ridin' the grub line."

"Anytime you're not satisfied with my work, all you gotta do is say so."

"I'm talkin' about your tone of voice, not your work!"

Horn drew a deep breath, reminded himself to go slow. Only with a supreme effort of will had he made the adjustment from outlaw to rancher. Yet there were times he felt like two men, and it was a constant struggle to beat the callousness of his old self into submission. Men hired to steal horses could be dealt with summarily, even cruelly, but a ranch foreman was another matter altogether. Harry Birdwell was honest and dependable, a proud man, and that made the difference. He had to be treated with respect.

At length, Horn yielded with a casual gesture. "Forget what I said, Harry. I've got a lot on my mind these days, and I guess I'm a little quick to take offense."

"Anything I can help with, Mr. Miller?"

"No, just a personal matter, doesn't concern the ranch."

"Sorta figured as much, after you come back off that last trip, I mean."

Horn regarded him without expression. "What's that supposed to mean?"

"Why, nothin'." Birdwell sensed he'd overstepped himself. "Just that you're generally pretty obligin' after one of them trips. This time you wasn't, that's all."

"Suppose we stick to business and let me worry about my personal affairs. Fair enough, Harry?"

"Hell, suits me. I've got enough trouble of my own."

Birdwell smiled inwardly. The allusion to *personal affairs* convinced him Miller was suffering from a busted romance. All along, he'd thought the trips involved a woman— probably a courtship of long standing—and now the boss had gotten himself jilted. It made perfect sense, and accounted for his virtual seclusion of the past month.

"Now, about these contracts," Horn resumed. "How far are we overdue?"

"Couple of days with the slaughterhouse, and pretty near a week with the army."

"All right," Horn told him, "cut out some beeves and get 'em on the road. Tell your boys to push 'em hard."

"Well, not to pour oil on the fire, but that sorta brings us back to the original problem."

"Which is?"

"The payroll." Birdwell shrugged. "The boys ain't gonna be too happy about hittin' the trail when they ain't been paid."

Horn stared at him for a time, seeming to deliberate. Finally, he tilted back in his chair, fingers steepled. "I'll give you a letter to the bank. You ride into town, pick up the payroll, and then beat it back here. That'll solve that."

Birdwell looked at him, astounded. "You want me to pick up the payroll?"

"Wasn't that what I just said, Harry?"

"Yeah," Birdwell replied doubtfully. "Only I don't get it. You've always looked after that yourself."

"So now I'm sendin' you to look after it for me! Why all the questions?"

"Well . . ." Birdwell shook his head. "I don't know, Mr. Miller. We're talkin' about better'n a thousand dollars."

Horn waved it away. "I trust you, Harry."

"That ain't exactly the point. See, the thing is, Mr. Miller, I'd sooner not take the responsibility. Cows are one thing, but cash money . . . that ain't rightly my bailiwick . . . it's yours."

"Are you tryin' to tell me my business?"

"Nope." Birdwell hesitated, studying the floor. "I'm only sayin' I don't want no part of the payroll. I wasn't hired on to ride shotgun."

"Jesus Christ! Are you afraid somebody'll rob you?"

"Yeah, I reckon that's partly it."

"Partly?" Horn demanded. "What's the rest of it?"

"Call it anything you want, Mr. Miller. I just ain't partial to handlin' another man's money. That's the way she stacks up, and I'm a little too old to start changin' now."

Horn slammed out of his chair and walked to the window. Before him, spread out along the banks of the Arkansas, some thirty miles southeast of Pueblo, was the Diamond X ranch. His ranch! As large and thriving as any outfit to be found in the whole of Colorado. But it had taken time and vast amounts of money to make it a reality. Now, for the first time in his life, he knew fear. The fear he might lose it all, everything he'd built.

Scarcely two years past, with the Texas Rangers at his heels, Horn had called it quits. At the time, he led a pack of hardcases who specialized in bank and train robberies. Over a period of months, he had enjoyed a long streak of luck, staging successful holdups across the breadth of Texas. But after a near disaster in the town of Waco—and a week-long pursuit by the Rangers—he had decided to end it while he was ahead of the game. With Ranger companies constantly on the prowl, and a telegraph network throughout the state, robbery was fast becoming a hazardous occupation. Severing all ties, he had disbanded the gang and made his way in secret to Colorado.

There, after assuming a new identity, he had determined to go straight. With the money he'd saved, he bought the Diamond X, a ranch that had fallen on hard times during the financial panic of '73. Soon enough, he discovered that ranching, on the scale he envisioned, required resources far beyond his means. The banks, which loaned money only to people who didn't need it, turned him down cold. Faced with the choice of a hard-scrabble existence, or devising another source of capital, he had reverted to the way he knew best. But this time, with great fore-thought and planning, he'd taken care to re-main in the background.

The result was a horse-stealing ring, with Chub Jones and some of the old gang members recruited in strictest confidence. None of them knew of the ranch, or his new identity, and his personal risk was limited to the meetings in No Man's Land. The scheme had worked to perfection, and over the past year he'd poured upward of $100,000 into ranch improvements and land acquisition. The Diamond X prospered, his personal fortune seemed assured, and the future had never looked brighter. Perhaps of greater significance, Frank Miller had become a man of prominence and stature throughout southern Colorado. To Dutch Henry Horn, who had ridden the owlhoot all his adult life, it was no small accomplishment. He took immense pleasure in the fact that his Pueblo banker not only loaned him money, but now considered him a personal friend.

Since fleeing No Man's Land, he'd been obsessed by the thought that he might lose all he'd worked so hard to attain. From the volume of gunfire at the campsite, audible for a mile or more as he rode west, he felt reasonably certain the entire gang had been killed or captured. Either way, he had little fear of anyone betraying his whereabouts.

None of the men, not even Chub Jones and the other gang leaders, had the faintest notion as to his new life. His fear stemmed instead from the man who had gulled him with such uncanny subterfuge. The one called Starbuck.

Quite obviously, Starbuck was an agent in the employ of one or more cattlemen's associations. It was common practice these days, and would account for the large force that had attacked the camp. All the more apparent, Starbuck was a man of resourcefulness and great tenacity. There was little doubt his search would continue; though the gang itself had been wiped out, his employers would insist he take the trail of the ringleader. For that reason, Horn had thought it best to stay out of sight over the past month. Having underestimated Starbuck once, he had no intention of doing so again. By far, the wiser course was to lay low and allow time to work in his favor.

Yet, in a perverse twist, he'd gradually come to the conclusion that he owed Starbuck a debt of gratitude. Except for the debacle in No Man's Land, he might have gone on with the horse-stealing operation. The money was simply too tempting to have done otherwise. On the other hand, the Diamond X was prospering, and he no longer had need of outside funds. So in his greed, he would have continued to run an unnecessary risk and court disaster on an even larger scale. All in all, Starbuck had done him a service of no small consequence. By concentrating solely on the business of Frank Miller, he would at last put the old life behind him. And in the process, lay Dutch Henry Horn to rest.

Thinking about it now, it occured to him that today's squabble over the payroll was really quite timely. Harry Birdwell had jolted him out of his funk, and that was precisely what he'd needed. The fear was probably all in his mind, anyway, and after a month, whatever danger might have existed was no longer a factor. By now, for all his determination, Starbuck would have concluded that the trail had gone cold. Even if he persisted, there was no great cause for alarm. With no leads, nothing to go on, he'd been working blind from the day of the shootout. The chances of him wandering into Pueblo were one in a million!

Horn turned from the window. He walked back to the desk and resumed his seat. His manner was now brisk and business-like, assured.

"Harry, I'll be leaving for Pueblo at first light. You can tell the men they'll have their pay before suppertime."

Birdwell nodded, grinning. "That's fine, Mr. Miller, just fine."

"Get those beeves ready to go, too. While I'm in town, I'll telegraph the slaughterhouse

and the quartermaster and hold 'em off with
some sort of excuse."

"Good idea," Birdwell agreed. "I'll put the
boys to work on a gather first thing in the
mornin'."

"One other thing."

"Yessir, what's that?"

"I've been thinkin' it over, and you're
right about the payroll. It's a lot of money."

"Folks have been killed for a lot less, Mr.
Miller."

"My thought exactly. You never know
who you're liable to run across these days."

"Ain't that the goldurn truth!"

"Better safe than sorry, and it occurs to me
I've been takin' some damnfool chances car-
ryin' all that money by myself."

Horn considered it a moment, almost as
though he were wrestling with some inner decision. Only when he had Birdwell on ten-
terhooks did he glance up, eyes snapping
with authority.

"Harry, I want you to pick out a couple of
good men to ride with me tomorrow."

"How d'you mean . . . good men?"

"I mean good with a gun. Damned good!"

CHAPTER TWENTY

The hotel veranda was pleasantly shaded from the noonday sun. Almost hidden in the shadows, Starbuck lazed back, one leg thrown over the arm of a cane-bottomed rocker. His expression was downcast and his mood somber. Smoking one cigarette after another, he sat mired in his own gloom.

Passersby scarcely seemed to notice him. After nearly a month, he'd become something of a fixture on the veranda, and the townspeople had grown bored speculating about his silent vigil. When he'd first ridden into Pueblo, there had been considerable gossip, and a few attempts at tactfully phrased conversation. But the questions were blunted on his reserved manner, and the prying soon stopped altogether. Everyone went back to tending their own business, and now it was as though he'd staked out squatter's rights on the cane-bottomed rocker. Except for an occasional stroll around town, he sat there from early morning until late evening. Seven days a week.

The hotel occupied one corner of Pueblo's main intersection. Anyone entering or leaving town was almost certain to pass the corner, and the veranda afforded Starbuck a commanding position. From there, without making himself conspicuous, he could observe virtually all the street activity on any given day. At the outset, having discarded various alternative measures, he had resigned himself to a long wait. Yet his vigil, prolonged beyond anything he might have imagined, had slowly drained his spirits. He was bored and disheartened and assailed by a growing sense of doubt. He now thought it quite possible he'd staked out the wrong corner in the wrong town. He seriously questioned that Dutch Henry Horn had ever set foot in Pueblo.

All morning, his patience worn thin, he'd sat there considering his options. A month ago, upon entering Pueblo, none of the ideas had borne up under scrutiny. Convinced that Horn was using an alias, he knew it would start the grapevine churning if he went around town asking questions. All the more so since he had nothing to go on but the man's description. Once the talk began, it would have spread quickly, for an inquisitive stranger in a small town was prime news. A tour of the countryside presented even graver problems. Aside from fueling the gossip mill, it was entirely possible he might stumble across Horn without warning. In light of the man's cunning, that was a situation to be avoided at all costs. This time out, Starbuck wanted the odds on his side. Or, if not the odds, then at least a reasonable chance of walking away alive. Either way, it was imperative that Horn not be alerted to his presence.

To compound matters, Starbuck was in a touchy position regarding the law. Whatever face he put on it, there was simply no argument that would explain away the slaughter in No Man's Land. With more than twenty men killed or hung, he couldn't very well enlist the aid of local peace officers. The law looked askance on vigilante justice, regardless of the provocation, and horse thieves were no exception. At best, since he was again operating alone, the law would consider him little more than a bounty hunter. At worst, if he attempted to explain the killings in No Man's Land, he would be considered little better than a common outlaw. So that eliminated any chance of support from the town marshal. He was on his own.

Over the past month, Starbuck had pondered that very thought. Seldom reflective, his vigil had left him nothing to do but think, and he'd come to the conclusion he was on his own in many ways. His search for the horse thieves had effectively removed him from the influence of Ben Langham. For the first time in twelve years, he'd answered to no one but himself, felt beholden to no one. Slowly, almost without awareness, his streak of independence had once again exerted itself. Only at the very last, during those final moments in No Man's Land, had he fully realized the extent of the change. Without hesitation, he'd taken command of the ranchers and their men. No counsel was sought, nor had he brooked any interference; he'd simply laid out the plan and told them how to proceed. All the more revealing, none of them, not even Langham, had questioned his judgment. In some curious way, their roles had been reversed, and everyone understood he had assumed leadership of the operation. Looking back, he saw that it had marked a passage in time, a point separating past from present. Perhaps a point of no return.

Still, for all he'd discovered about himself, he found that hindsight had its troublesome moments. He kept thinking back to the words of one of the outlaws they'd hung, the older one who had spoken out near the end. The man had accused them of exacting too harsh a price for simple horse-stealing. At the time, Starbuck hadn't given it much thought. Later, upon reflection, he'd begun to wonder if the man wasn't right. A life in exchange for a horse—even a bunch of horses—was most certainly a stiff bargain. Yet the thief knew the price in advance, and by stealing the horse, he had tacitly accepted the risk. After mulling it over at great length, Starbuck decided it was not so much a matter of right or wrong, but rather whose rights would prevail.

Unless a man defended what was his, there were always other men who would come and take it away from him. The meek of the world, so far as Starbuck could determine, inherited only a portion of the earth. More often than not, it was a hole in the ground, six feet of sod, marked by a headstone attesting to their gentle nature. So a man either defended himself and his property—resorting to violence if necessary—or he forfeited the right to live in peace. Which resulted in dead thieves and honest men who slept fitfully, troubled by bad dreams. Each in his own way paid the price, and since No Man's Land, Starbuck thought perhaps the honest man got the worst end of the deal. His own dreams were of a gallows tree . . . and buzzards . . . and sun-bleached bones. And late at night, awakened in a cold sweat, he wondered if he would ever purge himself of Hangman's Creek. He thought not.

For all his ruminations, however, there wasn't the slightest doubt regarding Dutch Henry Horn. If anyone, it was the ringleader himself who had brought about Hangman's Creek. The terrible price paid there, by the living and the dead alike, demanded justice, swift retribution. Now, more than ever, Starbuck saw himself as the instrument of that retribution. Having arranged the death of so many men, he wanted very much to kill the one who had led them. It seemed somehow important, necessary. A thing not to be left undone.

Yet it was undone!

Staring blankly at the street, Starbuck knew he was at a dead end in Pueblo. The matter was no closer to resolution than it had been a month ago. If he was to find Horn and force a showdown, it wouldn't be accomplished by sitting on his butt in the shade of a hotel veranda. However risky, he must now fall back on the options previously discarded. The first step would be to inquire around town, attempt to turn up a lead that would give him a new direction, a fresh start. Failing that, he would have no choice but to scour the countryside, widening his search to include the whole of Southern Colorado. Up until now he'd played a waiting game, hopeful his quarry would come to him. But it was long past time to switch tactics. Today he must start a hunt, the only kind that would get the job done.

A manhunt.

Starbuck's spirits immediately improved.

With a course of action laid out, he felt some
of the old vigor return, and decided not to
waste so much as another minute. After a
quick meal, he would begin making the
rounds, asking questions, and it occurred to
him the place to start was the town's saloons.
Bartenders were a gabby lot, and a steady
drinker on a slow afternoon would encourage
them to talk.

On the verge of rising, Starbuck caught
movement out of the corner of his eye. He
glanced to his right and saw three riders pass
by the far end of the veranda. A quick once-
over, then he looked away, pegging them as
cowhands. But suddenly his head snapped
around and he looked closer. His jaw fell
open as though hinged.

The man in the middle was Dutch Henry
Horn!

Struck dumb, Starbuck watched as they
rode across the street and halted at a bank
catty-corner from the hotel. He sat as if
nailed to the rocker, unable to move, hands
clasping the chair arms so tightly his knuckles turned white. The men dismounted, leaving their horses at the hitch rack, and entered
the bank. His mind whirled, and his first
thought was that they had him outnumbered.
The other men clearly worked for Horn—that
much was obvious—for they had trailed him
into the bank at a respectful distance. Whether

they were cowhands or members of another gang . . .

Starbuck took a tight grip on himself, collected his thoughts. Where they had come from, why they were here—even if they were robbing the bank!—none of that mattered. Only one thing counted. Horn had him outnumbered, and one pistol against three was pure suicide. He needed an edge.

Bolting out of his chair, Starbuck went down the hotel steps and hurried toward the corner. Crossing the street, he walked to a hardware store directly opposite the bank. As he entered, he spotted a rack of long guns on the wall. A clerk approached, and he quickly dug a wad of bills out of his pocket.

"Gimme a shotgun!"

"Yessir." The clerk swept the rack with a proud eye. "We have the finest selection in town. Now, would you prefer—"

"A double-barrel!" Starbuck cut him short. "Any double-barrel, twelve gauge, and some buckshot shells. C'mon, man, move . . . pick a gun!"

The clerk gave him a startled look and pulled a Greener from the rack. Starbuck snatched it out of his hand and tossed the wad of bills on the counter. Watching nervously, the clerk produced a box of shells and stepped back, ignoring the money. Starbuck dumped the shells on the counter, broke open the shotgun and stuffed a load in both barrels. All the while, glancing through the fly-blown window, he kept one eye on the bank. As he snapped the Greener closed, Horn emerged, followed by the two cowhands, and crossed the boardwalk.

Starbuck hurried out the door, cocking the hammers on the shotgun. As he stepped into the street, the men circled the hitch rack and separated, moving toward their horses. He halted, planting himself, and threw the Greener to his shoulder.

"Horn!"

The shout brought several passersby to a standstill, and Horn turned. His expression was grave with wonder, a look of raw disbelief in his eyes. For an instant, perfectly motionless, he stared at Starbuck over the barrels of the shotgun. Then his mouth opened in a leather-lunged cry of alarm.

"Holdup! It's a holdup!"

Even as he yelled, Horn spun and dove headlong beneath one of the horses. On either side of him, the cowhands reacted instantly, clawing at their guns. Starbuck hesitated, saw the pistols coming level and ripped out a command.

"No! Wait!"

A slug whistled past his ear, and another tugged at his shirtsleeve. The cowhands had fired almost simultaneously with his yell, and now they frantically thumbed the hammers on their pistols. Starbuck triggered both barrels within the space of a heartbeat. The scattergun erupted with a blinding roar and sent a double-load of buckshot hurtling across the street. The cowhands were flung backward, almost as though their backbones had been snatched clean, and slammed to the ground. Peering through a dense cloud of gun smoke, Starbuck broke open the Greener, then remembered he hadn't brought along extra shells. He tossed the shotgun aside and jerked his Colt.

Advancing on the fallen men, he spotted movement beyond the horses, which were now rearing and fighting to break free of the hitch rack. A quick stride took him past the corner, and he saw Horn sprinting west along the side street. He snapped a hurried shot and splinters flew off the building above Horn's head. Ducking low, Horn raced to the end of the building and turned south into an alley.

Starbuck ran after him, vaguely aware of faces in the bank window and men crouched in doorways. At the alley, he paused and took a cautious peek around the corner of the building. A bullet pocked the earth at his feet, followed by the report of a gunshot. An instant later, Horn darted from behind a pile of rubbish at the far end of the alley. Starbuck threw up the Colt, firing as he caught a blur in the sights, and missed. Before he could fire again, Horn had crossed the street and vanished into a small adobe.

Walking swiftly, Starbuck moved through the alley. He kept his eyes on the adobe, shucking empties and reloading as he went. When he reached the end of the alley, he was at the edge of the business district. He flattened himself against the last building and slowly inspected the adobe. It was a Mexican cantina, set off by itself on the outskirts of town. The door stood ajar, and inside he saw movement, heard the chatter of excited voices. A sudden hunch told him Horn was no longer in the cantina.

Crossing the street, he hurried to the rear of the adobe, and eased around the corner. There was a back door, which was closed, and several yards away stood a one-holer outhouse. Beyond that was a stretch of open ground, then a cluster of adobe houses. He saw no one, and for a moment he debated whether to try the back door. Then his gaze was drawn to the outhouse, and his eyes narrowed. The door was shut and the latch bar firmly in place. But the latchstring stopped swaying even as he watched. Someone was in the outhouse.

With a casual glance around, Starbuck started toward the opposite side of the adobe. In mid-stride, he suddenly whirled, leveling the Colt, and drilled a hole through the outhouse door. Thumbing the hammer back, he drew a steady bead on the door, then called out in a hard voice.

"Dutch Henry, you got a choice! Come out with your hands up, or I'll turn that privy into a sieve."

"Hold off, Starbuck! I'm comin' out, you win!"

The latch bar lifted and the door creaked open. Horn stood in a spill of sunlight, his arms raised above the door sill. He blinked, watching Starbuck with a sardonic expression.

"You're a regular bulldog once you get started, aren't you?"

"Toss your gun out of there, Dutch! Slow and easy, nothin' fancy."

"I laid it on the seat before I opened the door."

"Then lower your hands—one at a time!—and you'd better come up empty."

"Hell, I know when I'm licked." Horn lowered his left hand, palm upraised. "See, no tricks and no—"

His right arm dropped in a flash of metal. Starbuck triggered three quick shots. The slugs stitched a neat row straight up Horn's shirtfront, bright red dots from belly to brisket. Knocked off his feet by the impact, Horn crashed into the back wall of the privy, then sat down on the one-holer. A pistol fell from his hand, and his head tilted at an angle across one shoulder. His eyes were opaque and lusterless, staring at nothing.

Starbuck walked forward and halted at the

door. He lowered the hammer on his Colt, gazing down on the dead man. He thought it ironic that Horn would have attempted the very trick he'd once pulled on Sam Tate. A smile tugged at the corner of his mouth, and he slowly shook his head.

"You should've known better, Dutch. You sure should've."

"Hands up!"

Starbuck tensed, but the voice behind him was cold with menace. "Go ahead, sonny, just gimme an excuse."

With great care, Starbuck dropped the Colt and raised his arms. He glanced over his shoulder and caught the gleam of a tin star. Though he'd never spoken with the town marshal, they had occasionally exchanged nods during the past month. Now, as the lawman moved forward, he slowly turned.

"What's the problem, Marshal?"

"You're under arrest."

"On what charge?"

"The murder of Frank Miller."

"The murder"—Starbuck stopped, suddenly frowned—"who the hell's Frank Miller?"

"He's right behind you, sonny . . . sittin' on the crapper."

CHAPTER TWENTY-ONE

"Yessir, sonny, you're a mighty lucky fellow."

"I sure wish you'd quit callin' me 'sonny.'"

"I will, soon as you get the hell outta my town!"

Walt Johnson unlocked the door and swung it open. Starbuck glanced around the cell, his home for the last three weeks, and stepped into the corridor. With a dour grunt, the lawman turned and walked toward the front of the jail. His gray hair and stout build belied his reputation with a gun. A man of few words, he was hard-eyed and astringent, and possessed little or no tolerance for lawbreakers. He had an even greater dislike for honest citizens who took the law into their own hands. High on his list at the moment was Luke Starbuck.

In his office, Johnson moved to his desk and opened a bottom drawer. He removed Starbuck's gunbelt and laid it on top the desk. He stood for a moment, studying the holstered Colt, then glanced up at Starbuck.

"You load that thing before you hit the town limits and I'll toss your ass back in jail."

Starbuck smiled. "Thought you'd be glad to get rid of me, Marshal."

"You just mind what I'm tellin' you. I don't want nobody else killed, and you'd do yourself a big favor by seein' it my way."

"Seems to me it's the other way round."

"Yeah, how so?"

"What if someone braces me before I make it out of town?"

"They won't," Johnson assured him. "Not that I'd blame 'em, but I'll see to it you aren't bothered."

"Still stuck in your craw, isn't it?"

"Folks around here thought a lot of Frank Miller."

"How about Dutch Henry Horn?" Starbuck replied. "Or don't that part count?"

"Guess it all depends on whose ox was gored. He kept his nose clean in Pueblo, and that's the way folks remember him."

"What about yourself, Marshal? You keep sayin' folks, but I've got an idea you're still wearin' blinders, too."

"I'm a lawman," Johnson noted sternly.

"Sometimes I don't like the way things work out, but I enforce it all the same."

Starbuck was forced to concede the point. His first night in jail, a lynch mob had formed on the street, demanding Frank Miller's killer. Only Walt Johnson, armed with a sawed-off shotgun, had dissuaded them. With chill dignity, he'd warned the crowd they would have to kill him to get the prisoner. The citizens of Pueblo knew him to be a man of his word, and there was no more talk of lynching.

Yet there was every likelihood the prisoner would be brought to trial and hung legally. Johnson had never heard of Dutch Henry Horn, nor was he impressed by Starbuck's tale of a horse-stealing ring. It all sounded improbable and highly far-fetched, particularly as it involved Frank Miller, one of the area's leading ranchers and a man of impeccable reputation. Still, in his own hard way, the marshal believed that justice afforded the accused certain rights. Fending off the county prosecutor, he set about checking Starbuck's story.

A telegraph inquiry to the sheriff in Fort Worth brought an astounding reply. There was, indeed, a horse-stealing ring. Some weeks past, the Panhandle Cattlemen's Association had delivered more than fifty head of stolen stock to the sheriff's office. How they had come by the horses remained a mystery—for the ranchers were stubbornly silent on that score—but there was no doubt the brands had been altered. Moreover, the ranchers vouched for one Lucas Starbuck, and confirmed that he was employed by the Association as a range detective. Almost as an afterthought, the sheriff's reply verified an outstanding warrant on a man known as Dutch Henry Horn. A wanted poster, bearing the man's likeness, would be forwarded by mail.

The wire itself caused a furor. It substantiated Starbuck's story and indicated he might very well be telling the truth about Frank Miller. The townspeople, however, refused to believe the allegations. There was a concerted effort to bring him to trial, and only at the marshal's insistence was a postponement granted to await the wanted circular. When it arrived, some two weeks later, Pueblo was rocked to the foundation. The likeness it bore was excellent, and erased all doubt.

Frank Miller and Dutch Henry Horn were one and the same. One man leading two lives.

Starbuck was cleared regarding Horn, but it took another week to resolve the matter of the dead cowhands. A certain element in town was of the opinion that a bounty hunter—even though he'd escaped the noose for the murder of Frank Miller—most assuredly deserved to be hung for shotgunning innocent men. In time, and again at Walt Johnson's insistence, witnesses to the shootout came forward. It was established that the cowhands had fired first, under the mistaken impression Starbuck was a robber, and that he'd acted in his own defense. The killings were ruled justifiable homicide.

Acting at the marshal's request, the court had also ruled that Starbuck spend one last night in jail. Walt Johnson, sensing the mood of the town, thought it best to release his prisoner at sunrise, while most of Pueblo still slept. In that, Starbuck heartily agreed, and now, as they faced one another across the desk, it occurred to him that he was in the marshal's debt. He was having trouble with the words.

"I'm not much on thanks"—Starbuck faltered, doggedly went on—"but I want you to know I'm obliged. You've treated me square."

Johnson frowned. "You don't owe me nothin'. I was just doing what I'm paid to do." He paused, considering. "Tell you what, though . . . you do me a favor and we'll call it even."

"Name it."

"Don't you never come back to my town."

Starbuck laughed. "You can take it to the bank, Marshal. As of today, Pueblo's scratched off my list."

Walt Johnson nodded, and led the way outside. Starbuck's horse was tied to the hitch rack, with his bedroll and a bag of provisions strapped in place. There was an uncomfortable moment, then Starbuck smiled and patted the holstered Colt.

"You said the town limits, didn't you?"

"Sonny, let me give you a last piece of advice. Put some distance between yourself and town before you stop to load that thing. You'd be surprised how quick folks forget once you're gone."

"Yeah, I reckon you're right."

The men looked at each other, then nodded. There was no offer of a handshake, nor was it expected. Starbuck mounted, and as dawn gave way to sunrise, he rode past the hotel. At the edge of town, he twisted around in the saddle and saw the solitary figure still watching him. With a mock bow, he swept his hat off, but there was no response from the lawman. He laughed aloud, then swatted his horse across the rump and turned away from Pueblo.

A few miles out of town, he reined to a halt on the north bank of the Arkansas. On the opposite side of the river, the road snaked south toward the Staked Plains. By continuing on, he would eventually strike the headwaters of the Canadian. From there, it was a matter of a hard day's ride to the Panhandle and the LX range. Fall roundup would be underway, and if he chose to do so, he could resume his duties as foreman within the week. Ben Langham had made that clear when they parted in No Man's Land. Yet the alternative was still open. An experienced range detective was always in demand, and with Hangman's Creek to his credit, he could find work wherever he chose to ride.

Anywhere, in any direction.

Thoughtful, he pulled the Colt, thumbed the hammer to half-cock, and opened the loading gate. As he stuffed shells into the chambers, it occurred to him that the decision was not all that difficult. Even in random moments, he seldom gave any consideration to the old life. His thoughts of the LX and Ben Langham were more like memories, and try as he might, he could no longer summon an image of Janet Pryor in his mind's eye. Events and time had dulled that life, altered all the days ahead. To whatever purpose, he'd been brought to the point of no return.

A slow grin creased his mouth. Another image flashed through his mind, vivid and clear, shiny-bright. He saw Lisa, radiant with bawdy laughter, rushing to greet him. Her arms were outstretched, and she hurried across the floor of the Comique, calling his name. The image evoked warm stirrings, a sense of need, and he knew everything else could wait. There was time enough ahead, a lifetime.

Starbuck lowered the hammer on an empty chamber and holstered the Colt. Gathering the reins, he feathered the gelding's ribs and turned downstream. He rode into the sunrise toward Dodge.

Whistling softly to himself.